WITHDRAWN

Lewis, Beverly, 1949-
  The preacher's daughter
FIC LEW
MPLD619563

The Preacher's Daughter

BEVERLY LEWIS

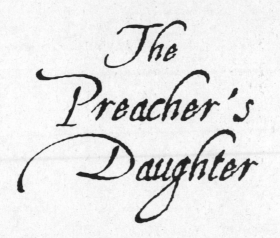

The Preacher's Daughter

BETHANYHOUSE

MINNEAPOLIS, MINNESOTA

The Preacher's Daughter
Copyright © 2005
Beverly Lewis

Cover design by Dan Thornberg

Unless otherwise identified, Scripture quotations are from the King James Version of the Bible.

All rights reserved. No part of this publication may be reproduced, stored in a retrieval system, or transmitted in any form or by any means—electronic, mechanical, photocopying, recording, or otherwise—without the prior written permission of the publisher and copyright owners.

Published by Bethany House Publishers
11400 Hampshire Avenue South
Bloomington, Minnesota 55438

Bethany House Publishers is a division of
Baker Publishing Group, Grand Rapids, Michigan.

Printed in the United States of America

ISBN 0-7642-0120-4 (Hardcover)

Dedication

To
Madge S. Bowes,
a preacher's daughter times two . . .
and dear family friend.

By Beverly Lewis

ABRAM'S DAUGHTERS

The Covenant
The Betrayal
The Sacrifice
The Prodigal
The Revelation

❖ ❖ ❖

THE HERITAGE OF LANCASTER COUNTY

The Shunning
The Confession
The Reckoning

❖ ❖ ❖

ANNIE'S PEOPLE

The Preacher's Daughter

❖ ❖ ❖

The Postcard • *The Crossroad*

❖ ❖ ❖

The Redemption of Sarah Cain
October Song • *Sanctuary**
The Sunroom

❖ ❖ ❖

The Beverly Lewis Amish Heritage Cookbook

www.beverlylewis.com

*with David Lewis

BEVERLY LEWIS, born in the heart of Pennsylvania Dutch country, fondly recalls her growing-up years. A keen interest in her mother's Plain family heritage has led Beverly to set many of her popular stories in Lancaster County.

A former schoolteacher and accomplished pianist, Beverly is a member of the National League of American Pen Women (the Pikes Peak branch). She is the 2003 recipient of the Distinguished Alumnus Award at Evangel University, Springfield, Missouri. Her blockbuster novels, *The Shunning*, *The Confession*, and *The Reckoning*, have each received the Gold Book Award. Her bestselling novel *October Song* won the Silver Seal in the Benjamin Franklin Awards, and *The Postcard* and *Sanctuary* (a collaboration with her husband, David) received Silver Angel Awards, as did her delightful picture book for all ages, *Annika's Secret Wish*. Beverly and her husband make their home in the Colorado foothills.

*M*oonlight created a silken halo around two small figures as they emerged from the dark covered bridge. The younger boy dragged a shovel, while the older carried a handmade wooden box carefully so as not to tip it, having sanded the miniature coffin smooth with his own hands.

They hurried around the north side of the bridge and down the grassy slope to a grove of black locust trees. Near the creek bed, they determined the location for burial—eight long steps past the first tree, then a sharp turn and four short ones to the soil most pliable from recent autumn rains. The box laden with the beloved pup was placed on the grass, and the older boy took up the shovel and began to dig.

When the hole was deep enough, the box was laid gently inside. The little boy inched back, sobbing at the grievous sound of dirt hitting the small coffin. Big brother worked the shovel faster, and with each heave and thud, the younger boy winced, squeezing hard a peach stone in his tiny palm.

Farther he crept back, away . . . away from the shadowy grave.

Soon the hole was filled. A proper burial. The boy responsible for his small brother peered into the darkness, calling repeatedly. When there was no answer, he scurried along the creek, then out to the road, seeking but not finding.

In short order, the People began to comb the area by horse and buggy, and on foot they joined stalwart arms in an unending thread to search for the wee child who had vanished into the silvery twilight. . . .

Ever let the fancy roam,
Pleasure never is at home.

—JOHN KEATS

Prologue

A gnawing sense of guilt defines my life, yet I am too obstinate
to fess up to the sin which so easily besets me. What I want to
do and what I *ought* to do get *ferhoodled* in my head and in my
heart. This is especially trying when it comes to my twice-weekly
visits to Cousin Julia Ranck's, where I am hired to help with her
two young children and do some light housekeeping . . . *and*
where I spend time working alone in the little attic room created
just for me, my undisclosed haven. There, I take a measure of
joy in the world of forbidden color—paint, canvas, and
brushes—this secret place known only to my Mennonite kinfolk,
and to the Lord God himself.

Deep on the inside, though, where it matters most, my heart
is torn. I have striven to follow in the Old Ways since childhood, to match the expectations of my parents and the church,
only to fail.

It annoys me no end that some Amish bishops allow for
artistic expression, permitting their people to create and sell art,
while our bishop does not.

I was just six when my preacher-father's probing brown eyes
did all the reprimanding necessary to stir up shame in my soul
when I was caught wistfully drawing a sleek black kitty, high in

the haymow. From then on, I learned to hide my art from prying eyes, even though I wished for a way to put a stop to it altogether.

Usually *Daed* had only to read out loud the Fifty-first Psalm for me to see the folly of my ways: *Have mercy upon me, O God . . . blot out my transgressions. . . .* King David's words rang ceaselessly in my ears until the next "holy scolding" for other acts of childish immaturity, though not again related to my pencil drawings . . . till I was caught again at age fourteen.

Have mercy, indeed.

There were times as a girl when I would sooner have welcomed a lickin' than the righteous gaze of my lanky, bearded father. It seemed he could see straight through to my heart. He had an uncanny way about him when it came to that, as well as the way his sermons stuck in my head for months on end. More times than I can count, I endured his deliberate silence, followed by his deeply drawn sigh and then a belabored reading from the Scriptures.

Unlike my six brothers—three older and already married, and three younger and looking to get hitched—I have never had the switch applied to my "seat of learning." Seeing as how some mules round these parts are less stubborn, it sure says a lot for the patience of my father, at least toward me.

Here lately, I have been urged to join the communion of earthly saints—our local Amish district. And since I marked my twentieth birthday back the end of April, I am keenly aware of concerned faces at nearly every gathering. Daed is doubly responsible under God on my behalf, *Mamm* says frequently, beseeching me to heed the warning. If I keep putting off my decision, well, that alone will become a choice, and in due time, I will have to leave the community of the People. I don't see how I could ever up and leave behind my family and all that I know and love.

But what gets my goat is the intense expectation regarding my upcoming decision. Joining church won't make me a good person. I know that. I live in this community; I know what makes most of these folk tick. Some live double lives, just as I'm living now—teen boys who take advantage of tipsy girls behind the bushes at corn-husking bees, and young women who parade around in pious cape dresses but whose hearts do not measure up to the Holy Scriptures. Most of this comes from our unbaptized youth, during *rumschpringe*. Still there is plenty of two-facedness. We're all human after all.

Alas, another sin has embedded itself within my soul: loving Rudy Esh and leading him to think I would marry him one day. Rudy formerly held the number one spot in my heart, even ahead of the Good Lord. But now, after three solid years of courting me, he has found a new sweetheart-girl. I'm obliged to show kindness where they're concerned, the utmost tolerance, too . . . things expected of me but increasingly difficult to demonstrate with any amount of sincerity. Handsome Rudy is soon to become a baptized church member and, no doubt, husband to his new sweetheart. Although I cared deeply for him, and he for me, I never shared with him my obsession with fine art. And since I wasn't ready to put any of that aside to join church, which is required before a wedding can take place, I am largely at fault for our breakup. He must surely be relieved, having pulled his hair out, so to speak, because of my resistance. "Heaven sakes, Annie," Rudy would say time and again, "why can't you just make the church vow and be done with it?" My answer always exasperated him: "I'm not ready." But I couldn't say why.

So I've lost my first and only love, which saddens me no end. Not that I should be bold enough to plead for his affection again, even though I was steady in my fondness for him from age seventeen till he decided he preferred Susie Yoder's company. All this adds up to three wasted years of faithfulness, to be sure . . . and now I am as lonely as ever a girl could be. A few years ago I would have shared this sorrow with my best friend, Essie, but lately my former playmate seems weighed down with her own set of grown-up problems.

Truth be told, only one other person knows about my fractured heart. My secret thoughts are safe with Louisa Stratford, an English girl who lives far away in Colorado. At twenty-two, she is engaged to be married, and for that I am most happy, seeing as how we're wonderful-good friends. Even though Louisa is fancy and I'm Plain, she's been reading my letters and writing back since she was nearly eleven years old. And if she hadn't sent that first drawing in her little letter—those delicate blossoms of forget-me-nots—so long ago, I might never have wondered if I, too, possessed any real talent.

I wish I could honor her by attending the splendid wedding she and her mother are planning. The thought of a big-city wedding in a faraway place surrounded by flowers and candles and girls in colorful dresses entices me terribly . . . things never, ever seen at an Amish wedding. Such things described in Louisa's letters have me completely intrigued, I daresay.

Naturally, I would stick out to kingdom come if I were brazen enough to go. Still I stare curiously at the pretty invitation with its raised gold lettering and wonder what it might be like.

Mamm would say it is out of the question to consider such a trip, even though I'm a grown woman. I can hear her going on and on about her fears. *You might get lost or worse in the maze of the hustle-bustle. You've never left Lancaster County, for pity's sake! You might get yourself kidnapped, Annie Zook!* Even so, I have yet to turn down my dear friend.

Honestly, my mother is wound tighter than a fiddle string when it comes to her children and grandchildren, often reminding my eldest brother, Jesse Jr., twenty-six, and his wife, Sarah Mae, to keep close watch on their two youngest, especially come dusk. *"You can never be too careful,"* she has said for the ten-thousandth time. It's not her fault, only an indication that not a soul has ever forgotten how dreadful it was for one of our own little ones to be stolen away, right here in the middle of Paradise. A heavenly-sounding sort of place, but one that's seen its share of heartache and mystery.

Here lately I've been going and standing beside Pequea Creek, staring at the well-known thicket of trees where little Isaac was snatched from the People . . . where I sometimes would swing double with him on the long tree swing. Where Isaac and I—and our brothers—often tossed twigs into the creek, watching them float away to who knows where.

Now I can't help wondering if I dare paint that setting in all its autumn beauty, as another side to the sad story. Perhaps by spreading the radiance of pastel gold on a canvas, I might somehow lessen the ominous side of the now-tranquil scene . . . even though my hand will surely tremble as I do, recalling Mamm's telling of the terrifying ordeal. When a bad thing happens to one family, it happens to us all, my mother says.

If that is true, then Rudy breaking off our courtship will also cause a wrinkle on the page of my life and everyone else's, too. For one, my future children—Daed's and Mamm's would-be grandchildren—will not have his gentle eyes and auburn hair, nor his fun-loving disposition. But even worse, I may never have babies at all. Yet if I were to abandon my paints and brushes in order to join church and marry, would I ever be truly happy? And yet . . . since I gave up the chance to wed a good Amish boy like Rudy, will I ever again know love? Oh, such a troublesome dilemma I face, and one that continually torments my soul.

Chapter 1

A late October mist draped itself over fields beseeching the harvest as Annie Zook walked along the narrow road to her Ranck cousins' house. Waving at a half dozen Amish neighbors out raking leaves, she felt all wound up, hoping for at least a few minutes to slip away to Cousin Julia's attic to work on her latest painting. Once her chores were done.

A gray and dismal sort of day was quite perfect for artistic work. Something about the anticipation of eventual sunshine, its warming glow held back by the cheerless clouds, made her feel full, yet achingly empty . . . and terribly creative, all at once. Even though the desire to express oneself artistically was considered by her particular district as wrongdoing, she saw no way out whatsoever.

She was still in her *rumschpringe*, the "in between" years—that murky transition between juvenile immaturity and adulthood . . . and church membership. Still, being the daughter of an ordained minister put an unwelcome clamp on her as she struggled to find her bearings. And yet, the thought of disappointing her parents went against the grain of her existence—it was the primary motivation for concealing her love of art.

Annie turned her thoughts away from her life struggle to

17

adorable two-year-old Molly Ranck, Julia's youngest, who had been scratching herself nearly raw with chicken pox two days ago. *Dear thing.* It had been all Annie could do to keep her occupied, what with the oatmeal bath and repeated dabs with calamine lotion. So there had not been a speck of time to work on the waiting canvas last visit.

She quickened her pace, somewhat surprised to see Deacon Byler's new house under roof already, and just when had *that* happened? Then, when she came upon the intersection, she became aware that the Lapps' corn was already going down and they must be filling silo, thus making it easier to see at the crossroads once again. *How'd I miss that?*

She realized she must have been walking in a fog of her own making since Rudy's parting words three months ago this coming Saturday. How had the changing landscape not registered in her brain?

This must be grief! When you hurt this bad, you push it way down inside. She remembered feeling this gloomy once before in her life, when, as a little girl, she'd stumbled upon Mamm in a mire of tears. But there was no sense in pondering to death *that* day.

She made a point to be more mindful of the details around her now—shapes, shadows, and depths of color. She took in the hazy morning splendor as it arched freely over muted green stalks, the burgundy-red barn of their English neighbors—the Danz family—coming into view, and the dark roof of the red-sided covered bridge not far from the old gray-stone London Vale Mill.

I'm painting God's creation! she thought, justifying her ongoing transgression.

She thought of her pen pal in Colorado, wanting to squeeze in a few minutes to write a letter to Louisa, who seemed to understand her best these days.

She contemplated the first time she had unintentionally embarrassed her English friend. It had happened early on in their letter writing, when brown-haired Louisa sent a small wallet-sized school photograph of herself, asking for the same from Annie. Not wanting to put Louisa on the spot, Annie had explained that the People didn't take pictures of themselves, carefully following the Ten Commandments: *Thou shalt not make unto thee any graven image.*

So she'd attempted to get around the Scripture and simply drew a colored-pencil self-portrait, showing the oval shape of her face, the single dimple, the soft blue in her eyes, and her golden-blond hair. She had also sketched the sacred symbol—the white heart-shaped head covering with its white ribbons dangling onto the bodice of her light green cape dress.

Such a long time ago, she thought, remembering how Louisa had written back with praise about the drawing, saying she'd immediately framed it for her bedside table. Annie wondered if Louisa still had it.

Here recently Annie had spent a rainy afternoon, counting her letters from Louisa, only to quit after reaching nearly five hundred. Smiling now at her amazing connection, not only with the outside world but with her English friend, she began to swing her arms, enjoying the pleasure of walking instead of having to hitch up the horse and carriage, as she often did to help Mamm on market days.

Yet even as she pretended to be carefree, she could not ignore the pangs of guilt.

Good thing Daed has no idea. She pondered the significance of her actions, or when it came to joining church, her lack thereof.

Sighing, she spied an enclosed gray buggy up ahead, pulled by a prancing steed with shiny new horseshoes. The young woman driver waved urgently. "Annie, is that you?"

Rhoda Esh!

Pleased as pie, Annie waved back just as enthusiastically. "Hullo, there!" she called, hoping Rudy's younger sister might stop and chat a bit.

"I'm so glad I ran into you," Rhoda said, pulling on the reins. She motioned for Annie to get in the buggy. "Come on 'n' ride with me, won't ya? We best be talkin' some."

Annie lifted her skirt and climbed into the buggy.

Right away, Rhoda spoke her mind. "I'm not s'posed to know, prob'ly, but Susie Yoder's cousin's big-mouthed sister said Rudy has been seein' Susie 'stead of you." Rhoda's brown eyes were about as big as gingersnaps.

Annie shrugged. "My lips are zipped."

"Aw, surely ya know *something* . . . after all, Rudy was your beau all them years." Rhoda eyed her curiously and slapped the reins, getting the steed moving again.

"Well, if ya must know, ask him."

"I'm askin' you!"

Annie kept her eyes forward, wishing she might've continued to walk instead of accepting the ride.

"Can't ya give me a hint . . . the least little one?" Rhoda pleaded. "Honestly, I'm in your corner. I wouldn't want Susie Yoder for my sister-in-law."

"Oh, why not? She's a right nice girl."

Rhoda paused a moment. Then she said, "Well, I'd have to say it's because she's nothin' like you."

Ain't that the truth, thought Annie.

"Surely Rudy didn't have a fallin' out with ya, did he?"

Puh! Truth was they'd fussed like two cats toward the end. One of them feistier than the other. Even so, Rudy had been the most wonderfully kind—even affectionate—boy she'd ever known during the years of their courtship. She had accepted rides home from Sunday night singing with several other fellows before him, but the minute she'd met Rudy, there was no other for her. Rhoda knew as well as anyone there was nothing bad to report about her own brother. He was not a troublemaker like some fellas. If anything, *she* had been the problem, unwilling to join church when he was ready to.

"We've parted ways, Rhoda, and that's all I'm gonna say."

Rhoda sniffled, like she might burst out crying, but Annie decided no fit of temper was going to change her mind. What had transpired between Rudy and herself was nobody's business. Least of all Rhoda's, who Annie just realized was something of a tittle-tattle.

They rode a good quarter mile in silence. Then, hesitantly, Rhoda asked, "Where're ya headed?"

"To my cousins, Irvin and Julia's, but I can get out here and walk the rest of the way." She wished Rhoda would take that as a hint to halt the horse.

"No . . . no, that's all right. Ain't so far out of my way."

In a few minutes, they arrived at the redbrick house, set back a ways from the road. Irvin Ranck owned a harness shop across the vast meadow behind the house, in a barnlike structure he'd built years ago. Daed had always spoken well of his first cousin. Irvin was a good and honest man, one Mennonite the Amish farmers didn't mind paying for their stable gear. Just maybe that was the reason her father hadn't protested her working for the Rancks, even though Irvin's family had left the Amish church many decades before.

"*Denki* for the ride," Annie said, hopping down from the carriage.

"I'll be seein' ya" was all Rhoda said with a quick wave.

Hurrying up the walkway to the prim house, Annie spied four-year-old James pushing a toy lawn mower over a pile of leaves in the side yard. "Hullo!" she called and was delighted to see his eager smile.

"Cousin Annie!" the towheaded tyke called, running toward her with open arms.

"How's your little sister?" She gave him a quick squeeze and let him go.

"Oh, Molly's got lots of bumps . . . you'll see." James hurried alongside her as they rounded the corner of the house, entered through the back door, and walked upstairs to the nursery.

James was quite right. Molly had oodles more chicken pox bumps than two days ago, wearing mittens now so she couldn't scratch. She was plumped up with several pillows, sitting in her toddler-sized bed made by her father.

"Annie's here . . ." said Molly, trying to smile.

"*Jah*, I'm here, sweet one. And we'll look at lots of books together, all right?" Her heart went out to the little blond girl with eyes blue as cornflowers.

That brought a bigger smile to Molly's face, and James promptly went to the small bookcase and picked up a stack of board books. "These are Molly's favorites," he said, placing them gently in Annie's hands.

Bright-eyed Julia sat on the edge of her daughter's small bed, looking pretty in one of her hand-sewn floral print dresses. She wore her light brown hair in a bun, similar to Annie's, only Julia's was set higher on her head. Atop her bun, she wore the formal cup-shaped Mennonite head covering.

"I need to visit one of my expectant mothers in Strasburg today," Julia said softly. "She wants me present at the birth of her baby in a few weeks. I hope you don't mind."

"Ach, no, we'll be fine," she said. "Won't we?" Annie looked at both children, who were bobbing their heads and smiling.

Cousin Julia went on to say that the word was getting out about her being a "gentle midwife, although I'm not certified at all."

"But you have such a comforting way," Annie commented. "I can see why folks depend on you."

Later, after Julia had left and Annie had read each little book twice, she pulled up the quilted coverlet and smiled down at Molly, already asleep and clinging to her favorite dolly. Annie turned and raised her pointer finger to her lips as she and James tiptoed out of the nursery. "Time now for your nap, too, young man," she whispered, and the boy willingly followed her down the hall.

When James was tucked in, Annie hurried to the attic. Instead of closing the door behind her as usual, she left it wide open, tuning an ear to the children.

Over the years, she had managed to purchase everything she needed to create her landscape paintings, as well as her few attempts at portraits: Irvin and Julia's children, either from memory or from photographs. Naturally, she didn't dare bring even James up here for a sitting. And both Irvin and Julia knew her love for creating was to be held in the closest of confidence, even though Julia had admitted to being tempted to hire a professional tutor for Annie.

Mixing paints on her palette, she dabbed some purple onto the sky, making repeated attempts to blend it to create a rich lavender streak. Next, she gave the clouds a wispy sweep with her brush.

She eyed the canvas and scrutinized the creek bed and cluster of trees. She had stood on that very spot some weeks back, studying and pondering what precisely had happened there so long ago. But now she checked off each aspect of the painting in her mind . . . the sunlight twinkling on the wide stream, the covered bridge, the density of the trees, the depth of gray and the basket-weave texture of the trunks, complete with thorns protruding from trunk and limb. And the pale autumn yellow of the leaves.

The trees could not be climbed due to the wicked thorns, yet locust wood was the toughest kind, much stronger than cedar. It made the best fence posts, too, according to her eldest brother, Jesse, soon to be considered a master carpenter.

Annie stood in the middle of the unfinished garret where the easel had been positioned so that light from the two dormer windows, especially in the afternoon, could spill around the canvas like a crown. But the grayness outdoors was hardly adequate today, so Annie turned on the recessed lighting, which Irvin had so kindly installed last year. She always felt a thrilling sensation when flicking on the light switch.

Going back now to stand before the painting, she contemplated the waft and wisp of clouds. Several bluebirds populated the painting, one in flight, two others perched on a distant branch—feathery flecks of color.

Something's missing. . . .

She moved closer, her brush poised. The connection of hand to brush and brush on canvas sometimes triggered something important, something subconscious pulled into awareness.

Holding her breath, she touched her brush to the first tree.

The long swing, that's what!

Steadying her hand, she drew a thin line down. *Jah . . . good.*

Suddenly, she heard her name being called. "Annie!" The

sound came from downstairs. "Are you up there, Annie?"

Someone—*who?*—was coming up the staircase!

"I'm here," she called back, her heart in her throat.

"What the world are ya doin' up there?"

Now she recognized the voice as her sister-in-law Sarah Mae.
No . . . no, dear Lord God, no!

Dropping her brush, she grabbed the nearest rag and began
to wipe the paint off her hands. She heard Sarah Mae's footsteps
on the wide-plank hallway at the base of the stairs and her heart
began pounding.

She's going to discover my secret!

Quickly Annie stepped out of the studio, pulled the door
closed behind her, and ran down the staircase, bumping into
Sarah Mae as she did. "Oh, hullo," she managed to say.

Sarah Mae's round face was flushed and her blue eyes were
inquisitive. "I knocked on the front door but guessed the children were asleep, so I just let myself in."

Annie nodded, feeling nearly dizzy with fright.

"What're ya doin' clear up here?" asked Sarah Mae. Then,
without waiting for a reply, she added, "Does Julia have you redd
up her attic, too?"

Not wanting to lie, Annie paused, thinking what to say,
stumbling over several answers in her head. She stared down at
the rag and said, "Jah, I'm cleanin' up a bit."

"Well, I stopped by to see if you'd be wantin' a ride home,
since it looks to be turning a bit cold . . . and I'm headed there
to drop off some blueberry jam to Mamm."

"I need to stay put till Julia returns. But denki—thank you."

Sarah Mae nodded, "All right, then." She inched her way
backward down the narrow staircase.

Whew! Annie blew out a puff of air. *I must be more careful!*

Chapter 2

Following a supper of lamb loaf, scalloped asparagus, buttered carrots, homemade bread with Sarah Mae's blueberry jam, and topped off with Mamm's well-loved misty mint salad, Annie washed and dried the dishes, taking pleasure in redding up. Mamm put away the few leftovers in their new gas-powered refrigerator, then swept the floor.

Soon her father wandered to the corner cupboard and took down the big family Bible for evening reading and silent prayers. He went and poked his head out the back door and called for Yonie, just turned nineteen last week, Luke, seventeen, and Omar, fifteen months younger than Luke—all courting age.

Annie had heard Daed refer quite often to his "empty wallet" now that Omar was sixteen. The price of a good road horse was twenty-five hundred dollars, not to mention her father's purchase of a new open buggy for Luke, close to three thousand dollars. All this with Daed being something of a penny-pincher, too. But a new horse and buggy assured each boy attendance at the all-important Sunday night singings, as well as other necessary activities during rumschpringe—the running-around years before a young person settled down to marry.

Later, when evening prayers were done, Annie hurried

upstairs to her room and lit the gas lamp. She sat at the little
maple desk Daed had made for her twelfth birthday, pulled out
the narrow center drawer and found her floral stationery. She
was mighty curious to know how things had turned out with
Louisa's mother's idea of having dozens of white doves released
from cages as the bride and groom hurried out of the church to
something called a stretch limousine, whatever that was. Annie
had not the faintest idea about most of the things Louisa shared
in her letters. Nonetheless, she began to write to her best English friend:

> *Wednesday, October 26*
> *Dear Louisa,*
> *Hello again. How are you doing?*
> *I've been thinking so much about you lately. I hope you're
> not as tired this week as you said you were last, what with all the
> places you and your mother have been rushing to. Hither and
> yon, goodness me! Do you ever feel like just going to bed with the
> chickens, the way I do?*
> *Which reminds me, did you decide what to do about the
> doves? Or has your mother changed her mind yet again? (I'm
> sure you're still wishing to have your guests simply blow the little
> bubbles, as you described in your last letter. To be honest, I think
> that would be the most fun.)*

She stopped writing, trying to picture thousands of bubbles
with every color of the rainbow gleaming within each tiny cir-
cumference. Smiling, she daydreamed about being present on
Louisa's special day, to witness firsthand the peculiar yet fascinating way the English celebrate a wedding ceremony and reception.

"What would Daed think if I just upped and went?" she

whispered to herself. *I really ought to. . . .*

But Mamm was entirely right—she had never set foot outside Lancaster County. So what made her think she could be high-minded enough to get herself a bus or train ticket all the way to the Rocky Mountains, which is nearly where Louisa's well-to-do family lived? Somewhere south of Denver, in a place called Castle Pines. Louisa had herself an apartment in the town of Castle Rock, just a hop, skip, and a jump from her parents' home.

According to Louisa, the prime location had been her father's first choice some years ago—five acres, a custom-built home set high on a ridge with sweeping views of the mountains, with three rock fireplaces, a separate library large enough for a writing desk and three overstuffed chairs, and five large bedrooms, each having its own bathroom. And although only the two of them resided there, they had four living areas, a "separate dining room big enough to entertain thirty for sit-down dinners," as Louisa described it, a butler's pantry, and a kitchen with every imaginable appliance, including electric everything—refrigerator, a regular oven, convection oven, dishwasher, garbage disposal and compactor, and the list went on and on. All this in a room the size of the entire downstairs of the hundred-year-old farmhouse where Annie lived. Most of these things Annie had never heard of before in her life.

She couldn't begin to know why Louisa's parents needed so many rooms, but it was not her place to question. *Englischers* were often frivolous, Daed had always said of outsiders. Still, in spite of that, Annie felt mighty happy all these years to have ended up with such an interesting pen pal. A true and faithful friend.

She let her mind wander back to the day the first letter from

Louisa had arrived in the mailbox.

The afternoon had been unseasonably cool and rainy. Fall housecleaning was well underway, with plenty of hands making light the work. Annie kept herself busy whitewashing the picket fence that bordered the main pastureland.

When the mail truck came with a letter postmarked Denver, Colorado, but with the recipient's name and address all soiled, Annie opened it, planning only to read enough to see who the letter was meant for. The inside salutation had read simply: *Dear New Friend,* so Annie began to read the first few lines. The letter writer introduced herself as Louisa Stratford, named for her paternal grandmother. Louisa was obviously not Amish and said she was almost eleven. But she'd written that she wanted to be an artist when she grew up, "with all of my heart, I do." Declaring this in the first few lines immediately grabbed Annie's curiosity.

Reading further, Annie soon realized the letter was not intended for her. She knew she ought to check at the next farmhouse over, to see if the English farmer's daughter, Jenna Danz, had signed up for a Colorado pen pal at school, maybe. Yet eight-year-old Annie was compelled to read on, especially because some pretty drawings in the margins caught her eye. And before she knew it, she'd read the entire letter, so captivated by this faraway modern girl and the way she described herself. Most of all, her keen love of drawing.

Quickly Annie wrote down Louisa's name and her return address. Then she put on her galoshes and raincoat and promptly marched down the road stepping in all the mud puddles, taking the letter to its rightful owner. She also apologized for having opened the letter and read it all, but dared not admit why . . . that she, too, loved to draw. She left that part unsaid, hoping

Jenna would forgive, and she had.

Returning to the house, she had scarcely any hope of ever getting a letter back, even if she did have the courage to write to the Colorado schoolgirl. But since she was still learning English grammar at the one-room schoolhouse, she reasoned childishly that writing to Louisa Stratford would be extra good practice for her, too.

The rest was history, as Louisa liked to say. Besides that, Annie had always felt it providential—meant to be—her getting the letter from outside the Plain community . . . the two of them so completely worlds apart, yet opening up their hearts to one another by mail. Daed had never said one word against it, though Annie was fairly sure he had no clue how often the letters flew back and forth.

But Mamm knew and was good enough to keep it to herself. Annie supposed her mother assumed there was no harm done, what with all the miles between the girls. Up until just this year, Annie never would have given a second thought to a wedding invitation such as the one she held now in her hands.

What would it be like to see the colors of all those cut flowers . . . and the golden candelabra, and satin bows, and . . . ?

She shook herself, knowing she must simply pick up the pen and politely reply on the RSVP card that she would not be going. Even though with all of her heart, she would be there in her mind's eye when Louisa took her father's arm and strode the lengthy walkway along the rows of church pews, the "aisle," Louisa had called it, covered with an ivory runner and sprinkled with red and pink rose petals by the five wee girls dressed as miniature brides and carrying flower baskets. All this to get Louisa on her way to her smiling and handsome husband, who was to stand with nine other men also in fine black suits, lavender shirts, and matching cummerbunds high at the chapel altar. *Formal tuxedos*, Louisa had written to describe them and had sketched them, as well.

Annie easily read the words, but without the aid of the drawings tucked into each letter, she would have been completely bewildered about the upcoming wedding ceremony of Miss Louisa Victoria Stratford to Mr. Michael Logan Berkeley at twelve o'clock noon on Saturday the nineteenth day of November. . . .

Chapter 3

Louisa Stratford parked her silver Mercedes in the circular driveway in front of her parents' home at Crown Pointe Place. Opening the car door, she headed for the house, already missing her signature jeans and ankle boots. At her mother's urging, she had donned one of the few ultraconservative outfits hanging in her closet—a chic blue-and-gray-plaid woolen skirt and coordinating blue cashmere sweater.

"Hello, dear!" Mother called as she emerged from the front door. "Shall I drive today?"

"My car's warmed up," Louisa said. Making note of her mother's prim navy suit and pumps, she went to open the passenger door and waited for her mother to get settled in the front seat.

When they were on their way, heading north on I-25 to Denver, Louisa absentmindedly slipped in an old Sheryl Crow CD, one of her favorites. "I'm exhibiting my art students' work in two weeks, so I can't be late for class today," she said, hoping to keep their outing as brief as possible.

Suddenly, the plaintive wail of *Every Day is a Winding Road* blared into the car, and she quickly poked the eject button. "Sorry about that."

Off to a classic start, she thought, restless, even preoccupied. She was eager to meet with her students again, having grown weary of the wedding preparations, more than a full year of them already. Each week's schedule of events, teas, and luncheons was a reflection of her parents' tastes, but she had learned from her childhood to acquiesce to Mother's wishes to avoid making waves.

Her dream wedding—hers and Michael's—bore little resemblance to the plans being carved out for them. Both families had decided their children, their *only* offspring, deserved something of a gala *to die for.* Well, Louisa was dying all right, and it had nothing to do with the composition of the gift sachets—satin or netting?—for three hundred dinner guests, nor whether the reception china should be rimmed in gold or silver.

Gold, her mother had insisted, with full endorsement from Ms. Tyler, the wedding planner. The reasoning was linked to the gilded birdcages with large satin bows tied to their gleaming posts to be positioned strategically along the wedding aisle. No mere candelabra or flowers with simple bows along the aisle, no. Nothing ordinary in *this* wedding. And because the embossed invitations were also gold, it was only fitting the dinnerware be etched with the same.

On the other hand, the groom had early voiced his humorous opinion to the bride, but the notion of saying vows before a justice of the peace was out of the question. Not with his family connections. And *hers.*

In fact, Michael paid little mind to their wedding plans. If anything, his primary interest seemed to be the exotic honeymoon cruise package. She smiled to herself. *Typical guy.*

"Driving a little fast?" her mother commented as Louisa navigated the wide streets of Littleton, a suburb of Denver, to the appointed boutique.

She tapped the brake. "Sorry."

Today's quest was to select gifts for the bridesmaids and junior bridesmaids, as well as the guestbook girls—*why three?* Louisa knew the answer all too well. Everything was about Daddy's prestigious law firm. It was essential, as it had been explained to her, that the upper echelon of her father's company—their up-and-coming progeny, at least—be well represented in the Stratford/ Berkeley wedding, whether Louisa and Michael had ever made their acquaintance or not.

At least I chose my own maid-of-honor, Louisa consoled herself, smiling at the thought of Courtney Engelman, her outspoken, even cynical, but fun-loving college friend.

The addition of bodies had begun to aggravate her, including three of the supposedly "charming" yet nameless flower girls whom Mother had lined up without her knowledge until just recently.

Sighing, Louisa parked in front of the boutique, then pulled her keys from the ignition.

"Darling." Mother turned and touched her arm lightly. "Is something the matter?"

Louisa sighed again. "I'm fine . . . maybe a little tired." Not only was she tired physically, but weary of attending to the infinitesimal details of a full-weekend wedding celebration, from calling to double-check room reservations at Denver's most exclusive hotel, the Brown Palace, for out-of-town guests to a zillion and one bridal showers in her honor—both lingerie and household—all happening in the next two weeks. Not to mention the post-wedding announcements to be sent to newspapers on the never-ending list: the *Denver Post,* for their present location, the

Chicago Tribune, where most of Daddy's side of the family lived, the *Los Angeles Times*, where Mother's people still resided, and several more small-town papers her parents had decided were a "must send."

Why did we hire a professional planner at all? she wondered, wishing she and Michael might have arranged a simple but elegant wedding.

"We mustn't tire you out, darling. You tell me when you've had your fill, all right?"

Louisa forced a smile.

Growing up in opulence, Louisa was accustomed to the niceties of life. But once this wedding hoopla was past and she and Michael returned from their honeymoon—once the hundreds of thank-yous were properly addressed and stamped, with the proper return address label on the proper day—the life she now led was going to screech to a halt. She had little interest in kowtowing to the almighty dollar. Daddy's riches hadn't brought joy to Mother's heart or peace to her perfect plastered smile. Oh, they were content and at ease with their friends and societal functions, but deep down weren't they as frustrated as everyone else on the planet, well off or otherwise?

However, in the midst of this crazy and contrived world, Louisa knew someone who had long embraced a simple and unpretentious life. A young woman who knew well the meaning of genuine beauty, laughter, and love, although without a boyfriend at the present time. Annie Zook understood how to live to the fullest and on very little means monetarily, or so Louisa assumed. The Zooks supplemented the sale of cow's milk and butter by raising peacocks, and from the honest and caring letters Annie wrote so frequently, Louisa had enjoyed a front-row seat to the Plain life—the daily routine on the back roads of Paradise.

Perfect name for a honeymoon resort, Louisa thought, smiling.

While her mother paid for each of the two-hundred-dollar bracelets to be presented to the attendants at the bridesmaids' luncheon in a few days, Louisa wandered toward the lace-covered bay window. She looked out to the horizon, past the flurry and cacophony of traffic, and considered the Pennsylvania barnyard where Annie often ran barefoot up until the first frost, bringing home their herd of cows twice daily and feeding the peahens and their chicks. She closed her eyes and visualized the fall plowing which was happening this week, with the help of Yonie, Luke, and Omar, the three younger Zook boys.

A "closet" artist, Annie also had a surprising knack for word pictures, even though she had only an eighth-grade education. The real-to-life descriptions in her letters helped Louisa envision the foreign world of the Old Order Amish.

Her curious connection to Annie Zook all these years had created within her a yearning for a less-complicated life, even though it was clear that brokenhearted Annie was caught in an ominous situation with her secret love of art, which was forbidden by her strict church community. *A train wreck about to happen*, she thought, wishing she could do something more than write letters to support her friend.

"She's as trapped as I am . . . in a different way," she whispered into the air, thinking how ironic it was that she had not been able to pry herself away from her parents' wishes for her own wedding. Just as Annie had not been able to please her parents by abandoning her art and joining the Amish church.

"Louisa," her mother said, tugging her back from her reverie, "let's have lunch. Somewhere wonderful."

Conscious of her mother's anticipation, she surrendered. "Sure, if you like, Mother."

Her mother waved at the thirty-something wedding planner, Katrina Tyler, who was pulling into the parking lot. "Why don't we head downtown to the Brown Palace Hotel and kill two birds with one stone?" Mother suggested. "Would you like that?"

Translation: *Why don't we sample the reception dinner entrée?*

"I'd really rather not." The words tumbled surprisingly off her lips.

"Beg your pardon, dear?"

Pardon, indeed . . .

Louisa shook her head. "Can't we trust the head chef, the wait staff, Ms. Tyler, and everyone else you and Daddy have shelled out tens of thousands of dollars to, to get it right? To make *my* wedding day the perfect memory. Can't we, Mother?"

Her mother's brow pinched up and her tone turned icy. "We're scheduled to meet the caterer there."

"I'd much rather grab some fast food. I'll ask Katrina to meet us at—"

"The luncheon is already set, Louisa."

Why didn't you say so? She glanced over her shoulder and noticed the boutique owner's face crumpling while whispering to the clerk.

Louisa turned to leave and politely held the door. She forced herself to slow her pace and wave at Ms. Tyler when she opened her car window and called a perfunctory greeting. "I can drive if you'd like," the wedding planner offered.

"I'm driving!" Louisa said. "We'll meet you there." She matched the dignified slow tempo of her mother's stride. Everything these days—*everything*—was a corresponding link to the Stratford family name and fortune. The way things were expected to be. All the years of finishing school—how to walk and not to, how to point toes, cross legs at ankles, how to present oneself perfectly in public . . . whether dressed in scanty swim attire, tea-length tailored suit, or floor-length evening gown. She knew the drill.

"I'll spring for burgers, okay?" she said, making one final attempt when they were settled in the car. "We could eat them on the way. Consider it appetizers." She snickered at her own mouthy joke.

"Far too much fat for a bride who must fit into her size two gown." Mother said, shifting into her most-determined mode.

"I'm not worried about clogged arteries or zipping up my gown. You never saw what I ate during art school."

"Well, we fed you the very best food growing up."

The very best . . . How often had she heard that?

At Seventeenth Street, they pulled up for valet parking at the Brown Palace Hotel, and Louisa was told they were lunching at Ellyngton's, the place to be seen and home to the "power meal." Maybe Michael might wander in for lunch with his attorney pals. She could only hope so.

After all, she thought wryly, *we're on the brink of marriage . . .*

When they were settled at a window overlooking Denver's lively financial district, Mother suggested the baby greens and three-tomato salad on the starter section of the menu, to which Louisa quickly agreed. In doing so, she would improve her chances of ordering what she really wanted for her main course, which was neither the spinach and wild mushroom salad nor the lemon-marinated salmon. The Angus burger would satisfy her hunger. She had enjoyed it before, several months ago when Michael had met her here during his short lunch hour, to discuss a prenuptial agreement his attorney had drawn up. She'd found it to be rather annoying at first but was informed of the "necessity" of such an agreement, as explained to her later by Michael's private attorney. And, silly her, she should have figured this might happen, with the amassed Berkeley fortune being "old money," unlike her family's more recently acquired wealth. After cooling down, which took a few days, she had signed on the dotted line, with a wink and a nod from Michael, who assured her there was "no need to worry."

Now she reached for her glass of sparkling mineral water, studying Katrina, who had taken her checklist out of her briefcase. No older than thirty-two, *this* wedding planner was earning her keep. She would not derail with an impertinent approach and had way more style than her predecessors. She also possessed the single most important ingredient of all: the ability to persevere.

Yep, Ms. Tyler will cross the finish line.

Later, when Mother and Katrina ordered identical desserts of apple beignets with lingonberry jam, Louisa went for broke with the black bottom pie, having chickened out on the burger and ordered a chicken entrée instead.

But it was following the meal, when the schmoozing with the caterer started, that Louisa stifled her opinion. She followed Katrina's lead, feigning interest in the reception entrée options: Filet Mignon, Roast Prime Rib of Beef, Chicken Edgar, Chicken Italia, Sesame Seared Salmon, and Herb-Crusted Haddock. Or a trio of three to please all palates.

After an hour and a half, she was no longer able to sit demurely by. She glared up at the chandelier, fidgeting idly with her smart phone and keys, wishing she dared call Michael. But his day would be demanding as always, tied up with important clients, as a busy junior partner at a competing law firm some miles from her father's.

Mother continued to deliberate the selection of ivory versus ecru linens, now kindly conferring with Katrina on the matter. Louisa let her mind drift away to the perfect daydream . . . to gorgeous Michael, who planned to drop by her apartment after work tomorrow evening. Together they would grill the steaks marinating in her fridge, but he would insist on making a walloping big Mediterranean salad while she stir-fried his favorite snow peas, oyster mushrooms, young asparagus spears, and strips of red and yellow bell peppers. Once dinner was over, she would share what was troubling her, confiding her dire frustration, asking if it was too late. *Too late for what, babe?* To make their mark on the most important day of their lives. Or, better yet, to go back to the drawing board and do it their way. He would assure her, pull her into his arms, and fervently kiss away her stress, while Muffin, her blue-gray cat, would blink his green eyes all curled up on Louisa's funky secondhand black-speckled Garbo sofa.

A good dose of sanity . . . soon! She could hardly wait.

Chapter 4

Sunlight played chase with yesterday's fog, and the newly painted clapboard farmhouse beamed like a white moon against the backdrop of a considerable willow tree in the backyard. There, dozens of scarlet cardinals flocked to its branches in the early evening, as if drawn to the thousands of golden leaves.

A stand of sugar maples on the opposite side yard made a show of their dazzling red tresses, and each day more crimson blanketed the ground below.

Never in disrepair, though more than a hundred years old, the three-story house stood as a testament to hard work and constant care. Out front, just steps from the yard, a scarcely traveled ribbon of road divided the property in two—the house on one side and the barn and several outbuildings on the other.

Annie stared out her bedroom window at the radiant foliage bursting forth from nearly every tree, the array of colors reminding her of an artist's palette. She chided herself a bit. *No time for daydreaming during the harvest*, she thought, *what with everyone keeping busy—men filling silo, womenfolk making applesauce and cider, this very morning, in fact, in Mamm's big kitchen.* She headed downstairs. *I must do my part, too. For now. . . .*

Annie and her mother were soon joined by more than a

dozen women, each assuming a different task. Looking around intently, she saw that one very important helper was missing. Annie held her breath, thinking of her dear friend Esther Hochstetler, hoping she might yet arrive even at this late hour.

Mamm's three older sisters, Aunts Suzanne, Emma, and Frannie were on hand with their married daughters, Mary, Katie, Suzie, Nancy, Becky, Rhoda, and Barbianne. Another half hour passed, and Esther was still not there, even though two weeks ago at Preaching service she'd told Annie she was definitely coming today.

I hope she's feeling all right. Esther was expecting again, and this pregnancy seemed to be the reason she gave lately for staying home.

Annie continued to help her cousins prepare the apples for cooking into sauce, cutting a neat circle in each apple to core the seeds and stem. All the while, Barbianne and Suzie chattered about the corn-husking bee tomorrow, the familiar light evident in their eyes as they talked softly of those "pairing up," unaware of Annie's hollow heart.

They continued whispering of the fun in store, hoping one of them might find the colored corn—Indian corn—for a special prize of candy or cream-filled cookies.

Then, for no particular reason, Annie happened to glance up. There was Esther coming through the back porch and mudroom area, hesitating slightly before stepping foot in the kitchen, looking awful tired and pale.

Lickety-split, Annie set down her paring knife and wiped her hands on her apron. She rushed to Esther's side. "Ach, I'm so glad you're here!" She pulled her into the kitchen. "Where have you been keepin' yourself?"

Esther blinked her pretty eyes, blue as can be. "Oh, you

know me . . .'tis easy to get caught up with the little ones."

"Well, two in diapers must be nearly like havin' twins."

Esther nodded. "Jah, seems so at times."

"Who's with them today?"

Esther paused. "Uh . . . Mamma came by, said I needed to get out a bit."

Annie agreed. "I'm glad she did!" She led Esther over to the section of the table where the cousins were still coring and peeling. "How does your big girl like first grade?"

"Laura thinks goin' to school is the next best thing to home-made ice cream." Esther gave Annie a quick smile. "But I miss her help at home . . . for sure."

They went over and began working on the first bushel basket. Then, after a bit, when the next group of women had the apples quartered and ready for the sugar, cinnamon, and water, they all took a short break while that mixture cooked.

Annie sat with Esther at the far end of the table, pouring extra sugar into her own cup of tea. "Laura's always been keen on learnin', seems to me."

Esther nodded, holding her teacup. "She's doin' all right . . . in school, jah."

"I remember I always liked spelling best." She bit her tongue and almost said *drawing*, too. But, of course, that subject was never taught in the little one-room schoolhouse over yonder. "I remember your favorite was geography. Am I right?"

Esther's lip quivered slightly and she was still.

"You all right?" Annie touched her arm. "Come, let's walk over to the outhouse right quick."

"No . . . no. I'll keep workin' here—you go on."

Annie was stumped. Esther looked to be troubled about something, so why did she clam up like that?

Hurrying out the back door, Annie headed around the side yard to the wooden outhouse. She hoped Esther was all right, really she did. Essie, as she'd called her when they were girls, had always been a most cheerful playmate. She and her family had lived a ten-minute buggy ride away, so she and Annie got to visit each other often, and Annie loved it, being the only girl in a family of boys. She also remembered that up until Essie's courting years, she'd worn a constant smile on her pretty face.

But sadly it wasn't long after Essie married Ezekiel that the infectious smile began to fade. Soon Essie was asking folk to drop her youthful nickname. "Call me Esther from now on," she insisted.

In the few months following her wedding day, Esther became sullen, even distant, and within the year, she was scarce at gatherings. When she did go to help can vegetables and fruits or put up canned meats, she didn't say much unless spoken to first. It was as if Esther had to be pried free of something each and every time.

Annie could not put her finger on the reason for the drastic change. But something sank in her like a rock in a dew pond whenever she thought about who her friend had become. What was it about getting hitched up that caused the light to go out of some girls' eyes?

Annie shook away her fretting and headed back to the house. She wished she could help, but there was a thick wall around Esther now and it seemed no one could break through.

Just then Annie spied her father and Rudy Esh's older brother, Caleb, across the road smoking cigars near the springhouse. How peculiar. In all her days she did not recall ever seeing Caleb Esh chewing the fat with Daed.

A little shiver went down her back, seeing Caleb, because he looked a lot like Rudy. *What on earth does he want with my father?*

But, alas, she'd worried enough for one morning. Taking a deep breath, she forced her attention back to applesauce-making and to dear downtrodden Esther. She opened the back door to the tantalizing aroma of tart Granny Smith applesauce.

Jesse Zook puffed on his cigar, exercising as much forbearance as possible, saying not a word as Caleb Esh gabbed away.

"My brother Rudy must have had a good reason for picking a different girl—it's just that I think your Annie's far and away a better choice of a mate, Preacher."

Jesse had not made a practice of knowing who was seeing his daughter and who wasn't. He wouldn't start speculating now . . . unlike some fathers who required a report from their sons of the scallywags who drove younger sisters home from barn singings and other church-sanctioned activities. Never had he cared to interfere that way with Annie's courting years. She was a level-headed sort and downright determined, too. *His* daughter would have no trouble attracting a fine man to marry, but only when she was good and ready to settle down.

"Rudy is makin' a big mistake, the way I see it," Caleb continued.

Sighing, Jesse removed his hat and inhaled his tobacco deeply. He contemplated the field work to be done yet, and here they were wasting time. "Well, I have to ask ya, just what's your concern in this?"

"Only that Rudy was in love with Annie. Sure as my name's Esh."

"But you say *he* broke off with her?"

"That he did."

Now Jesse was confused *and* perturbed. Seemed Caleb wasn't

making much sense for a man nearly thirty-five years old, married, and the father of nine children, last count. This here Caleb had also been talked about as a possible preacher nomination back last fall after council meeting, amongst some of the brethren.

A busybody, to be sure . . .

"Is all your plowin' done, Caleb?" he asked right quick.

"Well . . . almost."

Jesse shook his head a bit, looked down at his straw hat, and then placed it back on his head. "Why not let nature take her course where courtin's concerned. Seems the Good Lord works all that out just right fine, given the chance."

Caleb nodded his head quick like and said, "Afternoon, Preacher Zook." Then he sauntered over to his horse and carriage, where he'd left them smack dab in the middle of the lane.

"Be seein' ya at Preaching service come Sunday," Jesse called to him, attempting to keep a grin in check.

Louisa lit each of four candles on the table, two tall tapers and two votives. She softly blew out the match and returned to the kitchen, where Michael was putting the finishing touches on his organic dressing "experiment," as he called it: extra-virgin olive oil, French sea salt, freshly-squeezed lemon juice, dry Italian basil, fresh garlic, ground black pepper, and Greek oregano—leaves only, all mixed into one dressing bottle.

"Looks exotic," she said, smiling. "And the steaks await."

He carried the wooden salad bowl, tongs, and dressing to the table. "How about some dinner music?"

"Sure. What are you in the mood for?"

He winked at her in response, and she felt her face blush.

"You pick."

She went to the sitting area of the small living room and scanned the CD tower. This was not a night for anything heavy. *Keep it mellow,* she decided, thinking ahead to the topic of conversation, which must wait until they had enjoyed the jointly made candlelight dinner.

She reached for her old favorite, legendary Stan Getz—cool tenor sax—and slipped the disk into the CD player. Smooth jazz filled up all the spaces of silence, and she sat down across from Michael.

"Hold your plate," he said and forked one of the steaks.

She watched him place the medium-rare piece of meat onto her plate. She was aware of his hands, his well-manicured nails . . . and immediately she thought of her mother's plans to do an all-day manicure, pedicure, and facial with all the bridesmaids. Then, they were all supposed to go to a glitzy tearoom Mother had booked, where Louisa was to present the gold bracelets.

But here she was having a really terrific dinner with Michael, who was making nice remarks about the steaks she'd grilled. Saying other complimentary things with his eyes, as well.

Oh, she groaned inwardly. *Wrong timing.*

But later, during a dessert of peach sorbet and gourmet butter cookies, it was Michael who mentioned that his mother was asking about "all those groomsmen."

"Did you tell her it was *my* mother's idea to have a million bridesmaids, which meant you *had* to scrounge up that many groomsmen?"

He shook his head. "Moi?"

"Well, it's excessive, and it seems Mother has decided this

wedding is to be the most costly, the most lavish of any in Denver's recent history."

"Hmm . . ." Michael frowned. "I take it you're not happy."

"It's just that . . ." She spooned up a small amount of sorbet and stared at it. "I was hoping our wedding might reflect something of the two of *us*."

"Doesn't it? Our families aren't exactly collecting food stamps. Why not have a good time?"

This wasn't going as she had imagined. She looked at him. "It's gotten so out of hand, and Mother's calling all the shots."

He reached across the table for her hand but she stiffened. "What's *really* wrong?"

"Don't you get it, Michael? It's not a wedding anymore, it's a Las Vegas show!" She thought she might cry.

"Do your parents know how you feel?"

"It's not me they're trying to please. It's all about making impressions . . . Mother's society sisters, for one. And everyone else on the guest list."

Michael shrugged. "So? My mom's one of the society girls, too, remember? She's equally anxious to see a gala wedding for us. Everyone, both families, all of our friends, are on board."

"Except me." Her words came out like a thud, and Michael's eyebrows shot up. Until this moment, she hadn't realized how terribly disillusioned she had become. What had changed? Was it Annie Zook's friendship over the years, an Amish girl's influence from afar? No, it was more than that. Had to be.

She swallowed hard. "A quarter-of-a-million-dollar wedding won't make our day more special or meaningful, will it?" She had to hear him refute it. Instead, he pushed his chair back and reached for her salad plate, as well as his own, and carried them to the kitchen sink.

Returning, he brought along a bottle of champagne and two glasses. "Look, babe, who cares how much money our parents throw at this wedding? It's how we were raised. Our parents have more money than they know what to do with, so what's the harm?"

She shook her head. Either he hadn't heard a word she'd said or he simply didn't care. Or worse, he didn't understand.

Wealth is all he knows . . . it's all I know. Of course he doesn't understand.

"I'm tired of this life," she said softly.

He leaned forward, frowning. "I don't think I heard you. You said what?"

She was so frustrated, it was all she could do to measure her words, to keep from simply bursting. "I have no intention of living the way my parents—or yours—do. Look around here . . . at my apartment. This is the *real* me. I crave secondhand furniture and flea market treasures. Old stuff. Things with class but inexpensive, worn, and scuffed up . . . things that exude character." She paused. "I thought you knew."

Michael grimaced. "Isn't this merely a phase, your latest artistic flair? I didn't think you were serious." Casually he unwound the wire fastener from the bottle. "You want the look of poverty, well fine. That's cool."

She sighed. *He doesn't get it.*

"What does it matter about the wedding?" he continued. "Why not go along with the plans? You know your parents always get their way. Like they did with you and me."

His words slammed into her heart. "What are you talking about?"

He gripped the bottle and pulled up, grimacing slightly. "You know. The long-range plan." He popped the cork for effect.

She blew out a breath. "What?"

Their eyes met, and Michael flashed a smile. "Surely you remember how we met."

A *blind date.* "My dad ran into your dad. . . ." She struggled to remember. *Where?* "And they began talking, and one thing led to another, and then . . ."

He chuckled. "Well, yeah, but there's way more to it."

"More to what?"

"Oh, come on, Louisa. You can't tell me you didn't know."

She was unable to breathe. *It's so warm in here.*

He poured champagne into her glass first, then his own. He set the bottle to the side and raised his glass, proposing a toast, waiting for her. But she could only stare at him, too flustered to reach for her glass.

"Nothing changes the fact that we belong together, Louisa. Does it really matter how it happened?" He gestured toward her champagne. "I say we make a toast to the future—yours and mine, as well as to my partnership with your father's law firm . . . eventually, but certain."

She glared at him. "So that's what this is? An arrangement?"

"Louisa, don't play the drama queen."

"I thought we had something special."

"We do. Someone simply got the ball rolling, that's all."

She searched his eyes for some hint of insincerity, some indication he was teasing her. But he was incredibly earnest and more than eager to make the toast.

He winked at her, as though hoping to humor her. "To the Berkeley-Stratford merger."

Her mind whirled. *Surely we weren't merely pawns in our fathers' hands!*

He was smiling at her, attempting to charm her, still holding his glass high. "Our future is secure and rather limitless. Won't our children be perfect?"

She had not fallen for him for any of those reasons. She had been totally in the dark. "No . . . don't you see? Our beginning was a fraud," she whispered, blinking back tears.

He set down his glass. "What's the difference how it started? What matters is how it ends." His tone was one of impatience now.

How it ends. The words rang hollow and prophetic.

"It matters to *me*," she said.

"You're making too much of this."

She couldn't help it . . . she thought of her first boyfriend, a man a few years older whom she'd met at the start of her junior year—an art fanatic like her. Trey Douglas had loved her for who she was. But the timing was all off for them. She should have followed him to London. Instead, she'd fallen prey to her own father's misguided scheme.

She shook her head. "No, Michael! I don't want any part of this. I thought you loved *me*, no strings attached. I had no idea this was part of someone's plan to manipulate us. The whole thing is messed up." She rose and hurried down the short hall to her bedroom and closed the door.

"Louisa, baby . . . wait! Let's talk this out."

"I've heard enough." She locked the door, leaning her head against it, clutching her aching throat.

Even in spite of his repeated knocking and calling to her, she simply could not bring herself to open the door. It would break her heart even more to look into his face.

All a charade!

Chapter 5

Saturday's corn-husking bee at Deacon Byler's farm was off to a grand start, even though neither the shucking of ears of corn nor the stacking of stalks had begun. Young people, and a few married chaperones, were arriving, and already dozens of buggies were lined up in a row, parked along the side yard.

Annie and her sister-in-law Sarah Mae worked together, straining their fingers to unhitch Dolly from the enclosed family carriage. Pretty soon, Obed, one of Deacon Byler's sons, walked over and helped finish the task. That done, he led the horse up to the barn, where he would water and feed each of the driving horses stabled there.

"Denki, Obie," called Annie.

Suddenly she spotted Rudy Esh and several other fellows standing near the woodshed. *Ach, he's here!* She quickly looked away. Her hands grew clammy, and a sickening lump formed in the pit of her stomach.

I should've stayed home!

If he happened to take Susie Yoder home in his buggy later, it would do her in but good. She'd never actually seen them sitting side-by-side in Rudy's open carriage, and she didn't want to start now.

Rejecting the urge to wallow in self-pity, she found the courage to walk with her head high. *I'm not ashamed. I've done nothing wrong.* But she knew for certain she had, for her fondness for art had come between her and Rudy. Her paintings and drawings were a result of doing what she believed the Lord God had somehow implanted in her heart. *I paint the beauty I see around me. How can that be wrong?* Yet it was, according to the rules of their *Ordnung*, which governed much of their lives.

When she got to the house, she discovered a whole group of girls—mostly courting age—gathered in the kitchen. Some were pouring cold apple cider into paper cups; others were arranging cups on large trays.

"Hullo, Annie!" Deacon Byler's wife, Kate, called to her. "I heard tell your wailin' peacocks kept your neighbor, David Lapp, up all hours last night."

"Well, I heard nothing once I fell asleep," Annie replied.

This brought a wave of laughter.

"Must be mating season, jah?" one of the older girls said, and they fell silent, followed by a few snickers. "Them peacocks can yowl worse than an infuriated cat, I daresay."

"And they get awful lonely," Annie explained, as if the girls had never heard this about the bevy of beautiful birds she and her brothers raised. "They like bein' close to each other."

Several girls had their heads together, giggling.

"Once one of them flew off lookin' for his mate after she died. . . . I'm not kidding." Annie straightened her apron and pushed her shoulders back. "But for the most part, they stay put. They don't stray too far from home."

"Besides that, peahens are some of the best mothers ever," Kate Byler added amidst more peals of laughter. "Now, listen. What Annie's sayin' is ever so true."

More than amused by Kate's seriousness, Annie watched her dark eyes sparkle as she appointed different girls to carry the trays of drinks out to the men.

As if on cue, right then Rudy Esh appeared in the back doorway. His auburn hair shimmered clean, and he held his head at a slight angle, as if questioning her resolve even now. "It's time to team up and get to workin'," he announced.

His take-charge voice reminded Annie of all the happy yet frustrating years she'd spent as his girl. Here was a young man who knew precisely what he wanted in life, and she'd fully messed it up for him.

Turning her attention back to the girls, she refused to let on, but she missed him all to pieces.

———

Louisa kept to the speed limit as she headed up Highway 285 toward the town of Conifer, taking in the sweeping views of pine and evergreen. The highway was a two-lane sliver of concrete, crawling with cars filled with hikers, soon-to-be bikers, and tourists too late for peak foliage of aspen gold.

She was glad for a blue-sky day with not a threat of snow or sleet. This late in the season, a blizzard frequently enveloped the road within minutes of the first sign of snow-laden clouds moving quickly from the mountains to the eastern plains.

At Pine Junction, she made the turn south on Route 126, her ultimate destination being the cozy bedroom community called Pine a few miles from Buffalo Creek, another well-kept secret with an elevation of eighty-two-hundred feet above sea level. She knew of a secluded inn where she'd gone to work on several drawings sometime ago. The place was set back in the woods, with hiking trails that led to a spectacular overlook. She had called to reserve a room for the night, for the purpose of getting her emotional bearings. Of course, she could be reached if necessary, and she checked the time on her smart phone as the Mercedes climbed in altitude.

"Let's talk. . . ."

Michael's tense voice mail still ricocheted in her head. What was there to discuss? They had talked for more than an hour by phone following the superb steak dinner, only for Louisa to understand more fully how susceptible to the trappings of success Michael had become. Her fiancé's true motives had finally surfaced. *Just like Mother and Daddy*, she thought, *and all their friends.*

Excessive extravagance—the kind Michael continued to argue for, even on behalf of her own mother—had begun to slowly sicken her toward all she had grown accustomed to, although she had never known anything different. But now, enough was enough, and the way Michael had explained it, there was simply no room for compromise.

She pondered her life as Michael's wife. They were formed from the same mold, but she had come to long for something meaningful . . . the simple life, the way Annie Zook lived. At this moment such a peaceful existence strongly beckoned to her.

Most importantly, she could not marry a man who was so consumed with his career and making money that his wife—and eventually the children he wanted—would come in at second or third place. Or maybe fall right through the cracks.

She glanced at the sky now, at each tuft and curl of clouds, contemplating what she would give up by not going through with the marriage. Her father's favor and approval, for one. Possibly her eventual inheritance . . . who was to know? Anything and everything money could buy. She conjured up images of being disowned, destitute. At least she would have a say in how she lived her life.

If she were to call off the wedding, she would have to tell Michael first, then her parents. She must also be the one to tell her maid-of-honor. *Courtney will think I'm insane!* The rest could hear it from Mother.

She gripped the steering wheel as though clutching the remnants of her life. *Will my parents ever forgive me? Will Michael?*

What was she to be absolved of really? Hadn't they gotten the whole relationship started . . . that first blind date introduction?

At least she would give them an earlier heads up than most runaway brides. She would not wait until the actual wedding day, nor would she wait until the luxurious rehearsal dinner to call it off. There was still adequate time to alert guests, *immediately*. Most had not sent RSVPs yet, nor had many gifts arrived.

So much for the Fostoria crystal and the posh flatware, including two sets of silver-plated tableware. None of which reflected her taste—all chosen with Mother's plans for them in mind.

She thought back to the day Michael had accompanied her and her mother on yet another trip to register for wedding gifts; this one at Nordstrom in Park Meadows Mall, in south Denver. There had been tiny chinks in the armor again on that day. The hollow feeling she had when Mother kept insisting on the most impractical things—the one-of-a-kind placemats that had to be thrown away if ever soiled, the linen napkins, the too-delicate glassware for everyday use. Michael had seemed to approve of her mother's every selection, surprisingly.

And only the most exclusive honeymoon package would do for them. *Nothing but the best.* His mantra. And hers, as well . . .

until now. Something had snapped, and there was no turning back.

Adjusting her automatic seat, she hoped Michael's parents could get a good portion of their money back. Ditto for her parents. The last thing she wanted to do was rob them blind. But even with three weeks' notice, there was an enormous risk of loss.

She thought again of her pen pal, wishing Annie had access to email. Instant messaging would be even better. She needed to talk to her, but only one telephone serviced four Amish farmhouses, and those homes were well spaced, as she understood it.

There was something quite incredible about the wisdom of the unassuming girl who'd become her truest friend, though she lived in a remote area of Lancaster County, Pennsylvania. Louisa knew precisely where, because after only two exchanges of letters, she had searched out the town of Paradise in her father's big atlas. The one most highly prized by Daddy nestled on the first shelf nearest the writing desk, in his cherry-paneled home library.

Annie would understand. . . .

She pulled into the inn's wide dirt driveway and found a parking spot. Turning off the ignition, she leaned on the steering wheel, looking up at the historic rock-hewn structure of Meadow Creek B&B.

The fresh, strong scent of pine hung in the air, and the trickle of the spring-fed stream bordering the property welcomed her back.

If there's a God, He would definitely hang His hat here, she thought, getting out of the car and pulling her backpack behind her. She had never been one for church, the result of her parents being too socially busy to bother with religion. Their god was their lifestyle, and even they would not have disputed the fact.

Suddenly a strange idea struck her, and she stopped walking. *What if I went to visit Annie . . . to see just how long I can last without the good life?*

The notion was incredible—staying with an Amish family, if they'd be agreeable to it. Actually, it was quite perfect!

But she could hear it now. Her parents cautioning her, questioning her once their anger subsided over the called-off wedding. If they ever calmed down. *You're out of your mind, dear. What are you thinking?*

Michael would sneer, *You don't think you're just like us? Well, sure, try it for a while. But you'll cave, and then you'll come crawling back, ready to accept your real life.*

———

Annie absolutely refused to give up, keeping an eye out for the coveted colored corn on the stalks, hoping to find it, to be a winner of a special prize. She'd heard from Rudy, who was working on the same team as she, that the prizes were not merely homemade candies and cookies this time. *Why would he tell me that?* she wondered.

She couldn't get over how nice he had been to her for all the hours they had worked to husk the corn from the stalk, but then she'd never been ditched by a beau before, so she wasn't exactly sure how she should act. And what she did know, nevertheless, was how terribly difficult it was to stand in such close proximity to him, as they tied the stalks into bundles. She caught the occasional whiff of his sweet-smelling peppermint gum, which he seemed to continually chew, no matter what he was doing.

I must still love him, she thought. *But I love my art even more.* . . .

Rudy had been most pleasant during their courtship. For too long, she had simply taken his keen affection for granted, just assuming it would always be there, offered to her for the taking. But here they were working shoulder-to-shoulder, yet no longer planning a future as husband and wife. Quite the contrary. They'd gone their separate ways, so to speak, all the while involved in the same church district.

She wondered, *Can it be?* Was his thoughtfulness this day a way to show he still appreciated her? No animosity between them? If so, she was grateful, Indian corn or not.

"I found some!" Cousin Barbianne called out.

"Give that girl a treat," one of Rudy's buddies hollered.

"By all means!" said Rudy himself.

Barbianne blushed, obviously a little embarrassed yet thrilled to be a winner. But her big brown eyes sparkled as she was given the large whoopie pie, its icing threatening to trickle out between two homemade slabs of chocolate cookies.

Just then Annie spotted Sarah Mae motioning to her from the cluster of workers who were taking the nicest corn from the stalk for cornmeal. "Come over here and help us," Sarah Mae said, offering a sympathetic smile.

Annie went willingly, if not quite relieved. She was sorry . . . even sad to leave Rudy and his group behind.

How long before I don't give a care?

Sarah Mae chattered about the delicious ham bake to follow the husking bee. She also mentioned the anticipated full evening of singing and games geared to single youth.

The sun flickered and flashed light through leaves high overhead, and an occasional breeze made the work more pleasant. At one point Annie stopped and stretched a bit when several of the other young women did the same. Stealing another glance at Rudy, she couldn't help but wonder why Susie Yoder had not shown her face here at all today.

Chapter 6

Esther Hochstetler trembled as she made her way to the back door, glancing over her shoulder toward the barn. Time had simply flown from her, and she crept into the house, having just returned from visiting an elderly aunt.

Past time to start supper, she thought, pulling out the heavy black frying pan from the low cupboard. It was in her best interest to serve up a hearty platter of fried chicken this supper hour.

I could've stayed much longer, she thought sadly of ailing Aunt Rebecca. *If only . . .*

But she had known better than to risk it. As it was, she'd missed the imposed limit on travel time by two long minutes.

Scurrying about the kitchen, she set the table and made ready for the meal. All the while she heard her little ones upstairs, looked after by her widowed mother. Such a good thing it was to have Mamma so close by. *Maybe, just maybe I won't catch it bad this time. . . .*

Any minute now, her mother would come down, describing the cute antics of her wee grandsons, as well as saying what a big help Laura had been again this short visit. Mamma would also say, *Why on earth don't you take more time away, Esther? You rush off and rush back . . . makes no sense.* Mamma had made a point of encouraging her to get out to quilting frolics and such, frequently pressing her as to why she stayed home so much. Impossible it was to explain, so she bit her lip and never said a word, letting Mamma think she'd become a loner, content to stay put.

She'd never understand how I feel.

But today Esther was especially grateful for the help her mother could give with the children. While tending to her elderly aunt, she'd had the strongest urge to get out more, to pull her weight in the community. Helping Aunt Rebecca was only part of it. Actually, being in what she assumed to be a safe environment was altogether enticing to her, as well.

The potatoes came to a rolling boil, and she thought she best be calling up the steps. She leaned her head that way, getting ready to tell Mamma to bring the boys down and let them play in the corner of the kitchen on the floor for a bit.

Suddenly her heart leaped within her. *Oh no, I forgot again!* The thought of having little Zach and John play on the bare floor had triggered her memory. *What's-a-matter with me? How dare I forget this chore?*

But she knew too well. More and more, she felt angry, even defiant, having buried the resentment deep inside where it festered. Bitterness was beginning to take shape in her dreams, and sometimes she would awaken terribly frightened, being chased by a vicious animal or attempting to run to safety, only to be frozen in place. Just as she felt even now, nearly motionless with panic wondering how she could get supper on the table, the floor scrubbed well enough for an inspection, and Mamma out of the house and back home where she lived in the *Dawdi Haus* of Esther's brother and wife. All in the space of a few minutes.

O Lord God, it is not possible. I have failed once again.

Just then Esther heard her daughter running down the stairs. Did she dare ask happy-go-lucky Laura for help? And if so, she might be found out, having shirked her own duty.

Breathless now, she looked at the clock, calculating the time. "Laura, I need you to wash up the floor, quick as a wink. And you mustn't miss a single corner, ya hear?"

Her only daughter thus far, fair-haired Laura, tiny for six years old but quick on her feet, nodded quickly. Laura's normally bright blue eyes became suddenly dull and far too serious. "I'll help ya, Mamma . . . jah, I promise I will."

Poor dear, thought Esther. And her mind raced back to the day she had discovered herself expecting a baby, with her wedding day still six weeks away.

"*Show me how much you love me. . . .*" Zeke had whispered it so often she eventually believed that what he wanted from her was all right. And oh, how she'd loved him. Desperately so. But being in love at sixteen and getting hitched up soon after were two entirely different things. She had not waited till "the appointed time," like her mamma and *Grandmammi* and all the women before her surely had, although no one ever spoke of such things. At least not that she knew of.

Laura, their precious firstborn, was said to be premature, at least that's what Zeke had told the People. But she knew the truth. They both did. And she'd never forgiven herself, let alone her husband.

Sighing aloud, she tested the potatoes with a fork—still not quite done. Then she turned over the chicken pieces, careful not to splatter the grease, wishing she didn't feel so frantic.

Mamma . . . I need to call Mamma down this instant.

With a fleeting look at Laura down on her hands and knees scouring the linoleum, Esther made haste and headed upstairs.

There she found Mamma rubbing two-year-old John's "ouchie" on his chubby finger and watching three-year-old Zach build a tower with blocks.

Pausing in the doorway, she placed her hand on her chest, catching her breath. The last thing in the world she wanted to do was to worry her dear mamma. Nor did she wish to cause alarm in her tiny boys. *No need*, she thought.

"Time to wash up for supper," she said softly. "Mamma, can ya help with that?"

Her mother turned to look at her and her pretty gray eyes twinkled as she smiled. "Why sure. We'll be right down."

A great sigh shuddered through her and escaped unnoticed, she hoped, as she turned away from the boys' room, making her way down the hall. On the landing, she steadied herself a bit, feeling slightly dizzy as she stood at the top, looking down. *Dear Lord God in heaven, grant me added grace—*

"Mamma! I'm nearly finished." Laura was calling up to her.

Ach, good . . . good. She was careful not to slip as she hurried down the steps, securing her balance by holding on to the railing.

When she looked at the shining floor and saw that Laura had not only washed it but she'd also taken an old towel and dried it to a nice shine, she fought back tears. "Oh, *lieb*—dear—such a girl you are. Such a wonderful-gut help to me."

Laura ran to her, holding out her slender arms. Esther held her near, laying her hand on the top of Laura's head. "Denki, ever so much!"

"I'll help Mammi with the boys now," Laura said, and she was off.

Quickly Esther went to check on the frying chicken. She put the lid on it and removed the pan from the fire, then set about draining the potatoes for mashing.

Saved by the skin of my teeth, she thought, resisting the urge to go to the back door and peer out. No sense in that. Any minute now she would hear the swift sound of work boots on the walkway.

Willing herself to breathe more slowly, she took down a large mixing bowl from the shelf and began mashing the well-cooked potatoes by hand. She wished Mamma would hurry and come down as she pressed the masher deep into the bowl, the steam rising to her face.

In spite of the heat, she felt suddenly cold, recalling the last time she'd made mashed potatoes, standing here near the cookstove. A good portion of the potatoes—bowl and all—had fallen to the floor, splattering every which way, all over the floor. For the life of her, she hadn't known how the accident had even happened ... whether she'd momentarily blacked out or just what. But she'd ended up scurrying around as she had today, heart pounding in her temples at the thought of being *schlabbich*—careless. Never before had such a thing happened, and she couldn't help but wonder if her fingers had merely slipped. Nothing more.

Fortunately for her, no one but little Laura had known of the mess. And from then till now, she had been determined to be more careful, forcing herself to pay better attention to the work at hand ... not letting herself fall into an alluring daydream, where she had come to find a place of solace from the tempest. Where she was a young girl again, single and happy, enjoying the freedom of being as unhitched as can be.

Chapter 7

There's just something energizing about autumn—I feel it in the air," Mamm said as she cooked sausage early Monday morning.

Makes me want to paint all day, Annie thought, having just come downstairs to help with breakfast.

Mamm wore her old green choring dress and long black apron. Her face had been scrubbed clean and her silver-blond hair freshly parted and pulled back in a tight, low bun beneath a clean white *Kapp.* "I feel compelled to redd up everything in sight," she said with a bright smile.

"Happens that way every fall, jah?" Annie moseyed to the sink and washed her hands thoroughly before counting out eight place settings of dishes and utensils for *Dawdi* and *Mammi* Zook, Daed and Mamm, Yonie, Luke, Omar, and herself.

That done, she returned to the cookstove and broke twelve fresh eggs into the large frying pan, stirring the mixture ever so slowly, just as Mamm had taught her when she was a little girl. Being the only daughter had its drawbacks, she'd found out early on, especially because she cared little for domestic chores. Her head in the clouds, she couldn't help herself . . . there was a potential painting everywhere she looked: the sky both at sunup and sundown, pastureland, wheat fields, and the canvas was constantly changing with the seasons . . . even hour by hour.

"When do you want to start cleanin' for house church?" Annie asked, even though the thought of scrubbing down walls and woodwork and waxing floors made her head pound, as if she were somehow wasting brain power. She would never voice what she was thinking, because such words were considered prideful.

"Why put off till tomorrow what can be done today?" Mamm replied, a knowing smile on her round face.

I should've known. Annie began frying the bacon in a second skillet, recalling the meadowlarks she'd seen pecking away in the side yard yesterday, their bright yellow breasts adorned with a black crescent as they moved about like miniature peacocks with determined strides. *I could live to be a hundred and not run out of things to paint!*

She had no idea how long she had been daydreaming, but soon the bacon was spitting and curling sufficiently. She flopped each piece onto a doubled-up paper towel to soak up the grease.

"Jah, I'll help you clean, Mamm," she said softly. Daydreamers got lost in the shuffle of life, her father had once told her. Well, she certainly didn't care about that, because getting lost was the most fun, whether it was autumn or any season. Still, there was the pressing matter of when, or more rightly put, *how* she could ever join her parents' church. The clock was ticking on that issue, and she felt the pressure coming straight at her every time Daed and Mamm glanced her way, their eyes clearly conveying the question that weighed so heavily in their minds. *How long before I am asked to leave the People?*

She suppressed the fact that she must make a decision, pushing the urgency down into her soul, where it would resurface the next time her eyes caught her father's look of not only concern but disappointment.

How will I live with myself?

———————

It was midafternoon—between relining the dresser drawers with fresh newspaper and cleaning out the cupboards—when Annie heard the mail truck stop in front of the house. Quick as a wink, she took off running down the long, sloping front yard. She slipped her hand inside the mailbox and pulled out several letters for Mamm and one for her. Not waiting a second longer, she tore open the envelope and began to read the latest news from Louisa.

> *Thursday, October 27*
> *Dear Annie,*
>
> *Thanks for writing back so promptly. I hope you are well and enjoying all the beauty of autumn as we are here, although the earlier gold of our aspen trees is nothing to compare with your rainbow of colors there.*
>
> *A lot has happened since I last wrote, so I guess I need to get you caught up. Don't freak out when you read this, because I'm not at all sorry. Well, I am for reasons other than the obvious, but I'm not devastated.*
>
> *Things with the wedding planning had been going badly . . . in all sorts of ways. Totally out of control. And to get to the point: I won't be marrying Michael. This may sound horrendous, but I think you'll understand, because simply put, Michael is not the man for me. In so many ways, he's anything but Mr. Right. I'm so glad I discovered this before it was too late!*
>
> *I'm really wishing for a less complicated life right now, longing to get away. I don't mean to be bold, but is there any chance I might come and visit you for a few weeks . . . even a month? I*

know this is sudden, and I certainly wouldn't want to put you and your family out in any way, Annie. I'd be happy to pay for my keep and help with chores, as well. I really just need to 'get away from it all,' as they say, and clear my head.

I'll eagerly await your next letter.

With love,
Louisa

P.S. I'm exhibiting my art students' work soon, and I'll take some pictures to send to you . . . or better yet, take them on my smart phone and bring them along.

Annie was dumbfounded. "Her wedding's off and she wants to come here?" she voiced softly, feeling just awful for her friend. But she reminded herself that Louisa hadn't sounded heart-broken whatsoever, which was downright peculiar . . . especially considering how much in love she had seemed to be.

Funny how that is, she thought. *Head over heels in love one day and completely befuddled the next.*

But it was rather clear Louisa's situation was far different from her own. Still, Annie needed to think, to really ponder Louisa's letter, and while doing so, she headed across the road, spotting one of the peacocks strutting along, its enormous train of tail feathers spread to the full. These birds craved a peaceful setting such as their farmland here in Paradise.

Annie went and sat on the nearby fence simply observing the grand bird. *They need stretching room,* Daed had said some years back, when first he'd built the large pen and perches. With a wingspan of up to six feet, it was obvious a peacock could become stressed otherwise. Annie had seen this happen down yonder, at big brother Jesse's place, where he, too, raised the colorful birds.

Sounds like Louisa needs some stretching room, too. . . .

She opened the letter once again and read the part where Louisa was politely asking to come visit. Annie found it fascinating, especially because not too many days ago she'd thought of going to Denver ... to Louisa's wedding! The whole thing struck her as odd—and to think a fancy rich girl wanted to come here. To an Amish farm, no less, where peahens sat on their nests of eggs and cows came home for milking twice a day.

She has no idea what she's asking, Annie thought, yet she knew of other Englischers who'd come and stayed to sort out their lives. Some had gleaned simplicity, and others had even desired to learn to speak their language. Most of the time, though, outsiders simply did not fully connect with the Plain community and didn't stay long. But Annie was quite sure that's not what Louisa had in mind. Still, she hoped her own stonewalling—not joining church—along with putting Rudy Esh off, would not go against her now. Because, with all of her heart, she wanted Louisa to come and stay for as long as she pleased.

Watching the three-year-old peacock prance toward her now, she locked her gaze on the "eye" in the center of each of the feathers. What striking violet, green, red, and gold! Where on God's earth could an artist see such striking hues all blended on the same moving, breathing canvas?

She sat very still, not wanting to distract the bird, not wanting to stress him in the least. When he seemed to stare right at her, she said softly, "Goodness' sakes, you're a brave one."

The bird did not move, and she took this rare opportunity to lean forward, amazed again at the depth of color on each feather.

"If Louisa comes, you just might be one of her first paintings here," she told the peacock, feeling silly talking to an animal.

If Daed agrees, that is. He would put his foot down if he knew

Louisa was an art instructor . . . and I a disobedient daughter, hiding my sin in Julia's attic!

She waited till the peacock turned, at last, strutting back to the pen, slowly closing his train and letting it drag behind him.

Drawing in a deep breath, she realized now what Mamm had sensed in the air earlier. Not only was it the urgency of getting work completed before the onslaught of winter, she also felt a flood of excitement. She could enjoy it for the moment, because she was not at all sure what her father would say about Louisa's request. Especially because she was considered to be on the very fringe of the church, although she still attended Preaching service regularly. And there was the knotty problem of adding a single girl to the mix of three courting-age brothers in the house.

She climbed off the fence, anxious now to talk over Louisa's letter with her parents, particularly her father.

Won't Daed be chagrined to find out my close friend is a worldly Englischer? She trudged back toward the house, clinging to a small ray of hope.

Chapter 8

Finding Mamm alone in the kitchen having another tall glass of apple cider was a consolation. Neither Yonie nor Luke was in from plowing, and Omar wasn't in from the barn snitching the usual chocolate chip cookies, his favorite afternoon snack.

Annie had slipped into the room unnoticed and sat down at the table, observing her mother's purposeful movements—back and forth between the counter where she was chopping vegetables, then to the big kettle on her left, scarcely moving her feet, only her upper body, the graceful rhythm of an experienced cook. Mamm chanted the necessary ingredients, depositing diced potatoes, chopped carrots, small onions, and, last of all, the cubed stew meat, already browned in butter, into the kettle. A bit of paprika, two small bay leaves, some flour, and a dash of allspice, along with the sugar, lemon juice, a clove of garlic, boiling water, and plenty of ground black pepper, and the stew was ready for more simmering.

Mamm turned unexpectedly. "Oh, goodness, me. I didn't see ya there!"

Annie hoped now was the best time to bring up Louisa's letter.

Mamm tilted her head. "What's got ya lookin' like that?"

"I was just wonderin' . . ." She stopped.

"Aw, just spit it out, Annie-girl."

"All right. Louisa, my pen pal, wants to come for a visit." When Mamm seemed not the least bit flustered by the notion of having an Englischer around, Annie added, "She wrote that she needed some time away."

"Well, sure, tell her to come."

"But . . . she might need to stay longer than just a few nights."

Mamm nodded, still smiling. "How long would that be?"

"I don't know, a few weeks . . . maybe a month."

"She's not runnin' away from home, I hope."

"Nothin' like that." *Running from her beau maybe.*

"Well, it might be a gut idea to talk this over with your father, 'specially since there are three young men still living in the house."

She wasn't surprised at her mother's sensible response, but with all of her heart, she wanted to see Louisa face-to-face for the first time ever. She had daydreamed plenty of times about it. Now her chance was here at last, and she longed to stay up late talking with Louisa in person, to see her artwork, and to show her around the farm. And just maybe to get some pointers from a real art instructor who was a wonderful-good friend! These thoughts made her giddy with anticipation.

Annie made her way through the screened-in porch, where boots and shoes were lined up along the wall nearest the door. She hurried around the side of the house and down to the road, going to check for Daed first in the barn. Not finding him there, she climbed the hayloft ladder and walked the expanse of the barn's uppermost level to the wide outside door.

Pushing hard to swing the door open, she stood at the top of the grassy barn bridge, an earthen ramp where they moved the various farm equipment in and out. Looking out at the vast field to the south, she could see Daed and Luke and two teams of mules pulling the handheld plows.

I'll have to wait till later, she thought, feeling discouraged again as she stood there.

One of more than a dozen barn kitties skittered across the wood floor and rubbed against her ankle. "Aw, you cute thing. Where's your mamma?"

Going to the far corner of the loft, Annie raised her long skirt to climb onto one of the square bales stacked there. The kitten followed her. Annie sat down and picked up the black kitty. "My friend Louisa has a gray cat," she whispered. "If she brings Muffin here for a visit, won't that be fun?" Annie stared at the barn rafters, watching for the bats she knew were up there sleeping the day away. And she held the wee kitten in her arms, feeling its rumbly purring.

How can I convince my father?

She contemplated how her friend might be feeling now, getting so close to her wedding day and then changing her mind. But Annie knew she had done nearly the same thing to Rudy, though she hadn't waited till the last minute.

Just then, she heard shuffling below in the stable area. Silently she slipped down off the baled hay and crept to one of the hay holes, where they dropped bales down to the cattle. She peeked through the opening to see if Yonie was nearby.

Sure enough. Smiling to herself, she called to him. "Yonie Zook!" Then she darted back so he couldn't see where she was, teasing him.

"Who's there?"

She could see his wheat-colored hair through the opening in

the floor. Annie's favorite of her six brothers, Yonie was only eighteen months younger, part of the reason they were so close. And there was something uncanny about him—he understood her better than all her other brothers.

"Yonie!" she said again, unable to hold in her laughter.

"Ach, I should know you're up in the haymow, Annie. If ya want to talk, then ya best be comin' down."

She shrugged. "Well, you must have eyes on top of your head, brother."

"Nope, I ain't at all like Daed who sees and hears everything . . . nearly like almighty God." Yonie's head popped into view as he climbed up the ladder. He grinned at her, a long piece of straw stuck in his mouth. "If I was, maybe I'd already have me a girl to hitch up with."

"You shouldn't have a speck of trouble findin' a girl to marry." Annie figured her brother had plenty of time to find the right bride. After all, the boys could marry a girl several years younger . . . so if this year's crop of sixteen-year-old girls didn't take his fancy, then maybe next year's would.

Yonie sat on the edge of the hay hole, swinging his legs. "Well, look at *you*, Annie. I thought you'd be wed by now."

Climbing back up the hay bales, Annie reached for the long rope. She swung across the expanse of the loft, her legs tight against the rope so her dress would not billow out. Her feet were so callused from going barefoot early spring to late fall, she was able to cling easily, though her toes strained upward. "You goin' to the next singing?" she asked, riding all the way up . . . up toward the rafters and then back.

"Well, if you are, I guess I *have* to go and drop you off, now don't I?" His eyes shone with tomfoolery.

She laughed, keeping her back straight as a board as she flew.

"Seems to me you could go and stay a mite longer than five minutes. That way you might actually meet a cute girl to take out ridin'."

He shook his head. "Got no interest in Amish girls just now."

"Brave soul, you are."

"And . . . I have some plans, comin' up soon. But Daed knows nothing 'bout it, so keep quiet."

She let the rope take her across the loft once again. "Bet I can guess."

"Like fun you can." He patted his straw hat. "Unless you've been eavesdropping."

"Oh, I figure you're not long for here . . . that's what. Soon as all the plowin's done, you'll head out to do some hunting in the woods somewhere with your friends. Ain't so?"

"Well, if that don't beat all. How'd ya know?"

"I heard nothin'. Honestly."

"Well, then, you're a strange one, 'cause that's exactly what I have in mind to do."

Still holding the long rope, she said, "There's plenty of deer comin' down to the hay fields, nearly every evening now. Seems you wouldn't have to leave home to bag yourself a buck or doe."

Yonie frowned. "I've thought of spending daylight in a tree stand, but the deer can spot you a quarter mile away. Honestly, though, just gettin' away might do me good . . . for now."

"Well, if ya have to go, fine and dandy." She made her way down off the hay and joined him by the ladder. "I need to ask you something first, though." Quickly she told him about Louisa's hope to visit. "What should I tell Daed?"

"Do like I'm gonna do. Tell him right out."

"But I'm a girl."

He pulled the straw out of his mouth. "That's where you're ferhoodled, all mixed up, if ya think you can't speak your mind. Like Mamm does. I daresay he might just listen if you don't hem and haw . . . the way you do sometimes."

She thought on that.

But before she could say more, Yonie spoke again. "Daed likes folk to get to the point and be done with it. So if you're gonna ask him anything, do it with confidence—I know you've got it in ya."

She realized if Yonie was going hunting, then Louisa could have his bedroom upstairs for a week or so maybe.

"You go 'n' bring in the herd. I'll find Daed," she said, practicing speaking up to a man this minute, bossing her brother but good.

"Thataway." Yonie shooed her out of the barn, chuckling.

She ran hard as she could out to meet her father, who was walking her way, wearing the caked-on dirt from the field on his work boots and the bottom of his pant legs, looking like he could use a good hot meal and a warm bath. But the big galvanized tub wouldn't be brought indoors till Saturday night, like always.

Glad that Luke and Omar were nowhere near, she blurted her request when she reached him. "I'm hopin' you won't mind if my pen pal comes to stay with us for a while."

"What's that you say?"

"You know . . . my English friend, Louisa? She needs to soak up some of the peace here, I'm thinkin'."

"Why's a fancy girl want to come to Lancaster County? Is she lookin' to be Plain?" Daed's face grew more serious, and he reached up to tug on his long beard.

"Well, she's never written that." *Of course not. Louisa would never give up her art,* she thought suddenly.

His eyes were softer now. "Does she need a place to stay? Is that what you mean?"

"She just wants to visit."

"And what do her parents say?"

"I don't know."

Daed frowned suddenly. "Have ya given any thought to where she'd bed down? We've got a houseful of boys . . .'cept for you and Mamm." He paused, then he continued. "And what would she do durin' Preaching service? And there are plenty of weddings comin' up, too."

She couldn't mention Yonie's plans to be gone till he shared that with Daed himself. As for her father's other concerns, she honestly couldn't say. "I'm not sure 'bout church and the weddings." But just then she realized her chance, a way to make some sense of this. "Maybe she'd want to go along to church and the weddings and whatnot all. Might be interesting for her, don't you think?"

"A fancy girl would find a three-hour meeting, perched on a wooden bench, quite trying, Annie. Not interesting. And she won't understand much of what's goin' on." His eyes were serious. "You're not thinking sensibly, I can see that. And I best be warnin' ya, too . . . there'd be no shirking your chores with Mamm nor your work over at Cousin Julia's, you know."

She sighed, still hoping he might surprise her and say that Louisa could come.

He continued. "Honestly, I don't know how I feel about it, especially with my daughter still so apathetic toward the church. This girl might lead you astray, Annie."

"But I've been writin' to her all these years," she said without thinking. Then she bit her lip. "I'm sorry, Daed. I didn't mean to be rude."

"I'll be thinkin' on it." He looked away. "Don't ask me again. . . ."

She wanted to groan, but she squelched it. Besides, he had a point. She was at high risk for the world, the flesh, and the devil. If the people knew the truth, they'd think she was a hardened sinner already.

She shrugged off the annoying thought. It was much more pleasant to hope that she and her family might impart the peace Louisa was desperate for instead of dwelling on her own trans-gressions.

Chapter 9

Jesse watched his daughter hurry through the half-plowed field, making a beeline toward the barn. *She won't leave a single stone unturned,* he assumed.

He had not shown an iota of interest in Annie's pen pal through the years, and he didn't feel he'd been kept in the dark by either Annie or her mother. Still it was hard not to wonder about the young woman's motives. Was Louisa simply curious, as were the gawking tourists?

Thirsty now, he began to make his way across the furrowed soil, turning his thoughts to Caleb Esh's comments about Annie and Rudy. He hadn't been able to dismiss them, even though the grapevine was entirely unreliable. Yet knowing Rudy as he did, it was perplexing why a staunch young man had not been able to persuade Annie to marry. It didn't add up. *Something's peculiar with that. . . .*

Then it dawned on him—Annie was surely stronger-willed than her former beau, and maybe more so than a good number of the young men in the church district. He found this realization not only startling but secretly a bit satisfying. Annie knew her mind, that was clear. Having seen the earnestness in her eyes regarding her English friend's visit, for instance, Jesse thought he might at least run it by the other preacher, Moses Hochstetler, Zeke's elderly uncle. Then, if need be, he'd work his way up to the bishop.

We'll just see what's what.

All-in from the day, he made his way through the barnyard toward the road. When he came near to the back door, he caught a whiff of what smelled like beef stew and hurried inside to investigate.

A fine meal by the best cook ever, he thought, going and slipping his arm around his wife's stout waist. Accustomed to his furtive interest prior to meals, she lifted the kettle lid. Jesse leaned into the fragrant steam, eyes closed, breathing in . . . then turned to the woman he loved and planted a kiss on her soft face. "Keep this simmerin' a bit longer," he said, winking.

"Why, sure." She smiled knowingly, leaning toward him.

"I'll be makin' a quick trip out."

"All right then, love," she said. "Stew and corn bread will be waitin'."

With the memory of the mouth-watering aroma lingering, he hurried out to hitch up his fastest driving horse to the family carriage.

Annie found Yonie already starting the afternoon milking. She stood near the center aisle of the milking area, seeing two rows of cows' hind parts and tails, and below, the manure ditch. She waited for Yonie to see her, and when he did, she motioned to him.

He sauntered over to her once all the cows were hooked up to air compressor-run milkers. His hazel eyes were bright with the question. "Well?"

"I did what you said. But Daed's goin' to think about it. So who knows."

"You worry too much." He flashed an infectious grin.

"Seems to me I'm allowed to fret a bit. *You* haven't spent nearly a lifetime writing to Louisa Stratford. This might be my only chance to meet her."

He frowned momentarily, and then there came the twinkle in his eye. "Hmm. Stratford. Sounds like a high and mighty name for a *best friend,* ain't?"

She didn't know where on earth he'd gotten the idea Louisa was that close to her. Not unless Mamm had mentioned something, which was unlikely. Other than their mother, nobody knew of Annie's close friendship with Louisa except . . .

"Wait a minute! Have you been talkin' to Mrs. Zimmerman?"

Yonie grinned. She'd caught him. "That's for me to know and for you to find out."

"Well, I just did!" She should've put it together the instant Yonie had declared Louisa as her best friend. Mrs. Zimmerman was their busybody mail carrier, and her daughter, Dory, was one of the prettiest English neighbors around. So Yonie was interested in the local girls—just not Amish ones.

Yonie suddenly looked sheepish.

"Aha!" Annie exclaimed. "I'll keep your secret if you keep mine. Jah?"

"Nothin' to keep, you silly." With that he turned back to attend to the milking.

I know better, she thought, for she'd seen the blush of embarrassment on his face. Well, no wonder Yonie wasn't so keen on attending singings and other youth activities. She just hoped he didn't do something stupid, like fall hard for the wrong girl . . . like Louisa had surely fallen for the wrong fellow.

She headed back to the house, hoping to hear something soon from Daed, trying to remain optimistic.

"As a father, I'm concerned 'bout Annie's worldly friend," Jesse told Moses Hochstetler at the elder minister's kitchen table, where they drank their coffee black.

"What's that?" Moses asked, struggling to hear.

Jesse thought of writing down what he wanted to discuss, that his daughter's pen pal wished to come for a lengthy visit. And he sure wouldn't want to tempt his youngest sons with a modern girl in the house.

He moved closer to the elder minister and proceeded to speak directly into his ear. "Our Annie's got herself a worldly friend who's lookin' for a dose of the simple life."

A glint of recognition passed over the furrowed brow. "Ah, jah, she's a right good one . . . your daughter."

"I'd like to keep it that way," Jesse muttered.

As if Moses had heard, he adjusted his glasses, studying Jesse. "What's this 'bout an Englischer? She's not comin' to spy, is she?"

Jesse reiterated that the girl, as far as he knew, was looking only for some respite from the world.

"Well, sure. Why not have her come, then?"

"I've got myself three sons still in the house. It wonders me if it's such a good idea to bring a fancy girl under my roof." He pondered Yonie, especially, who seemed to be working his way toward the fringe. "Sure wouldn't want my boys taking a shine to Louisa. We can't be losin' any more of our young folk."

Moses cupped his ear with his gnarled hand. "In all truth, the Englischer might just be the thing to push Annie off the fence, so to speak. Could be a wonderful-good idea."

Jesse couldn't imagine such a thing.

"Well . . . I know we must be patient with our youth."

Moses nodded his head, as though pondering further. "This worldly girl might be a godsend, the answer to your problem. Might move Annie closer to joinin' church, her friend bein' so interested in our way of life."

"Hadn't thought of that."

"But I hope the outsider won't cause any confusion in our midst, 'specially in your house, but that she'll receive the peace she seeks," Moses said. "I would also hope she might fit in with the womenfolk here . . . go along with Annie to market, quilting bees, and such."

Jesse finished his coffee, still thinking of Annie, who was not past her rumschpringe. He wished she would continue to attend the youth activities and find herself a new beau.

Getting up from the table, he waved his hat, thanking Moses for the coffee. He hurried out to his horse and carriage, anxious to return to his wife's delectable beef stew.

Riding along the countryside, Jesse waved at acquaintances in several passing buggies. Then, once he'd passed the most worrisome intersection, he leaned back, contemplating Moses' agreeable nature. Such a compassionate, upstanding man he was, but his days of prophesying were surely a thing of the past. Since taking a hard fall on the ice years back, not only had his hearing been greatly affected, but his ability to stand long enough to deliver the main long sermon had, as well. Old Moses, as some of the People referred to him, could no longer remember the required sequence of biblical stories and Scriptures to accompany them. So, then, was it even possible he was right? That spunky Annie might simply need to encounter firsthand a worldly friend to nudge her closer toward making her lifelong vow to God and the church? Only time would tell.

Chapter 10

On Friday Annie made haste to Cousin Julia's. Once her work was done, she would have more time this afternoon to paint, since she'd finished up every piece of ironing last Tuesday. Still holding out hope for Louisa's visit, she thought of her present painting in light of her friend's artistic achievement. Far as she could tell, the scene depicting the setting of the kidnapping was her best work yet. All that was left was the highlighting of tree trunks and branches, as well as making sure the sunbeams skipped off the creek water as it made its way past the old bridge.

I want Louisa to see it, thought Annie.

As she walked, she thought of all the places she wanted to show her friend, but most of all she wanted to share with Louisa her private little artist's sanctuary. *She's heard all about it in my letters . . . and she'll keep my secret, for sure!*

When Annie reached the Ranck home, she caught sight of James and Molly playing "horsy and buggy" in the side yard, where James had his little sister tied to a cardboard box, with the rope "reins" in his hands. Molly appeared to be quite a lot better, and Annie was glad of it.

"What's that you're doin'?" she called to them. "Seems to me

Molly ought to be the one riding in the carriage, and James, you could be the big strong horse."

That got big smiles from both children, and right away James began untying and switching the horse and driver. "Molly's bumps aren't so itchy no more," he said, pointing out several on his sister's arm to show Annie.

"Jah, I can see that." She stood there, watching James work the knots out of the slender rope he'd put around Molly's little arms. "You must think you're Amish today, both of ya."

"That's right," Molly said, eyes sparkling with excitement. "We're just like you."

"But you never bring your father's horse and buggy over here, do ya, Cousin Annie?" James never even looked up at her, just kept untying the rope.

"By the time I hitched up, that would take a good thirty minutes, so why not just walk over here in the same amount of time?" she explained.

"Or you could hop in a car, like we do, and get here even quicker."

She tousled his hair, thinking he was mighty smart for his little britches. "Jah, there's a lot of things one could do, I 'spect. But we Amish do what we do for a reason."

"What's that?" Molly said, obviously glad to be free and on the other side of the box now, holding the reins big as she pleased.

"Well, we obey our church rules. And, besides, it's much better for us to walk when we *could* be riding. Even better is to hitch up horse and carriage than to drive a car. It keeps us slowed down some . . . not in such an awful hurry." She thought she might be stepping on some toes, so she stopped right there. After all, the Rancks were as fancy as anyone around here, being Mennonite and all.

"I wish we had a horse and a buggy," James said, moving his head as if he were a prancing steed.

The grass is always greener, she thought.

James was off running now, with Molly behind him, hurrying to keep up. She smiled over her shoulder at them . . . so adorable. She thought again of Rudy and what a fine father he might have been. But he was off going to singings and taking someone else home, and rightly so.

Refusing to fall into a quagmire of self-pity, she hurried toward the house and got right to work redding up the children's rooms upstairs. Then she set about cleaning the large bathroom, thankful not to have that chore to do at home. With an outhouse, there was much less upkeep, she decided, although there were plenty of times, especially in the winter, when she would have liked to close the door on herself and the large tub Daed brought into the kitchen from the shed, where she and Mamm got the Saturday night bathing routine started. At least she was usually first or second, not nearly as grimy as the boys and Daed always were. Of course, she and Mamm often took sponge baths in the privacy of their rooms, using a large washbowl and a kettle of hot water. Same thing her grandparents had to do, because they were too frail to get in and out of a tub anyway. The boys and Daed would slip out to the makeshift shower in the barn and rinse off every other day, though they complained of it being cold as ice in the wintertime. Still, there was nothing worse to Annie than feeling dirty.

She and her sister-in-law Sarah Mae had often had conversations about such things. And now, Sarah Mae and Jesse Jr. and their children lived in a farmhouse with two large bathrooms—

approved by the ministers, because they were merely renting the place. Occasionally Annie had even hitched up the team and gone over to enjoy their bathtub in the heat of the summer, soaking away the cares and soil of the day. Sometimes, too, Sarah Mae let her use her very own bubble bath, which was a special treat.

Ach, no! She was nearly aghast at the thought of Louisa, who was used to taking as many as two showers a day. *Oh, goodness! Shouldn't I write and tell her?*

But she would do nothing at all to discourage Louisa from coming, if Daed allowed it. Annie found herself grinning. *Louisa might just wish she'd never longed for the simple life!*

———

Exhausted from precious little sleep, Esther felt her muscles beginning to relax now as she tucked in both Zach and John for, hopefully, a long afternoon nap. Little John had awakened with an asthmatic attack at midnight, and she had held him while sitting up in the rocking chair in his room, making sure he was breathing. Making sure his struggling cries would not awaken Zeke, too.

Now she sat on the double bed, reaching over to put her hand on John's tiny forehead. "Close your peepers," she said to both boys, and they blinked their eyes shut obediently.

Sitting there, she gazed down fondly at them, nearly like twins in looks, and so close in age, but quite different temperamentally. Zach was similar to big sister Laura as a young one, easygoing and anxious to please. Baby John, on the other hand, was restless and more apt to have upset stomachs, like Esther herself was these days. He had started out quite frail due to his breathing problems—*a predisposition to upper bronchial problems,* the Strasburg pediatrician had told them early on.

She realized how awful small her little boys looked in their big bed. "Sleep tight," she whispered, absently touching her abdomen, where yet another baby grew. She left the door open enough to hear John should he begin to wheeze again.

Sighing, she tiptoed to her bedroom, in desperate need of rest before Laura arrived home from school. The thought of standing and making supper was beyond her at the moment, and she dismissed it till later. She wished she might simply slip into her nightclothes and sleep soundly, dead to this world, and absolutely irresistible was the urge to do so. Yet she shuddered at the thought of making herself too vulnerable. Two other times she'd done so, but no longer. These days she kept all her clothes on, including her long apron, even on the hottest summer day during a rare short nap. Today would be no exception.

She turned to close her door but thought better of it, still on edge from last night's frightful spell. Not knowing if their wee boy would live to see the light of day had caused her an ongoing heartache. Yet he had, and she attributed his recovery to the inhaler she kept near for such alarming occurrences, although five months had passed since the last episode. What a true relief the rather long reprieve had been. Still, her heart feared there might come a day when she would merely sleep through his nighttime attack.

But, no, she had some confidence that young Zach would be aware, sharing the same bed, and come to get her help. On the other hand, her husband, once asleep for the night, was out so soundly that not even a lightning strike could shake him awake. She knew this to be true, as he'd slept through a deafening thunderstorm not so many years back, their barn hit by lightning in the night. In some ways, her husband's unusually deep slumber was a blessing, but in the case of their youngest, it was a tremendous point of ongoing concern.

She walked to the window and sat on the small cane chair, one her father had made for her hope chest the year before she met Zeke. *I miss you, Pop*, she thought, wishing her father might have lived to see the births of Zach and John, and the new little life she was now carrying. She had never forgotten his grandfatherly delight over Laura, as a brand-new babe, despite the fact Esther knew he suspected baby Laura too hearty an infant to be called premature. But he and Mamma had never questioned that, were never outwardly skeptical.

She had yet another reason to wish Pop had survived his heart attack. A terribly selfish one. Even so, had he lived, she wondered if even he would have seen fit to help her, since all men were considered ordained of God, the sovereign head of their families. And, invariably, what they wanted they got, no questions asked. She'd never had the nerve to ask another married woman, not even Mamma, only silently observing those whose expressions were consistently cheerful and those who were merely marking time, as she was.

Waiting for my number to be called, she thought woefully, staring at the woodshed and the outhouse beyond. *Why was I born a woman?* She was convinced if she were a man she would not treat anyone—human or beast—the way Zeke treated her. But, of course, that was a futile thing to ponder. Truth was, the Creator-God had seen fit to make her a woman. A woman whose needs were ignored by a man who did lip service to cherishing her but who never once considered her hopes and wishes. Such thoughts made her feel terribly guilty, as though she were going against everything she knew she was called to do—under God and man. *Submission is my only choice.*

Since childhood, she had been taught compliance, observing it in action. It spilled into all areas of their lives, including acquiescence to the ministers, who ruled as they deemed best. So the façade of peace saturated the community, but she knew better.

Hearing John's sudden cries, she rose and went to him. As if by some punishment for her lamentable contemplation, her time of rest had been cut short.

Not to awaken Zach, she went around the side of the bed nearest the wall and picked up whimpering John. She carried him to her room and closed the door.

Walking the length of the room, she felt too weary to calm him. "Shh, I've got ya . . . Mamma's right here," she said, fighting her sad little tears as she held him near.

Chapter 11

Saturday morning, Nov. 5
Dear Louisa,

I'm so excited!

Oh, before I get carried away with my news—how are you? I hope you're doing all right and not second-guessing your decision to back away from your marriage plans. Honestly, though, I've been doing some of that here, but for different reasons, of course.

Well, here's why I'm so happy. My family wants you to feel free to stay with us for as long as you wish. My brother Yonie is going off hunting, so he'll give up his room for the time being. If you decide to stay for longer, there are two empty bedrooms in our Dawdi Haus, if you don't mind my grandparents. That's entirely up to you. Just let me know so we can have everything shiny and clean for you!

I must hurry off to a quilting bee. We're making a wedding quilt for my eldest brother's niece (his wife's niece, that is, but here we're all family, no matter by marriage or just what).

I'm looking forward to seeing you, face-to-face!

With love,
Annie

She was thrilled to be able to send the written welcome to Louisa, indeed. She pushed the stamp onto the envelope and then quickly wrote the address.

She headed down the stairs and out the front door to the mailbox at the end of the lawn. Daed had been as agreeable as she'd ever known him to be, which seemed to delight Mamm no end.

"That's good . . . keep everybody happy," Annie said, pulling up the little red flag on the hefty mailbox. "Not the easiest thing in the world."

———

By the following Tuesday, on her early morning walk to Cousin Julia's, Annie had what she guessed might be a brain wave, as Yonie liked to say of a sudden—and terrific—idea. And when Julia agreed that she most definitely could eat her lunch in the attic, Annie took advantage of her time to paint.

Studying the canvas, which was still resting on the easel, she knew exactly what she must add to the picture. *The final touch* . . .

The account of the small boy's disappearance was quite clear in her mind, and she was convinced the tale was incomplete without the peach stone. A boyish token, of sorts. As a young girl, she'd heard other children talk of squeezing a peach pit hard enough and long enough, till it would eventually sprout. A made-up story, most likely. But little Isaac, long presumed dead, had carried the stone with him everywhere, as she recalled from hearing the details of his kidnapping time and again. She'd known this firsthand, as well, from having spent many happy hours in the company of the imaginative boy.

Isaac, my little friend . . . lost forever. The thought never ceased to put a grind in her teeth, this fiery anger she'd never voiced.

So solemnly, even crossly, she painted a tiny oval-shaped peach pit on the board of the long tree swing. Hard as it was to spot in the picture, she impulsively brush-stroked a pale yellow ray of sunshine falling on it.

Now the painting's complete, she thought.

Minutes later when Julia brought up a big slice of apple pie, she was so taken by the image on the canvas, she stood there and stared.

"Is something the matter?" Annie asked.

"My word, no . . . this is beautiful. I never would've guessed you could paint such splendor." Julia's smile was as radiant as the sunbeams shining on the locust trees and the stream. "Wait here just a minute . . . I have an idea." With that, she turned and hurried back down the stairs.

Where's she going?

But Annie wasn't worried what Julia was up to, for the woman was as keyed up as anyone she knew. She could burst out laughing at the most unpredictable thing, and Annie believed because of this, young James and Molly were the most contented and carefree children. Even more so than her own nieces and nephews. No, there was truly something remarkable about spontaneous laughter in the home, and Julia had a corner on that happiness, for sure. She was also quite eager to extend herself to others—taking meals to sick neighbors and driving elderly folk to doctor appointments. A true friend, indeed.

In no time, Julia was back and waving a paper that looked to be clipped out of a magazine. "Here now, and don't say no till you hear me out," she said. "In fact, why don't you sit right down a minute and I'll read it to you."

Annie did so, listening as Julia read about an "artistic opportunity," where the first-place winner would receive some classes with an experienced artist.

"Now what do you think of that?"

Annie had no idea what she was getting at. "I just don't know. . . ."

"I'll take a digital picture of your painting and submit it for the contest."

She could see Julia was convinced. "Then what? If I should win—which I know I won't—what then?"

"Well, it says here the first-place winner will be featured on the January cover of *Farm and Home Journal* and will receive three art lessons by a master artist. Oh, Annie, you'd finally have the chance to study art."

Annie shook her head. "No, no, this is a bad idea." *Such education smacks of headiness and high-mindedness . . . frowned on by the People.* "I don't have a scholarly bone in my body."

"That's where I think you're wrong. You know I believe in your work. This is a wonderful opportunity for you. It's a fine magazine; Irvin and I have read it for years."

"Well, it may be good 'n' all, but that's not what I'm concerned 'bout."

Julia's face grew more serious. "What, then?"

Annie gritted her teeth, but she felt sure Julia knew already. "Bein' found out—this place here where I work and all. I wouldn't want anything to change, wouldn't want my father to know what I'm doin'."

"Honestly, Annie, you're taking a risk every time you come up here. But you haven't joined the church yet, so why's this such a concern?"

Julia had a point. "Still, I haven't made my decision on that."

Julia reached out a hand. "In your heart you're just not sure, Annie. . . ." She paused, tears welling up. "Maybe the Lord has something more for you."

Annie inhaled slowly. She knew what Julia believed—that a person could know the Lord in *an intimate way,* as she liked to say. Annie sighed. "I've never said I wasn't going to make my church vow. If it weren't for my art it would be ever so easy . . . I might have already. But my first love tends to get in the way."

Julia nodded. "I know you want to improve and keep working on your craft, getting better with each painting, just as Irvin and I see you doing every time you come here."

She offered her thanks, grateful Julia hadn't pushed with all her talk of salvation, as she had in the past. "You've been so kind to me, and I appreciate it. Really I do."

Julia's bright eyes held Annie's gaze. "What's to lose if you let me submit your painting to the contest? I'll even pay for the fee."

I'll never win anyway, thought Annie.

"Pretty please let me do this for you?" Julia entreated. "At least for a chance to have a few pointers from an instructor."

Annie suddenly thought of Louisa. "My pen pal is comin' to visit, and she's an instructor, but that'll have to be kept quiet, I'm thinkin'." She went on to say how Louisa even held exhibits for her students and was doing so this very week.

"Well then, if you should happen to win the prize, your artist friend could go along with you to the classes. Maybe so?"

"I don't know. . . . I can't see myself taking classes out in public. Besides, as I said, there's no way on earth my painting can possibly win."

Knowing Julia as she did, she would be trapped right here in the attic today unless she agreed. Even if she didn't, Julia might simply snap the picture with her fancy camera and send it off on her computer—by something called email, which both she and Louisa knew all about—and submit her painting anyway.

She rose and went to look at the image once again. Closing her eyes, she cleared her vision. Then, opening them, she attempted to look at her own work through different eyes. She had in mind that her paintings should have a purpose, but just what she didn't know. Surely it was not to vent her anger over Isaac's long-ago disappearance? *I must forgive whoever took Isaac away.* . . .

"All right, dear cousin," she whispered, "if you must. But I'll be payin' the fee."

Julia hurried to her side. "Oh, this makes me so happy! Wait till I tell Irvin. He'll set up some lights in here and we'll use the digital camera until we get it just right."

"Best not let the word slip out," she reminded her. Constantly she felt she was repeating herself about this secret . . . this beloved place. "Promise?"

Julia nodded, pushing the paper in front of Annie's nose once again so she could sign her name. Once that was done, she grinned at her. "You won't be sorry. I just know you have a very good chance!" Then she disappeared down the steps.

Annie leaned against the far wall, looking at the painting, at the swing hanging from the tree. She stared so hard at it, for a split second she thought it had moved slightly, but that was impossible. The painting was as real to her as her memories of her childish bond with the missing boy.

She hoped Louisa might not be troubled if ever she were to

hear what had happened. But Annie knew she would not be able to keep the tragic story from her good friend, especially when she showed Louisa this painting. *We won't visit this spot right away,* she thought. *No sense starting things out on the wrong foot!*

Chapter 12

Louisa wondered when she might have the opportunity to recharge her smart phone, since Annie's family lived without electricity. She took her time going over her address book and calendar, making note of the date, Saturday, November 12, and checking on the weather forecast while riding in a cab from the Harrisburg airport to Lancaster County.

A red letter day. Paradise, here I come!

She called home to let her mom know she had arrived safely and then put her cell phone away. Glancing at her laptop in its case, she wondered how often she would get to use it, wanting to keep in touch with her art students by email. Some by instant messaging. She longed for a less complicated life, but she could not leave behind her ability to communicate, which was essential to her work—even if Mother's voice *had* been cold when Louisa let her know she had arrived safely. At least she hadn't pulled the martyr routine . . . yet.

Louisa wished now she hadn't given out Annie's mailing address. *Too easy for letters from home to reach me. . . .*

Looking out at the farmland whizzing by, she replayed Michael's outrage at her supposedly "playing runaway bride for effect . . . nothing more," as he so angrily had said. Mother, of course, had had her say, as well. Interestingly, though, her dad had not voiced displeasure, but his squinted eyes had exposed his annoyance.

As for the pre-wedding expenses, Louisa had offered to pay her parents back, over many years' time. *At least the next twenty or so.* But Mother would not hear of it, most likely because she assumed Louisa might snap out of it and return to Michael's waiting arms. To put that belief to rest, Louisa insisted on canceling everything herself, from the Brown Palace reservations to the white stretch limo.

At this moment, she felt more relaxed than she had in months, and much of it had to do with Annie putting out the proverbial welcome mat. She was bemused as to how the Zook family could have possibly understood her wishes, that she needed a clean break from Michael, not to mention some distancing from her parents, as well as hoping to infuse herself in the simple life for as long as possible. Annie's open-ended invite proved once again her opinion that she and her Amish pen friend were on similar wavelengths, having shared rather confidentially in their letters.

Leaning her head back, she spotted a billboard for the Rockvale Square Outlets. *Discount malls abound even in Amish country.* . . .

But most alarming was seeing firsthand precisely what Annie had been writing about for years, that the business sector was encroaching on precious farmland. Too many non-Amish farmers were selling their land to developers. Town houses, patio homes, and large custom homes were rising up out of the world's most fertile soil.

Stunningly sad, she thought. *Actually stupid!*

Having grown up in Denver, she might easily have viewed all the new development as a nonissue. But because of her close relationship with Annie, she had some empathy for "the People," as Annie liked to refer to her church community, and their problems.

No wonder the Amish are searching for land elsewhere!

Well, there was certainly ample land in other states. Take Colorado with its wide-open spaces such as the sprawling ranches situated between the small cities of Monument and Castle Rock. And thousands of acres of grazing land stretching out to the east, toward the Kansas state line. But the semi-arid climate and high altitude were not conducive to the array of crops Annie's People were accustomed to growing.

She leaned up to ask the taxi driver, "How far to Paradise?"

"Oh, a good ten miles or so, miss."

Miss. The bleak realization hit her once more. The sadness, no, the deception hurt the most.

Shaking her head, she found herself exasperated anew at her father's interference in her life. One of the reasons she had desired to come to Pennsylvania was to sort out her feelings. She needed to put things together in her head . . . and in her heart. Remaining in Colorado had not been one of the options she allowed herself. Except for her enthusiastic students, nothing held her there any longer. She had seen to it that they each had plenty of assignments to keep them busy. That way if she decided to be away longer than a month, she was set.

She stared down at her "Palm," the minicomputer, organizer, cell phone, and camera all rolled into one very cool gadget, and wondered how she would ever manage without it, along with her fabulous car, her favorite DVDs, and her many jazz CDs. Despite any small misgivings she felt now, she couldn't wait to see

Annie, to talk with her in person. That alone she hoped would make up for the abandonment of all her high-tech toys.

Weird, she thought, *having such affinity to a Plain girl.*

Next to her on the seat, in the pet carrier, Muffin opened his kitty eyes and looked at her through the mesh window as if to say, *Where are you taking me?*

Leaning over, she whispered, "You'll have lots of company where we're going." She almost laughed, but smothered it so as not to call attention from the driver, who had been noticeably surprised when she'd given the Paradise Township address. *"Isn't that Amish farmland?"* he'd asked, and quickly she agreed that it was, saying no more.

She closed her eyes, weary of the day, having gotten up at three that morning to shower, shampoo, and dress in order to catch the first flight out of DIA. Then there was the mad rush to the connecting gate at Chicago's O'Hare. She was glad to be this far into her travels and could hardly wait for some of Barbara Zook's home-brewed coffee!

Annie pushed a wet rag deep into the corner, back where the bed hid the floor from the doorway. After dry mopping, she had taken great care to get down on her hands and knees, making sure all stray dust bunnies beneath Yonie's bed, or anywhere else, were gone. She had also given the front porch a good strong sweeping, very glad the potted mums were still blooming due to no frost yet, a rarity. She had even done something rather "fancy" by bringing in the pots at night, hoping to preserve their beauty for Louisa's arrival.

Just now she wondered about the time and excitedly ran downstairs to check the wall clock in the kitchen.

She asked Mamm about the apple dumplings. "Are they done yet?"

"Ach, calm yourself, dear."

One look at Mamm and she knew they were *both* wound up. The whole family was. Yonie, of course, was out deer hunting with friends over the weekend and most of next week, but Luke and Omar would be around and grinning to beat the band. Jesse Jr., Christian, and Abner and their wives and children, too, would meet Louisa after Preaching service tomorrow. No question, her pen pal's coming was a first for all of them.

"I made sure Yonie's room was spotless," she told Mamm, hurrying to the front room to look out the window.

Her mother followed close behind. "Why don't you give me that rag?" Mamm held out her hand. "And why not comb through your hair once? Worry less 'bout the cleanliness of the house now and be thinkin' how ya want to look yourself."

I'm all mussed up, she thought, recalling the only other time Mamm had ever spoken to her like that. Back when she was a little girl and not even close to being ready to leave the house for Preaching.

Now she considered tomorrow's house church meeting. How would the People react to Louisa sitting in their midst? And would her friend even want to join them?

I'll know soon. . . .

Louisa released her seat belt and stared at the Zooks' property—the old two-story barn with its picturesque windmill to her right. And the tall white farmhouse with distinctive black shutters on the other side of the road, the south-facing porch dotted with clay pots of gold- and bronze-colored mums. A lofty willow, minus its leaves, hovered near the back of the house, gracing the yard. The distinct vision she had formed in her mind since childhood had been merely a reflection of the real thing. Now, here she was.

This is Annie's world!

Nearly speechless, she jumped when the cabbie announced the fare. "Oh, sorry," she said, digging into her purse for a wad of cash.

When her suitcase and matching overnight case were unloaded from the trunk, she thanked the driver again. Then, hooking the two pieces of luggage together, she rolled them across the road, carrying Muffin in his pet tote up the dirt lane leading to the house.

She heard the first little squeal of glee and looked up to see Annie running toward her, arms outstretched, long skirt flying as she came. "Ach, you're here, Louisa! *Willkumm*, friend!"

Letting go of her luggage, she set down Muffin in his carrier just in time to receive the warm and welcoming hug. "It's great to see you," she said, feasting her eyes on her friend. "You're so pretty, Annie! You didn't do yourself justice in your descriptions through the years."

They locked eyes on each other, and Annie said, "I'd have to say you look just like the picture you sent."

"The engagement picture or the one with my art students?"

"Well, both. I'd know you anywhere."

Before she could stop her, Annie grabbed her luggage, talking all the while. "I'm so glad you're here safely . . . flyin' on an airplane and all . . . what was that like?"

Louisa smiled at her exuberance. "Oh, it's really lots safer than driving a car, according to statistics."

"But how's it feel to go so fast?"

"Surprisingly, you don't realize the speed, except for the

takeoff and landing. You mainly sit in a chair, buckled in, of course, and if you're like me, you pick up a magazine and read. Some people actually sleep through the entire flight, if it's not too choppy, which it certainly can be flying out of Denver." She explained the updrafts and stronger currents near the mountains. "One of my friends flies a small aircraft—a four-seater—and she nearly crashed it because of the bizarre wind currents out there."

Annie's blue eyes twinkled. "Did you say a girl flies the airplane?"

"Well, she's my age . . . a year older."

"Ach, what a life, goin' ever so fast!"

No, this is the life . . . right here, thought Louisa as she walked with Annie, as energetic and delightful in person as she had always been in letters.

They walked through the well-landscaped side yard, around the house to the screened-in back porch.

Annie's mother met them with a winning smile, as overweight as Annie was slight. "Come in, come in, Louisa. Make yourself at home," Barbara Zook said, wiping her hands on her long black apron.

"Thank you, Mrs. Zook. I'm so pleased to meet you at last. Annie's talked so much about you . . . well, written about you, anyway."

That brought another cheery smile. "Oh, you mustn't call me something so formal sounding. Honestly, Barbara's just fine," she said. "How was your trip in?"

"Uneventful . . . a good thing, thanks. It's really wonderful to be here." Louisa took in the unique surroundings and wondered how the large kitchen with its massive black wood stove and long table with wooden benches on either side would have looked to her today if she hadn't already visualized this house from Annie's letters. "What a beautiful place," she said, as if standing in the middle of a dream.

But it was Annie's demeanor, composed and demure, that struck her. She was as attractive as any of Louisa's friends. Simply remove the head covering and the long cape dress, and she could pass for a modern girl. But Annie's remarkably blue eyes grew suddenly wide as she caught a glimpse of Louisa's long earrings.

Annie is startled at the sight of me, Louisa thought, wishing she hadn't worn either her pencil-thin jeans or her jewelry.

Chapter 13

Annie sure hadn't expected Louisa to be dressed the way she was. She honestly wasn't sure how she expected Louisa to look, really. She was quite sure Daed would be distressed, though, once he came in from the barn and met their English visitor.

A mite taller than Annie anticipated her to be, Louisa also looked much too skinny. Like the painfully thin catalog models in tight-fitting blue jeans and hyacinth-colored linen shirts over matching camisole tees. She knew of such descriptions and colors only from having paged through the ads at Julia's. She had no idea why the catalogs came in the mail there, since her cousin sewed all her own clothes, as well as little Molly's dresses and nightgowns. Still, it was interesting to see the different types of shoes and purses and whatnot. She'd even peeked at the fine jewelry section—rings, bracelets, and necklaces—knowing she'd probably never wear such things, but they were awful easy on the eyes.

"Come, I'll show you where you'll be sleeping. Yonie's out hunting, hopin' to get his first deer this year, so you'll have his room for the time being." She started up the stairs, still holding the two pieces of luggage, the nicest-looking suitcase and tote she'd ever seen, and motioned for Louisa to follow her.

"Hey, I'm not helpless," Louisa said, trying to wrestle away the suitcase while still carrying Muffin.

Annie laughed. "If you want to help so much, then you can finish washing and drying all of Mamm's dishes for tomorrow's noon meal. We'll feed about two hundred and fifty people, how's that?"

"That's a bunch."

"Well, wait till you see how many attend our weddings." She stopped at the top of the stairs and waited for Louisa to catch up. "Ach, I'm sorry to mention that right off."

"Don't worry, Annie. I'm not super sensitive about it."

"Well . . . you know. I think we both need some pampering, jah?"

"For sure." Louisa smiled.

"By the way, breakfast comes early on Sunday mornings, 'specially when we have Preaching here."

"I'll be awake in plenty of time," Louisa said. "Remember, I'm a morning person . . . like you."

"But your body clock's two hours behind us here, jah?"

It was Louisa's turn to laugh. "I'll just set my Palm to go off before dawn." Then she seemed to remember something. "Oh, no! That won't work."

"What won't?"

Louisa shook her head. "There's no place to recharge, right? No electricity here. Duh . . . I should know this!"

"Unless you want to head down to Cousin Julia's right away. She and Irvin have electric," Annie said. "But, honestly, you won't have any trouble wakin' up. Our peacocks have a built-in alarm clock, trust me on that."

She led Louisa down the hall, stopping to point out her own room. "See there? That's the desk where I write to you."

"Sweet." Louisa hurried into Annie's bedroom, cat carrier and all.

Annie set down the luggage and moved the desk out from the wall to show the date and initials carved into the back.

"Your dad made this?"

"It was a big birthday surprise when I was twelve. I got spoiled that year." Annie watched her friend sitting on the chair where she'd pondered so often what should or shouldn't be shared in her letters to an outsider.

Just then, Louisa turned and looked up at her. "This is so wild. I've tried to picture you, your room . . . everything. You have no idea how terrific this is."

"Ach, I feel the same way, havin' you visit." Annie suddenly thought of their bath routine tonight and cringed. *What'll she think when she finds out about Saturday night baths? Will she turn right around and make a beeline for home?*

But she didn't reveal the bath routine. She just kept smiling, and Louisa did, too, like they were long-lost friends; except they knew they weren't that at all.

"Come, let's get you settled."

Annie was amazed at the "slide show" in Louisa's Palm, as Louisa called it—one image after another of the watercolor and oil paintings in the recent exhibit. "You must be so happy 'bout your students," said Annie, looking intently, and then holding the gadget when Louisa handed it to her. "What do I do with it?"

"Just watch."

"It goes all by itself?"

"Yep."

She'd heard of some of the womenfolk in other church

districts being allowed to own cell phones, but she'd never seen anything like this. "It's hard to believe . . . such clear pictures in a little device." She looked at Louisa. "What will your students do without you while you're here?"

"Oh, don't worry . . . they have plenty of assignments."

"A whole month's worth?"

"At least." Louisa turned off her Palm. "That's enough for now," she said. "Want to help me unpack?"

"Sure." But as Louisa removed her colorful clothes from her suitcase, Annie was quite surprised. There were a number of out-fits, and for all different occasions, it seemed—dress up, work, play, and everything in between. Foreign as anything she'd ever seen, as fancy as the catalog pages at Julia's. There was even a separate pull-out case for Louisa's bracelets, necklaces, and earrings.

Annie bit her lip, wishing she might persuade her friend away from such ornamentation while she was here, at least. Contemplating the potentially awkward situation, she continued helping Louisa organize her clothes.

Out of the blue, Louisa stopped what she was doing. "It's surprising that you and your family would open your home to me. I'm really grateful."

Annie touched her arm. "You're truly welcome." She leaned over to line up Louisa's shoes beneath the wooden wall pegs. "We enjoy havin' company, believe me. My mother loves to cook . . . likes havin' lots of feet beneath her dinner table."

"Cooking is one of *my* passions, too. Sometime while I'm here, I'd like to treat all of you to one of my favorite recipes. Deal?"

"I'm sure Mamm will be more than happy to take you up on it, but we'll help you with the wood stove, of course."

"Oh, I didn't think of that." Louisa's eyes were mischievous. "I might present the family with a burnt offering, which would never do." She reached down and unzipped the pet carry bag. "I hope my kitty's welcome to stay . . . here in the bedroom. Is it all right?"

Annie wondered when Louisa might mention Muffin. "Well, since he's a city cat he must be used to lots of pamperin', jah?"

Lifting out the lump of grayish-blue fur, Louisa snuggled her nose into his neck. "There's my sweet boy. Aw, such a good traveler you are."

"Our mouse catchers in the barn never had it this fine." Annie laughed, enjoying the sight of Louisa and her cat. She'd heard so much about "precious Muffin this," "darling Muffin that" for the past year or so, since Louisa had gotten her new place after college graduation.

Louisa set her kitty on the floor, and immediately Muffin disappeared beneath the ruffled white bed skirt.

For good measure, Annie hurried to close the door. *In case he decides to make a run for it.* Returning to sit on the bed, she decided now was a good time to tell Louisa about the evening's activities. "Since we're hosting the Preaching service tomorrow, there'll be a group of men comin' later this afternoon to remove some of the interior walls—to make an open space large enough for the meeting. The bench wagon will arrive soon after."

Louisa nodded. "I'm fascinated to see how everything is set up."

"Well, some of Mamm's helpers will start arriving at seven-thirty tomorrow morning. It gets awful busy round here on Preaching days."

"I don't want to be in the way," Louisa insisted. "Just tell me what to do and when."

Should I say something about fitting in just yet? Annie wondered, not wanting to stare at Louisa's shiny pink lips or her dangling earrings. Rather, she zeroed in on her thoughtful aqua blue eyes, but even they were made up too much.

Then, as though sensing her concern, Louisa said, "I brought along several skirts and dresses. Wouldn't want to stick out like a sore thumb here." Promptly Louisa held up a bright red shirt-dress, a tiny flap-style pocket on the upper left bodice. The other dress she showed Annie was a solid lime green, a bit low cut, and the color shouted, *"Lookee here at me!"*

Annie held her breath. The dresses, if they were Louisa's only choices, were much too loud for Preaching service.

"Knowing your people as you do, Annie, which would be best for church tomorrow?"

Ach, neither one! She was at a terrible loss for words.

Right away, Jesse was in a quandary, seeing Annie's friend enter the kitchen looking like Jezebel herself.

What have we done? Even as he thought this, he scooted his chair back from the head of the table. He felt strongly the importance of showing respect to their guest even though she was bejeweled, made up to kingdom come, and wearing fancy clothes . . . a man's pair of trousers, in all truth.

"Welcome to our house." He extended his hand.

"Thank you, uh . . . Mr. Zook. Well, Preacher Zook is better, isn't it?" She shook his hand and smiled.

He could see she was trying hard to be polite, though he was also mighty sure she was terribly uncomfortable. Still, he recalled the curious words spoken by Preacher Moses regarding Annie and her visitor and hoped that just maybe Louisa's coming might prove to be providential indeed.

Annie insisted on Louisa sitting next to where Mamm always sat at the table. Louisa offered repeatedly to carry over the serving platters, but Mamm was adamant about her being "waited on" for the first meal with the family.

Meanwhile, Dawdi and Mammi Zook came over from the Dawdi Haus, the connecting addition to the main house, Mammi leaning on both her cane and Dawdi's arm. "Well, who do we have here?" she asked, eyes bright as she leaned forward, wobbling a bit.

"Louisa Stratford has come to stay awhile," Daed spoke up.

"Well, it's very nice to meet you, young lady," Mammi said, nodding her head and smiling.

"Where'd you come from?" asked Dawdi, his pure white beard touching his chest.

Before Louisa could answer, Annie volunteered. "She's all the way from Denver, Colorado." *Not from Mars!*

"Well, now, I hope ya didn't walk," said Dawdi, a twinkle in his eye.

Louisa shook her head, smiling. "Two thousand miles is a long way."

"She flew on a plane," Mamm spoke up. The comment put a slight damper on things until Luke and Omar wandered in from the barn, looking disheveled. Annie waited till both had washed up at the sink, and then she introduced them to Louisa, as well.

Luke blushed and muttered "hullo," as though he ought not to be looking at such a fancy woman.

But Omar stuck his hand out and smiled big, his brown eyes shining. "Nice to meet ya."

"And you, too," said Louisa, smiling back.

When they were all seated, following Daed's silent mealtime

prayer, Mamm carried the conversation, asking Louisa about her family. To this Louisa summed up her father's work, saying merely that he was a busy attorney and that her mother kept occupied with her social groups, including a monthly book club.

"Oh, a book club, you say?" Omar's eyes shone. "I'm curious 'bout that."

Mamm clammed up quickly, casting a glance at Annie, a question mark on her face.

Louisa continued on. "Last count, there were eight book-worms in the group. Two men, the rest women. They choose a book to read each month, then meet for coffee and dessert at someone's house and talk about it."

"Sounds interesting," Daed spoke up suddenly. "What sort of books?"

Here we go, thought Annie.

Louisa shrugged. "Oh, all kinds. This month it's Grisham's latest novel."

"Who's that?" Omar asked, his left suspender drooping off his shoulder.

"The author, John Grisham, writes courtroom thrillers, for the most part." Louisa said this with such certainty that Annie was sure Louisa had also read them. "My mother's book club reads everything from CIA suspense to alternate reality," Louisa added.

Daed frowned, clearly mystified. "I can't say I've ever heard of this alternate reality. What do you mean by it?"

Louisa paused, reaching for her water glass. She looked so peculiar with her eyelashes long and dark, as showy as the English tourists who visited the quilt shops and the many roadside stands up and down Harvest Road. "What if you could wake up and discover the dreams you have at night are actually real—

your *true* life? So you're walking around in your dream, but it's really your life."

Luke chuckled and put his head down quickly, but Omar latched right on to Louisa's comment. "I could go for a book like that, really!"

Everyone laughed, including Daed.

"I could go for 'bout any book if I could see the print," Dawdi added.

Mammi wore a sly grin. "Oh, go on with ya, Pop."

Annie felt herself relaxing a bit. Her family was attempting to make Louisa feel comfortable. Still, a downright awkward predicament, to be sure.

Chapter 14

Louisa was bowled over when Annie said she could be first for the Saturday night bath in the kitchen. "You mean you all use the same bath water?"

Annie grinned, though it was apparent she was trying her best not to. "It's the fastest way to get done."

"Well, that's nice, but . . ." She felt positively speechless. *What was I thinking . . . leaving my Jacuzzi tub behind?*

"You all right?" asked Annie as they talked in the privacy of her bedroom.

"Oh, sure." But Louisa was convinced her mascara was smudged and her face oily from the humidity here and the long day of travel. A brisk scrub or even a facial would be wonderful if she could actually see what she was doing. *No large mirrors?*

Annie explained further. "For the baths, the kitchen is closed off, really 'tis. We simply hang a big curtain between the kitchen and the adjoining room. We tape cardboard up on each of the windows so no one could possibly see in."

"I guess I'll adjust." But Louisa wasn't certain the required adjustment would kick in within the next few hours. So . . . this was the real introduction to the simple life she had been craving.

The next shocker awaited her in the outhouse. Her eyes watered at the horrendous smell, and she refused to sit down on the wooden opening. *I'm going to have to expand my lung capacity immediately!*

Louisa lathered up with the scratchy bar of oatmeal soap, unquestionably homemade, resisting the slightest urge to relax or soak. Sitting knees up in the tub, she wondered wryly what her friends would say if they could see her now.

Thinking back to supper, right here in this room, she recalled the flabbergasted looks on each of the Zooks' faces. *I must seem like an alien!*

Following the inelegant bath, she was glad for the warmth of the grand old cookstove and wrapped herself in a thick towel. She fought off the lingering concern that Luke or Omar might forget and walk in on her, and dried off quickly.

Putting on the long pink bathrobe from home, she thought, *I must be nuts to stay here longer than a few days!* Laughing softly, she slipped her well-pedicured feet into matching slippers.

She remembered Annie had said her mother would be the third to bathe after Annie, followed by the preacher and so on down the line of boys. Annie had also reminded her that since Yonie was out hunting, there was one less person using the communal tub this night. Lucky Omar would be the final one to wash off in everyone else's dirty bath water.

The thought repulsed her, but she tried to distract herself by fluffing her hair with the towel, missing her blow dryer. *No wonder Annie gets by shampooing only once a week . . . her hair is covered up!*

Still feeling exposed, she peeked through the curtain. Seeing no one, she dashed to the stairs, hair still dripping. Upstairs, she knocked on Annie's door to say it was *her* turn.

"Already? Goodness' sakes, you're fast." Annie smiled, her gaze falling on Louisa's pink robe. "I'll hurry, then we can talk, jah?"

"Sure, I'll go dry my hair."

Annie smiled. "Sorry 'bout that. We use the air, ya know."

"So do I—only forced air . . . all at once." She laughed.

"I won't dawdle," Annie said, heading down the hall to the stairs.

Louisa went to her room and closed the door. She swished her thick hair around, patting it with the towel and combing through it with her fingers.

Going to the tall bureau, she picked up her Palm where she'd left it on. Not expecting to see any messages, she was actually pleased to see four. *Who's thinking about me? Maybe Courtney or one of my students?*

Sitting at the window, on the only chair in the room, she punched in the numbers for her code, then listened for the first message. "Louisa, we need to talk. . . ." Michael's voice jarred her.

"We have nothing to talk about," she whispered, deleting his message and going to the next.

"I have an idea, babe. Please call!" Another from Michael.

Yep, I have an idea, too. Get over yourself!

But hearing his voice made her feel miserable. She really hoped all four messages weren't from him, because she wanted to fall asleep in the stillness of this stark bedroom, not with Michael's desperation ringing in her ears.

Sighing, she listened to the third, finger poised to skip over it if she heard his voice again. But this time it was someone else.

Cybil Peters, one of her newest students, was calling to say she'd sold an oil painting from the art show. "It's my first, and I owe it to you, Louisa. We definitely have to keep in touch while you're on your sabbatical."

Sabbatical? Did I say coming to Amish country was that? She didn't recall, in the midst of all that had transpired prior to her flight to liberty.

She pressed to return the call and was thrilled to hear Cybil's perky voice. "Hey, there!"

"Cybil? It's Louisa. Got your message . . . and I'm so jazzed. This is great news."

"Don't I know it? And guess who bought it? You remember that older gentleman, the one who kept circling back to stand and stare at my painting? Well, he's the one. I got a whopping three hundred bucks . . . so I'll be hitting Aaron Brothers tomorrow, to stock up on art supplies." Cybil continued chattering, and Louisa was more than happy to oblige her by listening.

After a few minutes, Cybil said, "Well, it sounds like you've got another call coming in, so I'll let you go."

"Hey, keep in touch," she said. "See ya!"

Catching the incoming call, Louisa was surprised to hear her father's voice. "Honey, we miss you. I know you're upset, and so are we." He paused. "Frankly, this whole thing with Michael can be unraveled."

"No, Daddy. Marrying Michael would have been a mistake." The lump in her throat threatened to choke her words.

She heard him sigh. "Your mother and I think—"

"I can't do this now," she interrupted.

"Listen, we need to discuss this. I see it as essential, Louisa."

Essential?

"I'm losing power," she told him. "I really need to go. Bye, Daddy."

She pressed the off button. It was true, the Palm needed recharging. *Perfect . . . I'll be unavailable for a while. . . .*

There was another voice message to check, but she turned off the power, not in the mood for more pleas from either Michael or her parents.

Going to lie down, she was happy to see Muffin jump on the bed and come purring toward her. "Oh, you . . . hiding again?" He snuggled down on her stomach, curling up like a kitten. "What would I do without my kitty?" she whispered. "You don't know it, but tomorrow's going to be a busy day. So I hope you'll be a good boy and stay right here in this room."

She considered the church meeting tomorrow, but not so much the length as the awkwardness of it. *Will I feel as out of it as I did at supper?* She couldn't stop thinking how strange it felt to be looked at with such curiosity. *Like Annie and her family must feel when they're in the minority.*

Lying there, it struck her that she was free of any home ties—especially those connected to Michael. She stroked her cat, aware of his persistent strong purring. "I think you must be as contented here as I am," she whispered, playing with his crystal ID tag.

Smiling to herself, she reveled in the solitude, thinking of Cybil's excitement at selling her art, recalling her own first sale ever. It had happened the fall semester of her sophomore year at California School of Art. The acrylic painting had been dear to her, inspired by a trip to Hampton, Virginia, when she was twelve. She had spent a few weeks that summer with her single great-aunt on her father's side of the family. Margaret Stratford was the only person Louisa had ever known to talk somewhat casually about God . . . as if she met Him often for espresso and pie.

Although she did not see Aunt Margaret after that summer, not until years later at her funeral, Louisa had never forgotten her tender, even intimate prayers, offered at mealtime and other times of the day. Seemingly insignificant things brought out her aunt's eagerness to chat with divinity. Margaret would blink back tears at the mention of Jesus and "that black and heartbreaking day—Good Friday," as she referred to it, when her dearest friend was mutilated and killed . . . a criminal's crucifixion.

At the time of her work in progress, Louisa's heart was fiercely bound up in the painting, fondly recalling the one-time connection with soft-spoken Aunt Margaret. The Virginia seascape was the ultimate inspiration, set at Grandview Beach at the nature preserve, where she and Margaret walked the two-mile stretch of beach. In Louisa's mind, the lovely woman in the picture, gazing out to sea, captured perfectly her devout aunt as a young woman "communing with the Creator," as she liked to say.

Terribly attached to the painting, Louisa kept wishing she might have set the price higher on the opening night of the show. Ridiculously high would have been much better than being forced to sell, but when a serious buyer approached her with cash in hand, ethically she had no choice.

Ironically, the easy sale opened wide the door to romance. The buyer, a captivating man five years her senior, wined and dined her often. Quickly she was caught up in the exhilaration of his keen attention and his admiration for her artistic talent. But the relationship distracted her terribly from her studies and her painting, so when he talked of opening an art gallery on London's posh Cork Street, she let Trey Douglas walk out of her life without even so much as a dispute.

After he left for Europe, she turned all her attention back to completing school, often wondering how her first love was doing. Was he happy in Europe? Had he found his niche?

The next year, Michael Berkeley entered her life with grandiose and surreptitious plans. . . .

Louisa was lifted out of her reverie by a tapping on her door. "Are you still awake?" Annie called softly.

"Sure, come in." She sat up, still holding Muffin. "I've been thinking. . . ."

"Well, that's a good thing to do!" Annie laughed.

"Seriously, do you happen to have an extra dress I could wear for tomorrow?"

Glory be! Annie squelched her enthusiasm. "Just a minute." She hurried to her room and chose from the wooden pegs two of her best and newest cape dresses. One blue and the other purple.

She took them to show Louisa. "Which one of these do you prefer—the color, I mean?"

Louisa looked at one, and then the other, and back again. "Umm . . ."

"Well, which?" Annie pressed her, trying to keep a straight face.

"Both are nice solid colors." Louisa seemed unsure. "We'd look like twins!"

"And what would ya think of that?"

"Well, it might be fun. The perfect way not to stick out, jah?"

Annie giggled a little at her use of the Dutch. "I can see havin' you here will be loads of fun. You'll be talkin' like us in no time."

Hopefully not the other way around! thought Annie.

"Which one did *you* plan to wear?" Louisa asked.

"No, no, you pick."

Louisa reached for her purse on the bed and rummaged inside. She pulled out her wallet and found a nickel. "Here we go! Heads it's blue, tails it's purple. Deal?"

"Deal," Annie said, using Louisa's word. She watched her flip the coin high into the air, letting it fall *kerplink* on the wide plank floor. Her brothers had often done this very thing, but mostly to decide which team would serve first in volleyball.

"Tails!" Louisa leaned down to retrieve the coin. She rose and pointed toward the purple dress. "That's the one. Mind if I try it on?"

"Sure, let's see if it fits." She removed the hanger from the dress, hand-sewn just last week, glad Louisa had picked this one. Especially since it hadn't been worn except while Mamm marked the hem for her.

Louisa had already kicked off her slippers and was untying her robe when Annie said, "You know what? I'll leave ya be."

"Oh, I'm fine . . . stay."

Even so, she felt nearly pained with her friend undressing right here. When Louisa's pink robe fell to the floor, Annie's face burned in embarrassment and she huddled in the corner, waiting for Louisa to request help if she needed it. Pinning the *Halsduch*, the cape part of the dress, to the waistline was a real chore.

"I guess you read my letters right close, then," Annie joked. Louisa seemed to know all about the pile of straight pins required for securing the cape to the skirt. She picked up a few and began pinning the front of the skirt.

"I read every word, silly." Louisa stood tall and still while Annie began pinning the back.

"This is my least favorite part of gettin' dressed," Annie admitted. "Takes a bunch of pins, as you can see."

"Ever stick yourself?"

"Honestly, I never have, but my friend Esther Hochstetler—oh, and you've got to meet her tomorrow—she's stuck herself by mistake. She's my closest Amish friend, I'd have to say."

"You wrote me once that you feel lonely sometimes with only brothers," Louisa said suddenly.

Recalling that, Annie replied, "Mamm and I are closer than some daughters and their mothers, prob'ly. But with three sisters-in-law, I'm not the only young woman in the kitchen at family gatherings, that's for sure."

When the final pin was in place, she said, "There. You look like one of us, 'cept for one thing yet."

Louisa's eyes widened. "Don't tell me . . . you're going to pull my hair back in a bun?"

Annie nodded. "Let's do this right. I'll be back." She headed to her room to get an extra head covering, terribly excited that Louisa should consent to this much Plain dressing.

Returning, Annie displayed the white netting heart-shaped cap. "This goes over your hair, and the strings are tied for church but no other time."

Louisa appeared to enjoy the process, while Annie took care to twist the sides of Louisa's parted hair, keeping any strays from escaping the tight, low bun.

When they were finished, Annie reached for a small hand mirror and held it up. "See?"

"Wow . . . I look like you. Well, sort of."

"No, you actually *do*," Annie said, wondering how long this new look would last with Louisa.

Chapter 15

Though it was late and Louisa was tired, she joined Annie in her room after changing out of the purple dress and into her pajamas. She remembered how strange it had felt wearing Annie's clothing. But there was something else, too . . . something incredibly positive about the Plain attire. She'd felt stripped of all pretense. Truly uncomplicated, just as she had longed to be. And now, wearing her pink and silky shorty pajamas, her damp hair brushed straight back, away from her face, she actually missed the mega modest dress . . . missed how she had felt in it, too. Like she was someone other than a member of the Stratford family. She wouldn't have known how to explain the feeling to anyone, being a thoroughly modern woman from the soul out.

Not wanting to stare, even though she was, Louisa couldn't get past the conspicuous contrast between herself and Annie now that they were dressed for bed. Her Amish friend looked almost childlike in her white ankle-length, high-collared nightgown, her golden-blond hair parted down the middle with loose waist-length braids. Louisa felt like a schoolgirl again, sitting there with Annie on her bed, happily whispering together. *An old-fashioned sleepover!*

"What's your favorite memory, besides Christmas or your birthday?" Annie asked unexpectedly.

"Let's see. . . ." But Louisa didn't know, couldn't think of an answer. "What about you? What's yours?"

"I believe it was the day I finished an entire painting—the first time I did—back when I was fourteen. It was a Friday—I go to Cousin Julia's to work on Tuesdays and Fridays." She paused, reminding Louisa of the attic room. "I can't decide which is my favorite memory, really. It was either that day or the first time Rudy asked me to ride home from a singing with him. Oh, Louisa, he was so awful cute. And he still is, but . . ." Annie looked like she might cry, but she composed herself quickly. "I remember my heart sure did flutter fast."

Louisa knew too well the feeling of exhilaration. "Torn between two passions?" She couldn't fathom having to choose between romantic love and her enthusiasm for her art. In fact, if she wanted to have both, she could. That was not the struggle of *her* life.

Annie leaned back on the bed, staring up at the ceiling. "You know, I never thought things would end up the way they did between Rudy and me. I thought for sure we'd be married, somehow or other. I loved him, really I did."

Still does, Louisa realized. "You're not telling me anything. It's excruciating letting go. It would be way harder for you, though, having been in a courtship for three solid years like you were." She pondered the many dates Annie and Rudy must have had, even though Amish couples saw each other rather infrequently—every other Saturday and the opposite two Sundays each month. The only other opportunities were flirtatious exchanges across the room at Preaching service or if they happened to be seated near each other at one of the many wedding feasts from November through March. Annie had written that since fewer farmers were raising tobacco currently, more time was freed up, and the bishops had extended the wedding season by three months. A good thing in the grand scheme of things—the more couples "hitched up," the more babies born. This, as Louisa understood it, was the way the Amish propagated themselves, not by seeking out new converts.

"Poor Rudy," Annie said suddenly. "He got awful tired of bein' put off. And who's to blame him? In the end, I refused to submit . . . turned him down."

Louisa wanted to divert the conversation. It was way too easy for both of them to get caught up in the "woe is me" thing. So she attempted to change the subject and asked about Annie's lovely walnut hope chest.

"Sure, I'll show you." Annie went to the foot of the bed and opened it wide. She removed a heart-shaped pillow with a tatted edge and held it up for Louisa. "Sarah Mae, my first sister-in-law, made this for me." Next she presented a set of starched white doilies. "Nearly all the gifts here were given on my sixteenth birthday." She took out a long tablecloth, neatly unfolding it and pointing out embroidered delicate pink roses. "This one's so colorful, ain't so?"

Ain't so. Louisa pursed her lips to make sure she didn't smile too broadly. Annie's exuberance was infectious, no question. She was incredibly excited about life in general and more specifically about making Louisa feel quite at home here, even though Annie was still terribly wounded, Louisa knew.

Watching Annie display one cherished item after another from her hope chest, Louisa realized suddenly she was quite okay about not returning Michael's persistent calls. In fact, she could not summon even the smallest fleck of guilt, entirely content to relax here in this room. A world apart.

Upon first arriving and sitting at the desk made by Preacher Zook, Louisa had noticed how sparsely furnished Annie's room was. A double bed with a solid maple head and footboard, two large multicolored rag rugs, a wide maple bureau—without a mirror!—and the petite writing desk in the opposite corner graced the room. Other than that, there was a single cane-back chair situated near one of the windows.

Definitely exhausted, she felt this first evening in Amish country seemed perfect, almost surreal . . . like being a character in one of the alternate reality books her mom's book club had read and discussed. Like dreaming you were in Amish country and waking up to find it was quite true!

Maybe this is my favorite day ever. . . .

———

Tears rolled down Esther Hochstetler's face as she lay on her side in bed, facing the door. She willed herself to take only shallow breaths, not wanting to awaken her husband.

Has he forgotten what it means to be a child? she wondered. *Poor little Laura. Her heart must be broken, for sure.*

It was all she could do to lie still next to him, her back toward his. He preferred to sleep like two spoons nestled together amidst warm layers of heirloom quilts. But she had made it a point to distance herself from his wrath, silently accepting some of the blame.

She had been frightened to intervene this time, as she always was. A submissive woman under God was not to question her husband's methods of discipline, according to their upbringing. The womenfolk toed the line without reservation or animosity toward their husbands or the church brethren. This was expected.

What's wrong with me? Why do I question Zeke's authority? She asked herself such questions nearly every day.

Earlier tonight, young Laura had simply rushed out the back door alone, making a beeline to the outhouse. Something she'd eaten had not set well. This had been the childish excuse given. Esther had believed her daughter's confession, for she'd seen her little one's ashen face soon after the supper hour.

Laura's transgression had occurred once the house had fallen quiet, several hours past dusk. Ignoring the standing rule, made when Laura was a mere toddler, her girl had not stood at the bedroom door and called out to awaken Esther. After dark, the children were required to have either Zeke or Esther accompany them everywhere. Other fathers amongst the People had imposed similar expectations for a good number of years now, as well.

Who knows what may lurk in the darkness, Zeke uttered all too often, but oddly enough, his urgings no longer put the fear of God in Esther.

Always before tonight she had managed to bite her tongue and keep her peace.

Honestly, I couldn't wait, Dat. I had to hurry. . . .

Little Laura's pleas ricocheted through Esther's memory now—her pleadings for Zeke not to whip her were followed by high-pitched screams that ripped through a mother's tender soul. Esther concluded that Zeke's heart was hard as stone, for Laura's cries had touched him not one iota. He had taken their wee girl out behind the barn, made her raise her skirt, and thrashed her with a willow switch, leaving welts up and down the back of her legs.

No longer able to stand by, Esther had gone out and hollered at him, "Stop hurting her, for goodness' sake!"

By some miracle, he had stopped, his face all flushed red, anger spent. Looking at Laura with glistening eyes, he pushed her back toward Esther. "There, now that you've learned your lesson, go to your mamma," he said, his voice cracking with a hint of remorse.

But now in the dark room she agonized anew. *Why must he be so?*

Boldly, she had ordered something by mail, from an ad she'd seen in *The Budget* a few weeks back. And lest she be found out, she'd watched the mail like a hawk till the order arrived. Yesterday! Oh, how eager she was to see if it would work. Starting tomorrow morning, and every day after, she planned to steep the tasteless herb into Zeke's black coffee. *This is desperation*, she thought.

Suddenly he turned and reached for her in his sleep. Her body shuddered at his touch, and she held her breath, frightened that he might awaken fully.

She lay there in the stillness, pondering her resentment. How could Zeke be kind, even understanding, one day, only to pester and belittle his family the next? He had already started in on young Zach, who, if childishly forgetting one of the rules—misbehaving in the least—was humiliated no end. Sadly, she was most perturbed by the helplessness she felt at her inability to protect her own offspring.

Her animosity was devouring her love, as each year passed. *Yet I will bear another baby for my husband this winter.* Her muscles tensed at the thought of one more innocent life having to endure the domination of such a moody and volatile parent. She hoped the new babe might be another boy, and a brawny one, to be sure. One who could stand his own against his father if ever things should come to that.

How did I ever fall for such a man? she wondered.

But she knew all too well and could not blame anyone but herself.

Outside, the late September day had been perfect in every way—full sun, warm breezes, and nary a cloud on the horizon. Inside, however, Essie was scared speechless as her heart pounded at the thought of mingling with young men at the church-sponsored youth activity. Her older brother had taken her in his open carriage, as good brothers did, to her first Sunday singing.

A buzz of voices wafted her way as she stepped out of the buggy and wandered toward the two-story barn. The sound of so many youth in one place—boys and girls alike—filled her heart with dread and her head with visions of being passed over.

Soon she and all the others were singing the "fast songs" in unison. At one point, she looked down the long row of young men on the opposite side of the table from her and a host of other girls. Like a magnet pulling hard on her, she caught the unexpected gaze of a boy she'd never seen at Preaching. He was staring and smiling at her, and making no bones about it, either.

Quickly, she looked away, her face burning with shyness. Try as she might, she could not continue singing, her mouth so dry and her brain so befuddled.

It turned out the boy with light brown hair and shining brown eyes must have kept his gaze focused squarely on her the entire time of singing and table fellowship, although she did not once look his way again.

When later she stood to talk with several girls, she was

astonished by his haste, and even his courage, in approaching her. She had turned only slightly and there he was, standing a smidgen too close. The girls who were with her revealed a certain alarm in their eyes, or perhaps it was astonishment. She didn't know which.

"You're the pertiest girl here" were the first words out of Ezekiel's mouth.

From that moment on, she was smitten with the good-looking boy from out of town, who had just happened to come for no apparent reason. His striking confidence in what he seemed to want, her as his *Aldi*—girlfriend—made her feel ever so good about herself.

After a mere two rides in his courting carriage, she embraced his wonderful-good declaration of her as "my precious little dove." He was constantly saying how he would take such good care of her all the days of her life. She believed him, deciding then and there this handsome, caring Zeke was the man of her dreams.

When they had been engaged for a short time, her father somehow found out and stepped in, pleading with Essie not to marry outside her church district. Preacher Zook also went to her father privately and strongly urged him not to allow her to marry Zeke, never giving any solid reason for the opposition. But she insisted she could not turn her back on her fiancé.

Zeke had spent his most recent years in Honey Brook, and he made it known he was not so keen on living in Paradise, though he had been originally from the area. A topsy-turvy time, to be sure.

Eventually Zeke was persuaded to change his mind about where they would live, and in the end, agreed to settle near Essie's parents' farm, accepting a thirty-acre parcel of land.

Without a doubt, Esther was quite sure they would be living far from here instead of a close distance to her now widowed mother had her father not intervened and convinced Zeke in the end with the whopping-good dowry.

Sighing now, she felt painfully hemmed in, wishing she could move away from the confines of her husband's unconscious embrace. But the slightest movement might set off an alarm in his brain—trigger his own persistent nightmares—so she kept her upper body completely motionless. Slowly she slid her legs down, stretching them carefully, glad for the coolness of the sheet against her skin.

Who can I talk to? Who would even begin to understand?

Esther wished she dared slip out of bed, if only for a moment, to comfort her wounded little girl. She longed to hold Laura close, soothing her with gentle strokes and kisses. Sleep evaded her as the muted sniffles of her firstborn echoed down the hall.

Chapter 16

At Sunday breakfast, Jesse nearly fell off his chair when Annie and Louisa strolled into the kitchen arm in arm. The Englischer looked every bit as though she belonged in the family, decidedly Amish. Aside from the unusual color of her bluish-green eyes and brown hair, she might even have passed for Annie's sister.

I worried for nothing, indeed, he thought, amused. In all truth, he was pleased at Annie's transformation of Louisa Stratford, because his heart had sunk instantly at seeing her saunter up the lane yesterday, modern as the day was long in such brazenly tight jeans and that loud shirt and gleaming gold jewelry.

But now, at this minute, Louisa's expression was nearly as soft as Annie's own. He thought of his mother—dear Mamm, who was cooking breakfast next door because Dat was ailing this morning. Still, Jesse recalled her words of long ago: *The way in which a child is dressed reveals a mother's true heart.*

Annie couldn't help but notice her brothers' reaction to Louisa's purple dress and full black apron as they settled into their places at the breakfast table.

"Didn't expect you to be lookin' so, uh . . . Plain this mornin'," Omar said, eyeing Louisa's head covering. "You oughta come along to the singing tonight over at Lapps' barn. Ain't that right, Annie?"

She hadn't yet mentioned anything to Louisa. "We'll see." She poured freshly squeezed orange juice into each glass, wondering if Louisa might be curious to see from afar who Rudy Esh was, having heard so much about him. After all, Louisa had been fully aware of Rudy and Annie's courtship from the very first night on. *Might be the only reason she'd want to go*, Annie thought, sensitive to her friend's own emotional state.

Severely disappointed in love, Louisa would not care to meet new young men. Not even the cutest fellows that hung around the singings, probably. Annie seriously doubted she would want to go at all, and now, seeing the distant look in her eyes, she wished Omar hadn't brought up tonight's singing.

Two sermons, one much longer than the other, were given in High German, followed by a few testimonies in Pennsylvania Dutch, a dialect of German. As a result, Louisa didn't understand what either the preachers or the deacon were saying, but she did manage to turn around and kneel in silent prayer at her seat whenever Annie and her mother did, which happened twice during the meeting. She also rather curiously observed the rise and fall of Preacher Zook's rhythmic discourse, noting the way both he and the other minister folded their hands beneath their long flowing beards, as if in perpetual prayer while they stood preaching to a packed house.

A unique subject for a painting, she thought, wishing she had the nerve to bring along a sketch pad to church in two Sundays, when the next meeting was to be held at Rudy Esh's parents' house. Annie had whispered this tidbit of news as they filled the feeding trough with a combination of cracked corn, cat food, and game bird food for the enthusiastic peacocks earlier this morning.

Louisa had awakened later than planned, and it was no wonder, since she and Annie had stayed up late talking. Even so, she had wondered why Annie hadn't knocked on her door, so she hurried out of bed, made it quickly, and peeked into the hallway. Annie was already coming with a pitcher of warm water for her washbowl and an extra hand mirror. "This'll help some, maybe," Annie said, all smiles, handing over the mirror first thing.

The second mirror *did* help, at least somewhat, although she still had no definite idea how she looked in her getup. But she certainly felt strange with her face pulled wide at the temples, the way Annie twisted the sides of her hair and then pushed all of it into a tight bun. She wondered how long before she would get used to this terribly simple hairstyle but was very glad it had worked out for her to appear this way, as Annie's sister or cousin, here today. She couldn't imagine which would be worse, however: wearing her own modern version of a simple dress and calling attention to herself in a sea of Amish women, or wearing this midcalf-length purple dress of Annie's with its full-length apron and dozens of straight pins poked into the waistline, holding everything together.

As for the lack of makeup, if she were to admit it to herself, it felt surprisingly good to go with a fresh face, although she'd never gone anywhere without her "lips." Lipstick made the world go round, and here she sat with scarcely any color on . . . only a bit of gloss.

At the moment, though, Louisa was becoming more preoccupied with the lack of padding on the seats than the fact that her eyelashes were mascara-less or that her lips were practically au naturel. The backless aspect to the wooden benches made her wonder how the four- and five-year-old children sat quietly for so long on either their parent's lap or next to them—girls with their mothers on one side of the room and little boys with their fathers on the opposite.

Not meaning to stare, she spotted a woman using a simple handkerchief to keep her preschool-aged daughter occupied. Soon a tiny cradle with twin babies in the center appeared from the hankie, and Louisa had to be careful not to smile too broadly, for she had never seen such a thing. Next, the handkerchief was transformed into a series of knots that, when the ends were pulled, gracefully vanished, bringing a look of surprise each time to the pixie-faced child.

All of a sudden, a flash of gray caught Louisa's eye, and she wondered if it was merely her imagination. But soon she heard a steady stream of meows.

Muffin . . . oh no!

Annie's eyes widened and she mouthed to Louisa, "Your cat?"

Louisa nodded.

"Just leave him be," Annie whispered back.

Muffin skulked down the narrow space between the rows of benches, back hunkered low, tail high, in prowl posture. Hemmed in as Louisa was, she couldn't get to him, but she leaned over, snapping her fingers gently, whispering the cat's name, desperately trying to divert his attention. But Muffin was headed straight for the front of the meeting—toward Preacher Zook, who seemed unaware of a cat approaching him despite the muffled spattering of *achs* from his congregation.

What's gotten into Muffin? Louisa wondered, mortified.

One of the bearded men up front rose from his seat and clapped his hands, which was the wrong thing to do to get a feline's attention, especially her cat. Perhaps the man was attempting to scare Muffin out of the room.

However, Muffin remained planted where he was. In fact, he was now poised for attack only a few inches from Preacher Zook's black shoes.

Annie's father paused suddenly, abandoning his German. "Well, now, seems we've got ourselves a visitor . . . though not such a saintly one, I daresay."

Louisa bowed her head, completely embarrassed. "I'm sorry," she whispered when Annie touched her hand.

"Not your fault."

I forgot to latch the bedroom door, she recalled.

Preacher Zook spoke again, this time chuckling as he declared the enticement for Muffin's humorous entrance into the house of worship. "Seems my shoes tracked in a small temptation for this mouse chaser."

Louisa looked and was shocked to see Annie's father holding up a peacock feather.

"Well, for goodness' sake," Annie said softly, followed by a stymied giggle.

Laughter rippled through the large room where yesterday, minus its removable walls, a living room, sitting area, kitchen, and bedroom had been well defined.

When Louisa looked again, Muffin was gone from view.

Scarcely skipping a beat, Annie's father resumed his sermon-making, and the People were lulled back to reverence by his singsong tone.

An hour later, Louisa was still contemplating Muffin's whereabouts, hoping he hadn't completely disappeared into the cat population residing in the Zooks' barn.

Nearby, a little girl strained to look under the bench ahead of her. *Is Muffin hiding there?* Louisa wondered. She could kick herself for all the commotion. *My first Sunday with Annie . . . and this happens!*

She was somewhat reassured by the way Annie's dad had handled the situation with a proper though quite ornery English cat in the middle of their sacred service.

Sighing, she was again taken by the incredibly close proximity of all these people—two hundred and fifty, give or take a few dozen—as Annie's mom had stated earlier, at breakfast. All of them smashed in like pickles in a jar. Louisa considered how good it was they took their baths the night before these Sunday gatherings. Half of the church district was made up of teens, children, and nursing babies, and she had already counted more than a hundred young people—a way to pass the time until she would help Annie and her mother serve the cold cuts and other food items for the common meal, as Annie had called it.

Thinking back to the rare times she had attended church with her parents, Louisa recalled a soft kneeling pad, pipe organ music, and stained-glass windows at the big community church in Littleton, Colorado. She remembered thinking the parishioners seemed distant somehow. Close vested. Far different from this quaint church experience, but Annie had addressed the closeness in one of her early letters, attempting to describe their concept of unity. Not until now did Louisa begin to understand that letter—the idea being fleshed out before her eyes. *A tight-knit group of people . . . close to each other and to God,* she thought as the final hymn was being sung.

Louisa still had not located Muffin by the noon meal, when she was to help Annie and her mother with the distribution of food. Deciding she had no real option but to wait—accepting

Annie's assurance that "Muffin will come back"—she cut through dozens of pies, having never seen so many kinds in one place. She also helped set the tables, marveling at the number of people who would enjoy a lunch of bread, cheese, cold cuts, jams, red beets, sweet and sour pickles, and hot coffee here in the Zooks' old farmhouse.

The ministers, both the local and visiting preachers and deacon, along with the eldest church members, sat down to eat at the first table setting. The children ate at the fourth and final setting, and Louisa was surprised at how polite and self-sufficient they were—the older children helping the younger ones.

By the time the massive cleanup was underway, she had lost count of how many introductions Annie had made on her behalf. Funny, because none of the women had ever heard of her before today. Not even Rudy Esh's sister, who looked eager to come over and get acquainted. Rhoda also went out of her way to tell Annie that Susie Yoder was at home, sick with a cold, the reason she hadn't attended the corn-husking bee, either, she said.

Louisa wondered why it was necessary for Rhoda to explain, but Annie seemed to take it in stride. Most interesting to Louisa was the secret Annie had evidently kept all these years . . . that she had a pen pal relationship with a non-Amish woman. *Wouldn't they be surprised at her other bigger secret?*

One after another, women came up to Louisa, repeatedly saying such things as, "Nice to have you visit—what church district did you say you're from?" or "Are you in from a long ways?"

To this, Annie's eyes sparkled with mischief as she apparently enjoyed setting them straight. "Louisa's from clean out west in Colorado. She's actually English, wearin' my for-good clothes."

Trying to fit in, Louisa thought with a smile. Yet Annie

avoided any mention of their years of correspondence.

Once all the dishes were washed, dried, and put away, Annie, her mother, and all three sisters-in-law, as well as several other women appointed to help, stood around the kitchen chatting. At one point, Annie grabbed Louisa's arm. "Come, I see Esther Hochstetler."

Louisa followed willingly to the corner of the kitchen, where Esther was standing, swaying with a toddler-aged boy asleep in her arms. She recalled having read letters about someone named Essie who had later returned to her given name, Esther. Annie had always indicated Essie was her dearest friend among the People.

"Hullo, Esther," said Annie, giving her a big smile. "I was hopin' I'd see ya today." She turned to Louisa. "Meet my friend Louisa. Doesn't she look ever so Plain?"

Esther cracked a smile. "Louisa's an awful perty name."

"Thanks," said Louisa. "Nice to meet you."

Annie reached over and stroked the sleeping boy's hair. "This is Esther's youngest, John. He's got an older brother, Zach, and a big sister, Laura." Annie went on to say how "awful sweet" Zeke and Esther's little ones were.

Louisa listened, intrigued by the dark circles under Esther's eyes, as well as the pallor of her face. She appeared to be six or seven months pregnant.

"You're comin' to the quilting this week, I hope," Annie said.

"Well, I wasn't plannin' to," Esther was quick to say.

"Ach, you should. I'm goin', and so is Louisa, if she wants to."

Louisa was fascinated by the interplay between Annie and Esther.

Annie continued. "Connecting with the womenfolk, well, it's the only way to make it through . . . at times, ya know."

"S'pose you're right, but I can't get away," Esther replied.

"I'll miss seein' ya, then. Honestly, I will."

Esther nodded, and Louisa thought she saw a glint of a tear in the woman's eyes.

"Take care of yourself, Annie," said Esther. Then to Louisa— "Have a nice time while you're here visitin'. It's good to have you."

"Thanks, Esther. It was very nice meeting you." She wished she might capture on canvas the pathos on the face of the saddest woman she had ever encountered.

Chapter 17

The first order of business, once the house was vacated of so many people, was to find Muffin. Annie helped with the search, suggesting the barn first, and to this Louisa cringed, visualizing mud and manure caked on Muffin's paws. She had taken care to have him freshly groomed for the trip here.

Climbing up the long ladder to the haymow, she suddenly missed wearing jeans for the first time since arriving here. But she kept up with Annie, following her to peer behind the square hay bales with a flashlight, calling for Muffin. They looked in the lower level of the barn, in the milking area, as well as the bedded areas, and last of all, the milk house, behind the milk tank and the cleaning units.

"He has to be frightened by now," Louisa said, hoping she hadn't seen the last of her pedigree cat.

Annie nodded. "Maybe so, but he's not lost . . . 'least not for long."

Louisa was concerned, but she didn't want to be priggish and mention the cost involved in purchasing such a well-bred cat.

"Have you looked in your room?" asked Annie

"Several times, yes." Louisa thought of Muffin's playful

nature. "He's been known to entertain children, so I hope he didn't follow one of them home. Except he's very intelligent, so I doubt that."

"I've never met a smart cat," said Annie.

"Then Muffin's the exception."

"Well, let's think like a cat," Annie said, making a decidedly feline smile. "She has a permanent smirk on her kitty face."

"It's one of the features of the Russian Blue breed," Louisa said. Then she heard a squeal—a catlike one.

"What on earth?"

"That's Muffin!" Louisa announced, relief washing over her.

"It's coming from the cellar, I think."

Quickly, Annie led her down the wood steps to what they called the cold cellar, where hundreds of quarts of vegetables, meats, and fruit were lined up on neat shelves. When they heard the squeal again, they followed the sound to find Muffin—his head stuck in an empty jar.

Louisa quickly knelt, making a fuss over her precious pet.

"Poor thing. He's stuck," Annie said, joining Louisa on the floor.

"This is nuts . . . he's never done anything so weird." *Smart cat, indeed.*

Then Annie, getting down to inspect the situation at eye level, saw the real reason. "Your city cat chased a country mouse, that's what. Look, part of the tail's still in the jar."

"Oh, Muffin, what will I do with you?" Louisa laughed.

"I know for sure one thing," Annie said. "We need a hammer."

"You sure we can't get him loose without breaking the jar?"

"Not unless he holds his breath." Annie burst out laughing now, too.

"At least the lost is found." Louisa stayed with Muffin while Annie went to get her father. "You've got the preacher coming now," she whispered, petting his haunches. "You're in so much trouble!"

Muffin peered out at her, his natural smile still evident.

"This is too funny!" Suddenly she wished she could share this with her parents, but the feeling was short-lived, and her Palm had very little power left anyway.

Annie's father came downstairs along with Annie, who had a big towel in her hand. "Well, now, just what do we have here?" He eyed the situation without cracking a smile.

"Can you get him out safely, Daed?" Annie asked.

He advised Annie to wrap the towel loosely around the canning jar.

Louisa helped hold Muffin's lower body and legs while the towel was put into place. She spoke softly to her cat. "You'll be out of there soon, little boy."

Annie's dad raised the hammer and struck the canning jar through the towel. With a muffled crack the jar broke into large pieces. Muffin was out and not even scratched for all his dim-witted curiosity.

"Thank you," Louisa said to both Annie and her father. "Muffin and I appreciate it."

The Preacher smiled and nodded. He looked at Muffin. "Seems this cat's lookin' for a bit of adventure . . . twice in one day, jah?"

Annie covered her mouth, apparently finding her father's comment amusing.

"I'll keep better tabs on him from now on," Louisa promised.

Annie's eyes twinkled with mischief. "Got to keep tabs on the tabby?"

"Aren't you the punny one?" Louisa cradled her beloved cat.

————————

That evening, Louisa and Annie stood on the back walkway waiting while Omar hitched up his horse to his shiny black buggy used for courting. The air was cold, and Louisa was not at all accustomed to wearing a woolen shawl. It reminded her of playing dress-up when she was little.

"Now, Omar, don't be leavin' us high and dry if you find yourself a girl to take home tonight, ya hear?" Annie said, smiling at her brother.

"Well, why not?" He grinned back.

"You know why."

Louisa found the tone of voice Annie used with her brother to be quite curious. For a girl who had been taught submission to male authority, she certainly felt free to banter with Omar.

Annie whispered to Louisa, eyes bright with mischief, "We best be stickin' together, jah?"

"Well, since I don't speak your language—or understand—it could get very weird." She didn't want to be put in the position of having to find her way back here without either Annie or Omar. "I'm not lookin' for a new boyfriend anyhow. The last one was somewhat of a disaster, as you know."

Annie shook her head, eyes flashing a warning.

"What? Did I say something wrong?"

"Come with me." Annie motioned with her head toward the well pump in the side yard. "We never talk 'bout a beau, present or past, 'specially not in front of another boy. Or a brother. That's how rumors spread, and goodness knows, that's not what you want to happen."

"Well, good," Louisa said, trying not to laugh. "I'm glad that's settled."

A few minutes later, Omar called to them. "Time to get goin' if yous want to be on time."

Annie reached for Louisa's hand and playfully pulled her toward the buggy. "Jah, we'll have us some fun tonight. It's 'bout time. . . ."

Louisa felt hesitant, but she was also interested to see first-hand the social scheme of things from the Amish perspective.

I can't believe I let her talk me into this barn singing, she thought, raising her skirt just enough, as Annie did, to get into the open carriage on the left side.

Omar sat on the far right, looking a bit impatient as he held the reins, but Louisa somehow sensed he was enjoying himself. Even though Annie kept poking fun at him.

Once they were on the road, Louisa asked, "Do you think I could ever learn to drive the horse and carriage, Annie?"

Omar leaned forward and looked at her. "I can teach you, easy."

"So can I!" Annie sat straighter, egging Omar on.

"That would be right nice," Louisa said, bringing a pert smile to Annie's face and a chortle from her brother.

They rode for more than a half hour, and as they did, Omar ribbed Annie with his words, looking over at Louisa every so often, no doubt trying to include her in the conversation.

At one point, Louisa asked about the theme of the morning's sermons. "It seemed like the ministers, including your father, were making eye contact with the young people. At least it seemed that way."

Annie spoke up right away. "You're quite right on that. Both sermons were about obedience . . . it's the theme of the day."

Louisa wondered why that should be. "What's up with that?"

"Well, I don't know 'bout up, but there is a downside to not following the Scripture and the Ordnung," Annie said. "For sure."

Omar piped up. "You can say that again."

"Well, like what?"

"For instance, there are several boys in the church district who are known to be runnin' with a wild crowd," Annie explained. "They call themselves the Mule Skinners and have guitars and carry on at Saturday night dances . . . nothin' like the expected behavior at our Sunday singings, I can tell you. If they were baptized church members and actin' like this, they'd be put under the shun."

"Most definitely," Omar said solemnly. "They don't care how they hurt their parents and younger siblings with the fancy clothes they wear and their English hair cuts 'n' all."

"More than likely, that's the reason for all the preaching on submission to God and the authority of the People," Annie said. "Nearly *every* meeting, here lately."

"*Authority of the People* . . ." Louisa considered the idea of kowtowing to the expectations of an austere group. Even Annie was struggling, and Louisa knew this to be true. All these years of hiding her artwork, Annie had been disobeying or "sinning," as she always called it in her letters.

The buggy ride afforded plenty of time to think—an evening for some hard thoughts, continuing with the jolting impressions she had experienced while enduring the hardness of the church benches earlier. One of the more positive things about Annie's people was their connectedness. Louisa didn't have to understand Dutch to get this. They cared for each other with unusual compassion, including their very young and their aged. High regard was given to the elderly men and women at the large church gathering, evidenced by their being served the noon meal first. But it was the concept of an integrated sharing community—putting everything into a common pot—that shook her to the core.

If only my mother might understand this, if not witness it for herself.

Such a perception was foreign to Louisa's upbringing. Instead of hoarding wealth or spending it on oneself, a person could supposedly lay up treasures in the hereafter by demonstrating kindness and extending love and thoughtfulness, as Annie had explained with great enthusiasm following the church gathering. She described a community where people shared not only their finances but also time and energy. Annie said this was one way to carry out God's will on the earth, helping one another. Even to the point of sacrifice, if need be.

The thought made her eyes swim, and she had an irresistible urge to continue dressing Plain. *I might even ask to borrow one of Annie's cotton nightgowns,* she thought, not understanding this new and peculiar yearning but wanting to follow wherever it might lead.

The tranquility of the buggy ride was eventually replaced with noise and laughter coming from a large barn as Louisa and Annie stepped down from the open carriage.

"I'll wait for you two," Omar said, tying the horse to the post.

"Well, you better!" Annie called over her shoulder.

Louisa was amused. "You and your brother are a hoot."

"You think so?"

"Omar enjoys throwing barbs, I can tell. And you give it right back."

Annie nodded. "Well, you haven't seen anything. Wait'll you meet Yonie if you think Omar's that way. Yonie and I are constantly carryin' on . . . never get our feelin's hurt, though. My brothers would be the first to defend me, I know."

Unable to relate to sibling camaraderie, Louisa was quiet as she followed Annie into the barn. She took in the curious scene, aware of not only the sights but also the noticeable farm scent, which her college friends would describe as a stench. None of which seemed to deter the crowd of Plain-garbed youth milling about, some in the lower area, near the stabled animals, others up in the haymow, swept clean for the gathering.

She heard the strains of country music. "Hey, check it out."

Annie leaned forward a bit . . . then frowned. "Someone's goin' to be in trouble. It's got to be a radio or a CD player, one of the two."

For a moment, Louisa wondered why an Amish barn would be rigged for electricity. "Must run on batteries," she said.

"Always batteries. Still, we're not s'posed to have radios at singings. My father's spoken out on this at Preachin' plenty of times." Annie began to explain the different groups of kids, called "crowds." Some who pushed the boundaries and were considered liberal, some who were more middle of the road, and about five different groups like the one assembling here, who were more likely to toe the line. "Even still, there's often a rowdy one who tries to influence everyone else."

Louisa had never had a reason to question the rank and file of Amish youth. She assumed they were all similar to Annie, merely wanting to have a good time mingling with the opposite sex, and ultimately, making a decision about their future. She had not expected to hear Kenny Chesney crooning "When the Sun Goes Down." Not here. And looking up, she spied the culprit perched high in the rafters. "Look, Annie." She pointed at the portable CD player.

Annie craned her neck. "I wonder how it got up *there*."

"Got a gymnast in this group?"

"Jah, it takes all kinds." Annie stopped walking and turned toward Louisa. "Don't stare, whatever you do, but over yonder's my old beau."

"Auburn hair, right?" She remembered from Annie's description in her letters and had already spotted Rudy standing with several other boys.

"Uh-huh."

He's gorgeous, she thought. *Amish or not.*

"Oh . . . no," Annie sputtered.

"What?"

"He's lookin' this way."

Not only looking, but Rudy was walking toward them. "Don't freak," she told Annie softly. "Be cool."

Rudy strolled right up to them. "Hullo, Annie. Nice to see ya." Then he smiled at Louisa, removing his straw hat. "You from round here?"

Annie spoke up. "This is Louisa Stratford, a friend of mine from Colorado."

Nodding, Louisa said, "Hey. How's it going?" But by the surprised look on his face she realized she'd said the wrong thing, the wrong way. *Too forward for a girl who looks Amish.*

Rudy frowned, scratching his head and eyeing Annie. "Stratford? Never heard of that one."

"That's because Louisa's English," Annie said.

"But I sure don't look fancy, do I?" Louisa couldn't resist, and it was all she could do not to burst out laughing. This Rudy was a wreck, absolutely on edge around Annie.

"You're as Plain as any girl here." He offered a quick smile at last. With that he waved, especially at Annie, then put his hat back on, turned, and marched back across the barn to the other young men.

"Oh," Annie groaned.

"Yeah, I see what you mean. He's cute." She studied Annie, obviously still pining. "Why not get back with him again? It's not too late, is it?"

"No . . . no, you don't understand" came Annie's woeful reply.

"Well, I'm not blind. I can see how miserable he is without you." She was convinced of this . . . she'd seen the way he looked at Annie.

"I can't have it both ways—Rudy *and* my art." Annie sighed, turning away from the growing swarm of boys. "In order to ever marry at all, I would have to turn my back on my drawings and paintings."

"Bummer," Louisa whispered.

"Time's running out for me . . . and the pickin's will become slim once I turn twenty-one. Most fellas get hitched up pretty quick once they eye the new batch of sixteen-year-old girls each year." Annie began to walk toward the barn door, swung wide for the evening.

"Sixteen? Wow, that's young."

"That's when we start courting, lots of us girls do."

Louisa shook her head. "Well, how can anyone possibly know who . . . or what . . . they want at that age? At twenty-two, I nearly made a huge mistake marrying the wrong guy."

"I know girls who marry and are expectin' their first baby by the time they're turning just eighteen."

"That's way too young," Louisa said again.

"It's our way."

Makes no sense to me. Louisa looked at the dark sky, glad to have escaped the din of the barn. Several lone stars cut through the blackness, and she sensed Annie's dire frustration—being trapped between wanting her art and wishing to be a wife and mother someday, which suddenly united with Louisa's own very discouraging position.

Chapter 18

Jesse was mighty glad for a morning without a single wisp of a cloud, and this being wash day, his wife would be, too. As for his own work, he had offered to help one of the older farmers, Al Fisher, extend a field by digging up a section of pastureland. Luke and Omar were going to lend a hand to yet another farmer— finishing the plowing—so the three of them would leave for the day soon after breakfast. Once Omar cut their hair, that is. Jesse was glad not to bother Barbara with the chore. *Anything to ease her duties. . . .*

Luke's and Omar's absence later today might benefit Barbara and Annie in that they could forget about cooking up a big meal at noon. Of course, with Louisa there they still might make themselves a nice hot meal, with plenty of leftovers for the evening meal, he hoped.

While Barbara cleared the table and put away the leftovers, Jesse sat mighty still as Omar snipped away at his hair. "Keep it just below my ears," he advised.

"Jah, Daed, I will," Omar said. "It got awful long this time. Your bangs, too. Nearly in your eyes they are!"

Luke sat in the corner drinking coffee while he waited his

turn. Jesse let his mind wander back to his sons' toddler days . . . how the three of them had come all in a row. Annie, too, being the only daughter—sandwiched between three brothers on either side. Barbara had been overly protective of Jesse Jr., Christian, and Abner. For all good reason, he supposed. There had been no more kidnappings in the area, and for this Jesse was most grateful. But he had never stopped thinking that if Daniel Hochstetler had not exerted his own will against that of the Lord God's, they all would be waiting for Isaac to make his baptismal vow and join church about now. *Just as someone else ought to be doing,* he thought.

When Omar was finished with him, Jesse hurried outdoors and quickly brushed the hair snippets off his neck and shirt. He could hear Luke grumbling about being next, the typical protests that occurred every six weeks or so, when haircuts were in order.

Later, while making his way south toward the far edge of Paradise Township—to a field near the Strasburg railroad station—Jesse contemplated the contents of his sack lunch. Annie and Louisa had made a fine one for him, and he'd overheard them whispering as they buttered bread enough for two sandwiches, then spread the dressing nice and thick, sliced the liverwurst and dill pickles and topped both sandwiches with lettuce. A hefty helping of potato salad awaited him, along with a fruity Jell-O salad and four oatmeal raisin cookies, his favorite. He'd taken note of Annie's exceptional cheerfulness—a distinct shift from her attitude prior to Louisa's arrival. Just why that would be, he had no idea.

He had much back-breaking work ahead of him today, so he must save his energy and let the women fuss over lost love and whatnot all.

Halting the field mules, Jesse set down the handheld single-bottom plow to pause a moment, mopping his brow. The sun was exceedingly warm for a November day, its rays bouncing off the silo in the distance. With more work to be done to smooth out this section of the former pasture, he was relieved to see one of Al's daughters, Becky, running across the field toward him, carrying a Thermos.

Something to wet my whistle.

At the edge of the field, Al was trudging along, working another handheld plow, and moving at a slow but steady pace. By midafternoon, Jesse figured they'd have this section of land plowed and fertilized with plenty of manure, ready for planting come spring.

"Would ya care for a drink, Preacher?" Becky asked shyly, her cheeks bright pink.

"Denki," he said. " 'Tis good of you."

She opened the lid with clean hands and poured the ice water, offering him the red plastic cup. He drank the water straight down, then another cup, and at last, a third.

"Be sure 'n' take some over to your pop. He looks all in." Jesse wiped his mouth, and Becky turned to leave, Thermos in hand.

Refreshed some, he resumed the mind-numbing work and eyed the double hitch, as well as the four hard-working mules ahead, making well-defined furrows in the soil.

He pondered yesterday's sermon as he steadied the plow. All day Sunday he hadn't been himself, although not physically ill; he knew that much. Too much of his time was spent in wonderment, pondering his daughter's standoffish attitude toward church membership. Preacher Moses and Bishop Andy had both urged him to give the long sermon, but had they known of his malaise, they would not have pressed him to stand for the two hours necessary to give the biblical account of Adam's fall to Abraham's faith, followed by an even longer retelling of the life of John the Baptist to the close of the apostle Paul's numerous missionary journeys. Jesse had known something was terribly out of kilter that morning. Then, of all things, Louisa's feisty gray cat had appeared, ready to pounce on his shoes, which further added to his distress, even though he thought he'd concealed it well.

Inhaling more slowly now, he was aware of the sun beating hard on his back, but he would not let the unseasonably warm afternoon deter him. He kept his gaze on the ground, watching the grassy chunks of sod turn over as the plow loosed and aerated the soil.

In the middle of the row, a flash of something light caught his eye in the dark soil. *Bone colored.*

Halting the mules, he let go of the plow and leaned down to look, thinking this must be a decomposed animal, nothing more. But as he moved away the dirt, he drew in a quick breath.

There before him was a partial section of what appeared to be a skeleton sticking out of the earth, which did not resemble that of an animal. Suddenly, he was compelled to dig deeper, using his gloved hands to burrow out the buried remains.

A human child. Small, yet complete, the frame was perfectly undamaged.

He recoiled at the sight, unable to speak. *O Lord God and heavenly Father,* he prayed silently.

He opened his mouth to holler at Al, but on second thought stifled the urge to call the man over. Indecisive, he wondered if he should leave the remains as they were and hurry to the bishop or attempt to bury the bones even deeper and simply keep mum. Never to speak a word of this.

But if his assumptions were correct, he would like to have more to go on than simply the size of the skeleton, which prompted his thoughts toward the small boy who'd disappeared years before. Emboldened now, he searched further, on his hands and knees beneath the plow.

Lo and behold, his right hand bumped something small and round. Scraping it out of the earth, he saw the lump to be mud-caked with hints of gold shining through. He removed an old work handkerchief from his pants pocket and warily wiped the face of a pocket watch, searching for a set of initials, unaware he was whispering to himself, heart pumping hard. "Anything . . . *anything* to go on."

But look as he might, there were no recognizable decorations or markings to point definitively to the missing child. Even so, a dozen thoughts flooded his mind, not the least of which was "Ichabod," and he knew beyond any doubt he must pay a visit to the bishop immediately.

———

Esther sighed, leaning against the doorjamb between the kitchen and the sitting room. Fondly she observed Laura, who was sitting on the kitchen floor, entertaining her brothers. She was building with a combination of wooden blocks and checkers, creating what looked to be a small village, while Zach and John watched.

Remarkably, little John had not swung his dimpled fist to knock down the creation as of yet, but he *was* wide-eyed and intent on Laura's placement of the final red checker.

"There we go," said Laura. "See? This is Dat's big barn and there's the woodshed."

"Big barn." John echoed, his babyish voice so cute.

"*Two*-story barn," Zach added, pointing to the second level.

Laura smiled, nodding broadly. "That's right. Dat's barn has two big stories."

"Wanna story." Zach got up right quick and hurried to her. "Story now, Mamma?"

Jah, she wished she might sit and rest alone. But with Zeke over chewing the fat and having coffee with their neighbor, now was as good a time as any, she guessed. Soon it would be bed-time, and she was all done in from the long day of washing and hanging out clothes. Tomorrow she would iron every single piece.

She thought of asking Laura to make up a soothing tale for the boys. But, no, Laura had spent quite a lot of time with her brothers already while Esther redd up the supper dishes. Young Laura needn't have so much responsibility thrust on her just yet, even though it was inevitable what with another baby brother or sister on the way.

Tonight Esther would do her best to recite a Bible story, hop-ing she wouldn't leave out anything important like last time. "I'll tell you a true story, 'bout baby Moses," she said, which got both Laura's and Zach's attention. "Come, let's sit together."

Going to her husband's rocking chair near the wood stove, she took John onto her lap, while Zach and Laura sat at her knee.

Laura's eyes sparkled with anticipation, and once again Esther was reminded of her daughter's sweetness. The Amish midwife who'd helped deliver her had declared the little bundle a "perfect baby . . . with nary a single flaw." And now as Laura reached over and placed a protective arm around Zach, Esther's heart was filled anew with appreciation for this wee angel of a daughter. The fact that Laura could endure a whipping one day and display such a lovely disposition in spite of it the next was truly a marvel. Esther's own childhood experience with occasional thrashings served not to soften her spirit at all, but rather had borne resentment in her, although she had long since forgiven her father for his quick temper. *As I must Zeke,* she thought suddenly, but there was not an ounce of mercy left in her for her husband.

"Once upon a time, long, long ago, a baby boy was born to a devout and humble woman named Jochebed, wife of Amram . . . daughter of Levi." Esther began the story for her attentive threesome, but this one was especially for Laura, who loved it above all others.

———

Jesse stood, legs locked, in the most concealed corner of the bishop's barn. "Well, sure, if you think we must keep this in-house, then so be it."

Bishop Stoltzfus folded his knobby arthritic hands and bowed his white head momentarily, exhibiting a well-known determined pose. "I will speak with our neighboring bishop on this, but I'm sure the decision not to call in the authorities will be made. The Hochstetler kidnapping was never reported, as you recall. And that's how it should be."

Jesse remembered, all right. He'd never forgotten the panic of the nighttime search, the days of waiting for news, the family's eventual moving from the area, and the silence lapsing into the stupor of years . . . the yearning to put the reprehensible incident behind them, needing to move on with life, which they all had done to some degree, he supposed. Some more than others. Till now.

No question, the abduction had altered their lives. His own wife's jovial nature and carefree approach to mothering changed overnight. And when Jesse Jr. married and his Sarah Mae began bearing children, Barbara began to fret and hover over each newborn grandchild, as well.

" 'Tis best we keep the police out of this, as we always have," the bishop said.

Jesse had never questioned the ordained man. Bishop Andy's way was best, prompted wisely by the Lord God, he knew. But it was the other minister, Preacher Moses Hochstetler, whose decision-making processes concerned Jesse. That and the fact he was related to Zeke Hochstetler and poor dead Isaac. Besides, Moses was as frail as any of their elderly church members. "Will you be sharin' any of this with Moses?" asked Jesse.

The bishop paused, clearly contemplating what to do. "I'll have to think on that," he said at last. "The cat is so easily let out of the bag, you know."

Jah, which means the womenfolk need not hear of this, thought Jesse.

"Mum's the word, I daresay," Bishop Andy stated. The two men locked eyes, considering the seriousness of the situation.

They continued talking quietly for a while longer in the solitude of the barn, bringing up the need for a suitable burial.

"You covered the bones up adequately, you say?"

"For the time being, at least." Jesse lowered his voice. "I marked the spot by countin' the paces to the cemetery. I can easily return to the location."

"By all means, get over there later on tonight. I'll meet you behind the stone wall . . . somewhere safe, where no one will ever notice a freshly dug hole."

Agreeing with the bishop's plan, Jesse contemplated what must have happened that fateful night. "The little fella surely put up a fuss—a feisty one, he always was, remember?—and the kidnapper must've dumped his body in that pasture at the time, on his way out of town."

"Just can't figure why a killer would seek out our farmland for such a burial," the bishop said, his brow crinkly now.

"In some circles, Amish land is considered to be hallowed ground . . . 'least by the English," Jesse said. "And this isn't the first time, either." He cited several cases where, over a period of years, Amish soil had been chosen as burial plots for victims of serial killers.

The bishop's eyes were suddenly bright with tears. "The pitiable family . . . what they surely have suffered all these years since. Ichabod included, poor fellow, not knowing what happened . . . aside from God's sovereign judgment." He sighed audibly. "But, then, we still don't know, do we?"

"Has anyone kept in touch with the family?" asked Jesse.

"As I understand it, not even the eldest son knows their whereabouts, sad to say."

Jesse shook his head, not in disgust but disbelief. It was impossible to imagine any of his own children abandoning family and faith. Not even Annie. "Knowing *something* just might bring some finality to the parents, jah?"

Bishop wiped his eyes and face with a blue paisley handkerchief. "I'll see what can be done. But this must not leak out amongst the People, mind you."

Indeed, Jesse would heed the older man's admonition. After all, such a bleak report would only stir up more sorrow and foreboding.

Chapter 19

Annie studied Louisa intently. They were sitting at the writing desk drawing each other's profiles, making a game of it, to see who could draw most accurately and most quickly. Louisa, seemingly anxious to do some sketching again, was all for it, and she held her kitty on her lap as she did.

So far the outline of Louisa's eyes looked just right on the paper, her thick and slightly curly eyelashes nearly exact. Several times Louisa asked if Annie could turn slightly, not blinking.

This is such fun! thought Annie.

As she worked, she experienced a sense of purpose and even peace, right here in her own bedroom. Doing something she never would have dared to do had Louisa not come. She knew she was terribly brazen, but who was to know? "Who would've thought we'd ever be doin' this . . . working together?" she said.

Louisa agreed. "Funniest thing. I never considered visiting you until . . . well, you know."

"Perfect timing, jah?" Annie knew what Louisa meant. "Daed often says 'God works in mysterious ways.' And I s'pose this could be one of those times."

"Well . . . I'm not sure how I feel about that," Louisa replied, her face more serious now. "God may be okay for other people, I guess."

"I'm not at all sure what I believe and what I don't," Annie said, then clammed right up, not wanting to discuss such things within earshot of Mamm, who was resting in her own room down the hall.

She turned her attention back to getting the curve of Louisa's brow just so, as well as the shape and length of her cute nose.

Some time later, a knock came at the door, and without thinking, Annie said simply, "Come in," only to see that it was Mamm standing there.

"Girls?" Her mother came closer, peering down at their sketchbooks, eyebrows high. "What's this?"

Too late to hide the truth, Annie thought glumly. "We're tryin' to draw each other" was her reply.

"Jah, I see that . . . and these are ever so good, I daresay." Mamm stepped back a bit.

Annie could hear Mamm breathing hard, and she cringed, waiting for the words sure to follow.

"I didn't know you could draw like this, Annie."

Louisa's eyes locked on her. *What to say?* The heat rushed to Annie's head and neck. At a loss for words, she blinked, too aware that she was holding her breath.

"I have a group of students back home," Louisa volunteered, speaking up, yet sounding hesitant. "But Annie and I, we're just practicing now, that's all."

Mamm sighed audibly. "Well, your father better not catch you, Annie Zook." With that she stood shaking her head and muttering something about never having heard that Louisa was a teacher. Then she turned and left the room quickly.

Annie felt frozen, her muscles taut as can be. She even wondered if her mouth had gaped open, like a fish. But she waited to speak to Louisa till Mamm's footsteps faded in the hall, and then in only a whisper. "We can never let this happen again. *Never*."

"I'm so sorry, Annie."

"No . . . no, it's not your fault." Annie closed her sketchbook. "Tomorrow, when we go to my cousin Julia's, I'll show you my art studio. You'll love it as much as I do. And there's no chance of bein' found out there."

Louisa frowned briefly. "This is a huge problem for you, I can see that. I can't imagine not being able to express myself artistically."

"Jah . . . a problem's putting it mildly."

"I don't want to cause further trouble for you." Louisa was frowning now, glancing back toward the door. "Your mother is obviously upset."

"At me, 'specially. So not to worry. Promise me ya won't?" Then she gasped, remembering Julia's insistence on entering her painting in the upcoming magazine contest. "Ach, no . . ."

"What?"

In all the excitement of having her friend visit, Annie had completely forgotten this secret tidbit. Now with Mamm's stern warning, and the likelihood of her father being told, Annie dreaded the possibility of word getting out—whether she should win or not. *I never should've let Julia twist my arm!* she thought.

"What is it?" asked Louisa. "You're suddenly pale."

Can I even trust my cousin to keep quiet? Annie inhaled sharply. "You'll never guess what dumb thing I did. . . ."

165

After Annie had turned in for the night, Louisa lay awake. It was hours before her usual bedtime and she couldn't fall asleep. So she crept down the hall to Annie's room, careful not to wake her. There, she set the old framed self-portrait of Annie on the dresser. Stifling the urge to giggle like a schoolgirl pulling a prank, she tiptoed back to her room and slipped into bed. Still, she was too wired to close her eyes, too worried about Annie. What would Barbara Zook tell her husband about her discovery tonight? And what would Preacher Jesse do about it?

Turning in bed, she was conscious of an owl's persistent hoot. *Right outside my window?* she wondered.

Curious as to the location of the loud and immediate call, she again left her curled-up cat and went to the window. She raised it easily. Then, deciding to remove the screen, she did so and poked her head out.

The night was a silent, glowing basin before her, as the moon lit the pastureland and plowed fields in all directions. She listened, straining her ears.

Once, as a little girl, she had gone with her grandfather into the woods on a full-moon night, as he had called it. Enthusiastic about seeing the wide-eyed swivel-necked creature in the Connecticut woods at Christmastime, she had been intimidated by the size and grandeur of the black forest. But she had been equally intent on the owling adventure. In the space of a mere hour, they had thrilled to the eerie call of several owls but had not been successful at spotting a single one. Even so, the memory of the breathtaking experience remained all these years.

Less than two minutes had passed since throwing open the window. Suddenly, as if on cue, Louisa felt a brush of air against her face. The realization was nearly jolting.

Where is he? she wondered, looking . . . looking.

Then she saw the extended graceful wings, silver-brown in the moonlight, thrust straight out in a thin, silent line above the open field. She memorized the longed-for image, wishing the owl were flying toward her instead of away.

Tears sprang to her eyes, and she struggled to see as he flew with seemingly little effort, gliding over the harvested cornfield. *After all these years, is it a sign?*

Suddenly from below, she heard a door open and there appeared Annie's father heading for the road, a shovel slung over his broad shoulder.

She stood there staring down at him until he disappeared into the shadows. *What sort of Amish work is required so late?* she wondered.

———————

Esther was sitting reading the old German Bible by the cookstove when Zeke came into the kitchen, looking for seconds on pie left over from supper. He sat down at his usual spot at the head of the table, as if planting himself anywhere else might give the wrong notion to Esther . . . that he was loosening the reins even for a moment. She was probably wrong, but she sensed it all the same, the unspoken aspects of his dominance.

Closing the family Bible, she leaned her head back, aware of the smack of Zeke's lips as he enjoyed the pie. She couldn't stop thinking of Annie's introduction yesterday . . . of her English friend, Louisa. And she found it ever so curious that the preacher's daughter should be entertaining a worldly girl, one who'd been kept very much a secret from the People, evidently, although Esther remembered Annie had mentioned a pen pal back when she and Annie were schoolgirls.

Still, there was something terribly enticing about Annie's

way. At times she had observed Annie in the line of young single women waiting to enter house church on a Sunday morning. Invariably, she would be the only girl with her hand perched on her hip. Not that Annie wanted to be bad-tempered, no. Neither was she known for being defiant. Even so, Esther thought she knew what made her tick, deep down. Preacher Zook's only daughter had some difficulty with the idea of wholly submitting. Rudy Esh was only one case in point.

Esther thought again of Annie's enthusiastic invitation to the quilting bee this week. Just the talk of work frolics and such left Esther feeling nearly overwhelmed. Too many prattling women sitting round a quilt frame gave her the jitters anymore.

Truth was, she enjoyed the company of the other women, but she felt out of step with them. As though *they* were doing what was expected and she was not. She privately questioned the whys and wherefores of submitting to male authority. It was impossible not to. She hadn't had the luxury of being born with the desire to simply say *jah*, like her female counterparts.

She sighed, acknowledging to herself that she made a consistent effort to put her best foot forward nearly all the time—at least giving the appearance that all was well. Yet she knew otherwise and was beginning to suspect that Annie may have been sensing it, too.

More often than she cared to admit, even to herself, she imagined rising up and shaking her fist at a man. Especially at Zeke.

She wished he might hurry and finish his snack so she could clean up after him. *Yet again.*

Rocking harder now, she clenched her fists, her breath coming faster as she stared a hole in the back of his head. She might have blurted out a terrible thing if someone hadn't come riding up the lane right then.

Zeke got up and looked out. "Well, I'll be. The bishop's dropped by," he said and hurried out through the back porch.

"Hullo, Ezekiel," she heard the minister say to her husband.

But the men's words faded quickly, and Esther rose and went to stand near the window. Curiously, she watched the two of them mosey out to the barn in the fading light, wondering what was up, even though it was not her place to know or to inquire.

When the bishop reached over and placed a hand on Zeke's shoulder, she knew there was definitely something off beam. *What on earth?*

Chapter 20

Waking up the next morning, Annie was thankful for a few minutes to stretch and relax beneath her colorful quilts before getting up for the day. She snuggled down in her warm bed, staring at the window across the room, noting the slowly-shifting glow as dawn inched its way into daylight.

Eyes fixed on the light, she pondered Louisa's visit thus far. She knew one thing sure, she was beginning to see her own surroundings through her friend's eyes . . . grasping a glimpse of the peace she and the People seemed to take for granted. Right along with the rigid expectations weighing her down at times, though she attempted to conceal any negativity from her family.

She thought back to Sunday night, following their buggy ride home from the singing, when Louisa had said the most surprising thing: "The peacefulness here . . . it's like a sort of blessing hangs in the air."

Funny, hearing Louisa say such a thing. . . .

Louisa had never expressed this before, and Annie hadn't ever thought of Paradise that way. But she guessed the immense contrast between city living and Amish country was rather severe to Louisa. The farthest she had ever ventured into the populace of Lancaster was to the town of Strasburg. Which was enough of a jolt to her, what with tourists driving here and there, milling about, and in and out of the quaint little shops on the cobblestone sidewalks.

Today, though, she was anxious to accomplish her home chores quickly and head to Cousin Julia's for the remainder of the day. Still upset at Mamm's discovery of the two artists at work, she decided it would be nice if her friend could possibly paint to her heart's content in the attic studio while Annie did her housework for Julia.

A wonderful-good surprise, she thought, slipping out of bed and hurrying to put on her house slippers and long white cotton robe.

She went to the dresser and picked up the small hand mirror. Pouring a bit of water from the pitcher to the ceramic basin, she began to wash her face in the cold water. Quickly, she patted her face dry with an embroidered linen towel.

Just then she spotted a gold-framed picture Louisa must have left on the corner of the dresser. "For goodness' sake!" She studied the long-ago drawing of herself. *I hope I've improved since this*, she thought, knowing without a doubt she had. The early morning surprise brought a smile, and she could scarcely wait to thank Louisa.

Best not have this on display anymore! She placed the picture in her bathrobe pocket and tiptoed over to Louisa's room.

Jesse rose earlier than usual, still both mystified and shaken by the unearthing in Al Fisher's pastureland. The bishop had been quite prompt in meeting him last night, and together they'd decided upon an out-of-the-way spot for the suitable burial—a safe distance, deep into the walnut grove, behind the

Amish cemetery, where they left no grave marker to signal the shared secret.

As for the bishop's plan to visit the Hochstetler farm last evening, Jesse speculated how Zeke had taken such hard news. The headstrong man was also known to be quite outspoken. But Jesse had always assumed the fiery nature had more to do with Zeke's inability to forgive himself for his brother's disappearance than anything else.

Jesse shuddered and considered how such information would have affected him . . . *if I were the son of Ichabod.* . . .

Then and there, he purposed to reach out to the younger man, the first chance possible.

For now, though, he best get himself across the road for milking, because following breakfast he must head to an all-day wedding, where he was expected to give the *Anfang*, the opening comments, prior to the bishop's main sermon. He also must shake off his impending feeling of doom, wishing to convey a cheerful countenance on behalf of the bridegroom and bride.

Annie offered to take the horse and buggy over to Julia's, but Louisa insisted they walk, just as Annie always liked to. "Look over there." She pointed to their neighbors' farmhouse as they made their way along the road. "That's where the girl lived who first requested you as a pen pal. See how the electric lines run right up to their house and barn?"

"So *that's* how you know who's Amish and who isn't?"

Annie laughed softly. "Well, it's one way. You also have to watch for horsey apples in the lane."

This got a sniggle from Louisa, who looked as Amish as Annie was, except she'd twisted the sides of her hair looser than Annie ever would have. *At least she's learning.*

172

"What's Jenna Danz doing these days?" Louisa asked. "Haven't heard from her in years." '

"If you'd like to, we could stop by the house and ask 'bout her. The Danzes are ever so friendly."

"No, I'm here to hang with you." Louisa was lugging her laptop in a leather case, evidently ready for some connection with the outside world.

"So . . . does hanging with someone ever hurt?" Annie tried not to giggle.

Louisa wrinkled her nose. "You're as bad a tease as I am."

"That's for sure." Several horse-drawn buggies went by, and Annie waved at each one.

"Where's everybody going?"

"It's Tuesday, so I'd have to say they're headed for weddings. Most families get multiple invitations. They might have relatives in other church districts, so they must decide which one to attend . . . a busy time." She hated saying it, worried that another mention of a wedding might upset Louisa.

"How many in a single day?"

"Oh, oodles, really."

"Do you ever stay home," Louisa asked, "just skip going?"

"Most of the weddings in the past few years have been for my first cousins—close in age—or friends of mine." She sighed, not sure how to explain that it was beyond rude not to attend. "For me not to go would be similar to shunning someone for a whole day. It's just not done." *No matter how difficult*, she thought, aware of the wrench in her heart again, relieved that the couples marrying today were not close kin.

"Fascinating . . . to set aside a time of year just for weddings," Louisa replied. "Like we moderns have our June weddings . . . ."

Annie smiled. "My father's glad to be finished with plowing, 'specially with his responsibilities for tying the knot for quite a few couples. He'll be busy for the next few months."

"Well, he certainly looked busy last night, too."

"What are you talking about?"

"I saw him carrying a shovel . . . out to the road. Must've been round nine o'clock."

Annie shook her head. "You must be mistaken. Daed always goes to bed with the chickens."

"Say what you like, but I saw what I saw."

"And you also must've spotted an owl, too, jah?" Annie covered her mouth, stifling a laugh.

Louisa pulled a face. "As a matter of fact, I did! Didn't you hear him?"

"I heard him, all right. I almost got up and went downstairs. Sometimes I creep out into the night and shine a flashlight on them. Daed's caught me several times."

"I felt the silent flap of his wings and saw the hind end of him. Amazing. So . . . can you guess what I plan to draw the moment my peacock painting is finished?"

"My father chasing an owl?" She couldn't help it, she burst out laughing.

"Very funny, Annie."

Annie was exceptionally surprised about Louisa's encounter with the owl—hindquarters or not. But she wasn't about to reveal the common superstition: if a person sees an owl up close it sometimes points to a death. No sense causing Louisa to freak out, as she liked to say. Still, the *bird of death* had flown over them.

They walked farther, soaking up the sunshine and enjoying the fresh air as the tension between them subsided.

Louisa brushed off her apron. "Does your cousin have an

indoor bathroom? I would love a shower!"

"Sure. Julia won't mind at all if you shower there." Annie found Louisa's need for soap and water interesting. Not even half a week had passed since their Saturday night baths!

"I've been thinking about something else, too, Annie. If it's not a problem, would you care if I washed my hair more than once a week? I don't think I can stand it for more than three days, which it is today."

"Oh, you can shower at Julia's on Tuesdays and Fridays, take a bath at my house on Saturday night . . . and, in between, there's always the makeshift shower Daed and the boys use out in the barn. Goodness sakes, you'll be the cleanest girl round here!"

They counted fifteen more buggies coming their way, and at one point Louisa said, "I've never felt so strangely miserable and wonderful at the same time. Except for maybe the summer I spent with one of my aunts."

"Why's that?"

"I think it comes down to the basics, and I'm not talking baths or showers or indoor plumbing." Louisa slowed her pace. "Sure, I miss all the conveniences of my home, yet I feel somehow closer to all that is good."

"To the Lord God, you mean?"

"I don't know." Louisa turned to look at her. She had an almost sad expression. "Do you ever wish, sometimes, that there was something way more tangible to believing? I mean, than just a bunch of one-way prayers?"

"Well, my cousin Julia has conversations with the Lord. I'm not kidding, she honestly does." Annie wondered if she should go on, but she forged ahead. "I say silent rote prayers first thing in the morning and the last thing at night. I've never considered addressing God the way Julia does."

"Really? You don't *speak* your prayers?"

"Never."

"Well, then, I'll have to get acquainted with this cousin of yours."

A lone horse and carriage was coming their way, and at a fast clip. When Annie spied Susie Yoder and her older brother, a surprising lump caught in her throat. Instead of calling out her usual cheerful hullo, she merely raised her hand to wave.

Susie, wearing her for-good blue cape dress and white apron, was quick to return the wave, smiling and glancing at her brother who held the reins, wearing his best black suit and bow tie. When Susie looked back at Annie, there was a noticeable twinkle in her eyes and a radiant smile on her dimpled face.

She looks too happy not to be in love. . . .

Annie's heart sank like a millstone. *Oh, what's-a-matter with me?*

After all, it was to be expected that Susie would spend the afternoon and evening, following the all-day wedding festivities she was apparently headed to, playing games and attending a late-night barn singing with Rudy, along with many other courting couples. There was no other reason for Susie's big brother to be driving her today otherwise.

Annie swallowed hard. *Since I refused to marry Rudy, why should I begrudge Susie her happiness?*

Momentarily she wondered what it might be like to somehow get Rudy's attention back for herself. To abruptly abandon the near-delirious joy of mixing colors, painting whatever her heart desired. But such thoughts troubled her greatly. No, she could not substitute a man—not even Rudy—for her dearest love.

Chapter 2-1

Esther did not know what to make of Zeke's peculiar behavior. Nearly all day he stayed close to the house, except for doing necessary barn chores. He was spending more time with their boys than any other weekday she ever recalled—playing with them indoors, in the yard, and even washing their faces after the noon meal.

But each time she looked at her husband this day, she was keenly aware of a painful softness around his eyes. Something she hadn't seen in years. Was it the herbal potion she furtively mixed into his coffee each morning? Or was it linked to the bishop's surprise visit?

Is someone dreadfully ill? Or has Zeke's father gotten in touch with him at long last? If so, wouldn't Zeke say something?

She couldn't stop thinking about the bishop's mysterious visit, the good half hour he spent alone with Zeke in the barn. To get her mind off whatever it was, she set about baking an angel food cake for their supper tonight. *Zeke's favorite . . . and Laura's, too.*

"Cousin Julia!" called Annie at the back stoop and let herself in, holding the door for Louisa.

Molly and James came running to meet them, and the sight of the children cheered Annie's heart. "I've brought along my very good friend today," she told the smiling youngsters. "James and Molly, can you say hullo to Louisa?"

James grinned, showing his little white teeth. "Hullo, Louisa," he said, mimicking Annie. "You look just like Annie."

"Well! I'll take that as a compliment."

Molly reached for Louisa's hand and smiled shyly. "Molly . . . that's me."

Louisa was clearly taken with the little girl. "It's nice to meet you, honey. Your long braids are beautiful."

Nodding, Molly reached up to touch her hair. "Mommy makes 'em."

"She does good work," Louisa said, touching Molly's head.

Soon, Cousin Julia hurried into the kitchen, face aglow at seeing Louisa.

"Julia, I want you to meet my English pen pal." Annie quickly explained that she wanted to "be one of the People, at least in looks, for the time bein'."

"How thoughtful!" Julia extended her hand to Louisa.

Annie was most grateful for the warm reception, especially since she'd never told Julia about this peculiar friendship. And once the children had gone outside to play, she asked if it was all right for Louisa to have a shower or bath sometime today while they were here.

"Oh my, yes. Help yourself, Louisa . . . anytime, really." Julia's eyes twinkled when she smiled. "I see you've brought your laptop along, but if ever you want to simply use our computer, you can do that, too."

"I appreciate the offer," Louisa said, looking a bit surprised.

"So . . . then, you're permitted to use computers?"

Julia nodded. "Well, yes, we are. You might not guess by looking at us, but many Mennonites embrace the whole gamut of technology. We are more conservative than some, but even our little church has its own Web site as an outreach ministry."

They stood and talked awhile longer, and then Julia gave Annie the list of chores for the day. Louisa offered to help, but Annie insisted she should get her shower done. They argued jovially about that, but Annie finally said she could have the ironing out of the way by the time Louisa finished upstairs.

"Well, if you're sure," said Louisa.

"Oh, jah, I am . . . now go and get yourself cleaned up."

Louisa shrugged and smiled, then followed Julia upstairs to the only bathroom in the house while Annie set to work ironing, realizing anew how much easier this task was with the use of an electric iron. But as she pressed Irvin's Sunday shirt, she pushed away envious thoughts, including what fun Susie would be having with Rudy tonight.

She thought instead of Louisa, ever so eager to show her the attic art stuio. *I'm truly gaining a sister, of sorts,* she thought. *If only Mamm hadn't caught us drawing. . . .*

"Come, it's time for you to see my studio," Annie told Louisa once the ironing was finished . . . and when Louisa's hair was dry from her shower, hanging loose over her shoulders.

"Well, hey, you've described it to a tee in your letters, but I'm dying to see it with my own eyes."

Annie motioned for her to follow. "I need your opinion on something else, too." She wanted to know what Louisa thought of her painting, the one featuring the London Vale covered bridge, the cluster of locust trees, and the nearby creek.

When they arrived at the top of the attic steps, Annie reached for the skeleton key high over the doorjamb and unlocked the door. "Have to keep this locked, for obvious reasons," she explained.

"Wow . . . this *is* a top-secret room."

Annie stepped aside. "You go in first."

Louisa walked into the room and slowly moved toward the center. She stood like a slender statue, simply staring. Then, slowly, she turned around, taking in every nook and cranny. Pursing her lips, she said, "What a place. It's terrific."

Annie felt like she might burst. "I want you to spend the rest of today painting here . . . if you'd like."

"You mean it?"

"Well, since you can't just turn it off or on . . . sure. It's been a while since you painted . . . since comin' here." She smiled at her dear friend.

"This is too cool, Annie. I love it!"

Annie paused. Was now a good time to reveal the painting that had been driving her lately? "Uh, just real quick, I want to show you something I've been working on."

Louisa went to stand near the empty easel. "I traveled a long way for this, Annie."

Turning to the artist's desk, Annie gingerly carried the dry canvas, setting it just so on the easel. "This painting has a sad, sad story behind it. For the longest time, I wasn't even sure what to call it."

Louisa stepped back, studying the picture. Then, finally, she said softly, "This is very good." She paused, tilting her head a bit sideways. "You have some really wonderful contrasts here . . . and I can feel the mood. It's an undertow of something portentous. Bravo, Annie."

"You honestly sense something?"

"Absolutely! It pulls me right in."

"It's titled 'Obsession.'"

Louisa turned to look at her. "Meaning what?"

"I'll tell you tomorrow. We'll go up to the covered bridge and walk around."

"Now you have me riveted. I can't wait."

"Well, since Julia's not payin' me to stand here and yak, I need to get busy." She turned toward the stairs.

"So, just like that, you're going to leave me hanging?"

Annie wiggled her fingers in a dainty wave. "You like 'hanging,' remember? Besides, I'll be anxious to see what you paint today!"

With that she headed back to her domestic work, most excited about Louisa's response to the Pequea Creek painting. Yet, once again, she was torn by what the People would think of her if Mamm's discovery got out . . . how disappointed Daed would be. She hated letting her parents down.

The Lord God must be terribly displeased, too.

––––––––––

Louisa sat quietly in bed snuggling with her sleepy kitty long after Annie had left the room for the night. They'd talked about their day, and Annie had been quite elated over Louisa's colorful peacock painting, saying she "just knew" this would capture her imagination.

But it was not her own sketching and subsequent painting that intrigued Louisa. Annie's startlingly real depiction gripped her even now as she propped her head up higher with an additional pillow. She wished for a way to offer Annie some technical pointers—to share a wealth of knowledge she had gleaned in

L.A. at art school—although Annie was unmistakably on her way to becoming a superb artist under her own steam.

Remarkable . . . considering her humble background, she thought. *Shoot, no one even knows!* Except now Annie's mother was on to Annie's talent. . . .

Louisa contemplated what Annie's mom might do at having accidentally discovered Annie's ability—at least in part. It was bad enough for the Zooks to innocently open their home, let alone allow Louisa to influence Annie.

Her eyes roamed the wide plank floorboards to the window-sill, the flush of a full moon all around, and she was taken with the pronounced difference in the wispy, nearly ethereal light she experienced here in this country setting. It was as if she were nestled on the edge of the world as she knew it. Annie's world. Nothing at all like the glaring light of Denver's metropolis.

Annie was born into this, so how can she possibly appreciate what she has? wondered Louisa.

But she also pondered the flip side. *What if Annie were to leave the only life she knows?* Louisa shuddered, aware of the fierce competition within the artistic community. *How could an Amish woman possibly survive?*

Louisa decided quickly that Annie was probably better off staying here . . . that is if she would even be allowed to remain for much longer. From everything Annie had shared regarding the strict denial of individual self-expression, Louisa didn't see how Preacher Jesse would allow Annie to stay past a certain age, barring some unexpected turn. And if Annie's pull toward art was as strong as Louisa's own, which she surmised it was, how could Annie simply walk away from that?

High in the cozy attic earlier today, Louisa had gotten so completely lost in her peacock painting she'd forgotten to charge up her Palm. She'd even snoozed checking her email or connecting with her students by IM, too. *Friday's soon enough,* she thought, relishing the hours spent in Annie's delightful studio. *Unless Preacher Zook sends me packing before then!*

Jesse cradled his wife in his arms as they talked in bed, careful to keep his voice low. "I wish I'd known years ago," he told her. Hearing that Louisa was an art teacher did not set well with him. Nor did his wife's recent discovery—Louisa's teaching Annie how to draw. Had Annie tricked all of them, bringing Louisa here? "You were right to tell me, love," he said.

"I do wish you might've seen what I saw. I think you would've been quite surprised. Our Annie, I daresay she may have a gift."

"Now, Barbara . . ."

"No . . . I mean it."

Her words troubled him greatly.

"The best gifts are compassion, serenity, and joy. You know that. Patience, gentleness . . . self-control. And surrender to God, the Ordnung, and the ministry." He paused, thinking how he ought to say further what was on his mind. "Annie's gifts dwell within the confines of the church, not in self-expression." He felt her body tense. "No matter how much talent you may think our daughter has, you cannot encourage Annie in this. We must, all of us, offer ourselves up to God as a community—pure, unspotted, and without blemish. Nothing less will do."

Barbara's breathing came more slowly, yet she did not verbally agree to abide by his wishes.

"Have we made a mistake, bringing the blind and perverted world to our doorstep?" he said.

"Well . . . maybe so." Barbara's voice quivered, and for this reason sleep did not come to Jesse for another wretched hour.

He could not bring himself to think about Annie rejecting the faith, yet he could see she was most surely on the path right out of the community. And having Louisa to talk to and spend an inordinate amount of time with, well, he could kick himself for agreeing to invite Louisa here. Beneath the façade of Amish attire and head covering, she was no more interested in the Plain life than any ungodly outsider. He'd heard her talking on her little phone late into the night, even thought he heard her singing threads of a worldly song alone in the room. Aside from all that, it was rather remarkable how she had made an attempt to fit in. *To please Annie, no doubt.* Despite Moses' prediction, Jesse could see no evidence of Louisa's visit moving his daughter closer to joining church.

I ought to give Annie a time limit, he thought. *At what point does a father simply give up hope?*

Chapter 22

First thing the next morning, Annie tiptoed to Louisa's room. She knocked lightly and whispered, "You awake?" Aware of a small groan, she inched the door open and peeked in. "Psst! Louisa? All right if I come in?"

"You're halfway in already, you goof."

Annie sat on the bed, smiling. "I want to show you around today."

"What about chores?" Louisa sat up and stretched her arms. "And when's that quilting bee you talked about?"

"You'll see how quickly chores get done . . . and we'll even sew you up a dress or two before noon." She was surprised Louisa had remembered the comment made to Esther about the quilting bee. "The quilting's tomorrow—would you like to learn how to make the teeniest tiniest stitches ever?"

Louisa looked at her, a sleepy haze still evident on her pretty face. "That's why I'm here, right?"

"Oh you!" Annie plopped down on the pillow next to Louisa's; her cat came right over. "What did I ever do without a sister?"

"Aw, you're too sweet, Annie."

"I mean it."

"Well, I feel the same way. *And* I have so much catching up to do if I'm going to be a *good* big sister . . . starting with you showing me how to cook on that funky stove of yours."

"Honestly? You want to make breakfast today?"

Louisa nodded, reaching for Muffin. "I'll give it my best shot."

"Sounds like Yonie and his hunting adventure . . . probably shooting everything in sight."

"I'll need time to de-feminize the place so he doesn't freak when he returns." Louisa glanced at the room.

"No matter what, you'll have to open the window and air it out." Annie laughed, but she meant it.

"Hey," Louisa protested, "I told you I wanted to bathe more often!"

"I didn't mean it like that—it smells far too perty in here, that's what."

"Mm-hmm, sure. . . . So, what did you want to show me today?"

"This afternoon, I'll take you to Pequea Creek, where little Isaac disappeared." She paused, looking over her shoulder to see that the door was securely shut. "And we'll smuggle along our sketchbooks, too, if ya want."

Louisa raised her eyebrows. "You're one rebellious chick."

Chick? "So now I've been reduced to a fowl?"

"You crack me up, Annie. Go get dressed."

"I'll meet you downstairs in ten minutes." Annie headed to the door.

"Too short. I need time for a sponge bath."

Annie gave a little laugh. "You showered at Julia's yesterday. How clean must ya be?"

Louisa shook her head, feigning a pout.

"Okay, I'll bring up some heated water in a bit."

"Thanks, Annie. Maybe I'll actually be able to live with myself now."

Annie wasted no time giving Louisa a thorough lesson on how to cook on a wood stove. She began by talking about a good grate and how important it was to have a tight fit when it came to tending a fire, as well as keeping it from smoking up the house. "The fire is the focus of your attention, really. Once you get used to how hot you need the surface to be, you'll be fine." She paused, watching Louisa's expression.

"Want to help me get the fire started?" Louisa asked.

"This time, sure. Next time, you'll be ready to do it yourself." Annie pointed out the vents, ash box, and dampers and explained their functions. "Actually, a firebox this size is wonderful-good, 'cause it can hold a fire longer and requires less tending."

"I've read that food cooked or baked on a wood stove tastes better."

"Prob'ly so, but I haven't had much experience otherwise." Annie remembered eating at Cousin Julia's and, once in a blue moon, when she and Rudy were courting, she'd enjoyed supper at Harvest Drive Restaurant, as well as at Dienner's.

"I'll try to remember everything." Louisa reached for the big iron skillet and set it on the counter.

"Do you want to gather eggs or set the table?" Annie asked, curious to know which Louisa would choose.

"You're way better at the egg thing, so have at it."

"Ach, you'll be doin' that in your sleep by the time Christmas comes." And then it dawned on her: if Louisa stayed put, she could attend the annual school program at the one-room school, along with all the other fun holiday activities.

Louisa was studying her. "You think I'll ever gather eggs without getting pecked to death by defensive hens?"

"Maybe not." She offered a smile. "When I return from the henhouse, I'll show you how to test the stove's surface for adequate heat, with water droplets. All right?"

Louisa nodded, smiling, and turned to wash her hands. When she'd dried them, she pulled out the utensil drawer and counted eight place settings, including enough for the grandparents next door. "You must be laughing at me, Annie."

"Now, why's that?"

"I must seem nearly helpless in the kitchen . . . at least to your way of doing things."

Annie looked her over good. "I daresay you definitely need another dress or two. That one's got a telltale sign on it, by the way—paint from yesterday's visit to the attic." Here, she lowered her voice to a whisper.

Louisa grimaced. "An apron will remedy that, jah?" She went to the back of the cellar door and removed Barbara's work apron off the hook. "There. Ta-dah!"

Annie had to laugh. "You've come a long way in a few days, Miss Lou. You look and cook Plain, and you talk our first language." With that, she headed for the mud room to put on her work boots.

Miss Lou? Hey, I like that.

Louisa watched Annie leave the house, then went to the trestle table and, remembering precisely where each person always sat at mealtime, she began to set the table. "If my mom could see me now. . . ."

At that instant, a little furry creature appeared from under the cellar door and skittered across the width of the kitchen floor. Louisa stifled a squeal, looking around for safety. The mouse ran toward the sink and hid in the shadows. In turn, Louisa dashed to the long bench pushed against the table and hopped up.

Shaking with fright, she spied the rodent running the length of the counter. Then it zipped behind the cookstove. Louisa got up on the table and sat cross-legged there. *This would never happen in my apartment!* she thought.

She contemplated the contrast between the black-and-white checkerboard linoleum floor here and her own high-end ceramic-tiled kitchen with its state-of-the-art Sub-Zero fridge and stainless steel sink. *Definitely no mice!*

Her pulse pounded in her head, because more than anything, she despised rodents—filthy, disease-ridden critters. She leaned down, putting her hands over her face, and groaned. Her mother would be appalled and Michael would be splitting his sides with laughter. Yeah, they were so sure she wouldn't last here, and at the moment Louisa couldn't see herself ever getting down off this table. *Never!*

Without a warning, Annie's grandma wandered over from the Dawdi Haus. "Mornin' to ya, Missy," she said, her head covering a bit cockeyed as she stared at Louisa. "You city girls do yogurt exercises on tables?"

Louisa squelched a nervous laugh. "Uh, no, this isn't exactly yoga." She hated to reveal what a total wimp she was. "I . . . er . . . saw a mouse." She felt ridiculous, but she was too freaked to budge.

Grandma flashed a smile. "Well now, that explains it." She

stood there staring. "Did I hear voices a bit ago? Annie's, maybe?"

Nodding, Louisa glanced at the floor. "I had a cooking lesson . . . before the mouse showed up."

"Annie's got you workin', does she?"

"I'd like to pull my weight around here." That struck her funny, and she imagined how strange she must look perched up here.

Grandma Zook shook her cane about, as if shooing away the unwelcome visitor. "There. I daresay it's safe for you to come down now, if you've got your wits 'bout you."

That was definitely her cue to start acting like the empowered young woman she believed herself to be. She unfolded her long legs and hopped to the bench, standing there for a second before entrusting her feet to the floor.

"Quite a morning, already, jah?" Grandma teased.

"I'm still getting acclimated to the country," she said with a smile. Then—"Any mousetraps around here?"

"No need, really, with all them barn cats. And your Muffin . . . where *is* that feline when he's needed?" Grandma's eyes twinkled with mischief.

Cringing at the thought of her beloved kitty's paws getting anywhere near another disgusting mouse, Louisa went immediately to the sink to wash her hands. Then, returning to the table, she folded the white paper napkins and placed one beneath each fork.

The older woman smiled broadly, nodding deliberately. "Annie will have you cookin' all the time, if you're not careful. She's a good teacher . . . but not much interested in domestic chores, seems to me." She hobbled over and sat in the chair at the foot of the table. "My granddaughter's got other things takin' up space in her head . . . ever since she was a wee girl."

Louisa kept her eye out for a return of the mouse.

Grandma Zook continued. "We just don't know 'bout that one. Good-hearted, for sure and for certain, but our Annie thinks her own thoughts." She shook her head in short, quick jerks. "If you have any sway over her, I should hope you can steer her in the right direction."

That's a tall order, thought Louisa.

"Her Dawdi and Daed are both worried, 'tween you and me."

Louisa perked up her ears. "Why would that be?" She wasn't playing dumb. She really wanted to know what this little demure grandma was thinking.

"It's a cryin' shame for Annie to snub her nose at the Good Lord." Sighing, Grandma continued. "Seems to me she should've been first in line to join church when she turned courting age, or soon after. Just makes not a whit of sense."

Louisa found it interesting that Annie's grandmother, whom she scarcely knew, felt comfortable opening up like this. "Well, I'm sure Annie will eventually do the right thing."

"I should hope so . . . for the Good Lord and the People," Grandma was quick to say with the fire of sincerity in her eyes.

When Annie returned to the house, Louisa was amazed at the large quantity of eggs in her wire basket.

Annie smiled big. "'Mornin', Mammi . . . I got me a perty big batch."

"Well," said her grandmother, staring at Annie. "You missed all the excitement."

Louisa shrugged, wishing to forget the appearance of the mouse. And when Grandma didn't attempt to tell on her, Louisa was rather pleased . . . as if the older woman and she shared a small secret.

Annie looked somewhat confused. Not inquiring, she motioned for Louisa to go to the sink for some water. "See if the droplets bead and roll . . . and hiss on the stove. You try it."

"Jah . . . bead, roll, and spit. Bead, roll . . . spit," chanted the elderly woman.

When Louisa tested the heat, the water did precisely that. "That's cool," she said.

"No, that's hot," Annie said. "You're ready to scramble up some eggs."

"Mustn't forget the bacon." Grandma Zook came over to observe.

Louisa welcomed her presence. She wasn't hovering the way Louisa's mom typically did. The woman, oddly enough, was most supportive and encouraging, though she merely nodded her little gray head, folding her hands now and then.

But in a few short minutes, even though she tried to keep ahead of the fire by continually scraping the eggs from the bottom of the cast-iron frying pan, Louisa had burned the eggs to a crispy mess. Chagrined, she wished she had attempted fried eggs instead. "I'm so sorry," she said, looking to Annie. "I'll have to start over. What about a back-up plan?"

"Such as what?" asked Annie.

"Peahens' eggs?"

Annie covered her mouth, trying not to laugh, but her eyes told the truth. "No . . . no, *those* eggs are our future peacocks and peahens."

Even Mammi Zook had to hold herself together, she cackled so hard.

"Maybe I'd do better with pancakes," Louisa suggested, hoping so.

Annie quit laughing long enough to say she'd help Louisa figure out when to flip the pancakes.

At that moment, Annie's mother entered the kitchen, looking quite stunned at seeing an Englisher standing at her cookstove. *And a worldly artist, at that!* Louisa was sure Barbara held her at arm's length and would continue to do so. And no wonder.

Annie offered no explanation but quickly began to mix up the pancake batter. Her mother, who must have sniffed the burnt offering, set about making coffee.

It was Mammi Zook who nodded her head silently, patting Louisa's arm before heading over to the table to sit. *What a sweetheart,* thought Louisa, wondering why the older woman hadn't coached her earlier. *Learning by doing.* A concept her own mom had ignored early on as a young mother, too eager to step in and do things herself instead of allowing Louisa to try and possibly fail.

Part of why I love this place, Louisa thought. *I'm free to fall flat on my face.*

Thinking ahead, she had difficulty envisioning the process of cutting out a cape dress and sewing it up in a few hours. But then, a few weeks ago she never would have believed she'd be running from an Amish mouse *or* wreaking havoc with breakfast for Annie's family!

———

Louisa was heartened by Annie's patience toward her . . . stretching the measuring tape from nape of neck to waist, and waistline to hem, as well as all the other vital measurements . . .

to marking the hem. "Good thing we're sewing another dress for me. I have to admit, I have a hard time wearing something more than once. And it might be nice to have a nightgown, too. If you think I can sew one of those."

"Oh, well, if you really want to sew your nightclothes, that's fine, but I usually get mine at Wal-Mart."

"No kidding?"

Annie smiled playfully. "They have a hitchin' post out behind the store for us horse-'n'-buggy folk."

"Wow . . . interesting."

"Yeah, we show up every so often in pictures on the pages of the *Lancaster New Era,* one of the local newspapers, I'm told."

Louisa was captivated. "The juxtaposition of the old ways and the modern high-tech world is really quite a clash—nearly startling, actually. Who would believe that people live this way . . . in the twenty-first century?"

She tried to focus on Annie's instruction. It was as if she were in seventh grade home ec class all over again. Except she'd never seen a treadle sewing machine, let alone operated one. It was so tricky to get the rhythm of her feet pressing back and forth. She felt absolutely inept.

"Here, I'll show you once more," Annie offered. "It's like eatin' watermelon, spitting out the seeds, and walking at the same time, jah?"

"I feel like such a klutz."

"You mean clumsy, jah? Here we say *dabbich.*"

Louisa repeated the Dutch word and smiled. "I'm slowly building my new vocabulary."

"That you are." Annie's feet worked the treadle, smooth as satin. "It takes some doin' . . . you almost don't want to think 'bout it too hard, though."

Louisa watched and was soon ready to try again. "Your grandmother said you're a good teacher, and you're proving it to me."

"Did she also remind you that I taught at the one-room school for several years?"

"No, but I remember *those* letters back then. You were waking before sunup to crank up the ol' wood stove so your students—all eight grades together—wouldn't shiver during the first hour of school."

"But I quit the second year Rudy was courtin' me. It looked as if I might be getting married that fall, but as you know, I didn't. By then, another girl had taken my spot as teacher." Annie explained how once she graduated from the eighth grade she was immediately eligible to instruct the younger students. "But the minute you're married, you're out."

"How come?"

"A bride is expected to put all her attention into makin' a home for her husband and preparing to bear many children."

"So you couldn't have gone back to teaching even if you wanted to?"

"*Nee*, wouldn't think of it," Annie said. "Such would set me up for tongue-waggin'."

Not wanting to press further, Louisa could read between the lines. Preacher Jesse's daughter was a conundrum to the community. Big time.

And my coming adds even more fuel to the fire, Louisa thought. Yet she felt no urgency to abandon Annie and cut short the visit. If anything, she was even more determined to stay and encourage her friend to follow her heart.

Chapter 23

The first thing Louisa noticed when they arrived at the covered bridge on Belmont Road was how very much it looked like Annie's painting, except for chips of missing reddish-brown paint from several roughly-hewn boards nearest the road. She recalled clearly the way Annie had set the tall craggy trees back away from the road in her picture—the locust grove gracefully bordering the creek—and the way the gray stone abutment seemed to vie for equal attention. The entire setting had been pinpointed precisely in the exquisite painting.

"Talk about quaint. This is definitely it." She and Annie strolled together, arm-in-arm, to the base of the first tree, carrying their sketchbooks.

"I've always heard the black locust seeds are poisonous," Annie said as if her mind had wandered.

"You must feel plagued by this place. Is that why your painting is called 'Obsession'?"

"In more ways than I can say." Annie pointed out the dark trunk furrowed with interlacing bark. "Ever see thorns like this on a tree?"

"Kinda creepy."

"And dangerous, if ever you've tried to climb it. Thorns are all over the limbs and on the trunk."

They stood there silently, peering at the grove.

Suddenly the light left Annie's eyes, and it looked as if she might start to cry.

"As pretty and serene as this is, it does have a haunting feeling," Louisa said.

Annie looked the other way for a moment, composing herself, no doubt. Then, she said softly, "My friend, Esther Hochstetler—you met her Sunday—well, her husband was the last person ever to see the boy who disappeared. Right here, where we're standing. Isaac was Zeke's little brother."

"Really? Well, what happened that night?"

"Truly, Mamm's the best one to ask, but I can tell you what I know at least."

Standing beneath the airy umbrella of branches, mostly devoid of leaves, Louisa listened as Annie began her story. "Something this awful had never happened round these parts . . . I can tell you for sure. Folk came and went—Amish and English alike—never thinking twice 'bout locking doors or being suspicious of strangers and whatnot. Never." Annie put her hand on her chest.

"If it's too hard to—"

Annie shook her head. "No . . . I'll be all right." She sighed loudly. "Every mother lost sleep, Mamm told me. Some parents were so fearful they got permission from the bishop to get indoor plumbing . . . abandoned their old outhouses and whatnot."

"To keep tabs on their kids?"

"Oh, jah."

"And what about Zeke? He must've totally freaked out, losing his brother like that."

"That's the truth. Esther's husband was hit terribly hard emotionally, I'm told. He was just a youngster, only eight when Isaac vanished into the air. He and Isaac had left the house after dark to bury their dead puppy. But Zeke acted against his father's will, sneakin' out of the house after supper when no one was looking." Annie paused, not saying more for a moment.

"Heavy stuff."

Neither spoke for a time. The air became eerily still before Annie began again. "Esther told me once that Zeke's father refused to forgive him and belittled him all through his growing-up years. Made a point of telling everyone the kidnapping was the worst possible punishment to befall a disobedient son, meaning Zeke, but that the harsh, even divine judgment had come for a reason nonetheless."

"But *Isaac* was the one who was lost," said Louisa. "Surely the father didn't believe that the so-called punishment for disobedience was to rest solely on his *eight-year-old* son. Seems unnecessarily cruel."

"And Zeke was, no doubt, already bearing the weight of blame."

What a horrendous guilt trip to put on a person, let alone a kid. Louisa was truly aghast.

"To this day, no one knows what happened to Isaac Hochstetler." Annie's eyes shone with tears. "Ach, not sure why this bothers me so."

Louisa reached out a hand. "Well, you're softhearted, Annie. One more reason why you're an incredible artist."

She nodded slowly. "Maybe so."

"You may talk big, but you're sensitive on the inside."

"I s'pose I am."

"Well, we both are," Louisa admitted.

She followed Annie down to the creek, where they stood silently and watched the water surge beneath the covered bridge.

Then they turned and walked down the creek a bit and, later, back again to the first tree. "In case you're wondering, the rope swing in my painting is long gone from here. My mother says it was taken down after Isaac went missing. But I have no idea who would've done that."

"Maybe Zeke's father?"

"Could be, but I never heard that."

"But you put it back in your painting . . . where it belongs."

"At least in my heart it's there." Annie glanced at the sky, then back at Louisa. "So, you see. Our village of Paradise hasn't always been as peaceful as you might think."

She felt inadequate to offer the slightest measure of sympathy. "I can only wish that Zeke's brother had never disappeared."

"Isaac would be getting married 'bout now, prob'ly." Annie forced a smile. "I remember playing there in the creek . . . his brother and my brothers, too. We were such good little friends."

"How do you remember what happened when you were so young?"

Annie shrugged. "Mamm says I remember things clear back to when I was only three. So, jah, I have a right clear memory of Isaac. It was just the most terrible thing when he was kidnapped. I even wondered if something like that could happen to me."

"Is it possible he simply wandered off—got lost in the night?"

"I don't see how, not with his brother right there. Every inch of the township was searched—the little waterfall across from the old stone mill, and the Eshelman Run, all through the community park and the fields. It's a nightmarish mystery, that's what."

"Did the police question Isaac's family . . . all his relatives?"

"I don't know." Annie frowned. "The church brethren handle things their way, so I doubt he was ever even reported missing."

Louisa was stunned. "You've got to be kidding!"

"It's the way we do things, that's all I can say."

"And the brethren? You mean all the men in your church?"

"Our *ministers*—one deacon, two preachers, and our bishop."

Louisa pondered the curiously unexpected answers. She couldn't imagine a child vanishing in the area of Colorado's Castle Pines without the authorities being called in. For that matter, she couldn't conceive of it happening that way anywhere on the planet. "How long ago was this?" she asked.

"Well, I was the same age as little Isaac when he disappeared . . . so sixteen years ago."

"An eternity for the family. . . ." Louisa couldn't begin to think how she would feel if one of her own family was taken . . . and a mere child, too.

Annie brushed a tear from her cheek with the back of her hand. "Plenty of folk put their lives on hold right along with the Hochstetler family," she said. "But Isaac's family didn't stay put here for long."

"You mean they left because of what happened?"

"Jah, never returned. They cut themselves off from the very church of their baptism and, eventually, from their son Zeke."

Foregoing their plan to sketch there, its beauty now overshadowed by somber thoughts and images, Annie and Louisa walked back to the waiting horse and buggy.

When they returned home, Louisa was surprised at Annie's insistence in discussing the topic of the kidnapping with her mother. Annie seemed to take advantage of the kitchen being deserted and began to pour lemonade into three glasses. Then she boldly suggested they all sit at the table "for a little while."

Louisa cringed inwardly, but at Annie's urging she reluctantly brought up the long-ago incident. "I was just curious about the events surrounding that night." Louisa went on to say that she and Annie had gone to the creek to look around. Nothing was said about Annie's painting, of course.

Barbara's round face became quite flushed, and she began to blink her eyes as she looked first at Annie and then back at her lemonade. It was obvious she was reticent to discuss what she recalled, at least with an outsider. Either that or she was still peeved at Louisa, especially, for the profile-drawing session two nights ago.

If I'm not careful, I'll get booted out and fast. . . .

Louisa immediately felt apologetic. "You know, that's all right," she spoke up. "You don't have to talk about this now, or at all."

"No . . . no, I want Mamm to tell you what she knows," Annie interjected. "Besides, it's been a long time since I've heard the story." She leaned forward at the table, eyes fixed on her mother.

"Well, all I'm goin' to say is that the perpetrator—the person who stole Isaac away, prob'ly killed him, too—will certainly be required to answer to almighty God for the treacherous deed." Annie's mother turned to look directly at Louisa. "And, I believe the Lord God and heavenly Father looks not so kindly on *anyone* who purposely sets out to harm one of His own."

Jeepers, I've been told. Louisa felt the heat of embarrassment rise in her face. Before she could make an attempt to excuse herself, Annie's mom said rather pointedly she wanted to speak with Annie "right away." Translated to mean—and Louisa was absolutely sure—that she personally needed to get lost as soon as she finished her lemonade so Annie could get an earful in private.

Frustrated and aghast at Mamm's pointed approach, Annie shifted in her seat. Her mother had never reacted in such a way, that she recalled. "You're terribly upset," Annie said softly.

Mamm sat solemn-faced, fanning herself with a corner of her apron, even though it was anything but warm in the kitchen. "I'm glad you're having a good time with your friend, Annie, but you daresn't be tempted by the fancy drawings she makes."

Tempted?

"Louisa's drawings are wonderful-good. Did you see how close to perfect her profile was of me?"

"Now, Annie."

"No, I'm serious. She has an amazing gift."

Her mother's face softened quickly, and she reached a hand over to touch Annie's arm. "Dear one, you must not allow Louisa's talent to draw you in . . . to entice you away from the People."

It already has. . . .

"Havin' Louisa here has been the best thing for me, Mamm. You just don't know." She bit her lip thinking about her breakup with Rudy just then, but she caught herself.

"I see in your eyes how happy you are, but Louisa certainly isn't Amish and won't be stayin' here forever. So you need to be thinking 'bout your future . . . who you'll settle down with and marry."

Annie shook her head, taking quick short breaths. "Well, you best enjoy your grandchildren from my brothers, 'cause honestly, I don't see myself becoming a bride now." It wounded her to admit it, but truth was the boys her age were all getting hitched.

Mamm's face fell. "You can't mean it."

Once the difficult words were out in the air, Annie felt some better. Now Mamm would stop bringing up this painful topic, just maybe.

"Well, it hurts me to think . . . another baptism season has come and gone already."

Jah, Annie, you've missed out on joining church yet again! Annie grimaced at her own thoughts. "Well, why's everything all tangled up with what's expected of me?"

"No . . . no, you mustn't be thinkin' on it that way. It's what is good and right and true, Annie. That's what." Mamm sighed loudly, her face ever so serious. "You may not know this, but there's much more to the story of little Isaac Hochstetler, and what with our talk about your future 'n' all, it just might be time for you to hear it, lest you yield to temptation yourself and turn your back on all that is right."

Annie hadn't the slightest idea what her mother meant.

Mamm began to explain. "Isaac's father committed a deadly error . . . no other way to say this." She paused, placed her hand over her throat, and then continued. "You see, Annie, the divine lot for Preacher fell first on Daniel Hochstetler one month before the kidnapping occurred. He out and out refused to accept the ordination."

Annie could not believe her ears. A terrible, bad omen. . . .

"'Tis a decision unto death."

"Oh, Mamm . . . I never knew of this."

Her mother nodded, face drawn. "It's scarcely ever talked about, even in a whisper, for all good reason. So . . . your father was God's second choice for preacher . . . no getting round it."

"I never would've guessed someone would be so unwise . . . turning away from the drawin' of the lot," Annie said softly.

"The People called him '*Ichabod*—the glory of the Lord has departed,'" Mamm whispered. "It was nearly like a shunning, and some of the brethren *did* banish him. Then, not long after, the family up and left, only to be heard from again when Ezekiel returned and wed Essie."

Annie listened carefully, wondering why on earth Mamm was sharing such ominous news.

But then quite suddenly she knew. Sure as a mackerel sky means rain, she knew.

———

Jesse accepted a mug of coffee from Esther. Then, when she'd left the kitchen, the little boys in tow, he looked at Zeke and motioned toward the back door with his head.

Zeke followed willingly, carrying his own coffee and talking all the while about the nice weather "this late in the season."

In the barn, Jesse offered Zeke a cigar, but he shook his head, saying he never cared so much for the odor. "Well, just thought I'd . . . pay you a visit," Jesse said, stumbling over his words. He felt downright awkward, but he wanted to know how Zeke was doing. "I'm awful sorry . . . 'bout your brother. Such a terrible shame."

Zeke stared a hole in him. He was silent for a time, taking one gulp of coffee after another. At last, he spoke. "Where's he buried?"

Shuffling his feet, Jesse hadn't expected this. "The bishop

and I took great care to find an out-of-the-way spot for your brother's bones. Bishop wants it kept quiet."

Eight big steps past the edge of the cemetery, four short ones past the first tree, thought Jesse.

Zeke ran his hand through his light brown beard. "I beg to differ with that. He's my kin . . . I have the right to know!"

"S'pose you do."

"No supposin' about it, Preacher. I want to pay my respects."

The fire in Zeke's eyes could not be missed, and Jesse wondered if he'd made a mistake by coming here. "I say we follow the bishop on this," he stated flatly. "No need to argue with the man of God."

Zeke shook his head slowly. "Well, seems a man ought to be able to quietly go and say good-bye to his own brother."

Seems so, thought Jesse. But he wouldn't budge where Zeke was concerned. The man was as volatile as any of the farmers he'd ever known. As headstrong as Zeke's own father had been. "The womenfolk . . . that's what the bishop's most concerned 'bout. Such an upheaval your Isaac's disappearance caused amongst the People. No need in stirring all that up again."

Zeke eyed the spare cigar. "I just might take you up on your offer, Preacher," he said, pointing at his pocket.

Jesse pulled out the cigar and handed it to the distraught younger man. "I best be headin' on home. Always plenty of chores to tend to."

When Zeke lit up and puffed some, but didn't say a word for a good long time, Jesse figured he was ready to get back to work, too. But Zeke followed him all the way out to the horse and buggy, and as soon as Jesse was settled in the front seat, reins in hand, Zeke said, "You ain't heard the end of this, Preacher."

Jesse looked at him, this man who'd suffered such torment

his whole life. To think that selfsame misery had turned to a stone wall in the end—something Zeke could not get past and apparently needed to.

"It's time to put this to rest," Zeke said, his voice cracking.

Compassion swept through Jesse. He couldn't just ride out of the man's lane without giving him something to go on, at least. "All right, then. I'll talk to the bishop for you."

"And I won't rest till I hear back," Zeke said. "Gut day!"

Jesse directed the horse forward slowly, and not even when he made the turn onto the paved road did he hurry the steed. *Such a can of worms!* he thought, hoping Zeke might simply forget and go about his farm work. Because there was no way he was going to get Bishop Andy to budge on this matter.

Chapter 24

Following breakfast and kitchen cleanup on Thursday, Annie hitched up the team with some help from Luke. She was anxious to take Louisa to the quilting bee, along with Mammi Zook, who required extra care getting in and out of the family buggy. Mamm had decided to remain at home in case Yonie returned from his hunting trip with a deer, so Annie headed out to Sarah Mae's with her grandmother and Louisa filling up the front seat.

The cold seeped into the enclosed carriage despite the heated bricks she'd placed on the floor, as well as the lap robes, to help ward off the nip in the air. Her nose became quickly chilled, but the tips of her ears were well protected with her black "candle-snuffer" style hat. She was amused, looking over at Louisa . . . the three of them looking rather alike in their winter bonnets. *Such a good sport is Louisa, dressing as if she were truly Plain!*

It turned out that Esther did not show her face at the quilting frolic, just as she had indicated on Sunday. But a dozen or so other women were on hand—half of them were married first cousins of Annie's; the others were hoary-headed seasoned quilters.

When it came time to sit at the enormous frame, Louisa

planted herself next to Mammi Zook. She seemed determined to imitate the smallest stitches, listening to the storytelling while heeding Mammi's gentle instruction. Louisa appeared to be quite taken by the bold reds, purples, and greens of the Center Diamond quilt. Annie wasn't surprised at all, for it had always been one of *her* favorites.

The only Mennonite woman present—a cousin of Julia's—commented that several women in her neighborhood had formed a "Scraps R Us" group, creating comforters from leftover fabric. "Some of our husbands are helping cut the squares," the woman explained, "and the youngsters tie the knots on the comforters."

Mammi Zook perked up her ears. "Well, I have hundreds of pieces—I'd be glad to donate 'em."

The Mennonite woman smiled and thanked Mammi, returning her attention to making careful stitches. Annie was content to sit across from them, concentrating on the process of quilting, saying precious little. Rhoda Esh and Susie Yoder were on hand, as well, and it was rather clear that Rudy's sister and his new girl had gotten themselves on much better footing these days.

Time heals. . . .

Annie couldn't stop thinking about Mamm's startling revelation last evening. *Isaac's father is Ichabod. . . .*

She shivered with the ominous feeling, the knowledge that one of their own had rejected the divine appointment. Could time heal such a thing as *that*?

The next day, Louisa worked diligently on her colorful peacock painting in the attic studio while Annie cleaned Julia's downstairs. Louisa didn't have to remind herself to charge up her

Palm. She was beginning to feel somewhat out of touch and was ready to make contact with the outside world. *I need to remember who I really am*, she thought as she mixed blue with green on the palette.

Julia knocked softly and entered, bringing a cinnamon roll and a cup of tea. She placed the tray down and stepped over to the easel, eyes wide with delight. "Oh, Louisa. What a wonderful talent you have! God certainly has given you a great gift."

"Well, thank you. I've never quite thought of it that way." Louisa paused, realizing this woman was absolutely sincere. "Do you really think God gives people certain abilities?"

"Oh my, yes. The Lord is the ultimate artist, you know, creating each one of us with special gifts. I should say so."

Louisa was stunned. Julia wasn't kidding . . . she believed this.

"There are gifts such as musical ability, as you know, writing gifts, and gifts such as friendship, loyalty, and courage. Honestly, the list goes on and on. I'm sure if you think about it, you'll realize this in your own life . . . and others."

Louisa thanked her for the "sticky bun," as the breakfast rolls were called here, and the honey-sweetened peppermint tea before Julia slipped out nearly as silently as she had come.

During lunch Louisa checked her email on her laptop, corresponding with Cybil Peters and several other art students, smiling at their waiting remarks about her abandoning them for Amish country. *They would snicker at my Plain getup*, she thought.

While she was online, Courtney sent her an instant message, reminding her unnecessarily that today was the eve of her once-planned wedding. "I'll be thinking of you—especially tomorrow. Just want to make sure you're okay, girl." She replied to Courtney, assuring her she was fine and happy to hear of her latest date to *The Phantom of the Opera,* at the Buell Theatre in downtown Denver. Louisa experienced a twinge of melancholy, having seen the musical years before on Broadway with her parents. Suddenly she decided to send individual email messages to her mom and dad, which triggered an interesting thought: *Am I becoming latently homesick?*

When her Palm was completely charged, she listened to all of her new voice mail. Starting at the beginning, with the call she'd snoozed the last time, she was surprised to hear Trey's voice in her ear. *Hey, Louisa . . . I just sold a large Joseph Bohler painting—man, what a style . . . earthy and honest. Anyway, Joe's work made me think of you. Maybe we can do Denver again sometime. Call me!*

Hearing Trey's voice did crazy things to her. She pressed "9" to save his message. When she'd heard each message, including three from Mother and two more from Michael, she replayed Trey's, savoring the rich tone of his voice, visualizing him making the call from London, within the confines of his fabulous art gallery.

Why did we disconnect so thoroughly?

But she knew. She had wanted to finish her degree at the California School of Art, and he was ready to get on with his life, having completed a master's degree in business management, his undergraduate degree in fine arts with an emphasis in art history, theory, and criticism. The perfect combo for an art dealer.

She humorously recalled his aversion to high tech anything, never having asked for her email address and avoiding the Internet as long as possible. If she could have reduced Trey to a two-word definition, it would have been *earthy sophisticate. But minus the deception*, she decided, smiling at the perfect description for her first boyfriend.

Why should he contact me now? Does he know about my split from Michael? She also wondered if he had ever known of her engagement.

She recalled her many dates with Trey, the way he seemed to enjoy treating her special—like a lady. Rushing around the car to open her door, insisting on paying for her expensive dinners, ordering for her . . . things most men overlooked, or women didn't value, being liberated and empowered these days. Trey appreciated fine quality and nice things, but he had always been just as comfortable in jeans and a sweater as he was in an expensive suit.

All day she contemplated his charming phone message, growing more introspective of their past romance as the hours ticked by. Even at supper that evening, Annie attempted to pry Louisa out of her blackout, asking occasional questions about Denver, her college years . . . as did Annie's mom, uncharacteristically so. But Louisa was preoccupied with Trey, struggling with the strong tug toward him yet somewhat stunned by the uncanny timing of his reappearance in her life.

During the evening prayers—always silent rote prayers, so she never really knew what the Zooks were saying to God anyway—Louisa considered returning Trey's call . . . perhaps in a few days. *I'll give myself more time to think. . . . But, no, we called it quits. It's over.*

Kneeling before the plain sofa next to Annie and her family, Louisa was so conflicted regarding Trey. She wondered if her back-and-forth state was itself a clue. *Should I pay attention to that alone?* In the past, she'd often listened to her psyche, making sure all systems were go, especially when it came to relationships with guys. So many things could go wrong, she had quickly discovered.

But since hearing Trey's voice, her old feelings continued to resurface. She wouldn't tell Annie, when she asked what was bugging her, in so many words . . . but Trey *had* been the all-time best kisser ever. A truly affectionate man. Was that *his* gift? she wondered, smiling and recalling Julia's strange remarks. She wished she'd thought more than twice about possibly following him to London. Had she agreed to go with him, she might have easily transferred her credits to the Sorbonne in Paris, where two of her girl friends had gone. If so, she would never have been around for the blind date setup with attorney Michael Jackanapes Berkeley!

———

The next morning, Yonie returned home without a buck to show for all his hunting. There was one good thing about his recent disappearing act—he seemed more relaxed, Annie thought. They promptly resumed their fun-loving bantering, including his comments about Louisa's "powerful cologne," which Yonie insisted still permeated his bedroom even though she'd aired it out but good. He hadn't seemed to mind Louisa staying in his room, however. If anything, he was intrigued by an English girl dressing in Amish clothes.

There was a decided spring in his step, so Annie guessed he'd also paid a visit to Dory Zimmerman en route home.

As for housing Louisa, Mamm was surprisingly agreeable, allowing her and Annie to move to the large upstairs bedroom in the Dawdi Haus, which put a surprisingly big smile on Mammi Zook's wrinkled face.

As Annie unpacked a box of her things, she ran across

Louisa's wedding invitation—the fancy wedding that had been scheduled to take place at high noon today. She slipped the invitation into the bottom of her drawer, thinking Louisa didn't need the reminder, especially considering how quiet and preoccupied her friend had been lately.

———

In the weeks that followed, various works of art began to emerge from both Annie's and Louisa's keen imagination onto the pages of their individual sketchbooks and the canvases in the sequestered attic. Louisa insisted, however, on taking time off to show Annie some advanced techniques, saying her brain needed time to be "re-inspired" between projects. Annie soaked up the instruction, which involved highlighting to set a mood, layering and glazing colors—moving from light to dark values in watercolor and pastel chalk—and the power of shading accents with pencil drawings. Louisa worked frequently with Annie to help her transform her simple still lifes into a three-dimensional look. But Annie needed less help with her landscape paintings—which popped right off the canvas—and Louisa focused on their fine details by using unexpected spots of color.

Annie savored these educational, yet creative hours, but had the growing conviction that they could not last much longer. Although she didn't breathe a word to Louisa of Mamm's revelation about Isaac's father's refusal of the divine lot, she frequently brooded about it, wondering what consequences might befall her, too, for refusing to submit to the will of the People.

She also found herself finishing her household chores for Julia more quickly than she had in recent months. And even though Louisa offered to assist with the work, Annie continually refused, urging her to "make good use of the time," knowing they must not risk a further run-in with Mamm at home.

Preparations for a Thanksgiving feast were in progress with oodles of baking—a half-dozen pumpkin pies and the same of mincemeat—which meant less time for drawing at home. Annie was actually glad none of her cousins were scheduled to marry that week, otherwise they would have been planning to attend the all-day wedding celebration instead of happily inviting all of her brothers and their families for a big get-together.

Later, when Louisa brought up the possibility of renting a car "for a few days" for the purpose of purchasing additional art supplies and exploring the art galleries nearby, Julia offered to drive her to several locations, including the Village of Intercourse. In short order the completed peacock painting and the ethereal owl in flight, as well as one of surrounding farmland, including Preacher Zook's barn, were quickly snatched up on consignment by a small art gallery and craft shop situated on Route 30, near Leaman Place Furniture.

Annie was delighted no end at Louisa's success in placing her realistic paintings where, given the heavy tourist trade, they could enjoy a wide audience of potential customers. Of course, Louisa's appearance, looking as if she were Amish, had an appealing influence on the owner, as well. Louisa was quick indeed to set the record straight, revealing that she was actually a modern young woman, though residing with an Amish family "for the time being." Annie was fairly sure the English owner didn't believe this for a single minute.

Annie secretly wished she, too, might sell her work. But that was out of the question for now.

One Saturday morning, Louisa, Annie, and Julia, along with her children, headed out by car to the Old Country Store in Intercourse. There, Julia shopped for precut fabric, color-coordinated in packs, ready for quilting.

Meanwhile, Louisa and Annie walked around, looking at the various handmade crafts—the embroidered items especially interesting to Louisa. "I can't believe someone actually makes this stuff by hand," she commented softly to Annie. "You know, it's really an art form—check out the colorful arrangements and the unique designs."

"Well, the whole upstairs is a quilt museum, if you want to see more," said Annie. "Quilts made before the 1940s."

Louisa glanced toward the stairs. "I'm in!" Then she ran her fingers over the intricate flowers in a basket stitched onto the wide hem of a pillowslip, studying the needlework. "Do you embroider like this?"

"Jah, all the womenfolk do . . .'specially during the winter. Some are better at it than others, though."

"Well, this is a talent, too, Annie, like painting. A gift, Julia would say."

Louisa became aware of two "English" women near the piece goods, looking their way and talking none too quietly.

"Look, Cari, they're Amish," said one.

"Oh, you're right," said the other. "Have you ever seen dresses like *that?*"

Louisa rolled her eyes and moved away. *They must think Annie and I can't hear them with our bonnets on! How rude!*

There was a sudden flash, and Louisa turned and came face-to-face with one of the modern tourists, now wielding a camera.

"Smile!" the woman said, with one eye squinting.

Louisa put her hand in front of the lens. "Excuse me. What

you're doing is impolite," she spouted, glancing now at Annie, who looked nearly as stunned as the tourists.

"But you're both so *cute*," the too-blond woman cooed.

"Your camera's not welcome here," Louisa said, stepping between Annie and the tourist like a shield. She stared at this pushy, insensitive person, the first bejeweled, made-up woman she had seen since coming to visit. *Was I ever that rude?* she wondered. *I hope not!*

She took a deep breath, suppressing the urge to speak up again.

Annie marched off, keeping her face from view. And Louisa followed suit, mimicking her Plain friend, quite proud to join ranks with Annie.

During afternoon milking, Annie mentioned to her father that Louisa had seen him out quite late one night, carrying a shovel. "I told her she must've dreamt it, Daed."

But it was peculiar how he did not return her smile. His eyes took on a serious, even stern expression. "No need talking 'bout this," he said flatly.

"Then I guess Louisa wasn't dreamin' after all."

"Ach, Annie . . . church business."

She knew by that she best hush up. Because whatever it was, Daed had no intention of revealing it to her. And now she was ever so curious.

Chapter 25

Toward the end of the fourth week of Louisa's visit, an important-looking letter arrived in the mail. Glancing at it, Annie noticed the inscribed address for the law offices of Louisa's father.

Dashing across the road, she found Louisa pitching hay to the mules with Luke and Yonie. "Mail call!" she announced, holding out the elongated envelope.

Taking a moment to study the envelope, Louisa promptly folded it in half and stuffed it into her dress pocket. "This can wait," she said softly, shrugging a bit.

But after supper, Annie sat on the bed with Louisa in their shared room in the Dawdi Haus. A small but cheery sitting room separated their bedroom from Dawdi and Mammi Zooks'.

"You're upset," she said, aware of Louisa's gloom. "Anything I can do for you?"

Louisa held the letter in her hands, staring at it, a wistful frown on her face. "My father wants me to come home—especially since I stayed here through Thanksgiving. They're thinking of having a family reunion, I guess you could call it, before Christmas. A get-together of sorts to take the place of my canceled wedding."

"Did he say *that?*"

"No, but it's implied, trust me. If I return, they'll fly the extended family out. If not, they'll skip it. So the burden rests on me."

Annie felt sad, knowing how terribly she would miss Louisa, who had become her dearest sister-friend. "Must you go already?"

Louisa returned the letter to the envelope. "Well, I doubt my parents would appreciate my Amish dress and apron. . . ."

This made Annie smile. "Then why not stay for Christmas?"

"You know, Annie, I have to say for as out of place as I felt when I first arrived, I can't seem to get enough of your Paradise."

Annie was heartened at this. "Have you considered stayin' for longer . . . like a full year? What would ya say to that?"

"I think I do need more time here. . . ." Louisa looked intently, even longingly, out the window. Her head covering fit her face and hairline quite perfectly.

"Then it's settled. You're stayin'."

Louisa's eyes brightened again. "If I can make all the arrangements—and if your parents consent to it—I'll take you up on your suggestion."

"Oh, this is such good news!"

"Let's not count our chickens before they're hatched," Louisa said, which got Annie laughing. "I'll have to sublease my place, and I need to touch base with each of my students. And to keep painting at Julia's and selling my art, too, if possible. I'm not a freeloader."

Annie wondered why Louisa hadn't mentioned contacting her parents. "I'll cross my fingers and hope real hard that everything falls into place." Blissful at the thought of Louisa staying on, Annie also knew this might well be her last year in her parents' house. She suspected the brethren of having spoken in private on the knotty problem of her hedging about church membership. If she didn't sign up for baptismal classes by next spring, there would be more to deal with than a multitude of raised eyebrows.

Leaning her head back on the bed, Annie stared at the ceiling. Then, sighing, she looked over at Louisa. "You goin' to answer your father's letter?"

"When I know for sure what I'm doing," Louisa said quietly. "Meanwhile, I think I might like to talk to your cousin sometime."

" 'Bout staying put here?"

"No, other things. Julia seems like a person who's actually interested in reading the Bible. That blows me away, because it's such a dry sort of read, from what I remember. But your cousin's got her nose in it a lot." Louisa paused for a moment, then continued. "There's just so much about God that I don't get. Ever feel that way?"

Annie definitely understood. "Jah, more than ever."

———————

Annie was sitting toward the back of the kitchen, closest to the sunroom at Deacon Byler's house, during the common meal. She was mulling over the sermon her father had given. Often she contemplated the way he told the story, as if attempting to communicate the Old Testament accounts in such a way as to draw in the young people more fully. And he'd certainly done that today. Sometimes she felt as if she were seeing a side to her father she rarely saw, except on Preaching days, and she savored the feeling.

She was so deep in thought she literally jumped when Esther

came over and tapped her on the shoulder. "When you're through, can we go walkin'?"

"Why sure." Annie pushed her dessert aside. "Let's go right now."

"No . . . no, finish your pie." Esther's face was drawn and she looked to be sleep deprived, the way she often looked lately.

"I'll tell you what . . . I can easily take it along." Annie scooped up the pumpkin pie and placed it on a napkin.

"Will Louisa be all right?" asked Esther.

A quick glance up the table and Annie could see Louisa well occupied with Mamm and several of Annie's aunts. "Looks like she's busy talkin' for now."

They headed out the back door and down a stony walkway. Annie asked which way she wanted to go, pointing out the narrow farm road as well as the paved but little-traveled road out front.

"Back road's best, I think."

By this Annie knew Esther had something personal on her mind. "I'm glad you asked me to come walking. You feelin' all right?"

Esther pulled a hankie from her pocket. "Oh, Annie, I've wanted to talk to you in the worst way. . . ." Her voice quavered. "Things have gone from bad to worse 'tween Zeke and me."

Annie didn't know what to say, having only suspected something amiss . . . never knowing what, at least not from Esther directly. There had been some things dropped now and then from Annie's mother to Sarah Mae, but nothing substantial. "I'm so sorry, Esther. How can I help?"

Esther stopped beneath a tree, gathering her shawl about her. "My wee babe's comin' soon, but something keeps tellin' me to run away. I even have dreams 'bout taking Laura and the boys and leaving Zeke."

Annie was aghast. "You'd do that?"

Esther hung her head. "Some days I want to disappear just like Zeke's little brother did back when. Other times, when Zeke's right kind, even thoughtful, 'specially toward the children, I wonder what the world I'm thinkin'." She reached for Annie's hand. "I believe I've come to my wit's end. Is it just me, or am I truly losin' my mind? Are things so terrible wrong at my house?"

Annie inhaled deeply, gripping poor Esther's hand. "Maybe you'd better tell me what you mean."

Esther's lower lip trembled. "Well, to start with, I need to know something." She took a great deep breath. "Does your father ever lay a hand on your mamma in rebuke?"

"Never in anger, no. But then Mamm respects and obeys him, no question 'bout that."

"Are you sayin' it's all right for a man to strike his wife if she doesn't?"

Annie thought on that. "Well, we both know there are plenty of men who demand submission . . . and they use the Ordnung to back that up." She was thinking of her grandfather Zook and some of his brothers, much too harsh in some ways. There were rumors, too, that Deacon Byler and some of his married boys were awful hard on their women, including the younger girls. "Usually, the men say it's the woman's fault. . . ."

"But I need answers, 'cause I feel like I'm walkin' in the dark." Esther let go of Annie's hand, moving slowly now.

"There aren't easy solutions, I don't think. But if you're ever in danger, you know where you and the children can come for safety." Annie meant this with all of her heart.

Esther shook her head. "I could never take you up on that. I doubt Preacher Zook would tolerate such a thing. He'd say I was diggin' in my heels, not yielding to my husband." She grabbed hold of her shawl again. "Truth is, one of these times, you just might not see me round here anymore, Annie."

"Honestly, you'd up and leave?"

"I'd find myself some peace, that's all. It's not like I *want* to go away. . . ."

"So it's your husband you'd run from, not the Lord God?"

Esther blew her nose as they continued walking. "Don't you see? I feel I may be in danger . . . and the children, too." She put her hands on her protruding stomach. "With the next baby coming, well . . . I just don't think it's a good idea to stay put."

Annie was at a loss to know what to say. "Are you afraid of Zeke?"

"Jah, awful much." Esther sniffled and began to cry. "He's impossible to understand, truly. I don't know what he's capable of doin'." She rambled a bit, telling tidbits about the ups and downs of her husband's moods.

Then her voice grew stronger. "I found the oddest thing here lately, while doing a bit of sorting. It was a small burlap bag . . . with dozens of peach pits inside. They looked to have been washed clean and set out in the sun to dry and bleach a bit."

"Sounds like Zeke's still grieving his brother's disappearance."

"Well, I've heard him whimpering in his sleep the past month . . . more than ever before."

Annie's heart went out to both Esther and Zeke. "Too bad there isn't some way for one of the brethren to talk with him . . . to let him pour out the bitterness somehow."

"Funny you say that, 'cause Bishop Andy came over one evening some weeks back. He and Zeke hurried out to the barn. The next day, Zeke was ever so kindhearted toward our little boys while Laura was at school. But then, later that night, he turned ugly again."

"Does he drink, do you know?"

"I've smelt it on his breath some."

Annie pondered what to do. "Would you want me to say something to my mother? In confidence, of course."

Esther's eyes flashed disdain. "Well, why would you do that?"

"Only that she would talk to Daed . . . see if something can be done."

Turning, Esther looked her square in the eye. "If I wanted to tell a preacher, do ya think I'd be whisperin' all this to *you*?"

Annie felt terrible. She'd said the wrong thing, she knew . . . hurt her friend's feelings. "Ach, I'm awful sorry. I just want to help if I can."

"I daresay you must want to tell it around, that's what."

"No, now listen, Esther. You have my word. I'll keep your secret . . . but is that the right thing? For you and your coming child? For Laura and Zach and little John? Is it?"

"I should've kept quiet, looks to me like," Esther said softly.

Annie felt empathy, as well as a good measure of anger at being misjudged. "Well, I'm warning you now, if I ever see you with a black eye or other bruises, I'll be goin' straight to my father. Hear?"

Esther shook her head, tearstains on her face.

"Look," Annie challenged, "do you believe the Lord God gave us women the ability to think or not?"

"Maybe so. . . ."

"I say don't let any man trample you into the ground. Who cares how some of the menfolk treat their wives and daughters, or how our great-grandfathers did back when. It's time Zeke started showing you and your children the kindness and love you deserve, Essie!" She couldn't believe she'd just spoken Esther's old nickname.

Letting out a little gasp, Esther turned away. She didn't even bother to say good-bye, just trudged back toward the barnyard on the rutted dirt path, the fringe of her black wool shawl bouncing as she went.

Well! Annie crossed her arms and took several slow, deep breaths lest she holler one final remark and cause even more strife in poor Esther. *Maybe it's good I'm not getting married anytime soon. Even if I ever meet a man who measures up to Rudy.*

Chapter 26

Much of the night and now this morning, too, Annie had been stewing over Esther and their impulsive conversation. Esther's comment about wanting to disappear upset Annie horribly. *Surely she won't lose her head and do something stupid!* Yet Esther had been clearly distraught out on the farm road.

Annie's thoughts were jarred by Yonie's voice as the two of them worked together, milking the cows before breakfast. "How do you expect your fancy friend to be content at all if she doesn't have any wheels while she's here?" Yonie asked her. "Louisa's used to drivin' a car, ya know."

Annie considered that. "Well, on one of her first days here, Louisa did say she wanted to learn how to drive the team. Both Omar and I volunteered."

"So, did ya teach her then?"

"Haven't yet."

"What're you waitin' for?"

She smiled. "Christmas, I guess."

"Which is almost here." He patted the backside of a cow.

Annie watched Yonie move from one cow to another, so at home with the farming routine. She was dying to ask him about his English girlfriend, but she thought better of it, aware that both Daed and Luke were coming and going, hauling five-gallon milker buckets between here and the milk house.

"You say Louisa's plannin' to stay longer." Yonie removed his black work hat and scratched his head where it was flattened and oily. "But if she does, it'll be right surprisin'. I can't imagine her giving up her car for too long. Downright odd."

She had to speak her mind. "You've got cars on the brain, ain't so?"

"Aw, Annie, why would you say that?" He looked sheepish.

"You're smitten with talk of wheels, that's what." But there was more to it. She'd heard through the grapevine that not only was Yonie taking joy rides with Dory Zimmerman, but that she was teaching *him* to drive, too.

He eyed her, holding her gaze. "I'm not ashamed of running around. If this is the worst thing I do, well, then . . ." He put his hat back on. "Besides, I'm doin' what I want to, just like you."

"What's that s'posed to mean?"

"Don't play pretend. You have your secrets."

Her heart was hammering. *What's he know?* "I think you'd better tell me what you're accusin' me of, Yonie-boy."

He looked over his shoulder and all around the milking area. Then, leaning closer, he said, "Where'd ya ever learn to paint a picture, sister?"

Her breath caught in her throat. *Who spilled the beans?*

"What picture?" she replied, trying to keep her composure.

He took his time answering, shuffling his feet a bit and looking away, as if he were in trouble. "Well, I've been spendin' a lot of time at the Zimmermans', to tell you the truth, and you best be keepin' what I'm going to say quiet, ya hear?"

"I won't say anything. What picture?"

He looked relieved and continued. "Just listen. Dory's father lets me sit in his office there at the house and read."

"What're you gettin' at?"

"Yesterday, I was sitting and soakin' up the sun, on such a cold day. And I happened to be poking around in one of his new magazines, and, well . . . your name was listed on the inside cover, as a winner in an art contest."

She gasped inwardly.

"There you were: *Annie Zook of Paradise, PA.*"

This was the last thing she'd expected to hear. "You're pullin' my leg, Yonie, I just know it."

He studied her curiously. "No, I think you're pulling *mine.*"

"What do you mean?"

"It seems you've won yourself a place on a magazine cover."

This cannot be! She froze, scarcely able to breathe.

His probing gaze held hers. "Unless there's another Annie Zook round here . . ."

She wouldn't lie. Yonie would see right through her.

Such horrid news! And, right then, the tiniest possible thrill, the joy of winning something, vanished completely.

Even so, on some uncanny and wonderful level, this was lovely news to her ears. Someone besides Cousin Julia and Louisa was now aware of, and appreciated, her work.

All of a sudden, the terribleness registered in her brain. *My painting will be seen by all who subscribe! My lifelong secret will be discovered.*

She leaned down and reached for a three-legged stool nearby. Daed's eyes would offer a stern yet silent warning at first, if found out. Then he would open his old Bible and read slowly, thoughtfully. If she did not adhere to the Ordnung and abandon her artwork, she would be asked to leave home.

"You all right?" Yonie frowned.

I'm sunk, that's what.

He squatted beside her. "What's-a-matter?"

"How large is the print—for my name?" She wiped her face with the hem of her black apron.

He looked at her with disbelief. The truth had definitely registered. "So it *was* you. Annie. What's this about? You lead a secret life?"

Slowly she began to explain how someone had talked her into entering a painting in the contest. She didn't say "one of her paintings," because she must keep him in the dark for as long as possible. "Being a first-place winner is a curse, for sure and for certain." She eyed him now, hoping he might understand her next request. "You must keep this under your hat. Promise me!"

He nodded. "And in return will you do a favor for me?"

"Say the word."

"Tell no one 'bout my visits to Dory Zimmerman, all right?"

"That's easy." With the mention of the mail carrier's daughter, the wheels began to spin nearly out of control. "Wait a minute! Which of the People subscribe to that magazine round here? Any idea?"

He shrugged. "Sure seems more geared to the English."

"Jah, good," she said, still thinking ahead. "But how can we know for certain? There's got to be a way, what with Dory's mother delivering the mail. Mrs. Zimmerman has a wonderful-good memory. . . . I daresay if she sees it, she knows."

Yonie nodded, then he hurried to empty one of the milkers, pouring the contents into the tall milk can. "I take it you want to find out . . . and soon. And you want Mrs. Zimmerman's help?"

"No, not hers . . . Dory's."

Just then, they heard their father returning from the milk house. "I'll tell ya what." Yonie leaned closer and whispered, "I'll talk to Dory tonight. See if I can figure out a way to get you out of this jam."

"Thanks, Yonie. Let me know what she says."

Annie made her way down the center walkway, cow tails flapping on either side. Between her and Yonie, they were a good team, and they might be able to save the day. *Just maybe.*

Letting her mind wander unchecked, she imagined confiscating next month's issue of *Farm and Home Journal* from rural mailboxes. Of course, she wouldn't actually consider committing a crime. Still, her mind was working overtime to devise a way to keep her father and the brethren from knowing of her secret hobby.

But what could she do? The December issue was already out ... with her name on the inside cover, along with other artists, although Yonie had said the print was rather small. Still what were the chances of *that* being missed? These farmers liked to read every word!

Feeling glum, she headed through the barnyard, buttoning her old brown work coat, glad for it, as well as her holey gloves. She contemplated all the happy days surrounding Christmas and knew she must enjoy them to the hilt this year. Because unless she and Yonie could cook up a plan to thwart the arrival of the magazine in neighboring mailboxes, the end of her artistic pursuit was clearly in sight. Maybe her future here, too.

Thank goodness Louisa's here! she thought. *My one supporter.*

She was also grateful for something else: Yonie had not asked where she'd hid out to do her painting. She was not ready to divulge that information anytime soon.

Talk about wanting to disappear!

The spare bedroom in the Dawdi Haus was large enough to accommodate two beds—a firm double situated between two windows, the other bed a plump three-quarter daybed pushed against the far wall. Annie had given Louisa first choice but then nearly insisted she take the larger bed with its attractive four posts after Louisa had picked the smaller. Now that they had been settled in for several weeks, Annie was rather glad to have the daybed, where she occasionally snuggled with Louisa's gentle and friendly kitty-cat. She and Muffin had become good pals, but only if Louisa was nowhere in sight. Then, and only then, was Annie a close second.

Tonight though, Muffin was nestled in Louisa's arms. Annie watched the kitty's eyes go half-closed each time Louisa stroked his little head. "Did you ever write back to your parents," Annie asked, "about the family reunion?"

"I wrote a long letter, but I haven't heard back. I'm sure they're peeved at me for snubbing my nose at their idea. No doubt I'm a total washup in their eyes."

"Well, I'm awful glad you're staying." Annie plumped her pillow. "How would you like to go ridin' tomorrow after we get home from Julia's?" she asked. "I think you need more fun in your life."

"Don't be silly." Louisa lifted the cat close to her face. "I'm having the best time, Annie. Do you think I'd want to stay longer if I wasn't?"

It was surprising to see how relaxed and cozy Louisa looked under several of Mammi Zook's heirloom quilts.

"Where do you want to go tomorrow?" asked Louisa.

"Anywhere, really . . . but with *you* holdin' the reins. It's time, don't you think?"

Louisa leaned forward, eyes alight. "You mean I finally get my first driving lesson?"

"Jah, it'll be you, me, and Yonie."

Louisa smiled at that. "He's nice . . . all of your brothers are."

"Yonie's fun loving, that's for sure."

Louisa asked if it was a good idea for her to be in control of a horse, "out on the road, I mean."

"No worry. Yonie can take over quickly if need be."

"Probably a good idea," Louisa admitted.

They talked briefly about the weather, that a cold front was coming in and what they might do if a snowstorm hit during the night. Annie hoped they could still go, all bundled up with mufflers and foot warmers . . . with the horse hitched to their small sleigh.

Later, when Louisa was still second-guessing whether or not she ought to try directing a horse, Annie simply said, "If you can fit in round here like you do, I don't see why you couldn't manage to drive us over to stock up on some candy for the holidays, maybe."

Louisa's smile inched across her tired face. "That could be interesting. But you might never want to ride with me again."

"I thought we could go to Sweets for Sweeties—you'll like that shop. They have every imaginable candy and then some," Annie said, recalling that Mamm had been asking for a purchase of some hard candy to give to the grandchildren at Christmastime.

Finally, she got around to telling Louisa her news of having won first place, although she was reluctant, not wanting to sound bigheaded. "I'm shocked, truly."

Louisa leaped out of her nest of quilts, coming around the bed to sit on Annie's. "This is so cool! How did you find out?"

"Oh, from the grapevine." She was stuck, had spoken much too soon. Yonie would have her head if she said more.

"Come *on*, Annie . . . don't be vague. How did you find out without me knowing it? You're with me twenty-four-seven!" The green in Louisa's eyes by some peculiar means seemed to overtake the blue suddenly. Annie had noticed this once before. Whenever Louisa became overly excited, the color in her eyes would change.

"You'll see for yourself the next time we go to Julia's." That was all she cared to say. She knew better than to say more. With Yonie working on his plan, whatever it was, she could not risk implicating him.

Louisa continued to stare at her. "So you're not going to cough up the full story? I'm dying here. I'm so excited for you!"

She'd never known Louisa to be this demanding. "It'll have to wait. I've said enough."

"I don't get it." Louisa shook her head, looking awfully befuddled.

"Well, it's late, that's what." Annie scooted past Louisa on her bed. She went to the bureau and reached for the gas lamp and blew it out.

"Congratulations, anyway," Louisa said in the darkness, finding her way back to her own bed.

Annie wished she'd kept the news to herself. *What was I thinking?*

Chapter 27

The bejeweled ice pattern on the windowpane was so thick the next morning Annie had a difficult time finding a clear enough spot to peer out. As the sun rose past the horizon line, over distant sticks of trees, she found a singular transparent circle on the glass, through which she glimpsed the barnyard below. "Goodness' sakes, what a lot of snow. It's a blizzard out there!"

She heard the rooster crowing repeatedly and remembered how Daed's father, Dawdi Zook, sometimes said the changing of seasons was a fearsome thing. The beginning of something, as well as the end.

Feeling the cold air whoosh through the space between the base of the window and the sill, she couldn't stop thinking about the astonishing first-place announcement. The news had wormed its way into her dreams last night, as well. *A startling end, and yet a beginning in some ways, too. The end of my terrible deceit . . . forced upon me.*

Across the room, Louisa stretched in bed, and Muffin moved from his spot near the double lump that was Louisa's feet and yawned widely before moseying up closer to the pillow. "This bed is so comfy," she said sleepily.

"My first nephew was birthed right there," Annie said.

"Argh! That's TMI!"

"What?"

Louisa laughed. "Too much information, Annie."

"Well, it's true. Jesse Jr. and Sarah Mae stayed in this room for a while after they were married." Annie turned her attention back to the window, peering out. "Too bad, but I'm afraid your driving lesson will have to wait. We'll have to take the sleigh over to Julia's today . . . one of the boys can drive us."

"Horses don't have trouble getting around in the snow?"

Annie shook her head.

"So I guess you never had to miss school for bad weather when you were a kid."

At least she's not asking about the art contest again, thought Annie.

She slipped into her bathrobe and made her bed. "I can't remember ever not getting to school, really. 'Least not for a snowstorm."

"Do you typically get tons of snow in December?" Louisa asked.

"We have plenty, jah." She told how the whole family enjoyed sledding, "except for my grandparents, of course."

"Your parents actually go?"

"Well, not every time. But Daed built a toboggan just for the two of them. Mamm squeals all the way down the hill . . . and she loves it."

Louisa nodded, stretching her arms above her head. "I can't imagine my mom doing that! But *I'm* all for it."

"Since Christmas falls on Sunday this year, there should be oodles of fun on both Saturday and Monday. Of course, we'll have Preaching service all morning Christmas, and then the most delicious feast afterward, which will be nothin' like the common meal every other Sunday, with cold cuts and Jell-O, no. It'll be more like a wedding feast with a roast and all the trimmings . . . and lots of candies and cookies."

"Food and feasting is a big part of your church life, isn't it?"

"Yonie likes to say, 'the three *f*s—food, fun, and fellowship.'" She smiled, recalling that. "As for food, I know of several Amish couples in Lancaster County who make extra money serving seven-course meals to English tourists two or three nights a week. So, I believe we *are* known for wonderful-good home cookin'!"

"I'll probably gain ten pounds while I'm here!"

Annie glanced at Louisa, who was making her own bed now. "A few extra pounds won't hurt you none." She tossed a pillow at her friend, then headed downstairs to heat water for the wash-basins.

———

Julia opened the side door as Annie and Louisa trudged up the steps. "Hurry inside, girls. Isn't this the most snow we've had in quite a while?"

Annie turned and waved to Yonie, who had been kind enough to bring them. "Looks like fallin' pigeon feathers it's so thick." She spied little Molly, her dress matching the fabric of Julia's, cleaning out a mixing bowl with her fingers, then licking them off. *Cake batter,* Annie guessed and hurried over. "Don't you look 'specially perty in your new dress."

Julia told how she'd found a bargain at the fabric shop. "I guess I really stocked up this time . . . bought enough material to make six or seven dresses. So I made me one, and Molly, too. I'll make dresses for my sisters and their daughters, too, sometime soon."

Annie smiled. "Mamm often does that. Why pay more when you can all look alike, jah?"

Just then, she spied the *Farm and Home Journal* lying on the telephone table over by the window. She didn't mean to stare, though she was anxious to see what Yonie had already mentioned to her.

Evidently the magazine was uppermost in Julia's mind, too, because she marched right over and picked it up. She opened the magazine to the first page. "I'm thrilled to show you something, Annie." Her eyes shone with happiness. "And I can't say I'm one bit surprised, either."

Annie waited, partly eager to see her name in print but dreading the conversation sure to follow.

"Your lovely painting—'Obsession'—has won first place." Cousin Julia pointed to the page and held the magazine out for both Annie and Louisa to see.

Annie looked hard at her name, seeing it for the first time. The recognition alone was more than enough honor, she felt.

Even though Louisa already knew, she gushed all over the place. Then little Molly came and gave Annie a little squeeze around the legs, congratulating her in her own way.

"Isn't it grand?" said Julia. "Here's a letter from the magazine. I imagine it's about the art classes you've won."

Annie nodded but remained silent. She went and sat down at the table, wishing someone else might've won. "It's so hard to believe, really." *Could it be a mistake?* "In the most peculiar way, this is the death of a dream, I'm sad to say."

Julia's smile turned to a quick frown.

"If my father gets wind of this—and how will he not?—I'll no longer be welcome to sit idly by, not joining church. I'll be a thorn in his side ... forced to make a choice, one way or the other!"

Louisa pursed her lips, looking concerned.

Julia folded her hands. "I never wanted to cause trouble for you. I hope you know that."

Annie contemplated the irony of it all. "Jah. . . ."

"This might seem strange, but I hope this might open the door for you to have a discussion with your parents . . . especially your preacher-father."

That's absurd, Annie thought. But to Julia, she said simply, "Honestly, I don't know any woman who does such a thing . . . speaking up to a minister, related or not."

Women are not to speak up to men at all, and especially not to the ministers. Anyone knew this.

Thinking on it, though, she recalled one time in particular when *she* had not only talked up to her father, but talked back. She had been one week shy of turning fourteen when Daed caught her sitting on a milk can out behind the springhouse, drawing the redbud trees in full bloom with a handful of stubby colored pencils.

When her father happened upon her, he did not have to stop and remind her of her previous disobedience, no. Without a doubt, this was the *second* time she had been in hot water with him, and they both remembered all too well.

Without speaking, he had reached down to take up her colored-pencil picture, deliberately tearing it into small pieces. Her anger soared beyond the limits of her ability to subdue it, and without thinking she uttered words that never should have been spoken to a parent, let alone a preacher. Still, she felt justified in spouting off, *"What right do you have?"*

Daed had not merely rebuked her with fiery eyes and his

words, but he had also struck her, once, as well. He forbade her to demonstrate such outright rebellion ever again. *"You're not old enough for rumschpringe, and yet you defy me!"* he said, eyes burning with his own fury. It was the first time he had ever raised a hand to her.

That night, all curled up in bed, she felt like a whipped puppy. And in the quietude of her room, with tears falling fast, she made a mental journey, going back to all the times she had drawn or colored little pictures for her pen pal, who seemed to appreciate them each time she slipped one into her letter, Daed none the wiser.

Later that week, when Julia happened to visit, asking Mamm about the possibility of hiring Annie part time, Annie jumped at the chance. But she'd had an ulterior motive from the start—remembering the empty little garret room. *I'll do my drawings there,* she decided before ever consulting with Irvin and Julia. Soon enough the Rancks' attic became the only refuge for her forbidden dream.

"Annie? I hope I haven't offended you," Julia was saying.

Offend was too strong. After all, Annie had given the go-ahead, although reluctantly, to enter her painting. "No . . . no. You mustn't feel bad."

Even so, Julia wore a concerned look. "The next magazine will be out in about a month . . . mid-January, I'd think."

Annie glanced at Louisa, who had been very quiet, perhaps deliberately keeping her nose out of it. "Honestly, it's beyond me how my parents *wouldn't* see or hear of this."

"Well, I happen to believe you could make it outside the Amish community, Annie . . . if it were ever necessary, I mean," Julia said.

Annie didn't feel like thinking about a future without the

People, nor did she wish to give up her art. What most begin-ning artists would have longed for, she wished to reject. The glory of winning had scarcely had time to register in her brain, and now it was gone from her altogether.

She could hardly wait to talk to Yonie the following night. Even at supper, Annie kept trying to catch his eye. Finally, she did . . . and her curiosity was piqued even more when he nodded his head toward the door later on while eating Mamm's pecan pie and homemade vanilla ice cream.

What'll he tell me? She hoped against hope something could be done to thwart the delivery of the January issue of *Farm and Home Journal* to local subscribers. Or, if not, that Yonie would have some idea how to keep their father's anger to a minimum.

Her hands trembled as she washed dishes, passing them off to Louisa to be dried. As much as Louisa already knew, Annie was almost certain she hadn't noticed the exchange of glances between Yonie and herself. At least if Louisa had, she wasn't commenting. *Thank goodness!*

When the kitchen was sparkling clean, Annie waited for Louisa to slip over to the Dawdi Haus and then headed for the wooden wall rack out past the cookstove. Pulling on her heaviest jacket and then her boots, she was glad for the peace—no one around to observe her leave by way of the back door. She tromped through the snow to the barn, heart racing.

In the lower level of the barn, she found Yonie rubbing his hands together. "It's freezin' out here, jah?" she said.

"So let's make it snappy. I've got good news for ya . . . at least I think you'll agree."

"What is it, Yonie?"

"There are only three farmers in our church district who get the magazine, and Daed's cousins, the Rancks."

"Who are these farmers, and do you think they'll be talking to Daed 'bout it?"

"Not till mid-April, prob'ly."

"What do you mean?"

"Well, one of the farmers is out in Nappanee, Indiana, for the winter, helpin' ailing relatives. The others are down in Florida—snowbirds, ya know?" He was smiling too much, the usual teasing glint in his eye. "I doubt you have much to worry 'bout till spring, Annie-kins."

"You mean it? They won't get their mail for another three months or so?" Oh, this was beyond her best hope. *So wonderful-good!*

"Far as I can tell, no one in our church district, at least, will be notifying Daed." He went on to tell her how he'd discovered all this . . . by asking Dory's participation and keeping it quiet from her mother, the mail carrier.

Annie breathed a sigh. *A bit more time to enjoy my art,* she thought.

"I think you need to know you're not out of the woods on this." His near-perpetual smile had faded.

"What do you mean? I thought you said—"

"The magazine is based near Marion, Kentucky, but it goes out to farmers and others all over the country. Daed has cousins near and far. 'Specially in Wayne County, Ohio, so who's to say someone might not notice your name in the December issue or see your painting on the next?"

She felt her shoulders droop and was suddenly as fretful as she had been at the thought of the magazine winding up in one of their church members' mailboxes. No longer did she care to know what the cover would look like with her beloved painting plastered on it.

"*Be sure your sin will find you out.*" Her father's words from long ago echoed in her mind.

"What will I do, Yonie? What'll happen to me?"

He shook his head. "I guess you should've thought of that sooner."

"Well, too late for thinkin'. If I catch it, I'm out."

"Won't be that cut and dried," he said. "But if I were you I'd walk away from this artist thing you're caught up in. Right away."

"Easy for you to say. You're being groomed to be a farmer."

He eyed her. "Well, it sounds like you think that's not such a grand thing."

"It's fine, all right . . . for you. What's expected." She felt bad now . . . didn't want to say another hurtful word. Not to the brother who had gone to some trouble for her. "You know what? I'm sorry," she said. "I don't mean to be sassy. I'm grateful for what you and Dory did for me."

"Good, 'cause I swore her to secrecy, too."

She looked warily at him. "You had to tell her?"

"No gettin' around it."

Puh! Too many folk know. . . . She shivered with the knowledge, as well as from the cold. "We ought to head inside lest someone misses us." She thanked him again.

"You owe me," he said as they hurried back to the warmth of the house.

"I keep my promises. Don't you worry none."

Chapter 28

Louisa had never been involved in making so many cookies of different kinds and shapes in her life. Baking and running errands with Annie and her mother, as well as attending yesterday afternoon's Amish school Christmas program, had taken up much of their time during the past week. Even at the Rancks' there was much to do to help the family prepare for the holiday. There had been little time to be taught to drive a horse and buggy, but she could wait for a better time.

Meanwhile, she had begun a new drawing of the quaint well pump coated with a fresh sprinkling of snow. She could easily view it from her vantage point in the Dawdi Haus bedroom, working without having to camouflage her art as Annie continued to do. Often she felt apologetic because Annie insisted she openly work on her drawings while Annie couldn't—or wouldn't.

It has to be a pain to hide what you love, she often thought and sometimes contemplated the apparent incongruity of it—a group of people following stringent rules they imposed upon themselves. The concept of an unwritten system of expectations and required behaviors—expounding what is good or evil, although discussed by the ministers and voted upon by the church membership twice yearly—was mind-boggling. Had she not come here to experience it for herself, she never would have perceived the riddle of the Amish from Annie's letters. The freedom she had always envied, which she believed Annie had managed to take for granted, seemed to come at an exceedingly high price.

The thing most amazing about deciding to stay on here was the notion that her coming may have bought some creative time for Annie. But now, with Annie's worry of being found out by her father—and she fumed over this constantly, even whispering late into the night—Louisa wondered if it wouldn't be a good thing if her friend's secret *was* discovered. That way some understanding could possibly begin. *Either that or she and I will be looking for an apartment somewhere off Route 30!* But she knew she'd never encourage Annie to leave her roots. What was the point? Her life was all wrapped up in being Amish.

Louisa still had not deciphered how Annie had known of the first-place win before ever going to Julia's. But she had more than enough on her mind today—up to her proverbial earlobes in cookie dough and chocolate frosting.

In the middle of the morning, a knock came at the front door. Annie and her mother and three sisters-in-law turned their heads to look in unison, appearing quite startled, as nobody, except outsiders, ever used *that* entrance!

Annie hurried off to answer it, and when she returned carrying a large vase of red roses, Barbara Zook let loose with a string of astonished Dutch. Soon, Sarah Mae was chattering, too, and all of them were observing Louisa, as if they knew instinctively this bouquet was not intended for Annie.

"These are for you." Annie held the vase up.

Amazed, Louisa couldn't imagine who would be sending her flowers *here*. A dozen at that.

Annie went with her to the table, where Louisa carefully placed the glass vase in the center. "Look, there's a little card with it," said Annie, seemingly eager to know what Louisa herself was curious to see.

This must be from my parents . . . or Michael. She pulled the small card from the plastic holder, opened it, and read: *Merry Christmas with fond memories of us. Thinking of you, Trey*

"Michael or a secret admirer?" Annie whispered, wide-eyed.

"Not so secret now." The surprise overwhelmed even her— the thought of Trey doing something like this. And how had he known where to send the roses?

Unless . . . did he contact my parents? That was the most likely scenario. Trey had not received a return call from her, so he'd called her parents' home. *Too weird.*

"Roses are for love," Annie whispered later in the day, when she was admiring them on the bedroom bureau. "Are you *sure* there isn't something still 'tween you two?"

Could there be? Impossible! Too much had passed since they'd parted ways. Besides that, she was on a quest for peace and understanding far from city lights and metropolitan madness, whereas he had gone to seek all the exhilaration one London town could offer.

"Trey was always very thoughtful, that's all it is," she said. "Probably . . ."

———

Louisa was amused at Annie's attempt to bundle them up for the ride once they were settled in Yonie's courting buggy. "Must be miles away to Esther's," she said while Annie continued to tuck lap robes around them.

"Oh, trust me, you'll be ever so glad for all these once we get goin'," Annie said as they waited for Yonie. "Your driving lesson's long overdue, ya know."

Louisa felt terribly restless now that she sat here staring down the long back of the enormous horse. "I had no idea we were going out this afternoon . . . with all this snow."

"It'll be fine, you'll see. There's little or no traffic out here, so we'll be safe from cars. The snow will be plowed to the sides of the road, but if too many cars get behind us, we'll pull off and let them pass. Then, when we return home, we'll all go ice skating on the pond behind our neighbors' barn."

"Danz or Lapp?"

"The Lapps . . .'cause we have a standing invitation from them anytime we want to skate," Annie said. "Awful nice, jah?"

Yonie came dashing across the yard, making boot-sized holes in the snow. "All right, let's go!" He climbed into the buggy next to Annie, but to Louisa he said, "All set?"

"As ready as I'm going to be."

"Well, if you want the horse to know you're in charge, it's best to hold the reins with confidence," he advised.

Louisa had no idea how to make the difference, but she sat up straighter and the reins became slightly taut. "Like this?"

"Much better." He was nodding and smiling. "That's just right."

"Now what? Should I say *gee*?"

Before Yonie could reply—and even with her rather soft directive—the horse began to move forward. "Wow, I didn't realize how easy *that* was." She laughed at herself, still as nervous as she'd ever been.

"This horse is very responsive," Yonie said. "Besides that, you're a natural, Lou."

Lou? There is it again, she thought. The nickname sounded so right somehow. "Do you really think I'm a Lou?"

"Seems fine to me, jah," Yonie said.

Annie nodded. "A good fit it is."

"A big departure from prissy Louisa," she admitted.

"Well, I like both names equally well," Annie said.

Louisa snickered. "Lou is much less fancy, jah?"

Now Annie and Yonie were the ones to laugh. "It strikes me funny when you say *jah,*" Annie said, her breath releasing little white puffs into the air.

"It's such a cool way to say yes, you know? And I think I do like being called Lou . . . it's new. A nice change."

"Hey, Lou is *you,*" Annie sang. "The new you!"

The new me. . . . She wondered if being called something different from her given name was a way to distance herself further from her modern life, to turn over a new leaf. Not that she was becoming enamored with the Plain culture, because being born into this subculture was the only real hope of successfully fitting in. Although Annie had told of a handful of folk she'd heard of, especially in other communities, who had attempted to join the church out of sheer frustration with the stressful life of the modern world. Most outsiders failed in such an endeavor, largely because they did not attempt to learn the language— Pennsylvania Dutch. The grueling work schedule also had a tendency to discourage them.

On the flip side was the idea that a Plain person, such as Annie, could make it on her own in the hubbub of the high-tech world. Louisa suddenly thought of herself, wondering how difficult it would be to reemerge into her former life . . . *when she was ready.*

A girl named Lou would not mesh so well in a complicated world. She smiled to herself, holding the reins for not only this powerful horse but for her own life, at least for this season of time. *I'm in charge . . . and I like it!*

"You're doin' just great," Annie said, instructing her to tug on the right rein just a little before the next intersection. "Then, after that, it won't be but a mile or so more before you'll see the Hochstetlers' driveway."

Louisa was careful not to move the reins too much, but when it came time to say *gee* and pull on the right rein, she did it with as much poise as she could muster, her body stiff. She held her breath, watching the horse strain on the harness as it made the turn.

Once they were headed on the next road, Yonie announced that she looked like "an old horse hand."

"If both of you weren't cheering me on, there's no way I'd ever want to attempt this," she confessed. "Way too much power at the other end of these reins."

"That's right," said Yonie. "You don't want to take a horse this size for granted, but I picked our gentlest and oldest for today."

"Well, thanks." She leaned up a bit, glancing his way, feeling edgy about moving around too much. The experience had taught her some interesting things, but after they made their cookie exchange with Esther, she would gladly give up the reins to either Yonie or Annie for the ride home. But she *would* like to try again on a road minus the snow pack.

Upon their arrival at the Hochstetlers', Louisa couldn't ignore Esther's swollen red eyes and suspected something was very wrong. She assumed Esther and her husband were having some conflict, because as soon as they headed into the house, he hightailed it out the back door, presumably to the barn. In turn, Yonie followed behind. Louisa had quickly discovered that most Amish males spent much of their time working outside. *Better than in bars*, she thought, wondering what could be troubling the tall man with haunting brown eyes.

Awkwardly she stood in the kitchen, much of it in disarray. Dishes were stacked high in the sink, and a bucket of sudsy water provided a needless obstacle in the middle of the room. The mop lay willy-nilly on the floor, while the youngest boy toddled around the bucket, leaning into the water to splash and cackle, oblivious to his mother's melancholy. One end of his diaper dragged behind him.

Louisa spied the older boy playing quietly with a mere five blocks in the sitting room, between the kitchen and the front room, talking to himself.

What happened here? She looked to Annie for clues, hoping Esther was not a victim of spousal abuse.

Annie, too, must have sensed something amiss, for she put her arm around Esther and guided her to the table, where they both sat and whispered in their first language.

Louisa wasn't sure where to put the several dozen cookies she'd carried in, so she set them inconspicuously on the far end of the table. Then, removing the plastic wrap, she chose one on top, with a big glob of frosting on it, to give to the little boy with the droopy drawers.

"Ach, no," Esther said quickly, turning toward her. "Little John's not to have much sugar."

"Oh . . . sorry."

"He has bad asthma," Annie volunteered, sitting close to

Esther. "And sugar seems to feed the problem."

Feeling suddenly useless, Louisa set the cookie back on the table and went to the wood stove to warm up, watching the little tyke mumble to himself as he continued making his futile yet contented circle around the bucket.

Annie and Esther eventually switched to speaking in English. And even though she had no interest in listening in on their muted conversation, Louisa wondered if this was Annie's way of including her. She couldn't quite understand why that would be, however.

But she could not ignore what was being said, that Esther was troubled . . . something about her husband threatening her with "the shun" if she didn't stop talking about a "newfound friend." Whatever that meant, Esther's tone of voice triggered a deep-seated alarm in Louisa.

From everything Annie could gather, Esther had stumbled into Cousin Julia, of all things, this past week at the Progressive Shoe Store. Esther was adamant now that their chat was "ever so providential." Talking with "this most wonderful-good woman" had raised her spirits, at least for a time, Esther said.

"Another dose of your Mennonite kin was just what I needed." Esther's blue eyes began to sparkle now with each mention of Julia. "She shared things I must admit to never havin' *ever* heard. Oh, I honestly ate up what she was sayin'." She lowered her voice, even though it was only Louisa and the boys hearing what she had to say.

Whatever had transpired between her cousin and her close friend, Annie felt at a loss to understand. Having known Esther her whole life, she wondered now why Esther had paid such little attention, if any at all, to *her* advice. And the more Esther talked of "saving faith," Annie experienced an empty sensation, wishing she might have been the one to help Esther instead of a Mennonite interfering, whether Esther thought it Providence or not. It was altogether clear that Julia's words had affected dear, distressed Essie.

"Why the tears before?" Annie asked her.

The sound of splashing of water ceased as wee John sat down on the floor patting the leather boots beneath Louisa's Amish dress. With the kitchen too quiet all of a sudden, Esther simply shook her head.

"C'mon, tell me," whispered Annie, reaching for her hand.

Esther looked about, then leaned forward, her nose bumping Annie's ear. "Zeke threatened to report me to the brethren," she confided.

Report her?

"Why on earth?" Annie whispered back.

"Oh, but he's right, ya know." Esther's face fell again, and tears sprang to her eyes. "The People will look on me as ever so haughty . . . jah, the sin of pride, they'll say. For sure and for certain."

Annie's heart was in danger of breaking. *Ach, she believes she's got herself saved!*

———

The lanterns rimming the shoreline were mesmerizing as Annie skated around the far rim of the Lapps' large pond. Louisa was close behind, doing "ice laps," as she jokingly called her everlasting loops. Annie wasn't sure, but she thought Miss Lou just might be determined to ignore Trey's kind gesture of the bouquet of cut roses. *What a shame to waste such pretty flowers!*

she thought, skating much more slowly now as Louisa whizzed past.

She had heard once, when she was a girl, the notion that if you wanted a boy to fall in love with you, a rooster's tail feather would easily do the trick if you pressed it three times into your beau's hand. That alone was supposed to make him love you forever. The old tale was the most outlandish she'd ever heard. Yet pondering romantic love made her wonder how Louisa's former beau had happened to resurface here and now, via the roses.

As for Annie, there was plenty on her mind to make her want to skate "till the cows came home," which had already happened twice today, as she'd helped put milkers on a good two dozen of the herd earlier this afternoon, following their visit to Esther.

Louisa slowed her pace and came over to skate alongside Annie around the rim of the pond. It was clear that she, too, had something on her mind. "What's with Esther and her husband?" she asked. "Is she always that upset?"

"That's between them."

"Well, what's he doing to her? Do you know?"

"Not for sure."

"But you must suspect something's wrong, don't you?"

Annie looked at Louisa as they made the turn at the lake's narrow end. "The women are to mind the men. That's what we're taught." She had promised not to spill the beans on Esther.

Louisa continued to press for answers. "Are you saying . . . even if you knew for sure Zeke was beating Esther, you wouldn't contact the police?"

"Never the police. It isn't our way."

"Then, what *is* your way?"

"Well, God's way, according to the church."

"So . . . let me get this straight. You simply turn a blind eye when husbands abuse their wives?"

Annie felt the sting of cold . . . and the harsh words.

Louisa must have noticed and quickly apologized. "I'm sorry, Annie. I know you care deeply about Esther . . . and you would help her if you could. I'm sure you feel quite helpless."

"Jah, 'specially when she looks so pale and exhausted . . . and expecting her baby soon."

Indeed, her befuddled friend's eye-opening disclosure weighed heavily on Annie's mind. That and the fact that Esther seemed to be losing the ability to keep up with her chores and her children. To help her catch up some, Annie and Louisa had finished mopping the floor and doing the dishes while Zach gathered up the toys in the sitting room at Annie's request. Annie even picked up little John and put him in a clean diaper, then into Esther's arms for a quick nursing. Esther had nearly weaned him, knowing full well she'd be kept busy with the new baby here before long. Besides, young John's baby teeth were becoming a problem, she'd said quietly.

Hemmed in on all sides, thought Annie.

Skating over a stray willow twig, Annie put out her arms to steady herself, then kept going. She considered Julia's involvement with Esther, which still flabbergasted her, in spite of Essie's ongoing struggle. *What right does my cousin have imposing her religious opinion on Essie?*

Oh, there had been occasions when Julia had talked about the Lord or heaven or what she liked to call "the gift of God—eternal life." But for the most part, Annie had paid little attention, letting it go in one ear and out the other. It wasn't that she wouldn't have been long-suffering enough or willing to hear Julia out; she just didn't see why she should compound her problems with unknown doctrine, or whatever it was her cousin was spreading around. Her own problems, though suppressed at this moment, were big enough to keep her up pacing the upstairs sitting room at night.

How long before one of our cousins in Ohio sees Annie Zook of Paradise, PA, is painting in her spare time and says to himself, Well now, isn't that Jesse Zook's girl back East?

Annie could hear it now, the ruckus such a disclosure would raise with her father first and foremost. Then it would filter into every crevice of the church district. People would wag their tongues like dogs catching flies. *That awful wicked girl . . . doesn't she know better?*

Annie had been noticing Louisa nearly every night sitting and drawing in her sketchbook in bed. Sure, she'd urged her friend to feel free to do so, but she hadn't thought Louisa would quite so often. Not with Annie propped up in her own bed nearly pining away for a graphite pencil and her own artist's pad. She often imagined what it would be like to openly convey her ideas on paper . . . or to sell her drawings unframed in small bins where customers could simply look through and discover a special gem. Louisa had recently sold several more paintings to the art gallery on Route 30, and Annie had decided to give Louisa the art classes she'd won as a special Christmas gift, since there was no way she would ever go.

What would it be like not to have to sneak around? she wondered.

Then it struck her like a brick out of the sky. *If the People would shun Esther for simply being led astray, what would they do to the preacher's willfully disobedient daughter?*

Chapter 29

Annie's stomach began to gnaw and rumble during the final hour of the second sermon on Christmas Day, and she couldn't resist breathing deeply to get a whiff of the roast and all the fixings warming in the bishop's old black cookstove. Each family remaining for the special dinner had also brought along a tempting dish. Some brought more than one. She only knew of a few who would be heading home for their own family dinners, so there would be a big crowd staying put at the bishop's big farmhouse today.

Smelling the delicious food, she was more than ready to hear from Deacon Byler, who rose to announce the location of the next meeting, as was customary. Then he continued. "Our brother Rudy Esh, along with our sister Susie Yoder, plans to marry next month, along with several other couples."

Annie paid close attention, although the words did not register immediately. Yet she had been expecting this "publishing" of the wedding news for some time now . . . and here she was, on Christmas Sunday, witnessing what might have taken place for herself and her former beau. *They're thick on each other, so they ought to marry*, she told herself.

Next thing, Susie's father walked to the front and stood

before them, announcing that a January tenth wedding—"on Tuesday"—was to take place for his daughter. "Those of yous sixteen and older are invited to attend the wedding service at our place."

In no time at all, Rudy will be a married man. Annie realized at that moment she was quite all right with the announcement. She actually had pleasant thoughts for the couple . . . not feeling regretful at all. Thankfully so.

Following the preaching service, Jesse situated himself among the group of older men just inside the barn, waiting for several of the younger men to move the benches around in the house, creating long tables for the common meal. He glanced up and noticed Zeke Hochstetler hurrying across the snow toward him.

Will he cause a scene on Christmas Day yet? Jesse wondered.

He anticipated what he would say if Zeke threatened to go to Bishop Andy with his malarkey. Truth was Jesse hadn't bothered with Zeke's request at all. It made no sense to speak to the bishop when he knew precisely what Andy would say. *What's done is best left alone,* he thought.

Zeke came right up to him and asked if he could have "a word" with him, and Jesse nodded, stepping out from the group, none of the men taking much note. "What's on your mind?" He almost slipped and said *son,* which would have been a bungle.

"I've been wonderin' where you've been." Zeke looked right at him. "I thought we had an understanding," he muttered.

Jesse wouldn't stir the fire by making an offhand remark. Instead he said, meekly as possible, "It's best all round to leave it be."

Zeke grunted. "No, I'm not going to rest till something's

done. If you can't get the bishop to move on this, then I will. And I won't wait."

"Well, I see no need for anything rash."

Looking around, Zeke's jaw was set in a dogged clench. "Where's the bishop now? I'll talk to him myself."

"I'm tellin' ya, Zeke, this is unnecessary." He reached out a hand.

Zeke brushed him away. "Isaac's dead, and I want the murderer caught." Lowering his voice as he looked around, he said, "I want some justice for the blood of my brother."

Jesse heard the misery seeping out. There was no getting around it, Zeke was unable to manage his grief or the knowledge of the boy's death. "Ain't our way, and you know this. We don't press criminal charges . . . or any for that matter."

"Well, this is the exception to that rule!" Zeke's words were biting now, and his eyes glowed with pain.

"It's best if we not bring the English world into our own. It is imperative."

But Zeke continued to urge, only for Jesse to put him off. "It is *always* best to err on the side of obedience. And that is my final answer," Jesse said. "It is Christmas Day, Zeke. Let's rejoice together in the advent of God's son."

Downtrodden as ever he'd looked, Zeke turned and clomped back through the snow, away from Jesse. *Will he bend his will and come under?* Jesse could only speculate, quite concerned that Zeke might do something foolish. Something to jeopardize all of them.

Louisa had charged up her Palm on Friday at Julia's, and by keeping it turned off since then, she had enough power to place several Christmas calls. She was hesitant to use it within earshot of Annie's church friends, all of them still hanging out at the deacon's place following the Preaching service. She'd kept the device tucked away in her dress pocket during the service, aware of the lump in the cotton fabric.

While the other women were preparing for the common meal, Louisa stepped out onto the porch and speed-dialed her home. She was relieved when her dad answered. They talked casually, and he did not once mention Michael's name this time. "We miss you, Louisa, but hope you're having a good Christmas there." Then, when he'd said "Good-bye, dear," he put her mom on the line, and even she was not pushy. *They've backed way off,* she thought while her mom rattled off about this function and that they had attended. "How *are* you, Louisa?"

"I'm doing well." *A safe answer.* "Thanks for the Christmas present. . . . I didn't buy any this year . . . needed a break from the mall scene. And, well, that whole shopping nightmare."

"We thought you might need a new watch, dear."

"It's beautiful," she replied. *But I won't wear it here.* She wondered if this was her parents' way of alerting her that it was *time* to get over her little fit and return home.

"Thanks for thinking of me." She wanted to be polite. Well, she did, and she didn't. The purchase of the diamond-studded watch was not the best choice for one who wished to loosen her grip on material possessions.

"Are you eating healthy food?" Mother asked.

"Straight from the moo to you."

Mother actually laughed into the phone, almost too loudly, too freely. And then Louisa realized why. They had been drinking, probably a few too many glasses of wine with Christmas dinner. *Dinner alone . . . just the two of them, and why? Because their only child had abandoned them. Perfect reason to get sloshed!*

"I hope you both have a Merry Christmas," she said.

"You have a nice time there, too, Louisa . . . with your Amish friends."

"Well, bye, Mother."

"Good-bye, dear."

Wow, Mother didn't fight to keep me on the phone. Weird. New tactic?

She didn't know, and she really didn't care to analyze the conversation to death. Instead she called Courtney and was oddly relieved when her friend didn't answer. Somehow she knew Courtney would give her grief about jumping ship. She left a cheerful Christmas greeting on her voice mail and disconnected.

Then she pulled her sleeve back and looked at her simple watch with its plain brown leather band. She calculated ahead five hours from eastern standard time, assuming Trey probably wouldn't be having supper yet at six o'clock his time.

Annie stepped onto the porch, startling her.

"What on earth?" Annie said, eyes blinking and very serious. "Best not be takin' any chances."

She'd pushed her limits. "Oops, sorry. . . ." Not wanting to cause further alarm in Annie, she eyed the area of the springhouse and set off tramping through the snow to the more private spot.

Louisa checked for Trey's current cell number, stored in her incoming list of calls. It was the polite thing to do to call, to thank him. A dozen roses of that quality—roses that actually opened beautifully—didn't come cheap.

He surprised her by answering on the second ring. "Trey here," he said, sounding nearly British.

"Hey, merry Christmas. It's Louisa."

"Well, it's great to hear your voice."

"Yours, too." It certainly was, and she was quite glad she'd found a quiet spot to chat. "The roses were so gorgeous . . . well, I mean they *are*. Thanks."

"I had the hardest time tracking you down, girl. What are you doing in Amish country?"

She laughed. "So you must've called my parents?"

"Your mom told me about the wedding. I'm truly sorry, Louisa."

"Don't be. I'm having a blast here . . . sorting out some head junk."

"So, let me get this straight . . . you ran away from the wedding altar to go and hang with your Amish pen pal?"

"Uh, close."

"Which part?"

"I didn't exactly bail at the altar." She paused a moment. "Let's just say I would've been out of my mind to take that plunge."

"I can't say I'm disappointed," he stated, followed by an awkward pause. Then—"I understand you're living in an old drafty farmhouse . . . probably not much different from the old digs I rent. Man, the winters chill straight to the bone here."

She smiled into the phone. "Yep, I wake up to the sound of peacocks, roosters, and cows every morning. Bet you can't believe that."

"It is surprising, Louisa . . . knowing you."

Not wanting to go there, she quickly asked, "How's the art business?"

"Booming . . . you'd be surprised. Actually, you wouldn't." He paused. "I hope you're still painting—you have the magic, girl."

"Well, I don't know about *that*," she said, beaming inwardly. "I do have a buyer for my work, though, here in Lancaster County."

"At a gallery?"

"Yep."

"Sold anything lately?"

She gladly filled him in, and he responded with the enthusiastic support she remembered so well.

"Well, let's keep in touch, okay?"

She warmed to his words. "You have my cell number now, but I don't have electricity here at Annie's. I charge up twice a week down the road."

He chuckled, that deep and jovial laugh she'd always enjoyed. "I hope you're kidding."

"Actually, I'm not."

"Really? No electricity?"

"None."

"Running water?"

"Some."

"This *is* interesting. Too bad you're not a writer. You could turn this funky experiment into a novel."

She let out a little laugh, feeling terribly vulnerable . . . the way his voice gave her goose bumps. "I just might, at that. But it's really not an experiment. It's a most needful thing." She'd picked up on this phrase at Julia's one day and liked it. Trying it out now seemed both strange and truthful somehow.

"Merry Christmas, Louisa. Terrific connecting with you."

"Same here. And a happy New Year, too."

"I'll call you soon."

"Bye."

She scarcely noticed how rough going it was getting through

the snow back to the house or how she'd begun to shiver. All she wanted to think about was the fantastic conversation she had just had with a most amazing guy, who, it seemed clear, was still interested in her.

I forgot to ask for his email address. She laughed at herself, questioning her own motives. *No, I won't chase him,* she decided.

Jesse sat enjoying his second dessert of carrot cake in Deacon Byler's kitchen, where a number of the older men had lingered following their Christmas feast.

He bit the inside of his cheek as he noticed Zeke making his way toward him, this time with Esther in tow. *What's this? Has he already blabbed the secret to his wife?*

"Esther here has somethin' to say," Zeke said, not pulling any punches.

Jesse got up from the table and motioned for them to follow. *Where could they go for privacy with a houseful of people?* He eyed the stairs and headed there.

When the three of them were shut away in the smallest of the upstairs bedrooms, Zeke blurted out, "Esther, go on . . . tell the Preacher what you did."

The young woman blinked her pretty blue eyes incessantly, cradling her swollen stomach. She looked at her husband, then back at Jesse, clearly nervous. "I . . . well, it's awful hard to explain."

Jesse was moved with sympathy and touched her elbow, guiding her to the only chair in the room. "Rest yourself," he suggested, and she quickly did so.

"Now, go back and start at the beginning." Zeke kept his distance, standing near the door.

"I've known a few Mennonites since I was a little girl,"

Esther said. "But this one lady, not so far from us, well . . . she's always been kind to the children and me. Seems to seek me out . . . as a friend, Julia Ranck does." She continued, reciting the various occasions she had encountered Jesse's own kinfolk.

Zeke became impatient and raised his voice. "Get on with it, woman. Tell what wrong thing you did!"

Esther immediately looked down, biting her lip. Jesse had a hankering to interfere, once again aware of the intense conflict between the two. But he waited, his heart entirely too soft to this lily of a woman who had often spent hours with Annie under his own roof.

"It's just this. Only this," she whispered. "I've found the Lord, at long last. Or maybe I should say He's found me."

"We are *all* followers of Christ and His church," Jesse replied.

She was shaking her head now. "I'm not talking 'bout man's rules."

Zeke spoke up, "She's fallen for this like a boulder in a fish pond, Preacher."

Jesse indicated with his hand that Zeke should calm down and be quiet. But when Zeke continued to rant, Jesse knew he had a larger dilemma on his hands. Not only was the man itching for conflict, he had more than one ax to grind. Jesse must firmly address the issue at hand and hope, it being Christmas, that Zeke's urgency for hunting down Isaac's killer might diminish.

Esther spoke again, eyes bright with tears. "I believe what my friend Julia reads from the Scriptures. I'm not ashamed to say I'm a follower of the Lord Jesus."

Zeke snorted a laugh. "See? Didn't I tell ya, Preacher?"

"I see no reason to ridicule your wife." Jesse turned to Zeke, putting a hand on the man's shoulder.

"Well . . . go ahead. Ask her!" Zeke was close to shouting, rebuffing him. "Ask her if she's saved."

Before Jesse could do so, Esther was bobbing her head. "I have nothin' to hide . . . and nothin' to lose, neither one. I've given over my sins—my very life—to the Lord. I'm redeemed by His blood."

All kinds of buzzers were going off in Jesse's head. He had only once encountered such a problem with a church member. *Embracing an alien belief*, he thought, suddenly feeling less merciful. "Well, now, ya know declaring yourself saved is the most prideful thing a person could possibly do, don't you, Esther?"

Zeke nodded his head fiercely. "Oh, she knows, all right. She's testin' ya and she's mighty good at it."

Apparently there was no limit to Zeke's smart-aleck approach. "I'll be talkin' with Preacher Hochstetler and Deacon Byler on this," Jesse said, presently feeling the need to distance himself from the couple.

"Well, and while you're at it, be sure 'n' see Bishop Stoltzfus 'bout that other important matter we discussed," Zeke demanded.

Jesse held his peace, but what he truly wanted to do was to cut loose on the younger man. But he squelched the impulse for a full-blown confrontation with their mouthiest church member. "You'll be hearin' back from me—both of yous." But he had no intention of squabbling with the bishop.

Turning toward the door, he opened it and walked as confidently as he could muster into the hallway and down the stairs.

Chapter 30

A gray smothering of clouds was suspended near the earth the whole week following Christmas, and although the atmosphere seemed conducive to snow, none fell.

The People marked the New Year by going from one relative's house to another, visiting extended family near and far. Some of the aging parents with more grandchildren and great-grandchildren than they could count knew they would still be having so-called Christmas dinner get-togethers come Easter. And many of those same youngsters displayed their Christmas gifts in the sitting room for visitors to see, especially teenage girls who had received a first "good china" cup and saucer or floral dish for a hope chest.

It was nearly Epiphany, the day often referred to by older church members as "Old Christmas." Annie's father asked her to pick up a new harness at Cousin Irvin's tack shop. Louisa hadn't been feeling well, because she'd caught a nasty head cold and was nursing a fever, as well. So Annie headed out alone with the team.

Her younger brothers were busy helping slaughter steers three farms over, and Daed was tied up with the ministers over at the bishop's place. Annie was glad the majority of the pre-

Christmas snowfall had turned to slush, at least on the main roadways.

Finding herself with the only horse left at home, one of the slowest driving horses Daed owned, she figured she might as well take her time to get where she was going. She settled into the front seat, glad for all the weight of the lap robes, as well as several heated bricks Mamm had given her for the trip.

Her thoughts meandered back to Christmas dinner—of observing Zeke coercing Esther to speak with Daed. Poor Esther's eyes were terribly pained and her big belly protruded like she was surely close to her time of delivery as she and Zeke followed Daed up the long staircase. Annie guessed Zeke was urging her to confess those things she'd already told Annie—of having found a friend in Jesus, in so many words.

Perhaps this is also the reason for Daed's meeting with the brethren today. She shuddered to think of her long-time friend being put under the *Bann,* if only for a few probationary weeks. Even still, knowing the tenacity Esther was willing to exhibit—rare for a woman—Annie wouldn't put it past her to endure the punishment without coming under the Ordnung. No, if anyone could hold her ground against the ministers it was Essie Hochstetler. *And her best sidekick . . . me.* Annie stifled a smile, knowing she ought not to be at all proud of it and wouldn't think of saying so to anyone. Least of all her father.

In the small parking area outside the harness shop, designated for horses and buggies, Annie tied her father's horse to the hitching post and headed inside, aware of the jingling bell on the door.

The first few days of Ben Martin's new job had blended uneventfully with the instruction Irvin Ranck had so kindly offered—the cleaning and refurbishing of harnesses. Ben enjoyed watching Irvin lay out the inventory of leather, using patterns to cut out and sew up harnesses. Some were quite ornate, as in the matching sets of six for a team of Belgian horses. He hadn't needed extensive training in the trade, having kept himself busy with horses in Kentucky—especially at the Saddle Shop near Marion, where he had been employed since high school graduation. A lover of horses and racing, he had spent many summers as a groom at Churchill Downs, home of the Kentucky Derby, and filled his other leisure hours with stints as assistant coach for the local high school's football team.

The obnoxious dinging bell alerted him to the next customer, and when he looked up, he saw a blond Amish girl coming through the door. She was so pleasing to look at he was caught off guard . . . failed to call out his usual greeting. He could not overlook the confident tilt of her head and the purposeful way she carried herself. She was now walking toward him, and he had to remind himself to breathe.

When he found his voice, it was excessively strong. "May I help you, miss?"

"Hullo. Well, I hope so," she replied, smiling, " 'cause it sure was a long ride over here in the cold."

Is she merely mischievous? He didn't know. Certainly not flirtatious, he didn't think, although there was a curious twinkle in her eyes. *Blue . . . they're definitely blue.*

"Cousin Irvin must've needed some help round here, jah?" she said.

He nodded, captivated by her demeanor . . . the fact that she did not seem put off by his being non-Amish and her being every bit as Plain as the four hundred or so horse-and-buggy-folk who'd settled in Crittenden County in Kentucky, where he had grown up.

"My father's in need of his order, and I s'pose you know what that would be."

"I'll look it up. What's the name?"

"Preacher Zook," she said. "That's not me, of course. My father's one of the ministers round here."

A *preacher's daughter*, he thought. And this one was made of pure spunk.

He pulled his grin into check and hurried off to look up the order for a Zook. He hadn't recalled a farmer with that name coming in to drop off a harness since he started the day after New Year's, but there had been so many unusual surnames floating around. Glick, Stoltzfus, Lapp . . . and more.

So . . . how does a guy go about getting a date with an Amish chick? he wondered, answering himself promptly, *He doesn't, nut head.*

Returning with the newly refurbished leather harness, he rang up the bill, aware of her fragrance there in the midst of leather and oil. Not the earthy, soil-beneath-the-fingernails kind of aroma he expected, but the spring-fresh smell of a young woman. Not more than twenty, if he was correct. He didn't care to analyze that his mouth had gone ridiculously dry, but he knew he had to at least discover her name.

"We checked the stitching, replaced what needed replacing, and made the harness as safe as possible," he said. "Here you are." He handed her the bill.

"Oh, just put it on the tab . . . that's how Daed always does it."

A dozen lines flew through his head. How to get her to

introduce herself? "Who should I say made this request of the outstanding charges?" he asked

Her soft blue eyes put darts in his toes. "Just tell Irvin his cousin's daughter was here . . . he'll know by that." She turned to head toward the door.

No . . . no, wait, his brain was saying. But he refused to make a fool of himself. He stood and watched her push open the door and head into the daylight.

The thought crossed his mind that he might not see her again. So the memory of the jangling bell was all he had of her.

On the ride home, Annie considered Cousin Irvin's hiring someone outside of his own conservative circles. It made no sense, because she could see the young man wasn't even remotely Plain . . . no outward indication, at least. With her Mennonite cousins being devout in their strict beliefs, she was baffled why that would be.

The hired help had seemed to have trouble keeping his eyes off her, which was a bit surprising because she'd never considered herself pretty. *Maybe he hasn't seen many Amish before,* she thought. *But, no, how can that be?* He would have to wear blinders on those irresistible brown eyes not to have seen the likes of her . . . head covering, cape dress, apron, and all.

But even if her initial impression was correct, she had little hope of speaking with him again, unless she volunteered to run errands for Daed and maybe even her married brothers, too. But that was absurd. *Why should I be thinking this way? He's an Englischer, for pity's sake!*

On the morning of January tenth, Annie sat straight and tall, keeping her full attention on the bride and groom as they stood before Bishop Stoltzfus.

Lou, who was feeling much better, sat next to her, far less fidgety than she had been during Preaching services. Annie guessed Lou found this wedding quite foreign to the extravagant plans made for her own wedding day last fall.

Mamm sat on the other side of Annie, nodding off from time to time, probably because the house was much too warm. Three hundred people provided too much body heat, packed in as they were.

At the feast, though, Annie was seated across from Obie Byler, the deacon's cutest son, but she did not care to engage in much conversation with him. Each time she looked up, he was smiling over at her, though, showing his teeth like he was proud of how straight they were . . . *like a horse, nearly!*

Truth was, she kept thinking back to her encounter with the new fellow at the harness shop, wondering what her father's cousins were thinking, being "unequally yoked" as they liked to say, between themselves and a modern employee. Mennonites came in all shapes and sizes, just as there were a myriad of Amish groups. Maybe the young man with eyes as big as a cow's—and an intense gaze to match—*was* actually one of them.

Ach, maybe he's someone Lou would enjoy getting to know. The thought crossed her mind just as she was putting her fork into her slice of apple pie. But perhaps Louisa was having more than her share of male attention presently, what with Trey's long messages on her cell phone every few days and Michael's enormously long letter through the mail.

Annie craned her neck to see where Lou had ended up, and when she found her, she wiggled her fingers in a quick wave and smiled at the interesting combination she witnessed down the table from her. Louisa was sitting across from Rudy's first cousin, Noah, who wore a noticeably deadpan expression, quite clearly aware he'd been paired up with a worldly girl in sheep's clothing.

Chapter 3-1

The clutter of her sketchbooks was beginning to annoy Louisa. She dry mopped the bedroom, and when that was done to her satisfaction, she sat cross-legged on the hardwood floor and began to organize. "Who would've thought I'd use up so many pages drawing here," she said more to herself than to Annie, who was cleaning her own side of the room.

Annie looked over, pushing several stray hairs behind her ears. "Is it more than you draw at home?"

"Hard to estimate . . . besides it's been two months since I left." She continued what she was doing, glancing over at Annie every so often, wondering how she was feeling with Rudy having given his heart publicly to Susie Yoder a week ago. "You okay?"

Annie nodded, coming over to sit on her bed. "You're talking 'bout Rudy and Susie, ain't so?"

"Whoa, that's scary. We're starting to think alike."

Annie's face lit up. "I like that part of bein' sisters with you, Lou. So, I guess you can never go home."

"Hmm . . . I don't know about *that*." She studied Annie and decided she looked tired. "You didn't think you could keep me here forever, did you?"

Annie's eyes were bright with some help from the blue light of dusk shimmering through the windows. "We both know this isn't permanent. And I won't be sad when you say you've had your fill."

"Promise me that?"

Annie laughed right out. "Ach, I doubt I should say such a thing. Who's to know how I'll feel when that day comes, really."

Before arriving here Louisa had never been much for asking pointed questions. Of course she had posed plenty to Michael the night of their breakup. But other than that, she hadn't recalled expressing herself so fully with another person. Not her parents and not even her almost-maid-of-honor, Courtney. "So . . . do you think Rudy and Susie are a good match?" she asked.

Annie took her time replying, removing her head covering and pulling the hairpins out of her bun. "It's not so much 'bout them being suited for each other as whether Susie will be a good housekeeper and cook, and if Rudy will be a good farmer who can make some basic furniture for the house. That's the real question. And knowing Rudy, I'm sure he'll be all of the above."

Louisa hadn't considered that the newlyweds might *not* be well suited. Wasn't everyone in the Amish community raised similarly, therefore a good match? She asked this of Annie, who was quick to shrug.

"We don't ponder ourselves silly over personality types and such . . . I happen to know 'bout this from the magazines I sometimes read at the doctor's office or at the library . . . well, I did back when my father let us go and check out books."

"No more?"

"Most everything's getting too worldly, he's decided." Annie's hair hung down over her shoulders, and she rose to get a brush from the top drawer of the bureau.

"Well, those 'winner's' art classes I took—thanks to you— weren't at all offensive. You easily could've gone."

"You know why I didn't go," Annie retorted.

"Yep, and you didn't miss much, as far as I'm concerned."

Annie frowned. "You must not have enjoyed it."

"Oh, I did. But I'm so not into abstract. You just never know, though. It might hit me someday." Louisa thought of Trey again. He adored abstract art—color-field painting and neoplasticism, especially Piet Mondrian's "Amaryllis."

"I would've been lost in a class like that," Annie admitted, staring at her now and then breaking into a big smile. "Do you realize you keep your head covering on till you slip into bed? And there's no need to, really. Once we're up here and the door's closed, it's all right to dismantle yourself back to bein' English."

The way Annie said it struck Louisa funny, and both girls broke out in peals of laughter.

When they'd composed themselves, Annie said, "Here's something to think 'bout . . . but I doubt you'll even crack a smile." She looked more serious as she brushed her hair. "There's an interesting fella you ought to meet . . . workin' for my cousin Irvin, Julia's husband."

"Yeah, I'm laughing. *Not!*" Louisa didn't care to tell Annie how weird it was to read a novella-sized letter from her ex-fiancé the same week as Trey's sweet-sounding words filled her voice mail.

"I'm not kidding, Lou. There's something special 'bout the guy."

"What's his name?"

"Don't even know."

Louisa eyed her. "So . . . he's not *your* style, is that what you mean?"

"He's English, that's all." Annie shook her head.

She's curious, though, thought Louisa. "When do you want to go back over there? Huh . . . huh?" She couldn't help it. Annie was so much fun to tease.

"Well, maybe Daed will have another errand for us to run for him. I'll see." Annie said this with a straight face—as naïve and guileless as ever.

She does like him! thought Louisa.

———

Her husband was in the process of rounding up the excess barn cats, and he might've shot them all in the head, in spite of what Esther had firmly suggested to do with them—put out a sign on the road: *Free Kittens.* And if Laura hadn't come wandering out to the barn just as he was loading his rifle, he might have done just that.

"Dat? What's that you're doin'?" their daughter asked.

The instinctive fright on her sweet face sent Zeke back to the ledge where he kept his gun. "Can you help me gather up some of the kitties to take to one of the farmers' markets—the Green Dragon, maybe?" He glanced disdainfully at Esther.

She ignored his glare, focusing instead on Laura, who nodded her little head and beamed a smile. "I'll go right now, Dat."

There was something that attracted cats to Laura. All animals, really. It was her gentleness and innocence, no doubt. Esther was secretly grateful Laura appeared when she had. Off Laura went to climb the haymow ladder, which was a good thing, because not but five minutes later, here came Deacon Byler in his family buggy, a long expression on his ruddy face.

"Zeke . . . Esther," the deacon said, removing his black winter hat. "I'd like a word with yous."

"Right away," Zeke said. He was raring to go, she could tell . . . mighty ready to have his whippersnapper wife shamed into repentance for *all this twaddle about being called by the Lord Jesus*," as he'd rudely stated right to her face a few hours before.

Ben Martin was unduly smitten. Preacher Zook's daughter, whoever she was, had his emotions by the throat, and he could only think of the next time he might glimpse her across the road, or far better, she might march back into the tack shop.

Or is there something I need from her father? I'll drive right over there. A good dose of religion, maybe?

He laughed at his own private joke as he worked, switching the hame strap on the front end of a harness. After all, if it was organized religion he was after, he would have nailed it by now.

During his short break time, he headed out through the snow to get a can of soda from the cooler he kept in his car. He inhaled deeply, taking the cold air into his lungs, totally jazzed to have signed a one-year lease on a 900-square-foot bungalow several miles from the harness shop. *Kentucky Ben walking on foreign but appealing soil, a long way from home*, he thought.

But where else could a guy work for an upstanding businessman like Irvin Ranck? Precisely the sort of man Ben had always wanted for a boss. None of the nonstop male chauvinistic blather punctuated by profanity, like at the last tack shop, his first job. Meek almost to a fault, Irvin was a man of few yet profound words . . . the most conservative man Ben had ever met. And he treated his wife like a queen.

Ben believed it to be sheer luck, among other things, that

had brought him to work in this little harness shop in a Podunk place called Paradise.

Taking a swig of his soda, he recalled looking out at the Amish girl's horse and carriage, wondering which direction she was headed. *This is silly*, he thought, picking his way back to the shop. But he shook the door enough to jingle the bell repeatedly, for the pure adrenaline rush of it.

———

She was out on her ear, or so Zeke seemed determined to remind her. Even after Deacon Byler left, Esther sat alone in the stillness of the kitchen, tears refusing to dry up. She had fully known what was coming, for she had been raised in the strictest of households, her own parents most mindful of the Old Ways. To think she had turned her back on the rigid expectations of her own church . . . *my own people*. And just today she'd been given yet another chance to renounce her new walk with the Lord. *How odd that embracing the assurance of salvation through God's Son is so frowned upon!*

Her lot in life, at least till such time as she "came to her senses," was for her to be separated from her own family while living under the same roof . . . here in this house where she and Zeke had made their home. Here, where she had been the ever-dutiful wife and loving mother.

She rose and moved slowly toward the stairs. Painfully she made her way to the bedroom where she'd shared all her married days with Zeke. But no more. If she was to be so arrogant as to declare herself "redeemed," then she was forbidden to engage in marital intimacy. *Who's going to check up on that?* She allowed the sarcastic yet comical thought to hold sway momentarily. *The deacon? Preacher Zook? Just who?*

She sat on the bed, collecting her wits, not wanting to be seen moving her personal items and clothing to the far end of the hall, to the tiny bedroom set aside for a toddler's nursery . . . where her next baby would reside, along with its mother, as she did not see herself bending her knee before the People. Not when what she fully believed was ever so right and good . . . and heaven sent, just in time.

I won't turn my back on this wondrous thing, she determined in her heart, unsure what the ramifications might be for her precious children. Not taking into account Zeke's husbandly needs and wishes, she must follow the shunning requirements, and what a pleasant respite . . . at least for a time. Zeke would surely hold her to the *Bann,* imposed by his own will and the church's. She shook her head, aware of the irony.

Esther held her stomach, so large now she could not see her own knees, let alone her ankles. A wave of sudden sadness, beyond the pronouncement of an impending permanent shun, was the stark realization that this child she was carrying would be her very last. And in her despondency, she prayed it might be a girl. If so, she would name her Essie, after her own lost innocence. That is, if Zeke deemed it acceptable.

When Louisa checked her voice mail, she was dismayed to hear Michael's voice. *Again!* Only this time he said he was booking a flight to Pennsylvania for this week—didn't say what day he planned to arrive—only that he was indeed coming.

"Oh, this is so lame!" she said while she hung out in the barn with Annie, who was inspecting the bridle and other parts of the many harnesses, in response to her father's request.

"What's lame?" Annie asked.

Sighing, Louisa groped for the right expression. "All right. It's the pits," she said. "Michael's determined to bust his nose in here and talk turkey."

"Himmel, not *that*!" Annie smirked. But then she must have realized the gravity of the situation.

"He says he has a new angle he wants to present in person." She wanted to have a royal fit—pull out her hair bun or throw something. But if she looked Plain, she ought to act it.

Annie looked at her stunned. She obviously didn't get it. "Well, why'd you say he could visit? Tell him to stay home."

Lou shook her head. "He left all this on my voice mail. Michael's like that. He doesn't wait for an answer . . . just barrels his way through."

"Honestly, I like a man like that," Annie said, surprising herself. "But is there anything he can do or say to change your mind, Lou, really? And if not, then it's a waste of money and time."

"Nothing will change my mind."

"Tell him to stay put, then." Annie could talk big. Louisa wondered if Annie would actually have done this if Rudy had decided to pull out all the stops after their breakup.

"Sure, I can do that. For the zillionth time," Louisa said. The last thing she wanted was Michael walking around here on Annie's turf. The thought of it made her livid, like it might desecrate the soil or worse. "I hope my Palm has enough power left for me to call him."

"If not, we'll go 'n' get some quick-like. We'll take Daed's fastest horse and the buggy and head straight to Cousin Julia's."

Louisa saw through Annie's suggestion. "By way of the harness shop, right? Hey, I know what you've got on *your* mind."

Annie blushed crimson, shaking her head all the while.

"I see right through you, Annie-girl." She was amused now. "I guess it's time for me to check out the harness shop dude for myself."

Annie blinked fast, and then gave a frown. "Dude?"

"Well, he'd have to be one if he's a modern boy hanging out at a tack shop, right?" She wasn't about to check the power on her cell now. "Come on, let's get going. I have a call to make!"

Chapter 32

Michael picked up immediately, and Louisa sensed he was at work.

"I want you to listen to me." She sucked in a deep breath.

"Hey! I'll be seeing you soon, Louisa. We can talk face-to-face."

He was not listening. He was railroading his way over her, the way he presented closing arguments in court. "No. The answer is no, even though you never bothered to ask," she said.

"What's wrong, babe?"

"Don't you get it? I'm done. We're finished. Cancel your trip."

"So . . . you've already hooked up with someone else?" This surprised her.

Immediately she thought of Trey . . . but that was so strange it was a sort of nothing on her radar screen right now. The fact was she'd found what she had craved: freedom to live her life.

She glanced over her shoulder at Annie, who was helping Julia in the kitchen. "It's not about another guy, which is really none of your business anyway."

He went silent on her, but she braced herself for the comeback. Definitely, there would be one. But *no*, she wasn't going to brace and she would not wait. "I'm going to hang up now," she said. "Good-bye, Michael."

Click!

Almost too easy, she thought, congratulating herself. And she knew Annie would be proud of her for standing her ground.

Ben followed the scent of woodsmoke, going to the door of the shop to look out. A quarter mile or so away, near Irvin's house, a lone Amish buggy was parked in the driveway.

Certainly he had work to do, but his feet were firmly planted as he waited and watched, curious to see who might emerge from the Rancks' door.

The phone rang a moment later, and he turned reluctantly. Answering, "Rancks' harness shop," he carried the portable phone over to the door and stood there, watching.

Paying attention to the broken English of the decidedly Amish customer on the line, he made a mental note. "I'll check on that order right away, sir. Have yourself a fine day," he said and hung up.

Fine day, indeed.

It was then that the horse began to rear its head, and one by one, the small pickets from the fence began to fly into the air. "He'll rip it to pieces," he muttered.

Grabbing his jacket, he hurried out the door. He considered driving the car over but quickly changed his mind, thinking the engine might scare the horse further.

Forget that, he thought, running across the wide field.

Annie heard the horse making a racket and excused herself from the kitchen, where she and Julia had been organizing all the lower cupboards and shelves while Louisa checked her email.

"Well, what's going on out there?" Julia asked.

"I'll go see." Annie said as she dashed to the door.

There, down on the driveway, the harness shop "dude" was attempting to steady her father's horse, and doing a fine job of it, surprisingly so. He had a hold of the reins and was stroking the horse's long nose and apparently talking to him, as well.

He's got a right gentle way, she thought, heading down the stairs to thank him.

"Hullo, again," he said before she could say it first.

"Well, now, looks like you just spared Cousin Julia's fence. Maybe she won't have to replace the whole stretch of it . . .'cause of you."

He nodded, extending his hand. "Glad to help. Any time."

She shook his hand, aware of his strength. "Thanks ever so much."

"I'm Ben Martin . . . and you are?"

"The preacher's daughter."

He handed her the reins, ignoring her impertinence. "This is one feisty horse," he said with a sly grin. "So then, you have no name?"

"Perty much," she said. And had it not been for Louisa coming down the back steps right then, Annie might've stood there wondering what forthright thing to say next, to keep this fellow's eyes from lighting up like an English Christmas tree every time she even uttered a word. But here came Lou, waving to them and smiling for all she was worth. "This is my good friend Louisa . . . she's decided she likes goin' by Lou, though. Say hullo to Mr. Ben Martin."

"Nice to meet you, Lou," said Ben, nodding politely.

"Same here. You're not from around here?"

"Good ol' Kentucky's my home. Fine horse country . . . you may have heard."

Annie had noticed the slight southern twang and was intrigued by the thoughtful drawl of his words. "Well, what brings you to God's country?" she asked.

That brought a laugh all around. Then, Ben seemed to focus his attention on her once again, which made Annie feel peculiar. "It's a long story how I ended up here, but for now I need to get back to the shop. Need to keep the customers satisfied."

She smiled, relieved to see he wasn't going to stand there and stare at her all day. "Cousin Irvin always says, 'The customer is king.'"

"And I agree. Nice meeting you both," he said, then turned to leave, patting the horse and whispering something to the animal before heading across the field back to the harness shop.

"Now there's a hottie if I've ever met one," Louisa whispered as the two of them stood watching him go.

"Oh, you and your English slang." She wondered if Louisa was at all intrigued by the newcomer. If so, too bad she'd decided to dress Plain while here. *Because Ben must surely assume she's Amish like me!*

So . . . she wants to remain anonymous! Ben was intrigued by such an outspoken girl and Plain, at that. He hadn't been in *such* a hurry to return to the shop. He'd used it as an excuse to hightail it back to privately consider the spark that had ignited when he touched the preacher's daughter's hand.

He wanted to see the Zook girl again. But he wondered what dark-haired Louisa was thinking . . . looking as if *she'd* like to go with him to Starbucks.

He knew he would probably second-guess this thing to

death. No doubt the girl who made his heart pound like a jack-hammer was probably already engaged. Nothing was ever this easy. . . .

Getting back to work, he decided to dismiss his ridiculous notions. What would an Amish girl want with an outsider anyway?

———————

They quarreled bitterly prior to retiring for the night, Esther pleading with Zeke not to raise his voice lest the ranting rise to the ears of their little ones who were supposedly asleep. But Zeke kept insisting she must "give up her silly little game."

"My devotion to God has nothin' at all to do with playing a game."

But, sadly, at the end of their disagreement, Zeke was more concerned about being without her in their bed. "Your punishment is mine, too," he stated fiercely, his fists clenched.

Her head throbbed with the knowledge of his anger. By her sheer ingenuity she managed to get away from the stinging words that spewed forth near endlessly. It wasn't that she lied to do so, not at all, for she surely *was* nauseated, even concerned with her baby coming in a few weeks. The stress of his confrontation was terribly taxing, and she needed a reprieve quickly. So she told him she must get some rest . . ."lest the baby come early." This seemed to help the situation, although he was surly all the way up the stairs.

His punishment, indeed, she thought, settling into the small bed in the corner room of the house.

Pulling up the layers of quilts, she knew that yet another punishment for her was the way the cold crept into this particular room, far from the heat source below them on the other side of the house. The lingering fires of the cookstove were located in the center of the kitchen, the warmth rising to the large bedroom where Zeke would sleep now, alone. And the only portable propane heaters they owned were situated in the children's rooms. Rightly so.

It was her darling children who encompassed her every dream this night, away from her marriage bed. First Laura, her oval face beaming with joy over the cuddly kitties she cradled in her arms, sparing them from a swift death. Then it was Zach and John pulling on a thick rope, laughing so hard they cried as they tugged . . . pulling . . . straining in their play. In helpless haziness, she was very aware of her dear threesome, and the baby growing within, in the vignettes of her many dreams.

Later in the deep of night, when she dreamt of her littlest boy struggling to breathe, she wakened with a start, sitting straight up in bed, wringing wet with perspiration.

Listening, she heard whimpering. *Am I still sleeping?*

Gingerly she raised her swollen self out of the foreign bed, rising as if in slow motion, unable to feel her bare feet on the floor at first. Then the familiar smarting—the sting of cold shot straight to the bone.

She moved about, attempting to locate her house shoes with her awkward feet, and quickly lit the lantern, keenly aware of Laura's small voice, calling . . . pleading for help.

Zeke sleeps through everything, she thought, shuffling herself along the long hallway, following the sound of Laura's voice.

"Mamma! Come help . . . Mamma, do come quick!" Laura called softly, having been programmed not to holler.

Then it was Zach's pitiful voice she heard. "Where *are* you, Mamma?"

The children knew better than to ever knock or call at the door of the main bedroom, lest they pay dearly for it.

Finally she stood at the door of Zach and John's room. What she saw made her gasp. There on the bed, being looked after by both his older sister and brother, was sweet little John, arms out at his sides . . . a frightening blue-gray pallor on his tiny face, evident in the lantern's light.

Oh, dear Lord, let him be alive!

She rushed to his side as fast as her weighted body would allow, and she leaned her ear down to his pale lips. Horrified, she began to press her own mouth over his, gently blowing a stream of her breath into him.

"Where were you, Mamma?" Laura's face was wet as she clung to her. "I was callin' ever so long."

Again she breathed for her wee son. And yet again. She could not simply let him slip away.

"Mamma . . . Mamma," Zach cried softly, hovering near them.

Live, my child . . . oh, you must live! She continued to coax air into his tiny round mouth . . . willing John to breathe.

At one point, between ragged breaths, she lifted him to her bosom, praying her nearness might revive him. *Somehow it must.*

"I'm here," she said to all her dear ones. "Mamma's here."

Chapter 33

Louisa awakened in the night, perplexed by her dreams. She and Ben Martin were riding bareback on a single horse through an open meadow of gleaming blue wild flowers, the wind in their faces and hair. She was no longer wearing Amish attire . . . she was back in her designer jeans and boots, encircled in Ben's arms.

Good grief, she thought now that she was fully awake. *What's that about?*

She had gotten up to use the chamber bucket beneath the bed, but on second thought she decided to pull on one of Annie's heaviest bathrobes and make her way outside for some fresh air.

The lingering visions remained even as she donned Annie's work boots and clumped out through the snow the short distance to the outhouse. The moon was bright enough to mark the way, and she smiled sleepily, wondering what could have triggered her subconscious to serve up such a weird dream. Sure, the blond-haired guy with inquisitive brown eyes was a hunk. But not her style, was he? And even if he was, he had eyes solely for Annie, of that she was convinced.

Maybe he's a temporary answer for her, she thought, even

though Annie had assured her she was no longer hurting over Rudy. Maybe this Ben guy could be her transitional man, someone to soothe her wounds and make her feel good about herself again. Like anesthesia.

Is that what Trey is to me? She surprised herself with the thought. And she knew better. Trey wasn't someone who was just filler in the larger scheme of things. He must have genuinely cared for her . . . simply stepping back while she completed art school, although he'd never stated this as his intention when he melted into the European woodwork back when. Now he was back in her life in a big way, calling several times a week, talking about a rendezvous in Colorado or even here in Pennsylvania. Emotionally, she felt she was keeping him at a safe distance. Even now. She wanted to be sure this time, wanted no residual stuff floating around. Nothing to get in the way of a new yet very warm former relationship.

On the way back from the drafty outhouse, where she'd encountered spiders galore earlier in the autumn—not so this time of year, when things were good and frozen beneath that disgustingly smelly place—she happened to see a car parked out on the road. She stopped walking, pausing against the cold. If she wasn't mistaken, one of Annie's brothers was leaning against the car, locked in an embrace with a girl. His silhouette—with a black winter hat—was stark against the moonlit snow.

Whoa . . . interesting. She was captivated by the thought of Yonie or possibly Omar sneaking around with an English girl, which it had to be, otherwise where had the car come from? Unless, perhaps, he owned a car and hid it from the eyes of their father, as Annie said some of the boys did during their running-around time. That, too, was another eye-opening concept. To think Amish parents allowed their teens to go pretty much their own way, offering freedom in the hopes of retaining them for the church. *The illusion of being given a choice,* she thought.

Shivering now, she made her way down the walkway and into the house, surprised that someone had been up and put extra logs in the belly of the woodstove. *Probably Annie's dad,* she guessed, wondering if he was also up checking on his absent son. She would ask Annie in the morning about what she'd seen tonight. *Love must be in the air!*

"Zeke! Wake up." Esther called to him repeatedly, even daring to shake him. "I need your help!" She was hollering now at him, Zeke lying there rather lifeless himself.

She heard Laura crying in the next room, where she'd left John and Zach. Now, attempting to rouse her husband, she called to him again, touching his face, his chest.

Getting down right close, she happened to detect the scent of alcohol. *Ach, no!* For the longest time, she'd felt he was staying away from his whiskey, but evidently whatever troubled him of late had gotten stronger footing once again.

Failing to wake him, she waddled back to the children, praying silently all the while, and feeling as panic-stricken as ever she had.

She lay down in the bed beside her tiny John, holding him near, praying aloud and asking the "dear Lord Jesus to return life to this child, just as you did to Jairus's daughter so long ago. This I pray, humbly . . . and not for my own sake. Amen."

She continued to cradle him, putting all her trust in the heavenly Father's love for her and her family.

Feeling a strange warm calm come over her, she placed her fingers beneath his chin, checking for a pulse. "Oh," she said, feeling the faintest beat. "Denki, dear Lord . . . oh, thank you."

"Mamma, what is it?" Laura tugged on her bathrobe.

"I believe your little brother is alive!" she said, looking into Laura's near hollow eyes.

Zach snuffed his nose and rubbed his face.

She sat John up and patted his back, talking softly to him, half praying, ever so near. He opened his small eyes, his long, thick lashes brushing his eyebrows, and he began to heave and cough . . . a deep, ragged rasp, spitting up as he did. The harsh yet all too familiar sound sent more shivers up her spine, but she was relieved to hear the coughing, which meant John was breathing indeed.

Going to the bureau, she opened the first drawer and took out his prescribed inhaler. Now that he was breathing, she would attempt to administer it.

She was determined to keep watch over her frail boy. *I'll put him right in bed with me!*—where she was now intended to slumber alone, for as long as she did not repent of finding the joy of her dear Savior and Lord.

O Jesus, it was you who spared my little one this night. I am ever so grateful! She prayed this silently as tears spilled down her cheeks.

———

Annie had something of a predawn ritual upon awaking each morning. If Louisa was even conscious that early she would sometimes drowsily observe Annie staring at the ceiling, as if contemplating her life. Or perhaps she was "saying" her silent rote prayers. Then, after a time, she would sit up in bed for a few minutes before slipping out from beneath the mound of quilts, going to the window to stand and look out.

This morning, however, Louisa did not wait for Annie to swing her long legs out of the bed and onto the ice-cold floor. She simply brought up what was on her mind. "I think one of your brothers has a girlfriend . . . and she doesn't look very Plain."

Annie was nearly angelic looking in her high-throated white nightgown. "He might just be pushin' the boundaries, but most of our boys do that."

"Well, there was lots of kissing going on, and I don't mean pecks on the cheek."

"Oh, that." Annie paused. "We're s'posed to just talk on those all-night buggy rides, ya know. But, honestly, many of the young people do way more than that."

"Don't we all."

"The main thing is gettin' all this out of your system before joining church."

"So, then, you must know for sure your brothers will." She was curious what Annie might say.

"Well, I'm perty sure they'll come to their senses."

"Like *you* will?" She had to say it . . . had to know what Annie was really thinking about her future as an artist.

Annie was on her feet all of a sudden, pushing her toes into soft slippers. "The difference 'tween a boy in love with a girl and . . . well, what I'm passionate about is awful easy: loving something that's not fickle. You know, like art. It's always there. Never betrays, never disappears, jah?"

She smiled at Annie's desperate attempt at honesty. "Hey, you don't have to convince me." Creating was such a big part of her life, she couldn't imagine having to choose art over a guy . . . or worse, over a belief system. "I'm not sure how you've managed to stay Amish this long, Annie."

"Well . . . it's the belonging . . . being connected to the community of the People." Annie patted her chest. "I know it in here. Like my father's faith in God."

What's faith anyway? Louisa thought. This was the hang-up of her life. The faith thing was so real and powerful and good that people from all walks of life embraced it on some level. Your "higher power," the AA folks called it, a confidence in something beyond oneself. But did it have to be all wrapped up in what *others* believed?

Whatever faith was, she didn't possess it. And she wasn't about to bring up the topic, not when Annie was eyeing the window again, preparing to race the dawn.

Work takes precedence over reflection in Paradise . . . most of the time, she decided.

Annie wasted no time talking to Yonie out in the barn. "You *Dummkopp!* Lou saw you with Dory last night!"

"How's she know it was me?"

"Well, she doesn't know for sure."

He squinted at her. "You didn't own up to it, did ya?"

"No, but even if I did, what would it matter? Lou won't talk it around."

He looked discouraged now. "We made a promise, remember?"

She nodded. "Louisa thinks what she saw was *one* of my brothers . . . and an English girl. Don't worry."

Yonie helped her pour the fresh milk through the strainer in the milk house. "You really have no room to talk, Annie . . . you sneak round, too."

"We aren't talking 'bout me, in case you forgot."

"All the same."

"I was only tellin' you so you'll be more discreet maybe."

Grinning, he said, "Well, now, aren't you quite the scholar? I've never heard you use such words."

"Seems to me, hangin' with Lou is one of the smarter things I've done."

Yonie walked with her back to the barn. "Just so she keeps her mouth shut 'bout what she sees past twilight."

They couldn't discuss this further, because Daed, Luke, and Omar were within earshot, getting ready to haul more milk cans to the milk house. For now she would take Yonie's remark at face value. Of course, Cousin Julia might call Lou's coming a blessing. But in *her* mind, having an Englischer visit here had opened her eyes to more things than she could begin to say.

Then and there, she purposed to make all their time together extra special, till that sad day when Louisa decided her "experiment" was over, that she'd had enough of country living and was ready to return home.

Chapter 34

Esther awakened to see Zeke leaning over and staring at her and little John nestled against her like a limp little lamb. She spoke softly, saying how grateful she was that John was better now, explaining what a horrid thing had happened—"our littlest one nearly gave up the ghost last night," she admitted, reliving the trauma.

Zeke frowned, shaking his head. "You mean you nearly let him die?" He straightened, and she realized how very tall her husband was, frighteningly so. He turned and paced the floor, then went to stand at the foot of the bed. "Sit up when I'm talkin' to you!" he demanded.

She trembled but quickly did as she was told, relieved to see John still resting, eyes closed, with a spot of color in his cheeks.

"If you'd slept in my bed, where you rightfully belong, instead of getting yourself put under the ministers' discipline, you would've heard John coughing and sufferin'. So it was your fault." Again he shook his head, looking down at the bed quilts before raking his big hand through his shock of brown hair.

His words cut through her, yet she refused to defend herself. Not with their little one lying here asleep, hair tousled, hands relaxed against the pillow.

"I hope you know it would've been your punishment—on your head—had our son died."

She did not respond, either in word or deed. He was picking a fight with her, she knew this well. Praying she might escape his wrath somehow—even this morning—she did not make eye contact with him further but turned to get out of bed. Reaching for her house robe, she lifted it and would have put her arm through the sleeve, but Zeke moved quickly to her side, as if he might help her do so.

Instead, he reprimanded her yet again. "How dare you disregard your own husband."

A soft answer turneth away wrath. . . .

In the case of Zeke, there was no indication that such an approach to communication worked at all. Evidently King Solomon had never met the likes of Ezekiel Hochstetler when he penned those words. In her daily experience, living with this oft-crazed man, no matter what she did lent itself to conflict. *It's no use trying,* she thought, no longer grieved but as angry as ever she'd been. But she contained her rage, breathing slowly.

She did not see it coming. In an instant, he raised his hand and slapped her hard on the face, the force of it pushing her whole body against the wall. "You will answer me!" he shouted.

Little John began to whimper, and she feared for him, as well. Her cheek smarting, she tenderly held her left side, worried she had hurt the babe within her.

Knowing from past incidents that she must respond or become the brunt of even more mistreatment, she nodded penitently out of sheer necessity. "Jah, Zeke, I do heed what you say."

He huffed and snorted like an enraged animal, and when she sat on the bed near her boy, Zeke miraculously exited the room.

The day she'd feared had come. *I must get away from here,*

she thought, aware of the throbbing pain.

"Come here to Mamma." She gathered John near. "You gave me an awful fright last night."

"*Millich*," he said softly, eyeing her bosom.

"Jah, 'tis nearly time for breakfast." She felt so terribly weak . . . too shaken to stand and cook. She longed to lie down and simply wallow in her pity like the big black and white hogs Zeke raised out back. But she was anything but lazy and wouldn't think of shirking her responsibility, not when she was so needed.

Filled with tremendous sadness, she opened her nightgown and lovingly offering her sweet breast milk to John as she rested against the pillow.

Setting the table for breakfast, Esther imagined herself knocking on Julia Ranck's door while the children waited in the buggy. *My only refuge,* she thought of her Mennonite friend.

Annie's house had never been an option, not really. For all the conclusions she'd drawn in her head . . . and for the reasons she'd given Annie the day they had been so plainspoken with one another, she simply could not flee to Preacher Zook's house. Neither was her widowed mother someone she could run to, because hers would be the first place Zeke would set out to look. She and the children would be welcomed at Julia's . . . safe, too.

For a time. . . .

Once there she could simply let the horse gallop home, pulling the empty carriage back to Zeke. That way he would have his best driving horse back and the family carriage.

On the other hand, Laura could easily walk the short distance to the one-room Amish schoolhouse, possibly attend tomorrow. Zach would entertain himself playing with James and Molly, and Esther could watch John closely. She'd thought of trying to have their doctor take a look at John first thing, but she knew why his asthma had gotten out of control and what to do to prevent it in the future. Such a thing would not happen again; she'd see to it.

As for birthing her baby, Esther knew that Julia would gladly, *lovingly* assist. Beyond that, she had no idea, but she wouldn't allow herself to worry over the future.

Not today. I'll put one foot in front of the other, nothing more. . . .

After Annie helped finish her milking chores, she hurried indoors to help Mamm with breakfast. Today it was fried eggs, apple fritters, leftover pumpkin nut bread, freshly squeezed orange juice, and black coffee.

The kitchen already smelled of her mother's dusting powder, which she patted on daily, even on the coldest winter days. That coupled with the frying fitters created a kind of fragrant cloud around her.

"Where's Lou?" Annie asked Mamm, who had set out the utensils already.

"Took off walkin' not more than twenty minutes ago."

Annie hurried to the table and began to place all the forks around, as well as the paper napkins and their biggest plates. "Did she seem all right?"

"Wasn't upset, if that's what you mean."

That's good, she thought, assuming Lou was perplexed, maybe even a bit stressed, too, over the many messages left by Trey.

"Are you girls plannin' to attend the quilting bee next Tuesday?" Mamm asked, flipping over the first fritters in the frying pan. "It's at Sarah Mae's this time."

"I'll go . . . but I'm not sure 'bout Lou." Honestly it seemed maybe her friend needed some time to herself, but Annie wouldn't mention it. Mamm had enough on her mind, what with taking oodles of baked goods to various markets several days a week.

Annie had also been thinking quite a lot about her best painting. Since she believed herself to be on the brink of being found out anyway, the least she could do was get her favorite work framed. She'd decided to ask Julia to drive her to the art gallery where Louisa had been successful in selling her own paintings. Since the magazine judges had chosen Annie's work for their cover, then, just maybe, the painting *did* have some merit . . . and she wanted to see it framed.

"Does Louisa ever seem homesick to you?" Mamm asked.

Annie sighed. She should've known a question like this might emerge at some point. Fact was, Louisa had settled in quite nicely . . . *for a fancy girl.*

"You'd think her parents would miss her something awful." Mamm was pushing for some kind of response; and out of respect for her, Annie knew she ought to speak up.

"Lou hears from her family some. She charges up her phone at Julia's and calls them now and then."

"She has no other close relatives . . . no brothers or sisters, jah?"

Annie shook her head. "Sadly, no." But her mother had known this for a good many years now . . . from all the letters.

"She must feel like she has a sister in you." Mamm forced a little smile, staring at the frying pan as if contemplating what she might say next. It was mighty clear Mamm had a talk on.

"Oh, we're sisters, all right. We've felt that way right from the start."

"And she shares her knowledge of art with you, as well?"

There it was! The thing Mamm was worming her way to.

"I watch her draw sometimes" was all Annie cared to admit. No sense volunteering more. The woeful day was coming, she knew, and she often had nightmares about it—Daed pushing her published art before her eyes, forcing her to behold her own sin, his eyes pinning her soul down but good.

Mamm turned and looked at her. "S'posin' I ought to rue the day your father ever agreed for Louisa to come here . . . but, Annie, I have to tell ya—'tween you and me—I'm rather fond of her."

"Jah . . . I've sensed that." Annie felt a tender pull toward her mother.

"Louisa certainly doesn't have to contribute money, and you must tell her this." Mamm was referring to Lou's sale of art, but Lou had never told them the origin of the money.

"Well, she's not one to wear out her welcome. She wanted to pay her way from the outset here."

"Oh, but she's been more than generous. She doesn't owe another cent."

Annie smiled. "Might be hard to get that through her head."

Their conversation turned toward the day's snowy forecast, and just then Annie recalled having heard from her brothers that the hill behind the meadow was "right slick and good for sleddin'."

Her mother remarked, "I trust you won't let Louisa's friendship lead you astray, dear one."

She feels she has to repeat this. . . .

Quickly, Annie set about making toast and then buttered it. "I'll go over and see if Dawdi and Mammi Zook are ready to eat," she said, looking for an excuse to slip out of the kitchen.

The smell of fresh-brewed hot coffee tempted her, and she could hardly wait to have some. Mamm's was the best. *I'll have it black,* she thought, as if coffee void of sugar and cream would alone serve to quell her apprehension.

Yet she would not allow her worries to overtake her. She must move forward and explore the possibility of getting her best painting framed.

Hopefully today. . . .

Esther sat down at Julia's lovely table to eat homemade potato soup and chicken salad sandwiches. She had gotten her own children settled into their chairs, with John perched in Molly's former high chair. Besides Zeke, Julia's husband was the only one missing at the meal, out on a company-related sales call in Allentown.

Julia bowed her head and said a heartfelt blessing, mentioning Esther's name as well as Laura, Zach, and little John. "And, Lord, please pour your abundant grace into the hurting places of our lives," she continued.

Esther held Laura's hand during the prayer, squeezing it and offering a comforting smile when Julia finished, saying "amen" in a hushed and reverent tone.

On the buggy ride here, Esther had said very little to the children, mainly that they were going for a visit to "Auntie" Julia's, even though they had never met either Julia or her husband and children. Laura had been full of questions, as always, asking if this was a day off from school . . . and why wasn't Dat coming along with them. Esther had not fibbed, however, careful not to alarm either her eldest or Zach and John, who seemed to be quite happy to get out in the "snowy land," as Zach called it.

Having kept an overnight bag packed and hidden for several months now, Esther had been able to gather her wits, her bag, and the children in record time, her heart in her throat, while Zeke was gone visiting at the neighbor's for his midmorning coffee break. All during the time of her escape, she'd prayed both silently and under her breath, mindful to carefully bundle up John, who looked surprisingly fit for having nearly suffocated in the night. She realized that if she should fail to escape this time, she might never have another chance. Zeke would see to that. Even her stay at Julia's was risky business.

Still, she felt justified in leaving, needing a safe place to deliver her baby. *My helpless wee baby must come first.* She did not know what the next permanent step might be, for it would be presumptuous for her to think she could stay for an extended period at Julia's.

Handing the large soup tureen to her, Julia said, "Help yourself to plenty. I made a double batch . . . one for our shut-in neighbors, too."

"Denki," whispered Esther, still stunned she'd made it this far into her unknown journey. She dipped the ladle into the thick soup, putting a small amount in Laura's bowl, then into each of the boys'. Last of all, her own.

The kitchen was pleasant, situated where sunshine could flood the eating nook as they all sat, the drop-leaf table extended out to accommodate all of them. With its refinished oak hardwood flooring, white cupboards and apothecary knobs, and hard rock maple butcher-block countertops, Julia's kitchen was more modern than anything Esther had ever seen. Bright touches of red cookie jar, sugar dish, and salt and pepper shakers, and the deep yellow sunflower toppers above the windows, made for an appealing room.

She felt her muscles relaxing as she ate each bite of food, not realizing until this moment how hungry she'd been. She enjoyed the simple offerings of tasty soup and sandwiches.

Later, when she was helping dish up the fruity Jell-O for Zach and John, she felt the sharp cramping of another contraction. Not wanting to upset the children, she would not let on.

After the children were finished with their cookie munching, she felt she ought to lie down, hoping to stave off the onset of contractions. She whispered to Julia that she was "all in," and Julia encouraged her to take the spare room, away from the traffic of the house, "back in a little corner, here on the first floor," said Julia. "I'll tend to the children. You rest."

Ever so relieved, Esther rose and thanked her for the good meal. Picking John up, she turned to Laura and Zach. "Be sure to mind Auntie Julia, ya hear?"

Laura's eyes were focused on her, but her daughter said nothing. Esther smiled back, wanting to ease any fears her too-perceptive girl might have.

"You go on, Esther. It's nice and peaceful back there," urged Julia.

"Thank you ever so much." She felt so appreciative of her Mennonite friend and longed to rest her weary bones . . . and to have little John near to keep a closer watch on him. "Come, let's get you washed up." She kissed his sticky face.

Dear Lord, be with my wee unborn babe! she prayed.

Chapter 35

Annie was bursting at the seams to share with Lou her sudden yearning—to frame her painting. But Omar was at the reins, having been kind to offer to drive them to Julia's. *This will have to wait,* she decided, trying to picture what such a large canvas would look like professionally framed.

And she couldn't wait to see the choices of beautiful frames. Of course she would be taking her chances at being seen out in the English world, but far as she knew there were scarcely any connections between herself and the fancy life here in Lancaster County. Next to none.

She kept still and listened to Omar and Lou chatting about upcoming farm sales, which Omar—and Yonie, especially—were always happy to talk about.

"What sort of things are sold at auction?" Lou asked.

"You name it . . . it's there." Omar was keeping a straight face, but Annie knew he was smiling inside. Anytime anyone wanted to talk about the sale of cattle, mules, driving horses, shovels, rakes, and all kinds of farm equipment, Omar was more than willing. "You oughta come along sometime. It'd be quite an experience."

"I'll say," Annie spoke up. "An all-day thing, with baked goods, quilts, and such for sale, and just like Omar said, everything under the sun, truly."

But not a speck of fine art, Annie thought.

By the time they arrived at Julia's, Annie could scarcely keep mum. But she waited till Omar had turned the horse and carriage around and headed toward the road before saying what was on her mind. "I want to tell you something, Lou."

"What's up?"

"I'd like to buy a frame for my painting."

"Hey, that's a terrific idea!"

"You don't think I might be seen there with it, do you?"

Lou shook her head. "I've never noticed any Amish people in that gallery. So . . . go for it." She opened the side door to Julia's house.

"All right, then. I'll do it today . . . if Julia will take me." Annie stepped inside the house, and right away she heard Laura Hochstetler's voice. "Well, what the world?" she whispered, going to investigate by peeking around the corner.

There in the cozy nook off the kitchen sat Esther's children with Julia, James, and Molly. "Well, hullo . . . we're late in coming today," Annie apologized first thing.

"No problem at all," Julia said. "As you can see, I have some houseguests."

Goodness' sakes! Has Esther suffered the last straw? Has she left Zeke? Annie went to Laura and touched her pretty hair, then leaned down to talk to her and Zach. "Looks like you had a nice lunch . . . here with Auntie Julia."

Laura smiled up at her, no worse for the wear. "That's just what Mamma calls her, too."

Poor little children. Annie stood up, thinking what an odd situation she was observing. *How will Lou occupy herself while I clean?* But she did not say what she was thinking, that the attic studio was surely off limits now. Instead, she asked, "Is Esther resting?"

Julia came over and guided her into the small front room, speaking in soft tones. "Oh, Annie, dear Esther needs our prayers . . . and some good rest, too."

"Well, I'll get the housework done right quick," Annie said. "And get out of your way."

"I'm glad you and Louisa came when you did. Is it all right with you . . . can you get the children tucked in for naps?" Julia explained she had a quick errand to run, out on Route 30, not far from Paradise Lane.

Right where I'd like to go! Her face must've dropped with disappointment, because Julia asked, "Annie? Did I say something wrong?"

"Ach, no . . . not at all. It's just . . . well, I have an idea . . .'bout my painting."

"Oh, that reminds me! With Esther coming, I almost forgot." Julia looked mighty pleased. "Irvin's copy of the new issue of the *Farm and Home Journal* arrived today. Come look."

Annie felt every possible emotion, from elation to sadness, as she held the small magazine in her hands. "This scene, by Pequea Creek . . . it just looks so real," she said softly, feeling as though she could fall right into the cover—*my own painting!*—and be right there, standing where she had so many times over the years.

Louisa paused at the window in what Julia always called the "front room," watching Annie carry her original painting, wrapped carefully in many pieces of newspaper, out to Julia's car.

Julia lifted the trunk and the two of them lifted the "Obsession" painting inside.

She's hung up on that place . . . and the secrets behind it, Louisa thought.

Sighing, she hoped her friend might not freak under the pressure of her own enormous secret.

Whim or not, she's painted herself into a corner. . . .

She went to look in on the children, who were soundly asleep in two different bedrooms, except for little John, whom Esther had taken in with her. Then she wandered to the kitchen, where she sat at the sun-strewn table with her sketchbook and a handful of colored pencils. Annie had indicated, in whispered tones, to avoid going to the attic to work today. *That will definitely have to wait,* she'd told her, and Louisa agreed. But it wasn't as if Annie's secret was secure anymore. The second hand on Annie's life clock was moving fast toward midnight.

Louisa turned her focus to her drawing, deciding to sketch Trey's handsome face from memory, only doing more of a caricature than the real thing. Casually she gave him a black Amish hat and brown beard, smiling at the juxtaposition of his modern attitude—evidenced by the wry grin and the charisma in his eyes—and the imposed plainness.

After a while, she rose to get some tap water at the sink and happened to glance out the window. She saw an Amish man rushing toward the side door. Bent forward, he was either angry or coming for help.

Zeke? she wondered. Thinking back to her only visit to Esther's house, Louisa couldn't recall what Zeke looked like. She'd only caught a glimpse of him before he disappeared into the barn. Besides that, the untrimmed beards and identical attire Amish men wore gave them the illusion of sameness.

In a few seconds the man was pounding at the side door. She felt nervous, being the only person fully awake in the house. *Should I even go to the door?*

She shoved her fear aside and walked through the little sun-room-sitting room, past the mud room, to the side door.

"Oh, I wish you'd have brought along the magazine," Miss Sauder, the gallery owner, was saying in response to Julia's cheer-ful prompting.

"Well, it's back home on the lamp table," Julia said quickly, looking at Annie. "But you have my word . . . she's a *very* good artist."

Quite embarrassed, Annie spoke up. "I'm interested in seeing some frames." She looked down at her painting all wrapped up, hidden from view.

The woman smiled kindly. "Come with me, I'll show you what we have in stock, as well as what can be ordered."

"Thank you," Annie said.

"Tell me again about your first-place award, please." The owner directed her question to Annie, but Annie deferred to Julia, since she seemed to derive such joy from sharing the news.

By the time Julia had described the contest in great detail, Miss Sauder was setting Annie's unwrapped painting up on a tall easel. She stood back and looked at it from all angles. "I've seen this place . . . I know I have," the woman said.

Annie glanced at Julia. "You have?"

"Oh my, yes."

"It's north of here, just down the slope from London Vale covered bridge," Annie told her.

"My sister and her family live a short distance from there."

The woman turned to Annie and surprised her by asking if she might ever consider selling it. "I believe I may have a buyer for it, even now."

Annie didn't have to think twice. "Why, no. It's not for sale."

"Do you have other work, perhaps?"

The question took Annie by surprise. "I do . . . but I think I might need some time to think on that. It's very nice of you to ask." Talking about selling something with her name on it gave Annie a dreadful sinking feeling. Like she was doing something unforgivably wrong indeed.

When the woman placed on the long counter the frame samples—traditional woods in classic and antique styles, composite moldings, and aluminum frames in twenty colors—Annie considered each one carefully. With Julia's good help, and taking up quite a lot of the owner's time, the three of them came to an agreement upon the best frame to "enhance the feeling of mystery," as Miss Sauder said.

Jah, mystery, Annie thought. *If only she knew. . . .*

Louisa stood at the door, looking into the face of the man who said he was Ezekiel Hochstetler, who babbled on about his horse and carriage having been returned by a young man. One Ben Martin. Evidently the horse had made the turn into the long lane leading to the harness shop, and Ben recognized the newly made harness as one he had created for Zeke himself. "That's why I'm thinkin' you've got yourself some visitors here," he said, frowning.

Before she could answer, Zeke turned and spit tobacco juice out the side of his mouth. "I need to see my wife," he said.

"She's asleep . . . can you return later?" Louisa felt she ought to say this, not knowing the real reason why Esther and her children had suddenly shown up here. She suspected something was quite wrong though, for a pregnant Amish woman to come with three children in tow, and a rather large overnight case, as well.

"No . . . I'm here now. I want to see Esther." He raised his voice slightly, his face growing ruddier. "You're Annie's friend from Colorado, ain't so?"

"That's right."

He shook his head, his mouth twisted in a sneer. "I don't understand why you want to dress like the womenfolk round here."

"I don't see how that's anybody's business but mine."

"Look, missy. . . ." He shoved his foot in the door and pushed his way inside. "Now, how about you get my wife for me!"

Her heart was pounding as she eyed the portable phone in the kitchen. Moving away from the door, she rushed to it, snatching it up. "Stay right there . . . I'm calling the police!" she told him. She began dialing: 9-1-1.

Zeke backed up and shook his head, waving one of his hands in surrender. "No . . . no, that ain't necessary. Put your telephone away." He eyed the sofa. "I'll sit over there while you go and tell Esther I'm here. I won't cause no trouble."

She aborted the call but gripped the phone nevertheless, wondering what this man might be capable of. "I *will* call the cops, if you even twitch an eyelid."

He went and sat on the couch, and she scrutinized him to determine if he could be trusted here in the house. She wasn't entirely convinced, but she found it startling when he turned to look at the lamp table. He let out a gasp, and she witnessed a cloud of sudden horror cross his face. He had reached for the magazine featuring Annie's painting on the cover.

She couldn't just stand there worrying that he might notice Annie's name printed in the lower right-hand corner. He was preoccupied now, though glowering at the magazine. Quietly she slipped away to the small back bedroom.

The door was cracked enough to peer into the room, and what Louisa saw took her breath away. Esther was resting peacefully with her little boy. Such gentle souls, no doubt having endured verbal abuse—if not worse—from the contemptuous man in the living room.

There's no way I'm disturbing her!

Tiptoeing back to the living room, she found Zeke with his hands over his face. "I'm sorry, but your wife is asleep, and little John is resting quietly, too," she said softly. She didn't care to have a ruckus on her hands, so she went promptly to the front door and opened it. "Why not return when she's expecting you? Tomorrow, perhaps?"

He looked up at her, his eyes shooting darts. "You don't understand." His voice was much too loud. "I want to talk to my wife, Esther. I need her back home."

Want . . . need. Big difference, she thought.

She wouldn't push too many of his buttons, because this guy was clearly a control freak. She had encountered enough people like this, and now she felt more certain than ever that Esther and her children had needed to escape from him.

"Good-bye," she said, glad for the phone still in her hand.

"Esther!" He planted himself in the middle of the room and hollered. "If you hear me, I mean to take you home with me. Ya hear?"

"No . . . get out!" Louisa raised the phone as a threat but intended to use it.

He caught her meaning. "Well, little missy, I'll be back!" He trudged out the door.

"I think you'd better stay away," she called after the brute.

Chapter 36

Louisa went around to the side door off the kitchen, making sure it was latched and locked. She felt uneasy here as guardian of this house, especially with all the little children . . . and a very pregnant woman, to boot.

Will Zeke return?

Pacing the length of the kitchen, she thought of Aunt Margaret, who had "talked to the Lord," whether it was out of concern or gratitude. *"Don't wait until you're in hot water to call on His name,"* she'd said.

"I'll bet Julia might say the same thing," Louisa muttered, returning to the living room. She caught her breath, glancing at the small maple table. In that moment, she saw that the *Farm and Home Journal*—the January issue—was gone.

What's with that?

She recalled how Zeke had been visibly affected by the cover. Most definitely so. She cringed at the thought of his causing trouble for Annie.

The house was peacefully still—so quiet, in fact, that when Esther called out suddenly, Louisa started and dropped her pencil.

"Julia? Julia!" Esther called urgently and Louisa hurried to explain that Julia had gone to run an errand and would be back shortly. "But the baby . . . it's coming . . . coming fast!" Esther clutched her abdomen and groaned.

Louisa took little John from Esther's bed and carried him in to Laura, where she, James, Molly, and Zach were already looking at picture books.

Esther cried out again and fear shot through Louisa, but she knew she must remain calm.

Her heart in her throat, she called 9-1-1, but the dispatcher said all the ambulances were out at the moment and it might be as long as another half hour until someone could get there. Completely ignorant about delivering babies, she did *not* want to handle this alone.

Oh, what can I do? She went to the window, on the verge of talking to Aunt Margaret's God. And in that unnerving moment, she spotted the harness shop, way across the field . . . and the car parked in the driveway.

Yes . . . Ben Martin's car!

She dashed back to check on the children—Laura was reading a story to all of them, holding little John in her lap now. "I'll be right back," she told them. "Stay right here. Promise?"

Laura nodded.

Hurrying back to Esther's room, Louisa gently told her to "hold on . . . you're going to the hospital." *For sure!*

It was an hour before quitting time. Ben was busy rubbing down a leather harness with oil when the door opened and there was Lou. He stood up, glad to stretch his aching back. "What can I do for you?"

"Oh, I hate to ask, but I really, really hope you can help

me . . . well, *us*." Her face had turned to crimson and she was out of breath. "Would you mind if I borrowed your car? I need to drive a friend to the hospital right away!"

She drives? he thought, surprised.

"A friend visiting Julia . . . is on the verge of having a baby. Julia's gone and I know absolutely zip about this."

Zip?

Ben removed his heavy work apron. "I'll drive you back over to the Rancks', then on to the hospital," he said, wishing he had time to scrub his hands clean. But he could see the panic on Lou's face, so he grabbed his jacket and they hurried out to the car.

When they arrived at the Rancks' house, Lou jumped out and rushed inside, leaving him to follow behind. "She's freaked," he said to the air, wondering why the birth of a baby should be such a troubling thing for a Plain country girl.

Inside the house, he heard a woman moaning and went directly to the kitchen to scour the leather oil off his hands. Then, waiting for Lou to return, he was suddenly aware of a stream of small children: preschooler James and toddler Molly— whom he'd met only once or twice—and three more he hadn't seen before . . . all coming into the living room.

Wow. . . . Who's going to watch all these little people? He stood in the middle of the living room and Molly tottered over and grabbed him around the knee, looking up at him with a grin.

In a few minutes Lou reappeared in the doorway, wringing her hands. "Esther's baby is coming *now*! There's no time to go to the hospital."

"If it's any comfort, I've helped birth dozens of foals," he said, wanting to reassure her. He hoped he didn't sound as nervous as he suddenly felt.

"Foals? Well, that beats anything *I* know." She looked at the children encircling him. "So . . . how about I watch the kids while *you* see if there's anything you can do to help Esther?" Her eyes were blinking ninety miles an hour.

He agreed, but for all his bravado, his heart began to pound and his hands felt clammy. He followed her to the bedroom where the woman lay, startled, no doubt, to see an English stranger—not to mention a guy—enter the room.

"This is Ben Martin, Esther . . . an employee of Irvin Ranck. He knows how to help you."

Ben sure hoped *that* was true.

"And, Ben, this is Esther Hochstetler . . . one of Annie's friends."

"Call me Essie," the woman said, her face flushed, her body covered with a thin blanket.

"Essie it is," Ben said, somewhat confused. *She must be Zeke's wife. So why would she send her horse packing without a driver?* Something was weird about that, because he had seen the same horse and carriage he'd returned to the Hochstetler pig farm show up later, here at the Rancks', with Zeke at the reins. But he didn't have time to think about that now. He must figure out how to help this woman.

Lou wrung her hands, clearly flustered.

"Listen, why don't you go hang with the kids," he told her. "I'll call you when I need you."

———

Jesse took pleasure in watching Yonie decorate his horse harness with chrome and a few brass buckles. Perched on an old barn bench, Jesse rubbed his hands together, blowing his warm breath on them.

Yonie looked up. "We've got ourselves an understandin' bishop, jah, Daed?"

"Well, he does seem to recall his young days better than some ministers."

Yonie continued fussing with the harness. "So if a bishop's got a good memory, then he doesn't mind us fellas deckin' out our horse harnesses so much, then?"

Jesse nodded. "Must be." He recalled his own rumschpringe days, shining up his courting buggy and whatnot, mighty eager to meet some nice girls at the barn singings. Pretty Barbara had caught his eye along about the second singing, but she had been seeing another fellow at the time. He remembered *that* even now.

"What were your running-around years like, Daed?"

"Oh, 'bout like yours, I s'pose."

Yonie laughed. "Now, how can ya say that?"

"What . . . you got something to hide, son?"

"Nothin' that most boys aren't doin', seems."

"Well, I don't have to tell *you*, now do I?" Jesse paused, not wanting to sound so overbearing as to shut Yonie up for further father-son talks. "It ain't the smartest idea to follow the crowd, is it?"

"How's a body goin' to know what they're missing then?"

Jesse stifled a smile. "Guess if a body's got to know everything he's missin', then he's not much of a leader but only a follower." He sighed. "I don't see you as the latter, Yonie Zook."

His boy looked at him. "Honestly, Daed, do you see me as a leader?"

"Since the day you came out squalling like a stuck pig."

"Well, then." Yonie squared his shoulders and twirled the shiny buckles on his new harness.

They heard the sound of a horse and carriage, and Jesse asked Yonie to go and have a look-see. Yonie poked his head out of the barn door, then came right back. "Ezekiel Hochstetler's here."

Jesse got up, his ankles cracking loudly, and did several upper torso stretching exercises before heading out to greet Zeke. "Better make yourself scarce now, son."

When he opened the wide barn door and marched out, Jesse waved when he caught Zeke's eye. Not that he cared to, really. He could feel in his bones this was going to be another unpleasant meeting. "Too cold out in the barn," he said, motioning him toward the house, in hopes Zeke might not cause such a ruckus round Barbara and all.

The two men walked together, crunching old boots through the fresh snow. "I want to know where you buried my brother," Zeke started in. "I want to know *now*."

"Snow's much too heavy to go lookin'."

Zeke snuffed his nose. "Don't matter none to me."

"We've talked this to death."

They were inside, in the enclosed porch now, removing boots, scarves, and coats. "I'm plenty tired of waiting," Zeke said.

"No changin' my mind."

"So you're goin' to keep stonewallin' me?"

"Call it what you will. . . ."

Zeke snorted like the pigs he raised. "Well, then, I have something to show you, Preacher." He reached in and pulled a magazine out of his shirt. "Here . . . take a good look at this." Zeke shoved it into his face.

"What's this got to do with anything?"

"Your daughter, that's what."

Jesse had no idea what he meant.

Zeke was adamant. "Annie painted the picture on this here cover . . . see?" He pointed to her name. "And if ya don't believe me, then ask her yourself."

Jesse stared at the picture. *Annie Zook?* "How many women with that name in Paradise?" he muttered, half to himself. "Must be dozens. . . ."

"Well now, Preacher, I guess that's for you to find out."

Zeke was heckling him, and it was all he could do to keep from rolling up the magazine and bopping Zeke with it. Even so, he was drawn to the picture—the way the sun spotlighted a single peach stone there on the swing. He looked closer and saw that peculiar symbol of hope, unable to forget all the village talk following Isaac's disappearance. How many times, years later, had Annie asked about the boy's fascination with a peach pit? The odd way little Isaac had carried it with him in his pants pocket. . . .

This is Annie's work, all right. But he wouldn't let on, so Zeke couldn't use it against him. Yet Zeke would, knowing him.

"Go ahead, Preacher . . . look at your own cousin's name on the address label." Zeke poked his finger on the name: Irvin Ranck.

Irvin and Julia. . . . Jah, they might just know something about Annie's artwork. But he wondered if he was jumping to conclusions.

"It's your daughter that'll be your downfall," Zeke taunted. "And you know what I mean to do if you keep mum about where you and the bishop buried my brother." He snatched the magazine back.

Jesse resisted his ire. "I'm following the bishop's bidding."

"Well, then, I'll be takin' this here magazine all round, first to the bishop, then to Uncle Preacher Moses and Deacon

Byler . . . see what *they* say 'bout your daughter's hobby."

He despised what Zeke was doing, putting him between a rock and a hard place. "I daresay you'll get yourself shunned yet, Zeke. Just like your wife."

Zeke scowled, mumbling under his breath.

"You wouldn't want to lose your pig farm, would you? Your ability to make a livin' for your family?" He could see he was making some headway, and right quick, too. "Better be thinking 'bout what you want to do." Jesse eyed the magazine. "And best be leavin' that here with me."

Zeke wilted, relinquishing his hold on the *Farm and Home Journal*. And seconds later, when it came to accepting Barbara's offer of coffee, he flatly refused. Donning his coat now, Zeke made an excuse about needing to get home.

Jesse put a firm hand on the younger man's shoulder. "Jah, you do that."

———

Annie led the way to the house, as Julia had insisted on carrying in her own purchases from the fabric store. They had made several stops following the interesting visit at the art gallery.

She noticed a car parked off to the side. "Got yourself more company?"

"Oh, that's Ben's car," Julia said. "He sometimes parks it here and walks over to the harness shop."

So Annie thought nothing of it, stopping at the side door, accustomed to it being opened. But she found it to be locked. *How odd!*

A little chill went up her spine just then, the slightest premonition. But she brushed off her jitters and waited for Julia to come and unlock the door.

Julia opened it and let Annie go in first. Right away as she entered the house, she heard a loud holler coming from the back room. "Hurry, Julia," Annie called. "Esther's cryin' something awful."

Julia rushed into the house behind her.

Annie hurried into the living room and found Louisa there, sitting on the floor and playing with Esther's three and James and Molly, too. "Who's with Esther?"

Lou got up quickly. "You'll never guess in a million years."

As if on cue, Ben Martin appeared in the doorway. "Oh, good, Julia . . . you're back. Your help is eagerly requested."

Lou was obviously relieved, as well, smiling almost too broadly. "Annie, I was so freaked. You have no idea what excitement you missed."

Julia had disappeared to assist Esther, and Annie felt Ben's scrutinizing gaze on her once again. "I'm going in to be with Esther," she said, hurrying past Ben.

Esther's face was wet with perspiration when Annie entered the guest room. But Esther's eyes shone with happiness as Annie came near. "Oh, I'm so glad you're here, Annie. It won't be long now . . . I'm ever so sure."

Clasping her hand, Annie apologized. "I'm so sorry . . . we never should've left you."

"Don't let go of my hand," Esther said, another contraction coming.

Soon, Annie witnessed the tiny life emerge into Julia's capable and loving hands, and the newborn's high-pitched squeal rang out.

Later, when the precious bundle lay resting in Esther's arms, Annie whispered, "She's so little . . . so sweet. I'm glad I was here right when she came."

"I'm awful glad, too." Esther nodded and smiled. "What do you think of Essie for my baby's name?"

"Sounds right fine. I daresay she's an Essie, through and through."

"And the dear Lord Jesus sent His angels to help . . . I just know He did." Esther's eyes were shining. "And Irvin's friend, Ben Martin, who was such an encouragement . . . and helped me stay surprisingly calm."

Annie didn't know what to make of Esther's remarks about the harness shop worker. She leaned down and kissed the wee babe's damp brow. "Honestly, Esther, I had no idea your baby was comin' so soon."

"Everything happened fast. I'd fallen right asleep, even before you and Julia left. It was after Zeke came and was so awful loud, that's when I was jolted awake and things started to happen."

"Zeke was here . . . in the house?" Annie's heart nearly stopped.

"Ach, I was scared he might come marchin' back here and haul me home."

"Aw, Essie, I feel just sick 'bout this."

"Well, don't fret. Your friend Lou sent him on his way. A tough one she is. Then she brought Ben to help. . . ." Esther's tears were not for pity but from exhaustion, and Annie wiped them away with her own fingers. "I'm ever so grateful for a healthy baby. That's what matters, Annie. Thanks be to the dear Lord."

"Well, now, you rest. Jah?"

Esther closed her eyes briefly, then blinked them open. "Do you really think this one looks like an Essie?"

Annie studied the tiny face. "Well . . . I'm not so sure now.

Maybe a middle name suits her." She pondered several. "What 'bout Essie *Mae?*" she asked. "That way we won't get her and you mixed up."

"I like Ann better—after you, Annie."

"Essie Ann. Jah, I *do* like it."

Esther's lip quivered. "I just pray my baby girl might grow up more carefree than her big sister, you know?"

Annie's heart went out to her dear friend, and she let Esther squeeze her hand ever so hard. "I know you do."

Chapter 37

Ben backed his car up and headed over to the harness shop, whistling all the way.

Annie Zook. The name had a distinct lilt to it. He even found himself wondering what her middle name might be.

"This is nuts," he said, returning to work. He breathed in the strong smell of leather and oil, taking it deep into his lungs, relishing the odor. He finished up the harness he'd begun before Lou had come bursting in two hours before.

Then he laid out the next harness on the big table, replaying the time at the Rancks'—observing and getting to know Lou better, and what an interesting Amish girl *she* was. He almost had the feeling she was playacting, going through the motions. The way she expressed herself really threw him, but then, he'd heard that some girls went a little crazy during their so-called "sowing wild oats" days. He wondered if Lou had been hanging out with some non-Amish friends, trying to pick up their lingo, perhaps.

Annie was also on his mind a lot. And about the time his thoughts of her seemed to quiet slightly, he would run into her again. Today he had even suspected she might be sensing something, too.

Meeting her had turned his whole world on its head. Never had he experienced anything like this . . . such all-encompassing feelings.

Annie, he thought. *Funny how perfectly the name fits her.* He had only known one other person whose name seemed custom-made. His mother, Sandie, with hair the color of a tropical beach and a complexion to match. He already missed his parents, and his four younger siblings, and all of them were great about keeping in touch by cell phone. None of them, especially his next youngest sister, understood why he'd had the urge to uproot so suddenly. And he still felt apologetic about it, all the while enjoying his new work here in Paradise.

He had been oiling down the last harness of the day, staying longer to make up for the time gone, when Lou knocked at the door and waved through the window.

"Come in . . . it's unlocked!" he called.

Lou hurried in, glancing at the many racks of harnesses hanging along the wall. "You know what? I don't think you have any idea how you saved the day . . . over at Julia's."

"I was glad to." He paused. "I must admit, I would have thought someone your age—from these parts—would have been accustomed to helping when babies are born."

"Oh, I'm not from here. I suppose it's okay to say—because everyone in Annie's church knows—I'm actually her friend from Colorado, just visiting. Annie and I, we've been pen pals since grade school . . . that's how we first met."

He listened attentively, wondering why Lou was volunteering this.

"I dress Amish so I don't freak out anyone here . . . especially Annie's dad. He's the preacher-man. Maybe you've heard," Lou continued. "Anyway, I was sick of the complicated world out there—the nutcase rat race. Not to mention materialistic madness."

"Hey, I hear you."

"Well, I just dropped by to say thanks."

"Not a problem." He smiled, not so much at her but with her. He found her story, whatever the rest of it was, irresistible.

"So, how can I ever thank you, Ben?"

He smiled, an ironic thought crossing his mind. He thought of Annie, the way he felt when they were in the same room together. Here in the shop, there at Julia's . . . with such affection for Esther and her new baby.

His mind was doing a number on him again.

"Well," he said, surprising even himself, "there *is* something. . . ." He paused. "What I mean is . . . is Annie seeing anyone?"

"Well, no."

"Would she consider dating someone like me?"

"An Englisher?" She smiled. "You know what? I am staying out of this. I think you'd better ask her yourself."

He nodded. "You're right. I will." *Soon as I work up the nerve!*

———

Annie should have guessed, by the stern set of her father's jaw during breakfast, what was coming. She ate as calmly as she could, making conversation with Louisa and Mamm, both of them eager to talk about Esther's new baby girl. And Annie couldn't help wondering if *that* was why her father looked so angry and disappointed, because she had spilled the beans about Esther's going to Julia's to have her baby. Of course, she'd been careful not to mention Zeke nor to let on that Esther went for any reason other than for help with the delivery, but maybe Daed had guessed the rest.

After redding up the dishes, she and Louisa walked back to the Dawdi Haus as usual. Annie was surprised when her father knocked on the door a few minutes later, saying he needed to talk to Annie alone. *About Esther?* she wondered.

Louisa excused herself and hurried off to the barn.

Then Annie spied the plain manila envelope in Daed's hand and her heart set to racing. *Could it be?* But, no . . . how could a copy of the magazine reach him so soon?

Everything that happened next seemed to Annie like staring through a cracked window—outside looking in. It shouldn't have felt like that at all, she surmised, having been on the receiving end before of such a harsh reprimand.

"You know what this means, don't you?" Daed's pointer finger tapped on the magazine cover. She stared at it, a lump in her throat, not for being caught—the third and worst time by far—but for the fact that her secret lay fragile and bare before her. The evidence not at all appreciated by a man who declared the glory of God and His handiwork each and every Preaching service. This disapproving man, who now stood over her . . . here, where she sat in her grandparents' kitchen, alternating stares between the perplexing landscape on the table before her and the honorable, yet smoldering, gaze of her father.

"You bring shame to our good name," he said.

She flinched, struggling with his pronouncement.

"What do you have to say for yourself?" Daed's finger stayed there, pointing to her name, emblazoned like an announcement from Hades itself.

I'm guilty . . . I've always been that. But she dared not express her thoughts in a negative manner. Self-expression had brought her to this moment, after all. This terrible black place. "My art was all I ever had, really. All I ever wanted," she managed to say, as if someone else were uttering the words.

He looked at her, disbelieving. "You never quit drawing, did you? You never stopped all those years ago . . . when I forbade you?"

She would not cower from him. *I must be true to myself.* Yet she could not bring herself to speak.

"You will answer your father, Annie Zook!"

She had forced him across a line. There was something merciless about his eyes now, the angle of his head as he looked at her. "This is who I am," she said softly. "It is not what I do. This painting . . . right here. That's the real Annie. Not who you see sittin' on the church bench at Preaching service or round Mamm's table every day." She patted her chest. "I've tried to be good, honest I have. But I don't have it in me, not if it means I can't draw or paint or study shapes and colors with the eyes the Lord God heavenly Father gave me."

"Be careful, lest you blight your Maker. Pride, after all, is who we are. All of us. Sins entangle us daily. Before Lucifer fell, he could've said to the Lord God, 'This is who I am!'" Daed folded his hands. "It is wrong to align yourself with sin, to say that it is who you are, Annie. You must reject it. Be set apart, as all the People are called to be."

She was crying now, unable to block her tears by sheer will. "To turn my back on my art would be impossible. I know this."

He shook his head but not sadly, she was sure. His attitude was either of righteous indignation or pure anger. "If you refuse to cease . . . if you will not submit to the authority of your own father, and under God, then you must leave the covering of this house."

She was not a baptized church member, therefore she could not be shunned. But many fathers required nearly as strict discipline of their rebellious youths.

Thinking of Louisa, she wondered what her friend would think *now* of the simple life she'd craved for so long. "Lou will leave with me," she said finally. "After all, she came at my invitation."

His eyes registered sudden concern.

Was he bluffing? She didn't think so.

"I'll go right away and pack." Looking at the painting on the magazine cover one last time, she rose to leave, even before her father dismissed her.

Upstairs, she opened the bureau drawers and began haphazardly pulling out her clothes, sobbing just as she had over Rudy Esh months ago. She felt betrayed even though she was not.

I had plenty of chances to obey. . . .

Hurriedly she folded each piece of clothing. Then, glancing around the room, she realized she owned hardly anything else, except for the contents of her hope chest. Largely, the room's furnishings belonged to her parents, the quilts to her grandmother. The rest was Lou's. Her English friend owned considerably more, in the way of sketchbooks and art supplies, than she. Except for Annie's precious items stored in the studio at Julia's.

What on earth will Cousin Julia think when she hears? Sitting on her bed, Annie covered her face with her hands and let go the tears. She felt sorry for poor Esther, and for her little children, and for helpless little Essie Ann, newly born. She felt sad for Louisa, who'd come here searching for something better than the modern world could offer. And she grieved for Mamm, who would be crying her eyes out when she heard what Daed had done.

Just when she felt so bad she couldn't feel a mite worse, right then, she heard a knock at her door. "Annie?"

It was Mamm.

She didn't know if she wanted to be seen this way, the way she surely looked just now, all tear-streaked and disheveled. But she longed for someone who might understand, and if anyone would, it was either Mamm or Louisa. "Come in," she said softly, brushing away her tears.

Her mother entered the room, face red, eyes swollen. Taking one look at Annie, she quickly closed the door. "Oh, you head-strong thing. My dear daughter." She rushed to her side and sat next to her on the bed. "Daed just told me." She didn't say anything at all against him, and Annie knew she wouldn't. But Mamm was clearly upset and sat there, reaching for Annie's hand.

Annie whispered, "I ought to be sayin' how sorry I am . . . but—"

"Hush now. We must keep our wits 'bout us. It won't look so good for the preacher to oust his daughter before she's baptized." Mamm was thinking out loud, which made Annie terribly nervous.

"I must do his bidding," she said. "Lou and I will pack up and find someplace else to live."

Mamm shook her head. "I just don't see how such a thing can be." She turned and looked at Annie, frowning and shaking her head.

"It's my fault . . . I deserve this. I do," she admitted. "I tried to give up my art. But it's got me—it's *in* me, Mamm. That's the best way to explain it."

"But where will you go, Annie?" Mamm asked, her voice quivering.

"I honestly don't know." She'd thought if Esther and her children weren't staying with Julia maybe that would have been an option. She recalled the day when Louisa had suggested renting a car. *Louisa's my answer*, she realized. But she couldn't think too far ahead, because Louisa had made it clear she would return to Colorado in due time.

Mamm wept, fumbling for a hankie in her sleeve. "I can't think 'bout this . . . it's much too hard." She rose and went to the bureau. "You were mighty quick to gather up your things, I see. Are you ever so eager to leave your family behind, dear one?"

"I guess I *do* need some time to think. . . ."

"Jah, we all do." Mamm turned, attempting to smile. "I'll leave you be for now." She made her way to the door, her shoulders heaving as she went.

Annie felt as forlorn as Mamm's dear face looked.

Lou had been outside helping in the barn. Now she came looking for Annie upstairs in the Dawdi Haus. "Can you help find me . . . er, us a place to stay?" Annie asked her right out when she appeared in the doorway.

"What for?" Louisa stared at the piles of clothing on the bed. "And what's all this?"

Feeling emotionally and physically weak, Annie attempted to explain, saying what had happened, how her father had in his possession the magazine with the incriminating cover. "He never said where he got it, but he has it. And he's madder than a sprayed hornet."

"Well, I think I might know," Lou said. "Zeke was looking at it earlier today at Julia's, when he came storming in to see Esther."

So Zeke came directly here? she wondered.

"You knew it was a matter of time before this happened." Lou sat on Annie's bed. "I think it's possible some good things can come of it . . . you know, finally getting all this out in the open. It doesn't really matter how freaked your father is right now. The truth is you haven't been honest with yourself."

She was stunned, Lou talking like this. "What do you mean?"

"Well, you say art is so much a part of you—*who* you are. And it is who I am, and everything I want to be." Lou pushed her head covering off suddenly. "But look at me, Annie." She began pulling her hairpins out, her bun falling out quickly. "Is this who I am, wearing my hair in a bun . . . these long blue or green dresses and black aprons? Is it?"

"You aren't Plain, no."

"But you *are*," Lou said. "Through and through. So, is being an artist more who you are than being Amish? I don't think so."

Annie watched Lou shake out her dark brown hair. "What makes you say this?"

"When I first came here, I thought you should follow your heart—your longing for art—but now I'm not so sure. Besides, I can't imagine how you could leave your family and the People behind for the modern world, Annie. I doubt there's any way you'd ever be happy out there . . . on the outside."

"How can you possibly know?"

"You've said it yourself, that you're like a sister to me. We've shared our hearts in letters all these years, and now we're like roommates in a college dorm." Lou got up and walked to the window. "So I guess you'll have to trust me, Annie . . . because I'm not going to let you walk away from here. You have to do the right thing."

"I don't even know what that is."

"Go to your dad . . . talk to him." Lou rose and went to sit on her own bed now. Her kitty came out from under the bed skirt and curled up on her lap.

"So you're not goin' to help me get an apartment?" It was her last effort.

"Listen, I'd love nothing more than to see you spread your wings . . . and for the whole world to witness your talent. But it's not the whole world I'm concerned about. It's *your* world, Annie. The Amish tradition. Right here. *This* is your world—your artist's canvas. You wouldn't be happy away from it—even with all the paint and freedom money could buy."

Annie almost wondered if Daed had taken Louisa aside and asked her to talk straight this way. She watched idly as Lou scratched Muffin behind his ears and stroked his long fur. "Sounds like you've thought all this through."

Lou's expression grew more serious. "I'm probably as surprised as you are—me, of all people, saying this—but why couldn't you express yourself in some acceptable way? Remember the lovely embroidery we saw at the Old Country Store?"

Annie nodded.

"Art is whatever you make it. It's actually a language . . . the way you express your emotions. Just think of the quilt designs and the placement and choice of colors in all those flower beds outside come spring."

"I s'pose you want me to follow the peacocks round, too, watching for the slightest changes in color on their trains, is that it?"

"Sure, why not?"

Annie smiled. "I'll think on it . . . that's all. I won't promise much else."

"Well, good . . . that's progress." Muffin suddenly hopped down off Lou's lap and ran over to Annie, surprising both girls. "See? Even my cat approves of you."

"It's nice someone does." She hugged Lou's kitty, dreading the thought of seeking Daed out.

Chapter 38

Louisa struggled over whether or not to tell Annie of Ben's keen interest in her, especially with all the upheaval in Annie's life. If she were aware would she entertain even more thoughts of leaving the People and feel justified in dating a non-Amish guy?

Louisa had no clue. Of course, the upside to it was the possibility that Annie might want to stay put, to be in close proximity to Ben . . . if it happened that she was interested in dating *him*. Bottom line, though, Louisa felt strange, knowing she held this romantic secret from her friend, having realized today what an amazing man Ben Martin was. Miles better than Rudy, in her humble opinion.

For someone to come in and do what Ben had done at Julia's—his gentleness in supporting Esther emotionally—was impressive. Not to mention his overall attitude and demeanor. She hadn't ever known a guy like that. And it was funny, too, because she caught herself sizing him up against what she knew of Trey Douglas.

That's ridiculous, she reprimanded herself, waiting not-so-patiently in the bedroom while Annie talked with her father downstairs. Louisa *had* laid into Annie, no question, but she truly believed everything she'd spouted off to her friend. *So, would it be wise to let on about Ben now?* Louisa wondered, even though she suspected Annie might be attracted to him, too. She was glad she'd had the presence of mind to tell Ben she was staying out of it and to ask Annie himself. She'd messed with Annie's life enough!

———————

Esther kissed the top of Essie Ann's little head, the peach fuzz tickling her nose. "I'm grateful to you, Julia, and to the Lord in every way," she said, glad for someone of like mind to talk to. "I must say, too, your husband's employee was like a messenger sent from heaven."

"That's the truth." Julia nodded, her soft brown hair beginning to come loose from its bun after the long day. "I can tell you, Ben's a fine young man. Though not a believer, far as we know."

Looking down at the baby in her arms, Esther was filled with love anew for her Savior. "I pray Ben might come to know the Lord, just as I have."

"Irvin shares Christ with him every chance he can." Julia's eyes were soft with tears.

"You all right?"

"Oh yes. Seeing you there, so safe and snug, with this new little one near, well . . . I just want to tell you that Irvin and I have decided you and the children should stay here for as long as need be." Julia pushed back the long stray hairs, her face rosier than before. "Irvin plans to speak with his cousin Jesse, Annie's father, about keeping Zeke away from you and the children. We'll pray something can be done to help your husband in the meantime."

A little sob caught in Esther's throat. "Ach, this takes such a burden off me, Julia . . . you just don't know!"

Julia rose and stood near the bed. "My husband won't allow any more visits like Louisa said occurred with Zeke. Not until you're ready, that is. In the meantime, the men will protect you should he show his face here again."

Esther felt lighter suddenly. "I'll sleep better tonight knowin' this. Denki, Julia. Oh, thank you!"

The afternoon light was fading rapidly when Annie found Daed at the far end of the barn, close to the door where the cows came in for milking. "I need to talk to you," she blurted to him, "'cause I'm all ferhoodled."

He had trouble looking at her, she knew. The anger had diminished some and in its place was great disappointment, that thing she had always wished to avoid.

"I heard you're packing already." His words fell from his lips like broken glass.

"Jah," she said in a near whisper. "But I don't *want* to leave. . . ."

"Well, I won't budge. I'll not have you flaunting your worldliness." His eyes looked hollow, colorless.

"I know this sounds peculiar," she continued, terribly tense, "but I need some time to say good-bye to my work . . . my art. Days or weeks . . . maybe longer."

His brow was deeply furrowed and he stood there, hay fork in hand, looking at her like he hadn't ever truly seen her before. "Cuttin' off a dog's hind leg is much harder done little by little, ain't?"

She sensed how difficult it was for one so deeply rooted in

the church. Ever so slowly, she nodded her head.

"You want time to do what . . . dabble further in the world?"

"No, Daed—"

"Well, you're askin' an impossible thing."

She sighed. "I wish you could understand *me*."

He set the hayfork aside and folded his arms across his chest. "Why must this be so hard . . . to lay down your will, as you must, in order to be truly happy?"

She had no answer. They stood looking at each other, father and daughter.

At last, Daed shook his head. "There will be no more discussion on this. I want you to agree to take baptismal classes come summer, to abstain from your drawings and such until then—for a full six months. It's past time to leave your rumschpringe days behind."

She swallowed the lump in her throat. "I could think on it, jah, but whether or not I can follow through . . . that's another story."

"Must I remind you? 'Where your treasure is, there will your heart be also.'" He took off his hat and began to fan himself. He was worked up again, and she ought to simply walk away—and do his bidding—not cause him this much grief in a single day. "Honestly, Annie, you're a lot like our peacocks when they get their long trains caught under the buggies on the road."

She felt dismayed with his comparison. Already, she'd hurt him enough for a lifetime. Even so, she didn't deserve to be judged against a slow-poke peacock, did she? Truth be known, she'd watched them strut along, unhurried as they were, getting their tail feathers all ripped up, away from the safety of the pen.

"After baptismal instruction, I would then expect you to join church next fall," he continued.

Oh, for his sake, she wanted to say she would. But how? "It would be foolish to make a false covenant," she said softly. "Even dangerous."

He put his hat back on his head and held out his hand. "You ain't a man, but I daresay it might be a good idea to shake on this, Annie. Will you agree to put aside your sin and give obedience a chance?"

She looked down at his callused hand, outstretched to her.

"I could try."

"No, you must cease to try, and simply do it."

Six months. . . . She was moved to tears, although she wouldn't dare blink and let them spill down her cheeks. No, she must accept the hand of her father, who was only doing the best he could, for goodness' sake.

Mentally, she marked the moment, wondering if she would recall this promise in her old age, many years from now. And if so, would she remember it with gladness?

Reaching out, she clasped his hand.

———

Lighting the lantern, Jesse carried it out to the sleigh. Zeke Hochstetler was heavy on his mind and it was imperative to get him hushed up, especially now that Annie wouldn't be leaving, at least not soon. He hadn't seen real signs of repentance from her, and he didn't know how long the promise of their handshake would stick with a free-thinking woman like his daughter.

He stepped into the sleigh and urged the horse down the road, thinking of his side of the family tree. A good and strong branch of it were some downright outspoken Mennonites. Not that they were necessarily an obnoxious lot, but they sure had differing opinions. Irvin Ranck was a strong limb off that particular tree, and from what he had come and told Jesse tonight, on the heels of supper, Jesse figured Zeke Hochstetler was a loose-fitting cork in a pressure-filled bottle.

He contemplated what Irvin had stated vehemently, that they would not allow Zeke to harm Esther or the children. *So Esther's run off for certain*, he thought, not liking it. Far as he could tell, Zeke was merely a loudmouth, nothing more. And if he had ever slapped his wife around, well, then he needed to be talked to. But the way he saw it, Esther was doubly in the wrong . . . claiming salvation and now shirking her domestic and wifely duties.

But there was a larger issue of worry, which was the reason for Jesse's after-suppertime trip to see the bishop. Zeke was a problem for the People as a whole and for Jesse in particular. With Annie possibly settling down some, it would work best all around if Zeke was finally told where his brother was buried. The bishop might not agree, but Jesse felt the distraught and unstable man should be tossed a crumb of information.

Zeke won't go round stirring up the People over Annie's art. Of this, he was fairly certain. And he was mighty glad he'd had the presence of mind to keep the proof. This way Zeke had no leg to stand on, except for shooting off his mouth, which he did like clockwork, anyway.

Jesse's greatest fear was the English authorities getting involved. Having followed Bishop Andy's demand from the start, the brethren had never reported the Hochstetler boy missing. *Best to keep it quiet*, the bishop had continually said through the years, whenever the matter was reviewed at the council of the ordained, twice annually. Preacher Moses had always had the biggest beef with it, Isaac being his kin. Which was where the rub came, far as Jesse could tell, yet the bishop had managed to keep a lid on a slow-boiling cauldron. Partly it was because not even Zeke had any idea where his parents had ended up after they left Honey Brook. Some thought they'd gone to a remote part of Ontario, Canada. Others rumored the family had left the Amish altogether.

Turning into the bishop's lane now, Jesse saw a single gas lamp burning in the kitchen window and assumed Andy was reading the German Bible to his wife. When he knocked on the back door, it took a while for the bishop to come and see who was there. Jesse should have called out, announcing himself, but he needed the extra moments to think again what he should say, even though he'd contemplated this visit all the way here in the dark and blustery cold.

"Well, Jesse Zook, what brings you out?" the older man said, ushering him inside.

"Zeke's on a rant." He kept his voice low.

"How's *that* news?"

They stood in the anteroom away from the kitchen. "I don't mean to go over your head," said Jesse. "I'm just wondering if Zeke shouldn't be allowed to know where we buried Isaac."

A gentle smile creased Andy's face. "He must've broken your will. All that flap comin' out of his mouth . . . is that it?"

Jesse wouldn't reveal his daughter's ongoing sin, wouldn't use it as the reason for his request. "Truth be told, if Isaac had been my brother, I might be askin' the same." It was his best defense. The only one.

Andy's jaw was tense, his eyes somber. "What with his missus on a probationary shun, do you think this is a good idea?"

"I see it as necessary." *An appeasement . . . a way to keep Zeke happy during this dismal time,* he thought. "Esther's left Zeke . . . took the children with her." He mentioned that the Rancks' place was her chosen safe haven.

"A whole new can of worms," Andy said.

"I say we give Zeke something . . . the one thing he wants, truly."

By his repeated sighs, the bishop seemed to acquiesce. "If it'll keep him from blabbin' to the police, then maybe so." His eyes lit up. "Jah, that's what you do, Jesse. You give him an either-or. Make him choose not to contact the authorities . . . not to hunt down the killer."

Jesse was surprised; the decision had been accomplished before he'd even gotten his gloves and scarf removed. "If this is your behest, I'll go and tell Zeke right away."

The bishop's wife called to him. "Who's there, dear?"

"Oh, it's Preacher Zook," he said over his shoulder.

"Have him come in for some hot coffee."

The bishop raised his eyebrows. "Care for some, Jesse?"

"Denki, but no."

The hoot of an owl rang out from the trees beyond the barn-yard. *Bird of death,* Jesse thought. The cadenced call echoed in his mind as he stared at distant floodlights on an English farm as he made his way through the snow to his waiting horse and sleigh.

Zeke will get his wish, he thought. *I hope it's the right thing. . . .*

Chapter 39

Ben was pleased at Julia's supper invitation, amazed in fact, as she already had a houseful of mouths to feed. But she'd called to urge Ben to join them for a celebration "at the birth of Esther's baby," now that Irvin was home.

He felt she was linking him to the joyous arrival of Essie Ann, and he couldn't take credit . . . wouldn't think of it. But he certainly wouldn't turn down a chance to visit more with Irvin or enjoy Julia's exceptionally good cooking. Not to mention all those cute kids with their contagious smiles.

Annie had not expected to run smack dab into Ben Martin as she was leaving Julia's by way of the side door. "Oh, goodness . . . I need to watch where I'm goin'," she said, backing up and looking at him full in the face.

"I guess we both do." Ben's eyes held her gaze. "You all right?"

She wasn't . . . not really. It had been months since she'd been that close to a man.

Ben stood there, not budging. And now that she'd stepped back, putting a better distance between them, she wasn't inclined to move, either. She did think it interesting that Louisa had chosen today, of all days, to go off by herself, taking pictures of barns and such with her fancy phone and computer gadget— "artistic research," she'd called it. Which put Annie right here in the Rancks' driveway, talking to Irvin's hired man alone, of all things.

"Would you think I'm forward if I asked you to have coffee with me sometime?" Ben asked unexpectedly.

"Are you askin' me now . . . or later *sometime?*"

He smiled and she did, too. She'd been much too hard on this fine-looking fellow. Downright difficult.

"Well, I'll ask now," he said.

She shied away from his shining eyes, instead staring down at her black high-topped shoes. *Doesn't he mind that I'm Plain?*

"I could meet you somewhere if that's easier," he offered.

She thought of the other options. "I doubt you'd want to ride in an Amish buggy. . . ."

He laughed. "And you wouldn't be caught dead in a car with me, right?"

"Better dead than alive," she was quick to say, which brought another chuckle from Ben.

"I didn't expect a Plain girl to have such a good sense of humor. So *is* it against the rules to ride in a car? Would your church fathers frown on it?"

"Well," she replied, "there are both angels and devils in those beards . . . but you never heard this from me."

Her comment seemed to catch him off guard. He looked at her curiously. "I'd like to know more about that."

Just then Julia poked her head out the side door. "Would you like to stay for supper, Annie?"

How do I squelch my smile? She needs to be more subtle about matchmaking, Annie thought.

"I can easily set another place," Julia persisted.

"Thanks anyway, but Mamm's waitin' supper."

So Julia approves of Ben. . . .

"I know of a wonderful espresso place," Ben said when Julia had disappeared back into the house.

I shook hands with Daed, she reminded herself. *I can't go out with an Englischer now!*

She took a breath. "Well, it's awful nice of you to ask . . . but I prob'ly shouldn't," she said. "But thanks all the same, Ben."

His smile slipped a bit. "I understand," he said softly.

Annie gave him a little wave and walked away, already feeling glum.

A dessert of chocolate silk pie was served, and the five youngsters eyed Ben at the table. He had consistently made comical facial gestures at each of them, off and on throughout the meal. He knew he had a way with little kids. His own father had first noticed it years back, when Ben's smile quickly soothed a howling baby on numerous occasions—his colicky nephew, one case in point. His mom and sister often said he would be a "terrific dad" someday. *Finding the right woman is the key,* he thought.

While Julia and Irvin worked together in the kitchen, he got down on the floor with Laura, Esther's oldest, and James. Esther had already whisked diaper-laden John and his infant sister back to the bedroom. Molly and Zach sat out in the kitchen playing with extra-large, toddler-safe Legos at the table.

Thinking how to entertain Laura and James, he pulled something from his pocket, keeping it hidden in his closed hand. "I have a secret hiding here."

"You do? I want to see it!" Laura said, moving right over next to him.

"Me too!" James said, folding his hands under his chin, sitting cross-legged like Ben.

"You have to guess first," Ben said.

"Give us a hint," said Laura, the older.

"Let's see." He closed his eyes, enjoying the tension-filled game. "I know. . . ." He opened his eyes.

"What?" Laura's face lit up.

"Well, you never find it unless you're hungry and start to munch. Then the secret will slowly start to appear. That's the hint."

James looked discouraged. "That's too hard."

Laura's pensive expression changed to a smile. "I think *I* know."

"Then tell me." He loved playing along.

She leaned over and whispered her answer in his ear.

How could she have guessed? he wondered.

"What *is* it?" James asked, his lower lip drooping now.

Ben kept his voice low and a bit mysterious sounding. "Here, I'll show you." He opened his hand to reveal a smooth peach stone. "Watch closely." He flicked the pit, fast as a sneeze, between his thumb and third finger. It stood on its end and spun like a little top.

James said a happy *oh,* while Laura wore a wide-eyed look of glee.

"How'd you do that?" asked James.

Ben spun it a second time. "Just . . . like . . . this."

"Do it again!" James scooted next to him, too.

He twirled it again and again, followed by the children's side-splitting laughter each time. At last, when James was called off to his bath, Laura asked to hold the "little top."

Ben placed the pit in her hand, and she looked closely at it. "Ach, it's ever so smooth. Dat's got himself a whole bag of these, but not a single one like this."

A man who collects peach pits can't be all bad, Ben thought.

Laura returned the peach stone, and he found himself looking down at it, aware of the overwhelming urge to squeeze hard, and not knowing quite why.

Epilogue

It would be downright pointless to deny that I'm waiting on pins and needles for the other shoe to drop, as they say—or as I've been saying to Lou: waiting for the next suspender to snap. What with my father eyeing me like I've got the plague, there's plenty on my mind.

I recently attended the quilting at Sarah Mae's with Mamm, while Louisa stayed at the Dawdi Haus with Mammi Zook, most recently intrigued by needlepoint. They talked about many things, Lou confided to me, and I know she and Mammi are becoming fast friends. It's interesting to hear Mammi talking in Dutch to Lou now and then.

Julia's in need of her attic to make room for Esther, little John, and baby Essie Ann. Having an art studio ready and waiting for me would be an awful temptation, I confess, so this is a good thing. It's already been more than a full week since my hand has held either a colored pencil or a brush. I can't say it's easy, but I'm taking one day at a time. For Daed's sake . . . and for the Lord God's. When I get the jitters of withdrawal, which is what Louisa calls it, I go and cut quilting squares and arrange them in unusual patterns on the floor in the front room. Mamm must think I've lost my mind, but if it keeps me from sinning, all for the better.

Louisa's friend, Courtney Engelman, says she misses "the runaway bride." I don't know what my father will say about Lou's fancy friend wanting to visit, too, but it'll just be for a long weekend. I figure if I keep myself away from drawing and painting, just maybe Daed will be in favor of yet another Englischer coming to experience the peace of Paradise. And *I'll* find all the satisfaction I need in the acceptable art of my people, as Louisa encourages me to do.

I don't know how many times I've bumped into Ben Martin recently, and not once has it been at the harness shop, not since the first time. For some odd reason, he keeps showing up where I happen to be—making a purchase at the Gordonville Bookstore and at the post office. Things like that. It's downright uncanny, and I have no idea what to make of it. He smiles real big and says, "Hey, Annie," and I say, "Hullo, Ben" back. Secretly, I'm beginning to hope he might ask me out yet again.

Lou's driven me in the buggy over to see Esther and little Essie Ann twice now. Lou's getting quite good at handling a horse, surprisingly so. I keep thinking one of these days she's going to wake up and decide to wear her brand name jeans again, but so far she hasn't. She's careful not to let me see her with her sketchbook and pencils anymore, which makes me kind of sad. There's no reason for her to hide *her* work. But I suppose if she were in the same boat as I am, I'd do the same for her.

Still, I don't know how long I can let her sneak round like that. It doesn't seem fair. She consistently sells her drawings, too. Takes them in for framing every other week. I suspect she misses our little hideaway in Julia's attic, and no wonder. The place was the most delightful location to give our creative minds wings to soar. If Esther decides to live with her widowed mother, the attic studio will become enticing to me once again. And that will be the real test of my will. For now my beautifully framed painting lies hidden there, wrapped up, like my dreams.

Sometimes I can't help but wonder if the Lord God didn't allow all this to happen, in just the way it did, to see what I'm made of. Am I ready to settle down and make my lifelong vow to God and the church? Some days I believe I could be, but then the hankering to draw one of the cow's black and white patterns or to paint the first red sunset of winter tugs hard at me.

Honestly, I'm staying clear away from it. Like an addict who goes cold turkey, Lou says. Nevertheless I *am* mixing paints on the palette of my heart, trying in vain to match the shades of blue in the Creator's ever-changing sky. God's ways, after all, are higher than ours, Cousin Julia says.

These days, my thoughts, even my convictions, seem to shift with the fickle hues of a Pennsylvania sky . . . a blending of what was true for me as the young preacher's daughter with what I now see and know. Is there no way to blend my opposing desires? Will I ever understand all of the shades of goodness, faith, and even someday, love?

Acknowledgments

I am blessed to have a small glimpse of God on this earth in the efforts and encouragement of some wonderful people. Among them are the following: Carol Johnson, Julie Klassen, David Horton, and Jolene Steffer, my remarkable editors; Dave Lewis, my husband, "first reader," and constant encourager; Hank Hershberger, Monk and Marijane Troyer, Fay Landis, and other faithful, though anonymous, research assistants; Marilyn Stockwood of London, England; Irmi Knoth and Joe Bohler, internationally acclaimed artists; Iris Stuart of Morton, Mississippi; and the good folk at *The Budget* in Sugarcreek, Ohio.

And, yes, the B & B mentioned in Pine, Colorado, is a very real and lovely place.

It must have seemed to my family as if I disappeared at times while musing, scribbling notes, and typing the pages here. But I was always gently nudged back to reality by their patience and love. Special thanks, especially, to Julie, Janie, and Jonathan . . . and to my darling parents, for steady prayer support. And to one prayer partner, in particular, abundant blessings for your faithfulness in lifting my work to the Lord Jesus.

CROSSINGS®
THE BOOK CLUB FOR TODAY'S CHRISTIAN FAMILY

A Letter to Our Readers

Dear Reader:

In order that we might better contribute to your reading enjoyment, we would appreciate your taking a few minutes to respond to the following questions. When completed, please return to the following:

Andrea Doering, Editor-in-Chief
Crossings Book Club
401 Franklin Avenue, Garden City, NY 11530

You can post your review online! Go to www.crossings.com and rate this book.

Title _____ Author _____

1 Did you enjoy reading this book?

❑ Very much. I would like to see more books by this author!

❑ I really liked_____

❑ Moderately. I would have enjoyed it more if_____

2 What influenced your decision to purchase this book? Check all that apply.

    ❑ Cover
    ❑ Title
    ❑ Publicity
    ❑ Catalog description
    ❑ Friends
    ❑ Enjoyed other books by this author
    ❑ Other _____

3 Please check your age range:

    ❑ Under 18   ❑ 18-24
    ❑ 25-34   ❑ 35-45
    ❑ 46-55   ❑ Over 55

4 How many hours per week do you read? _____

5 How would you rate this book, on a scale from 1 (poor) to 5 (superior)?
_____

Name_____

Occupation_____

Address_____

City_____ State_____ Zip_____